Rosemary
for
Remembrance

Rosemary for Remembrance

An Historical Novel

Peggy Reid Rhodes

Copyright © 2001 by Peggy Reid Rhodes.

Library of Congress Number: 2001119133
ISBN #:   Hardcover   1-4010-3439-X
                 Softcover   1-4010-3438-1

All rights reserved. No part of this book may be reproduced or transmitted in any form or by any means, electronic or mechanical, including photocopying, recording, or by any information storage and retrieval system, without permission in writing from the copyright owner.

This book was printed in the United States of America.

To order additional copies of this book, contact:
Xlibris Corporation
1-888-7-XLIBRIS
www.Xlibris.com
Orders@Xlibris.com

To friends – Jean Beam, a caring Martha; and a group that make reunions fun and renewing till next time – Alice Noble, Molly Johnson, Frances Ward, Sarah Hamrick, Nancy David, Jean Poston, Celia Homans, Frances Foreman, Susie Copeland

Miksch House and Manufactory sketch by Sarah

CHAPTER ONE

Martha Miksch pulled the white lace cap from the wall peg and set it on top of her blonde hair pushing the long, heavy braids so that they fell down her back. Her strong fingers tied the pink ribbons of the cap firmly in a bow at her neck.

"I don't see why I have to wear my cap just to go across the street," said eleven-year-old Martha as she picked up the water bucket.

"Rules, Martha," answered her mother Maria. Martha turned toward the door but was stopped by her mother's voice, "Your bodice, too."

"Oh, Mama. It's so hot," she protested as she jerked the checkered cotton top from a peg and put it on over her white blouse. "I'll just perspire and get it all wet, then I won't look good tonight at service."

"Don't run to the standpipe then. And be careful not to splash the water on your way back."

As Martha laced the narrow cording up the front of her snug bodice, Maria noticed that the cording was twisted a bit. She said, "Martha, come here a moment, the lacing needs a bit of straightening."

As she quickly smoothed the cording into a flat continuous line she notice how tight the bodice was on her daughter. She watched Martha turn, pick up the bucket and walk out the front door of the house.

"Leave the top door open," she called out. To herself she thought, Martha is really growing into a young lady. It won't be a year before her body will hardly be that of a child's. Matthew was right to have the town put that standpipe close by so Martha wouldn't have to go to the brothers' spring for water anymore. And I'll have to be more careful to watch her, too. It's a good thing she's in school all day when the shop is open. So many strangers and soldiers in and out.

With the thought of men around, Maria went to the front door and looked out. Seeing none about she returned to the small kitchen table that served the family for dining as well as for food preparation and a place to wash up afterwards. She stacked the few dishes she, Matthew and Martha had used for the noon meal of vegetable stew and applesauce.

Outside, on Main Street, Martha crossed over the hard dirt surface to the water pipe stand just opposite her house. She set the empty bucket she had brought, down in the street. She lifted the almost full bucket she had left early this morning to catch water and moved it aside, then she put the empty bucket in its place.

Martha looked down the street toward the public standpipe and the pump at the far corner of the fenced square that centered Salem to see if any of the other girls were getting their water. No one was in sight. Not even Anna Bagge. Martha knew it wasn't nice, but she was glad Anna had to walk further than she did for water. Everybody thought Brother Bagge was so important. He had more money than anybody else, and took more trips, but her father had been able to get the town to put the water stand right in front of his house—just by asking, and Brother Bagge hadn't. And he had really been mad. Martha had overheard some brothers talking about it one day while she was walking to school and they had been just in front of her.

Martha picked up the heavy bucket with two hands and held it to the right side, taking small steps so as not to spill any water.

She stopped to rest at her front door and saw two men coming up the street from the Brothers House where single men—masters, journeymen and apprentices – lived. Some worked there at crafts including a gunsmith (now making other items) and a tailor. Others like the baker, weaver, blacksmith and joiner worked at the brothers' workshop behind the house. She watched until the men reached Triebel's house next door. They stopped. One went up the narrow wooden steps, knocked and waited. Immediately the door was opened and both men walked inside.

She knew they went to see Brother Zillman, the night watchman, because that was his entrance. Brother Triebel always used the back door. Martha liked Brother Triebel. There was always activity around his house. He was a joiner. She was grateful for those logs that he bored to carry the water from the north spring to the standpipes and pumps. She missed seeing her friends at the spring and splashing about during the summer. Still, the full buckets had been heavy to carry so far uphill.

"Martha," she heard her mother calling from inside.

"Coming," she answered. Closing the lower half of the Dutch door and entering the kitchen, she asked, "Shall I pour some into the tub?"

"Let me do it. It's too heavy for you to lift so high."

"I can do it. Watch." With both hands Martha carefully pulled the bucket to the bench, let it rest halfway on the seat, let go one hand that she put under the bottom edge. Again she lifted, then tipped the bucket and the water flowed into the tub.

Maria beamed at Martha. "You're growing stronger every day. That's enough. I need to add some hot water."

Martha stopped pouring and put the water bucket beside the cupboard near the table. Maria went to the fireplace where the hot water kettle sat on a trivet. She took the corner of her apron and wrapped it around the tall handle of the kettle and walked the few steps back to the table and wash tub.

"I noticed your apron's smudged. You'll need a fresh one for tonight. Try to keep your dress clean this afternoon." She returned the kettle to the trivet. She took the poker and pushed the coals against the back of the chimney.

Martha noticed and asked, "Are we having a cold supper?"

"Yes. Boiled eggs, salad, apple cake, cornbread and buttermilk."

"Are we going to have company?"

"We might. I'm not sure."

"Mama, have we ever had an ordination service before?"

"Yes. Our first one was seven years ago. That was in 1773 soon after Brother Graff was made a bishop. A bishop has to perform the service. We really need the new ministers. There are so many congregations now for Brothers Graff and Marshall to look after."

"Mama, isn't Bishop Reichel going to ordain the three men tonight?"

"Yes. It makes the service seem very special tonight to have a visiting bishop from the central Unity headquarters in Germany in charge."

"Mama, it's so exciting that Bishop Reichel knows Grandfather Spanenberg. I wish he could come to Salem," said Martha wistfully.

"I wish you could know him. One of God's great servants. He came to Wachovia in the fifties."

"Do you think he'll come here again?"

"He's getting old for a trip across the Atlantic, Martha. Every since Count Zinzendorf died, he's been needed at Herrnhut, Germany."

"Is Herrnhut more important than Salem?"

Maria laughed as she washed a plate and handed it to Martha to dry. "No, dear. We're all important, but none of us more than the rest. Herrnhut is the central place for all Moravians. You know how Salem is the center of Wachovia. And Brother Marshall lives here. There are affairs that concern all of us that Brother Marshall has to attend to."

"Yes, Mama. Like when he goes to court and the assembly. And like when he was in Europe so long?"

"Yes. Well, Brother Joseph, your Grandfather, has those duties in Europe and gets reports and sees people going and coming from all our foreign missions."

"I'm so glad that Bishop Reichel brought us letters from him. Mama, could I write to Grandfather and Grandmother?"

"Why I'm sure they'd like to hear from you. You are their only grandchild. We could ask your father to find out if Brother Reichel could take it when he goes."

"I hope he will. I'll ask father for some paper to write, but I'll think first what I want to say. Mama," Martha said as she dried the last red pottery cup and placed it on the open hutch, "is there anything else you want me to do before I go back to school?"

"The salad would be better with some basil. Want to pick some?"

"Sure."

She bounced out the open kitchen back doorway, down the three steep wooden steps into the small fenced yard. She paused a moment under the apple tree, delighting in the coolness after the hot kitchen. There was no noise at the moment. There were so few quiet days during this wartime.

"Oh, God. The world is so beautiful. The apples smell so good. Please, let it be peaceful today and tonight. And don't let so many strangers come to town. Please, let us have the service tonight, if it is your will."

Martha prayed with a quietness, but an intensity, which was natural to all she did.

She liked the small yard of her house. She liked the trees: pecan, peach, apple and the fig bushes. She liked the smell of the fruit and the leaves. Before she had started to school, she would come out in the yard and play using the leaves for plates or books for her doll. As she had handled the leaves, she had noticed the difference in the fragrances. Later she played games with herself; mixing up the leaves, and with her eyes closed, selecting one, and guessing which tree or bush it had come from by its touch or its smell.

When she was a little older, her father had allowed her to go with him to the nursery that lay just beyond the backyard fence. While the yard around the house had a picket fence, the nursery fence was of rails, so Matthew could safely take his young daughter along as he checked over his stock or weeded the paths.

The garden soon became one of Martha's most favorite places. She wasn't aware of it, but whenever she neared the garden gate, her face took on a new look, one of eagerness, of anticipation of pleasant experiences. In the garden, she kept her glow; she was a natural learner, and her father was a natural teacher. He taught her various aspects of the nursery, as he thought she was ready for them. He let her watch him plant seeds, take cuttings, make grafts, layer some branches. He bruised the leaves of herbs for her to learn the distinctive fragrances. Here again she repeated the games she had played with the leaves of the trees in the yard. Matthew taught her how to identify the plants, too, by their shape and height, their habits of growth. Martha learned in the nursery that you get a bountiful harvest when you help God care for growing things. She was beginning to understand how the plants helped man.

She loved working close beside her father. To her he was wisdom and guidance. He knew so many things to share. Being with Matthew was to Martha like being with a good book in which each page was filled with new ideas to think about. Maria added much to Martha's library of knowledge, too, but her chapters were about cooking and housewifery, the many things a young Moravian girl was supposed to know in order to do the job that would be expected of her later. Maria's lessons were passed on in loving thoughtfulness with genuine concern, but it was the times with Matthew that excited Martha most.

A slight noise came from the direction of the potting shed and Martha looked over the picket fence, over the rose bushes and tried to see her father. She pushed open the gate and it swung shut behind her with the rock bumping against the post then settling on the chain. Martha ran down the center path.

"Father, I've come to get some basil."

"It'll be better if you wait till the sun goes down to pick it."

"We need it for supper. The salad is so much better with basil. I forgot it this morning. I've been so excited all day. I've just about forgotten everything. Isn't it a lovely day," she exclaimed and she ran up and hugged him, not noticing he had a plant in his hand. Some branches were crushed between them.

An aroma as clean as that of a young pine sapling suddenly wafted around Martha. She moved back and inquired of her father, "The pine smell. What is it?"

Matthew laughed, "That was a young rosemary plant."

He held in front of him a slightly crushed and limp young green plant.

"Oh, I'm so sorry. I hope I haven't killed it!"

"Love usually doesn't kill growing things, but a little less powerful hug might be better for such a young plant."

"How can we make it better, Father?" She asked as she looked at the bruised leaves.

"Well, first I'll be sure that I don't touch the young foliage with my hot hands. I'll put it in a pot, then I'll set it on the shelf here and keep it out of the sun a few days. Don't worry. The roots looked strong."

"Rosemary? Where did you get it? I can't remember rosemary in the garden."

"There hasn't been any here for a long time. I got my first starter plant at Bethabara when we first came down. Somehow all the plants were sold. I hadn't located anymore. Now one of the plants I sold from my original cuttings is so large that the owner was ready to divide it. I've just started separating all the roots. That's why I came out right after lunch. We'll set them in over there near the lavender border."

Martha looked over at the lavender and then at the rosemary. "They look so much alike, how will I ever tell them apart?"

"There's a difference. Very slight, but you'll soon know when you work with the two of them."

Martha bent to sniff a cutting of rosemary. The fragrance wasn't as strong as that of the leaves she had bruised. Still there was the scent of fresh pine. She ran over to the lavender bed and pulled off a narrow leaf. She had been taught early how to snip out one or two leaves with a thumbnail and finger so as not to disturb any other part of the plant.

As she rejoined her father in the shaded potting shed, she bruised the leaf and inhaled the fragrance. Then she brought the rosemary to her nose again. She closed her eyes and smelled both of the leaves once more.

Finally she announced, "I like rosemary best. It smells of the out-of-doors."

With this announcement, Matthew's heart warmed as he thought, she'll decide things for herself after comparing the choices. Aloud he said, "An interesting reason."

Martha leaned over the rough pine shelf to survey the plant she had accidentally bruised, "I hope it survives."

"How would you like this plant for your very own, Martha, after it has recovered?"

"My very own?" Martha asked incredulously. To have a plant of her very own was a wish Martha had long secreted in her heart, but had not dared hope could be fulfilled. She knew how the war had cut out all the treats for everyone. Money was so scarce, too, and her father kept track of all his plants. Each one was worth so much. It could be traded for other things they needed if people didn't have any money. Now here her father was offering her one these beautiful, fresh smelling plants. Truly this was a day to remember.

"Yes," Matthew said as he carefully centered the plant in a pot then packed dirt against the stem. When he moved aside, Martha cupped her hands around the little plant, careful not to touch the foliage.

"I love it. It's the best present I've ever had. Can I keep the pot, too?"

"Don't you want to plant it, maybe back of the house?"

"No. I want to keep it in the pot."

"It'll take a lot more watching. You'd have to remember to water it and . . ."

"I promise I'll take good care of it."

"All right. I think I can spare one pot."

"Father, if it wasn't for the war wouldn't this be just the greatest day of all?"

"We'll all be glad when the war is over and the trouble with England finished."

"Father, do you think the war will ever end?"

"Yes, my dear little Martha. I do. We must have faith."

"Do you think Brother Zillman will ever move into the little house built for him? It seems only soldiers stay there."

Both of them looked over the nursery rail fence on the lower north side to the little log house that the congregation had erected in June for the night watchman. Because Continental soldiers had been staying often in Brother Triebel's house, the night watchman had had difficulty sleeping and had requested other quarters. However, once the new log house had been finished, the Continental army, needing more sleeping space, had kept the house occupied all summer. But it had been vacant the past few days.

Before Matthew could answer Martha, the sounds of voices drifted from the south side. Matthew and Martha turned around and saw Brother Zillman coming across the back lot carrying a pile of quilts. He was talking as he walked.

"None too soon, I say."

Next, the two brothers Martha had seen going into Brother Zillman's a short time ago, came into view.

"Let's hope the soldiers didn't leave a mess," spoke the first. He shifted the little chair he had been carrying in front of him to a position over his head as he walked the narrow path behind Miksch's fence and the weeds of the back lot.

The second helping brother said as he saw Matthew, "Weeds kind of tall, Matthew."

"Frost'll kill 'em soon. It's a dry time of year to burn."

As the three men neared the little log house, the first observed,

"Zillman, this ought to be far enough back from the street, so you won't hear any noise all day long."

Zillman stopped and called out to Matthew as the latter came to the rail fence. "If I see any rats, we'll have to get rid of some of this brush, his eyes glancing sideways to the vacant lot north, that the brothers had recently fenced from Miksch's lot, up to the next house called the two-story house and over to Stockburger's farm.

Matthew replied, "If the vacant lot needs clearing, we'll talk about it in a Collegium meeting. We don't have any rats over here. We keep things picked up. This moving day for you?"

"Finally," said Zillman. He disappeared around the side of the house.

The only door to the house opened on the south side facing the back street, away from the Miksch house. There were no windows on the Main Street side either. Matthew was pleased with the arrangement. Martha was helping him more in the nursery now and he didn't like her having to work under the eyes of men now that she was growing up.

Martha was a pretty girl with fair hair and her mother's blue eyes. She possessed that glow that belongs to healthy young girls. She was almost as tall as Maria was now and larger framed. While Maria had been thin and frail in appearance as a young woman, Martha was strong and hardy. Matthew was glad he had moved from Bethabara; the land there was low thus damp most of the time. He himself had been ill the first years he had spent there. The first two children born to him and Maria had lived only a short time; one a few months; the other, a few days. So when Martha was born and seemingly healthy, he made plans to move to the central town being built. In fact, his house was the first private family house in Salem. He had such concern for their health that he moved the family to Salem even before his house was finished. They lived with others from December 1770 until the house was completed in April 1771. Matthew was remembering how his house had looked as a log dwelling for several years before he clapboarded it, when voices again brought his attention to the watchman's log house.

The three men reappeared.

"Need any help moving?" Matthew called.

"I think we can handle everything all right," Zillman returned. "Only have one room of things."

"Did the soldiers leave the place clean enough?" Matthew questioned the men filing past him, picking their way back to Triebel's house.

"Livable," the watchman commented over his shoulder and walked on.

"Well, Martha," Matthew stated as he turned back to the potting shed, "that answers your question. The watchman is now in his house. If the officers ask if there are any empty houses in town, we can assuredly say 'no.'"

Just then the bell in the square rang once. Martha gasped, "Father, I'll be late."

She raced over to the basil bed, deftly pinched several leaves from the stalks and dropped them into her apron. She ran up the dusty clay path, shouting goodbye to her father without turning around. One hand held the apron ends together, while the other tugged open the gate. She dashed up the back steps to the house almost tripping on her skirt as she hastily lifted it.

"Martha?" Maria looked up from the wooden bowl into which she was cutting up the vegetables for the salad.

"I forgot the time. I'll be late," Martha spoke hurriedly as she bent over then dropped the basil onto the table. She kissed her mother on the cheek.

"Did you wash it?"

"No. Sorry," she answered as she reached the front door and peered out. "The street's empty. You won't have to watch me. Bye." Martha disappeared down the steps.

Maria put the bowl on the table, got up and walked to the other side where Martha left the water bucket. She reached up and over to the middle shelf on the open hutch and selected a small dish. She dipped this into the bucket, then placed it on the table. She swished the basil leaves in the water. She took the leaves out, shook them, inspected them for foreign matter; not finding any, she added the basil to the bowl of salad. She sat again thankful for a few minutes rest. Although she enjoyed her busy life and never complained about any of her duties, and found pleasure in serving her husband and daughter and the congregation, Maria appreciated the quiet minutes in her house in early afternoon. Martha was at school, Matthew usually in the nursery, and the afternoon trade hadn't started.

Maria was forty-seven years old. She was beginning to feel that her body needed a little rest now and then. There was so much to do these days that she tried not to call attention to her needs.

She remembered that when they were first married back in May of 1764 in Bethlehem, Pennsylvania, Matthew had not thought her very strong. He seemed to doubt that she could make the long trip to North Carolina. But she had, and had fared well, taking only her regular turn at riding the horse or riding in the wagon, and walking the rest of the way. When Matthew had become ill soon after arriving in Bethabara, he was surprised at how well she could care for him.

"Poor Matthew," Maria thought. "He had such dreams of serving the community in Bethabara, running the store and being so helpful. But the illness lingered and he was in bed so many months . . . so tired . . . so little energy. How hard it had been for him."

The years melted before her eyes and she could see Matthew a young man, fresh from two years apprenticeship as a bookbinder in Herrnhut, coming down the street in Herrnhaag, Germany. He had been so erect, so handsome, and so ready to meet the world. When there were no books to bind in Herrnhaag, Matthew had easily turned his hand to leather goods. He knew good leather. Oh, he could bind the finest books anyone ever saw, like the one he was now doing for Brother Bagge.

Maria remembered seeing young Matthew come into the saal

for services. Of course, she never looked directly at him or he at her. Moravian boys and girls didn't pay attention to each other. There were no flirtations and no parties for meeting members of the opposite sex. All possible steps were taken to keep young men and young ladies apart. Even the youngest boys and girls attended separate schools. Boys left school at fourteen and were apprenticed to masters and lived in the single brothers' house. Girls moved into the single sisters' house at age eighteen when rooms were available.

Moravians called the unique groups, choirs. Overall, a choir was closely banded by mutual interest for a common purpose: such as little girls, single brothers, widows, and trombone musicians. An Altestan Conferenz oversaw concerns, especially the welfare, of the congregation. An Ausfer Collegium was responsible for trade matters and special military requests.

Maria had been baptized as an infant in the Lutheran Reformed church in Hinback, Watteau, Germany, where her father practiced the craft of stocking weaver. Maria's parents had been concerned about her upbringing. Later, when they came to know Sister Anna Nitschmann and heard how the Moravians took care of their children, educated all of them including the girls, they turned Maria over to her and the Moravians. Maria had been educated in the girls' school in Herrnhaag and later was employed in the school. However, when in 1749 conditions became uncertain in Herrnhaag, Maria went to England where the Moravians also had a congregation. In 1751 she crossed the Atlantic in one of Brother Joseph's early groups and went on to Bethlehem. Thus she was so busy learning and working that she did not have time to think of Matthew. She didn't see him again until he came to Bethlehem in 1754. Still, it wasn't God's will for them to be united that early. Maria was needed in the girls' school where she worked hard,

How many places she had been privileged to go: the countries she had seen, the people she had known, the long trips she had taken. The blessing she had of knowing dear Anna Nitchsmann and Count Zinzendorlf, the benefactor of the Moravians, and Bishop Spangenberg and Matthew's mother, Spangenberg's second wife; these thoughts flooded Maria's mind as she continued to tear the greens into bite size portions. As she smelled the sweetness so peculiar to basil, her thoughts shifted to Martha.

Where had Martha been? Nowhere except Bethabara where she was born, just six miles west of Salem. Martha seemed to like her home and her way of life. Maria wondered if her daughter would ever be uprooted. She knew that the Moravians believed that a person should be able to be at home anywhere in God's world, but Martha had been in one place so long, secure in the shelter and love of her parents and the congregation. Even in this wartime the town had offered a certain feeling of stability. All through the years of trying to get the Wachovia property deed transferred from England (the land had been bought from Lord Granville, one of the Lord Proprietors, and recently the deed had been stolen along with a coffer from Bishop Reichel at the Potomac during his traveling from Pennsylvania to North Carolina)—the Moravians had kept faith that things would work out for them to have a permanent home in Salem.

So many outsiders had threatened this security. Some had settled illegally on their land. Others had circulated unkind rumors that the Moravians were Tories. In spite of all the adversities, the congregation was staying on its land and trying to make the Wachovia area secure in every legal way possible.

Outsiders brought some disquiet to Maria's mind. Like Martha in her wishing a short time ago, Maria prayed they would not interfere with tonight's service. For once Maria was thankful that the soldiers who had been on good behavior where still quartered next door.

CHAPTER TWO

Martha, who didn't like to be late anywhere, ran along the road sending up flurries of dust behind her. She rounded the corner to the left and started the upward climb of the slight hill to the Gemeinhaus, a building with a room for worship, apartments for ministers and single sisters and schoolrooms for girls. As she ran up the tree shaded street, she saw something move behind the fence. She slowed down, glanced to her right and spied a small arm sticking through the fence. She hesitated a second, her keen blue eyes looking up the street in the direction of Gemeinhaus, then back at the flailing arm.

Her dislike at being late battled with her instinct to stop to investigate—to determine if someone needed help, and to render service if necessary.

After a brief debate, young Martha dashed to the fence. There between two rails she unmistakably recognized the hand and arm of a young boy. She stopped to peep between the rails to find out whose arm it was. Her gaze traveled from the stubby fingers, up the arm which showed several long scratches, above the white blouse sleeve and into the eyes of Peter Samson.

His head was resting on his shoulder.

"Peter, what are you doing here, crouching behind the fence?"

"Ssh, please, don't tell," the five-year-old boy whispered.

"Don't tell what?"

"That I'm in the square," he pleaded and shrank away from Martha and the fence.

Now Martha pleaded, "Peter, come out."

He made no move to come.

She tried again. "Peter, your arm is scratched. It needs looking after."

Between the rails she saw the little boy look down at his arm then jerk his blouse sleeve over the scratches.

Martha was almost frantic, but she tried to remain calm. She knew she must really be late for school now. If she were late, surely Peter must be also.

"Peter," she called, "you'll be late for school. Come on out."

"I can't."

"Why not?"

"I tried."

"You tried?"

"I tried to climb over, but it was too high. When I tried to climb through, my arm got scratched. Then you came along."

Martha looked around for a solution. "Peter, walk down to the Main Street and come out through the gate."

He hung his head, but he did not move. "Come on. I'm late for afternoon class," she implored.

"What will they do to you for being late?" he asked and raised his eyes so he could see her face.

"I don't know: I've never been late. But come on I'll walk down the street side and meet you at the gate."

Slowly, Peter began to trudge along at her pace.

"Why didn't someone walk to school with you, Peter?"

"Father had to go to the mill after lunch. Mama was taking care of the baby. I told her I could get to school by myself."

"How did you get into the square?"

"I was taking a short cut. I was hiding from the soldiers."

"Peter," Martha admonished him, "I haven't seen any soldiers in town today. Besides you're too young for them to enlist you."

"Papa said they were taking lots of young men and boys. He said Moravians had to be very careful. He said we should try to stay out of the soldiers way."

"You better go to school and learn your math and a trade. You can work and pay your taxes when you get older. You know Moravian men have to pay a three-fold tax."

"They do?" Peter came to the gate and Martha unlatched it for him.

"Sure they do. I heard my father say so."

"Gosh," Peter stopped and hung his head again.

"What's the matter now?"

"What will I tell them about being late?"

"Why Peter Samson, you'll say what everybody says, the truth," she stated firmly.

With that pronouncement she took his shoulders in her strong, young hands, turned him around, headed him in the direction of his school and gave him a gently but decidedly firm shove. After a slow step or two, his feet broke into a run.

She turned a second time up the street. When she was parallel with the new bell tower, she wished the bell were a clock so she could know exactly how late she was.

"Well, like I told Peter, just tell the truth."

And that's what she did to Sister Catherine Sehner, her teacher, who had just come to the top of the steps at the Gemeinhaus to look for her.

Unbeknownst to Martha, two other pairs of eyes had observed the episode in the square. Brothers Reichel and Marshall were upstairs in the Gemeinhaus discussing the plans for the evening service. Brother Reichel was near the window when Martha stopped at the fence and spotted Peter. He beckoned Marshall to the window.

"That's Brother Miksch's daughter, isn't it?"

"Yes, it is," said Marshall.

In silence they watched the children until Martha started back up the hill toward school.

Bishop Reichel commented, "I see she has good results with younger children."

"Martha is one of our most mature young girls," Marshall declared.

"She seems to have good instincts, stopping to help."

"Martha is always eager to help."

"Do you think she'll be ready to be admitted to the congregation soon?"

Marshall reflected a moment. He said, "She'll be twelve this October. By next year she should be ready."

"That will be some good news to relate to Brother Joseph when we return. How about her schoolwork? Is she a good student?"

"Extremely good. I'm glad we have a sister to teach math now. Martha needed a new area of study. Although I'll have to admit, she's learned a great deal from Matthew and Maria. People going to the shop have heard her call out exact answers to the various currency exchanges."

"Is she home much during the shop hours?"

"Not now. However, she was much later than the other girls were starting school. Maria needed her help at home and Matthew couldn't afford the school fee. You know, or did you, that Traugott Bagge pays for her schooling. Every time Matthew thinks he'll be able to pay the costs, something else comes along."

"The war has been hard on him, hasn't it?"

"Yes, indeed. Outsiders still want their tobacco and they come to town for it passing off their paper money onto him. Matthew is one of our strongest brothers in spirit and loyalty, that is. He's a good brother to deal with the public. As for Martha being home, she probably hears a bit of the trade talk from the kitchen or bedroom, when she's home during the short school vacations or from occasional late customers. She stays busy though, just like Maria and Matthew."

The bishop asked, "Maria worked in the girls' school, didn't she?"

Marshall nodded a yes.

"And Matthew was a teacher in Bethlehem?"

"He was for a time. Don't forget that Matthew's father was a teacher on one of the Unity's first mission efforts. He died shortly after he went out to Saint Croix."

"Do you think Martha might be a teacher later?" Reichel suggested.

"The indications are favorable. We'll keep a close check with her teacher," Marshall assured him. Thoughtfully, he added, "It might be wise for Martha to teach."

"Oh, how's that?" the bishop quizzed his friend in a puzzled manner.

"She's an attractive girl. As you just witnessed, she gets along well with young boys."

Marshall hesitated a moment then continued, "We have seen men turn to look at her."

"Anything serious, Brother?"

"No. Matthew keeps a very close watch. Martha has never been known to speak or act contrary to her upbringing. She just seems to have a natural rapport with some of the brothers. Going into service in one of the congregation homes might not be prudent for her."

"Do you think it wise for the fathers to have someone walk the girls to school?"

"Those who live furthest away do. Martha is so close they can watch her from their front door."

"When Brother Triebel is quartering soldiers, or when the town is full of outsiders, perhaps they should walk her, too."

"I'm sure they do most of the time."

"What about the little boys? We need to have someone go with them to and from school. Have the fathers and teachers discuss this soon. By the way, has a central place been decided for their school yet?"

"No. The Conferenz is looking over the town for a better site now. We'll talk to you before a final selection."

"Good. That reminds me, I want to get the copy of the Unity Elder's letter. I need to select some parts to read to the Conferenz."

"I'll join you later."

The two Moravian leaders parted for their private tasks.

Outside, Main Street echoed with the first sounds of the afternoon trade traffic. Visitors staying at the tavern in the southern part of town were climbing the long sloping hill to the brothers' house, Miksch's tobacco shop, and further north to other trade shops. Some men were stopping at Brother Jacob Bonn's house to avail themselves of his services as the community doctor, apothecarist or Justice of the Peace: he filled all those roles and filled them all well. Dr. Bonn's house and apothecary were on the same side of the street as Miksch's and just on the other side of the two-story, where Brother Meinung, surveyor and town clerk, lived.

Some Moravians from the outlying communities of Bethania, Hope, Friedburg, and Bethabara were beginning to arrive in town for the special service. Those who could combine the event with a business trip were coming in early. A few would be staying for the night with townspeople who had extra sleeping space, so Salem housewives were busy inside preparing extra food, making beds and checking lamps or candles.

Matthew finished dividing the rosemary. He took down dried sage bunches from the potting shed rafters. He anticipated that some of the people coming to town might want to buy the herb for seasoning sausage. Hog killing would commence with cold weather.

Matthew enjoyed these special days. He looked forward to seeing the brethren from all the settlements. He liked to hear what was going on. He missed the trips he used to take. In his time, he had traveled often with the brothers. In 1750 when the Moravians were expelled from Herrnhaag because of outside pressure following some of Count Zinzendorlf's religious attitudes and philosophies, Matthew moved with twenty-four other boys to Zeyst, Holland. What days of Grace he had known there. Working in the gardens of the Lord of Zeyst had brought him much happiness. His gratitude for those two years had been often mentioned in his prayers. His destined work, the work Brother Ettwein had insisted on his doing for the congregation in Bethabara, that of store keeper, had not turned out well. Now he was able to serve his fellow men with plants and seeds, and the harvests from the land were usually good. Matthew, now nearly forty-nine years old, remembered his younger days right after Zeyst in 1751. He had returned to Herrnhut where he had heard Brother Joseph, who had recently returned from a trip the colonies. Brother Joseph talked about the new country and the Moravian settlements in Pennsylvania. He spoke enthusiastically of the newly acquired land in North Carolina. What a pioneering trip that would be, Matthew had thought.

But Matthew wasn't called to the colonies until 1754. Earlier that year his mother had sailed along with Spangenberg and other Moravians on the congregation ship *The Irene* and had journeyed on to Pennsylvania. In May of 1754 Spangenberg married the widow Miksch. The following November, Matthew arrived in Bethlehem.

Coming to the colonies had proved as exciting as Matthew had dreamed it would be. He stayed with the single brothers in Bethlehem and for many years served as their treasurer. He taught in the boys' school and he traveled to the Indian mission of Pachgatgoch, New York.

The Moravians had ventured to the new world hoping to make a permanent settlement for members of their faith and to do mission work among the Indians. Matthew had felt privileged to go to the Indian mission. Later, when he was called to Bethabara, he had hopes of visiting the nearby Indian tribes. However, such was not the case. The French and Indian War broke out, and Indians were not friendly toward the white men in the area in general, so mission plans had to be delayed. Now there was the Revolutionary War and travel to Indian areas wasn't possible.

The trip to Bethabara was not only a trip to a new area, but a journey in a whole new relationship. As soon as he received the call, he was married to Maria Henriette Patermann. Matthew had seen Bethabara grow and watched Salem literally spring from the planning to the building. These were still expanding and missionary times for this small Moravian community.

The gardener finished gathering his herbs and headed toward the house. Mentally, he made notes of what needed to be done tomorrow and in the weeks to come as he passed through the nursery. He was glad to have this much land fenced now. He remembered when he had had to raise his first fruit trees in the town square because he did not have the funds to plow the yard or to fence it. What good help the brothers had been to him in those years when he first came to town. Money was still scarce but he had enough for essentials for his family these days. That little loan from the Collegium had been timely.

Entering the yard, he scanned the apple tree still full of fruit. Looks as if there're enough extra apples to sell a few bushels, he speculated to himself.

"Matthew," Maria came to the back door and called. "Oh, there you are. It's about time to open up."

"I brought some sage," he said as he walked inside.

"Good. Folks will be needing it soon. Slide the bench over here and I'll hang them now."

Matthew pushed the bench over the wide plank floor between the fireplace and the cellar door. Several pegs protruded from the overhead beams. She stood on the bench and Matthew held it steady. She reached as high as she could and looped the bunches over the pegs. He gave her his hand as she stepped off the bench.

"Thank you, dear," she said gratefully and pushed the bench back under the table.

"I'll go wash up before I hang the sign out," he announced as he picked up the water bucket. "That's a big bowl of salad. Expecting company?"

"Not for sure. Just wanted to have some extra."

Matthew carried the bucket through the kitchen, through the back of his front room and down a step into his bedroom. Maria followed him. While Matthew poured some water into a basin on the table, Maria sat down and took off her old shoes that she wore in the kitchen and backyard. She put on her other pair of black shoes that she wore in the afternoons and to services. With an old soft cloth she wiped off both pairs of shoes, then folded the cloth and tucked it neatly between the old pair. Standing up again she removed her large white apron, shook it, and retied it around her waist. She smoothed the peplum of her bodice over the apron.

"I'll take the bucket back," she said and picked it up. She closed the door upon leaving the room so that Matthew could have some privacy for his bathing. He liked to be fresh and clean when he greeted his customers. The bedroom opened directly into the front room and there were two windows on the street side. Although the first floor was fairly high from the ground, Maria had been in the habit for so many years of pulling curtains across the front windows when that one room had served them as a bedroom, front room and a shop; that was before the bedroom was added. She routinely closed the door now when someone needed privacy.

Taking the bucket into the kitchen, she stopped by the fireplace and refilled the copper water kettle. Although she was planning to have cool buttermilk for supper, someone might stop by and want a cup of tea.

Maria walked from the kitchen into the little front entryway, then turned left to the front room. The tobacco items for sale were on narrow shelves just inside the door. She straightened into rows the green pottery snuff jars and the clay pipes. The bowl holding reeds for the pipes was only half full. She'd have to remember to ask if the new reeds were dry enough to put in yet.

She moved over to the table set between the front windows. Everything seemed in order. She checked the ribbon supply wrapped around wide wooden paddles that were hanging on the wall. Sisters wore the narrow ribbons on their everyday caps, as well as on Haubes reserved for services.

She wondered if she should save some of the red ribbon for Martha. Whenever she became a communicant member of the church, she'd change the ribbons on her caps and bodice. With war, Maria didn't know when there'd be more ribbons. She decided that she'd better keep Martha spinning, for the rapidly growing girl would require a new dress and a new apron soon.

Matthew entered the room and teased, "Thinking of buying some ribbon?"

She laughed and stopped fingering the colorful ribbon, "I was realizing how Martha is going to need another dress, but she spins so slowly. She really doesn't take to housework or clothes making easily."

"She likes the nursery though. And does well in her studies."

"That's all well and good, Matthew, but she must learn to do these other things for herself."

"She stays busy."

"I'm not complaining that she's idle or that she doesn't help me, but there are some things that she needs to take more interest in. At least she must learn to do them. She'll have to do them someday."

Maria walked back into the bedroom. She took up an apron from the bed, picked up a darning needle and a long strand of linen thread.

"Take this mending. There's a rip in her apron. I'd leave it for her, but she needs this one for tonight."

Maria was sitting down in a chair when the sound of horse hooves was heard in the street. Matthew walked over to the open window and looked out.

"Soldiers," he reported.

"Many?"

He looked up the street. "Seems to be. Better get the sign out."

He took a wooden sign from his desk, stepped to the front door, reached over the bottom half of the door, around to the left and hung the sign. This was the signal that the shop was open for business. Since he had no separate shop room, he had made a practice from earliest days of placing the sign outside during regular morning and afternoon trade hours. Taking in the sign at lunch when Martha was home assured the family of an uninterrupted noon meal.

Matthew stood at the open door watching the soldiers ride past. He recognized some of them and he waved to those who greeted him. Then he saw Colonel Martin Armstrong ride by. Behind him came two soldiers who reined in their horses and halted at the tobacco shop. Matthew waited as the men tethered their horses to the post just at the street edge. They crossed the narrow walkway and started up the steps.

"Howdy," the soldiers said.

"Good afternoon," the tobacconist greeted them and opened the lower door, then preceded them into the shop. "How can I serve you today?"

"Got any twist?" asked the first soldier who was the taller of the two.

"Yes, indeed. How much do you need?"

"Oh, about a yard."

"A yard," mused Matthew. "You must not be planning to be back in town anytime soon."

"Never know with the army."

Matthew measured the brown twisted tobacco rope according to marks on the shelf. He pulled a small knife from his pocket and neatly cut the rope. He replaced the coiled rope in position on the shelf.

"What else today?"

The shorter man was hot and sweaty and he wiped his forehead with a neckerchief. "I need some snuff, but I don't want a pot. Got my own tin here."

The soldier reached in his pants pocket and yanked out a small tin box that had seen lots of wear. It looked as if it might have been painted black with some sort of decoration at one time. He handed the tin over to Matthew.

Matthew opened the container and set it on the shelf. He inserted a small funnel and poured some snuff from one of the pots into it.

"I saw Colonel Armstrong ride in. Is he staying overnight?" Matthew asked pleasantly.

"Nope. He had to get a few things down at the store."

"Anything more I can get for you? Need some soap today?"

The taller one said, "Shorty, get a bar. You need some sprucing up."

"I am plumb out. Yeah, I'll take a bar. But I'm warning you, buddy, if you want to borrow it, it'll cost you," the shorter one bantered with his friend.

"After you clean up, there won't be a sliver left. Better give my friend two."

"I'll buy my one. You buy your own," Shorty said and fished in his pocket and withdrew some Continental paper money.

"Now, men, I'd appreciate your paying in hard money."

The taller man also handed over paper money. "Well, I tell you, when this army pays us in silver, we'll pay you in silver."

"If you could pay part in silver," Matthew suggested.

"Are you saying you won't take *our* government money?" the taller bristled.

"No, but if you have hard money to spend, your spending it here would be appreciated," replied Matthew calmly as he accepted their money.

The soldiers ambled out of the building. Matthew could hear them through the open front windows as they untethered their horses.

"I'm holding on to my few pieces of hard money."

"Me, too. These Moravians have more'en anybody. They're not getting mine."

The two mounted their horses and rode down the street towards the community store.

Matthew shook his head. "If they only knew, if they only knew."

Maria finished mending the apron. She replaced it on the bed and the needle in a paper on her dresser. Just as she was re-entering the front room, Sister Samson came in.

"Good afternoon, Sister Maria. I need some candles. I've run out. What with all the fruit to put up, I haven't had time to dip any this week."

Maria opened the candle box on the front table, "I know. How many do you need? Have you ever seen so many apples?"

Sister Samson answered, "Better let me have four. I've pared so many apples, and the trees are still full."

"They'll be good when winter comes. Just wish there was more sugar available. I like sugar in my stewed fruit and in the pies."

"I could have used more myself to make some jelly with all those peelings, but you know I've about run out of things to put the fruits in." Sister Samson took the candles Maria handed her. She smelled them. "Don't you love the smell of fresh beeswax candles?"

"I do. Well, if we haven't had sugar, we've surely had honey. Guess all the flowers on the fruit trees were blessings in two ways."

"The Lord doth provide. Since the commissaries came in July and requisitioned all they could carry away, it's a good thing we're having harvest for so long."

"The corn fields surely have produced. I hear the single sisters were out helping with the late harvest yesterday."

"Yes. They were pulling ears down at the farm. I expect they'll have to go back for the husking later. Well, I'd better run on. I'm expecting some company in from Bethabara." Sister Samson withdrew some script from her apron pocket, paid Maria and left.

Maria went over to the big desk between the two side windows on the north wall and put the script in the appropriate box on the top. Congregation members used script among them and sold goods to each other for less than they sold them to outsiders. Matthew kept his desk closed and locked with the key in his pocket during shop hours. Any money taken in during shop hours was placed in one of the two boxes on top of the desk.

Matthew had been standing at the door while the women

talked. Now, he saw Bishop Reichel round the corner of Main Street and continue toward the shop. He stepped back into the front room and quietly told Maria, "Bishop Reichel is headed this way."

"Oh?" Maria looked surprised. Quickly her eyes surveyed the room to see if everything was in tip-top shape. She straightened an already very neat shelf.

Matthew had returned to the door.

Bishop Reichel stopped at Matthew's front steps. He looked around at the crowds up and down the street.

"Come in," Matthew cordially invited the bishop and stood back in the entry to let him pass first into the front room.

"Good afternoon, Sister Miksch."

"Good afternoon, Bishop," she welcomed him.

Matthew indicated the best chair and the bishop sat down and placed his hat on a nearby table.

"The town is busy, I see."

"We've had a few customers in," Matthew responded.

"We hope that your business has been good."

"It's steady. Of course, as we expected, the outsiders are paying in paper money. It seems they all come to town to get rid of it."

"Well, remember to pass it along, too, as quickly as you can."

"I'm planning to buy my next tobacco with it. A supply should be coming in soon."

"Matthew and Maria, you know in July, the new ruling was passed that the ministers' salaries would come from private pledges and not from the congregation business enterprises any longer. I thought I'd spare Brethren Marshall and Graff from this particular visitation duty. If you're ready to pledge, I'd be pleased to take the amount," the bishop finished without any tone of pressure.

Matthew spoke, "We've talked about it. Prayed about it, too." He rose and unlocked his desk. He lowered the large flat cover. From one of the small drawers he withdrew an envelope. He handed this to the bishop, saying, "We decided to save a bit each week, which we have done since mid-July. That's about what we expect we can do each three or four months."

Matthew turned and re-locked the desk.

Maria said, "Bishop, you know trade is heavier now that it will be during the cold weather."

"Yes, we understand. We can expect you to make your contributions from each week's income?"

"We think that best. We're sorry it's not more."

"Don't apologize, Matthew. It's known you've always been generous to our requests. Now, there is another little matter I want to discuss. The board has decided that the congregation should be responsible for educating the children in town and for paying a salary, a proper salary to the teachers," Reichel explained.

"We've expected that to come up. We talked about that, too. Did you know that Brother Bagge has been paying for Martha's schooling?'

Reichel nodded.

"We had hoped to pay for Martha ourselves this year. But this new expense," he indicated the envelope he had handed to the bishop, "well, we decided this had first claim. We simply don't know where to get anymore."

Reichel thought a moment, then said as his eyes swept the shop area, "What is your prime source of income?"

"Tobacco."

"Can you expand the tobacco business?"

"I'd like to. To make any real profit, I need to buy the leaf in larger quantities. Also, I need more room, or another building to process the twists and store the stem."

"I see," said the bishop thoughtfully. "Maybe after the war, when we can build again, you can proceed with whatever room you need. You use the loft now for drying your tobacco?"

Maria laughed, "We hardly need a sign out for the tobacco shop. You can smell the tobacco as you walk by."

"You have an extra room upstairs?" The bishop inquired.

"Really not extra. Part of the loft is enclosed for a bedroom for

Martha. It's fortunate that she likes the smell of tobacco," Maria remarked, "because the remainder of the loft is used to store tobacco."

"Perhaps Martha could share her room, then you could take in a girl boarder," he suggested.

Matthew replied, "We had a girl from Bethania for awhile. You know most families want to trade work around the house for room and board. With only the three of us, we don't need the help as much as those with several children."

Maria added, "Two young girls together don't accomplish the work that one does alone. But if we're ever really needed, we will do our part and double up."

"I'm sure of that. You both have always answered any call of the Unity. So there's no way you can spare any funds now for the schools," the bishop spoke more as a statement than a question.

Matthew questioned, "I trust Martha will be allowed to stay in the school. There aren't many years before she'll be ready to join the Single Sisters Choir."

The bishop rose then answered, "Oh, I'm sure she will be."

"As soon as we can, we'll pay something. Maybe we can add some items to the shop to increase the income," Maria offered.

The bishop nearing the door replied, "You two talk over the possibilities, then present them to the Collegium. I'll see you tonight at services."

"We're looking forward to it," they said as Reichel put on his hat and left the shop.

Matthew and Maria did not have a chance to discuss Reichel's visit because customers were entering the shop. In fact, there were people in all afternoon. A few more soldiers stopped for snuff or twists before Colonel Armstrong and his men left for their current headquarters near Bethabara.

Matthew felt some comfort with the Colonel in command of the troops. The soldiers behaved more civilly under his leadership. But Matthew knew not to put too much trust in the protection of men. It was the Lord he looked to for care of His people.

CHAPTER THREE

Brother and Sister Schmidt, a married couple the Miksches had known since their earliest days in Bethabara, stopped by near closing time. They had walked to town.

Maria warmly welcomed them. "I know you're tired walking on such a hot day. Please, sit down."

"Thank you," replied Sister Schmidt, "but it wasn't so bad. The September air is certainly dryer than the August we just had. The trees shade much of the road. Walking out was a treat after the days I've spent working in the wheat, rye, corn and vegetables all summer." The two women laughed together and shared stories of familiar chores. The men talked of business and war.

Maria asked Matthew if it was time to close up. Then she asked the visitors to stay and have a light supper, which they gratefully accepted.

Matthew said to Brother Schmidt, "I'll just bring in the sign, then we can walk out the front and down to the square. I like to watch for Martha leaving school. We might see who is in town."

After the men left, the women went to the kitchen to exchange news of their communities as they prepared to put out the supper.

The bell signaling "stop work" time had not been rung, but Matthew did not always adhere to it for his shop. Most of the craftsmen—the potter, weaver, tinsmith, cordwainer, tailor and such—worked on their wares right in the shops, but Matthew could not process his tobacco in his front room or work on his nursery chores there, so he kept more unusual hours and everyone had accepted this. Also, Matthew's health had not been good since the lingering fever, and he had "officially retired" upon leaving Bethabara even though he was only thirty-nine at the time.

Matthew inquired of Brother Schmidt, "Have you been to town since the new bell tower was erected?"

"No. Did Gottleib Krause build it?"

"Yes. A good job as always. Quite an interesting shape. Pyramid."

"Any trouble putting it up?"

"None. We were well blessed."

"And the waterworks still giving good results?"

"Generally we have enough water. In the fall, when the weather's very dry, we could use a faster flow. Someday we may have to dig wells again."

"Salem has how many people now?"

"One hundred fifty-two."

"That takes a lot of water a day."

"The standpipes help, and cistern at the square pump."

"What about when the militia goes through or camps over?"

"We try to direct them to the spring behind the Brothers House for their drinking water and to the Wach stream for their horses."

"I hear the British are on the move in South Carolina and are headed north."

"Let's pray the units south of here hold their lines or at least divert them to the east. Keep'em close to the coast I say."

"True." Schmidt agreed with Matthew. "But that does cut off our supplies from Europe. Puts them between us and Charleston."

"And when troops are north of here, our route to Pennsylvania is dangerous."

"War certainly does interfere with everyday living. We've seen a lot of it since coming to Bethabara, haven't we?"

"Enough. Maybe we'll see an end to it soon," Matthew said. "England can't keep forces up and down this long coast line and in all these inner territories many more years."

"I hope you are right."

Other married people were walking toward the Gemeinhaus now to meet their daughters. The door opened on the single sisters' side. One by one the older girls walked through the doorway and down the steps, while the teachers stood at the top watching. As soon as Martha was in the street and saw her father, she broke into a run.

"Father," she shouted, ran and hugged him.

He put his arm around her shoulders and patted her. "Still so much energy at the end of the day?"

"Hello, Brother Schmidt," Martha spoke. "Father, guess what we learned today? Some long division. And guess what I thought about?"

"What did you think about?" he asked with interest.

"The rosemary. As sister explained it, I could just see you dividing the roots. See my rosemary is already useful. It's helping me to remember my division."

"Martha, first thing we know you'll be dividing the clumps, knowing how many new plants you can get from one, then multiplying that number by the price. Then you'll know how much you can expect to realize," her father said in a pleased tone.

Schmidt commented, "Sounds as if you're going to have a good helper there, brother."

Martha did not respond to the compliment but looked down. From the corner of her eye she saw Anna Bagge still standing at the foot of the Gemeinhaus steps.

Martha looked back to her father. "Father, can we ask Anna to walk with us? Nobody has come for her yet."

"Be glad to have her."

As Martha ran back to get Anna and to tell the sisters she would see Anna home, Schmidt inquired, "Traugott's daughter?"

Matthew nodded.

"I hear her mother is still not well."

"No, afraid not. They say it's not safe to leave her alone," Matthew added.

"Expect that keeps Traugott nearer home."

"He's missed a trip or two. Usually he can get someone to stay with her."

"Having someone in the store all the time helps, too. That is having someone nearby."

Martha and Anna caught up with the waiting men. Anna was a year younger than Martha was and quite a bit smaller. Where Martha was growing rapidly, Anna was still very much the child. She was the prettiest young girl in town—blonde and blue-eyed with the features of her Danish ancestors. She had more material possessions than the other children did in Salem, although nothing in abundance. Her parents did not wish to spoil her. Because her father was out-of-town frequently, either on business trips for the store that he ran for the congregation or to the state legislature or to the court in Salisbury to take care of issues concerning the Unity, he could bring her gifts and unusual things.

Anna had store bought stockings, because her mother always messed up when she tried to knit. She couldn't keep the rows counted and the foot would be too long or the top too short. Anna also had beautiful satin ribbons for her cap and bodice. Martha didn't envy her friend all the things she had, but she surely wished she smelled as nice as Anna. Spring flowers, young pinks to be exact, is what she smelled like all year. Whereas Martha knew she always reeked of lye soap that her mother made and that was sold in the tobacco shop.

Suddenly, Martha thought as she walked beside Anna, the Bagges don't buy soap from us. I wonder where they get theirs? "Anna," she asked, "where do you get your soap?"

Anna answered, "Father buys it in Charleston. Mama likes one special kind."

"Is that why you smell so good? Is there an herb or flower in the soap?"

"It may be the soap, but it could be the sachet. Mama likes that, too. When she get's a new one, she puts the old one on the shelf with my dresses."

Anna didn't braid her hair and it hung long and loose across her back. As they reached the corner, the sun streamed down the street and Anna's hair gleamed like the satin of her ribbons.

Anna looked down the block and saw Brother Heckwelder, her father's helper, come out of the community store.

"He's probably looking for me," she said to Martha. "I can go by myself from here. Thank you Brother Miksch for letting me walk with you."

"Anytime Anna," Matthew waved her on.

Anna skipped on toward the store where her family had living quarters in the rooms in the upper section of the L-shaped building.

"Martha, you run along home. We are going into the Brothers House," Matthew directed.

She knew there would be no need to ask to come along. No girls, married or single, ever entered the Brothers' House, so she turned toward home.

Her father watched until she got to the doorway. She turned and waved and he and Brother Schmidt entered the Brothers' House.

Martha decided not to go in the front way. Instead, she scooted on back to the nursery. She wanted to check on her plant. It was still on the potting shed shelf. She really thought it looked a bit straighter. One of the tiny needle-like leaves was hanging as if it had almost been completely severed. She carefully tweezed it off with her finger and thumb and smelled the fresh green scent again.

"Please, get well again soon. I want to put you in my room."

Martha put the tiny leaf in her apron pocket and walked back to the house. At the open back door she saw Sister Schmidt. "Company for supper," she grinned happily to herself. She knew this meant her mother would use the cream she got at the dairy this morning for the applesauce tonight. Also, she wouldn't have to churn butter tomorrow morning.

"Mama, I'm home," Martha called gaily.

As Sister Schmidlt glanced out the doorway, Martha greeted

her, too. "Hello. Brother Schmidt and Father went in the Brothers' House."

When she stepped into the kitchen, she asked, "Can I help you, Mama?"

"Thank you, dear. We can get the dishes on. Please, go get some more water. Leave the front door open so we can see you from here. When you come back, you can wash up."

Martha took up the bucket almost empty now and went over to the standpipe. When she returned, she dipped some water from the bucket into a small piggin to take upstairs.

"Mama, what's a sachet?"

"It's a collection of dried flowers and herbs, tied together in a little square of cloth. Why?"

"I just wondered," she said as she quickly exited.

The steps to the loft were steep, narrow and without rails, but she climbed them easily. As always the aroma of drying tobacco filled the air. She noticed the leaves were turning a golden brown. She touched one on the closest stalk. It was still pliable. She pressed her nose close to the leaf and sniffed several times.

I still wonder how smelling tobacco helps you keep from getting smallpox, she thought as she crossed into her bedroom.

She remembered that two years ago there was an epidemic in town after one of the soldiers camping down near the tavern had brought the disease. Many people had come to the shop to buy tobacco leaves. She had caught smallpox herself, and had had a light case. She bore few scars. Her mother had taken excellent care of her. However, her parents had made her stay upstairs so that people wouldn't be afraid to come into the shop. Those who knew Martha was in with the pox would often call their orders at the half door. Martha remembered that every time Maria came up to bring her a tray or anything, she'd break off another leaf to take down.

Martha took off her bodice, blouse and cap. While laying them on the foot of her bed, she noticed the clean apron. She inspected it to see whether or not the rip had been mended. It was.

Martha poured some water into the wooden bowl on her little square table. She leaned over the bowl and splashed water from her cupped hands onto her face and neck. The water was cool to her warm skin. She reached over to the back of the door where her linen towel hung and jerked it from the two wooden pegs. The old towel was soft on her skin.

She continued to wash up noticing that the room was just beginning to get darker. Through the one window in her room, the sun was no longer visible over the treetops.

Martha wished she had a new dress to wear to the service tonight. She had one dress for summer, which she was still wearing because the days continued hot; and a dress for winter. The latter was a hand-down from an older girl. Funny, how mamas think about clothes. Maria had told her to make do with the one dress a season because she was little and didn't grow fast. Anna wore one to school and another to services on Sundays and special days.

On days when Martha's dress needed washing, Maria would get it done first thing in the morning, then iron it as soon as it was about dry. On those days Martha got to stay in her room and read for several hours. Her winter dress seldom got washed, but Maria kept the aprons and blouses cleaned.

Martha sat on the bed between the aprons. She reached over to the one on the foot of the bed and pulled it across her lap. She took out the tiny rosemary leaf and looked at it, still finding it hard to believe that she had a plant of her own. She smelled the leaf, surprised anything so tiny could smell so strong, and especially since the tobacco odor permeated the walls and lingered in her room. Then, the idea came to her to make a sachet.

How long will it take me to save enough leaves? Well, I can start with this one. How does father dry these leaves? I'll have to watch. Where can I put them?

She opened the closet door and peered in. No, there were too many things stored in there. She closed the door and opened her clothes press cabinet. She decided to place the leaves in the back in a corner until she had enough.

The bell rang in the square. She knew the men would be back soon. Everybody would want to eat early so that they could leave in time to get a seat at the ordination service. Moravians didn't turn visitors away although they were to sit in the back. Many communicants from nearby towns would be in the congregation and they could crowd the benches.

She was glad the soldiers were moving on to Bethania. Surely, they would not be needed tonight. Who would want to break the law or cause a disturbance on such an important night surmised the young girl who had been protected all her life. Quickly, she began dressing with the highest expectations of *peace* the very word that meant her town of *Salem*.

CHAPTER FOUR

Following a pleasant supper, the women cleaned the kitchen while the men lit their pipes and conversed in the front room.

About seven-thirty, everyone was ready for services. Matthew suggested they should start out as the saal would likely be filled early and the group filed out of the little house.

Just as Matthew locked the door, Maria spoke up. "Oh, Matthew, I forgot the lantern. Will you unlock the door?"

As he was putting the big iron key in the lock, Maria said, "I'm glad it is getting dark or I might not have remembered."

When she was going back inside, some people were coming up the street from the direction of the tavern. The loudness of masculine voices caused Matthew, Martha and the Schmidts to focus that way. Something in the men's manner disturbed Martha. She moved closer to her father.

The voices were loud, but not distinct. The almost darkness made it difficult to see the men clearly. Martha strained her eyes. One man kept swaying back and forth, back and forth. Then he leaned sideways against a man walking beside him. There was a third man on a horse. The group was moving slowly and erratically. The trio passed the intersection of Main Street and the street to the Gemeinhaus and progressed toward the Miksch house.

The stumbling man jeered, "We'll make a soldier of you, man. You wait and see." He swayed again and poked the man.

The horse rider on the far side boasted, "You'll be working for the loyal Continental Army."

"Yeah. Let's drink to the army," laughed the near man and tilted the flask to his mouth.

The men were about parallel with the Triebel house. Martha could see them more sharply. The walking soldier was lifting a flask to the man in the middle that shook his head.

"Won't drink after us now that we're Continentals, eh?" The men were opposite the Miksch house now.

The far man on the horse appeared to be a soldier, too. He sarcastically taunted, "Maybe he'd rather drink with them Moravians."

The near soldier halted awkwardly and leaned forward as if to see better the group standing in front of the tobacco shop. Then he straightened up as much as he could and jeered, "You mean these Tories?" He stretched closer again, nearer Martha. "Bet even this pretty young lass is a Tory."

He rubbed his bare hand across his lips and against his blue trousers. He staggered two or three steps toward Martha. Immediately, Matthew stepped forward, shielding her from the stranger. He was about to speak when the middleman muttered, "Come on!" and he walked briskly ahead.

The rider spurred his horse onward.

Martha clutched her father's coat, but she peered around his shoulder and saw that the man who had spoken to her wobbled in an attempt to steady himself.

"Don't be giving me no orders. You're not in the army yet. Besides, I don't want to pass the time with none of these English loving kind anyhow."

The rider called back loudly as he rode on, "Recollect, Tom, back when we worked here? There wasn't no passin' time."

"Nothin' but work."

"And preachin'."

"Go pray a heap tonight, Tories, 'cause we're gonna win this war; then we'll see who works for who," the foot soldier challenged as he staggered after his companions.

The middleman picked up his walking speed, but Martha heard him tell the others, "Oh, drink up and shut up."

The rider said crossly, "Tom's already drunk too much. And you talk too much."

The two soldiers commenced quarreling; however, Martha couldn't understand them. They were too far up the street. She thought she saw the rider reach over and grab at Tom's flask.

"Father," she said as her father turned toward her, "he smelled so awful. When he was near me, he—looked so terrible . . . like he was . . . oh, Father . . . his eyes—so unfocused. Father, does he have good sense?"

Matthew tenderly put his arm around her shoulder. "No, Martha, he doesn't right now. The strong drink is making him talk and act strangely. I regret you have to see such things."

Maria came out of the house. "Sorry I was so long. I had left the lantern in the basement this morning. I had to put a new candle in, too."

She noticed the strange quietness of the groups and Martha's head resting on Matthew's shoulder. "Is anything wrong?" she asked.

"Just some soldiers passing through. One was drunk," he said. "Well, let's be on. I see the brothers are leaving their house."

Maria started walking behind the men, "We really should instruct the tavern *not* to sell so much whisky to the soldiers." She moved over to let Martha walk between Sister Schmidt and herself. "Sister, do you have much trouble out in . . ."

Before she could finish her sentence, loud noises resounded from the direction where the soldiers had headed. The night was dark now. They could hardly distinguish anything up the street, but the men thought they saw someone dart across the road.

A horse whinnied, and then hoof beats echoed for a few seconds. Voices became louder, mounting to shouts. Matthew and Brother Schmidt looked at each other.

"Should we go up?" Schmidt asked.

Brother Triebel came from the back of his house. As he was checking the front entrance, he saw his neighbors, then heard the commotion.

"What's going on up there?"

"Some soldiers passed a few minutes ago. We don't know what's happening." Misksch answered as Triebel joined them.

Now Brother Zillman came along the path beside Miksch's lot. It was time for him to start his rounds. He joined the group and looked up the street, holding his lighted lantern high. It didn't cast its light very far.

"Sounds like the night is off to a loud start."

Triebel asked, "Zillman is anybody on watch with you tonight?"

"No. It's been quiet for a week. Thought we wouldn't need an extra."

"Want someone to go up there with you to see what the commotion is?" Miksch asked.

The sounds up the street were those of angry voices.

"Thanks. We'd better go." Zillman started off..

Schmidt put out his hands to stop Matthew. "I'll go to the saal to let them know you'll be late."

"Good. Take the women with you. They'll be better there than alone in the house, in case the men come back down here." Matthew wheeled around and followed Zillman and Triebel.

Faint sounds like those of shots rang in the air. Quickly, Schmidt guided the ladies in the opposite direction. A few other people were hurrying toward the Gemeinhaus.

The rapid climb up the slope took the women's breath. They were used to uphill walks, although not while talking and under such stress. When they reached the Gemeinhaus and were composed, Schmidt encouraged them to go in and be seated. He said he would find Marshall and inform him of the situation.

Inside the saal the women went to their benches where the

married women sat. Martha squeezed onto the end of a bench where her teacher sat with the older girls.

Schmidt spotted Marshal at the front of the room talking with the organist. He made his way up the narrow aisle, the benches having been pushed closer together so extra chairs could be placed on the sides.

"Excuse me, Brother Marshall," he apologized.

"Yes, Brother Schmidt?" Marshall recognized him. The organist moved to the organ.

"There's a disturbance up the street somewhere around Dr. Bonn's or the pottery. We don't know what happened. Brothers Miksch, Triebel and Zillman went up to check."

"Do you know who's involved?"

"Some soldiers. Three passed us in the street a few moments before we heard the shouting. They were drinking whisky and talking in unfriendly terms."

Traugott Bagge, sitting on an end seat near the front, observed Marshall's face as Schmidt was taking with him. Catching a word or two of the conversation, he arose and asked if there was any trouble.

Marshall spoke with a trace of worry, "Some disturbance up around the north end of Main Street. Perhaps someone will report in a few minutes. Let's look around. See if the brothers from that part of town are already here. There're Aust and Holder."

"Schmid is here. If there's trouble around their houses, they'll want to know," Bagge said empathetically.

"Yes. Can you slip out with them? We'll wait until you're back before starting the service."

Bagge strode over to Aust, Schmid, and Holder and gestured to them to follow him. They got up immediately and filed out of the hall.

The congregation, assembled in the hall, noticed the men leave. They exchanged glances, puzzled, and their eyes asked for an answer. Schmidt said something quietly to the brother beside him. Maria spoke to the sister next to her and Martha whispered to the girl at her side. Before long the saal was humming lowly. The congregation was concerned but was not panicked. The brothers and sisters waited quietly. They listened. There were no sounds of shots, no horses' hooves. Inside the saal, it seemed that the outside was quiet. The congregation felt the men who had left must now have the situation under control. They knew if they were needed, they would be called. Thus they waited.

Outside, Bagge and the men whom he had summoned walked rapidly up the street leading to the graveyard. It paralleled Main Street. Bagge briefly told them there was some trouble. They turned left at the first cross street, walked the short block and were on Main Street. Banging of wood was heard above Dr. Bonn's house.

The men proceeded as speedily as possible.

Zillman was shouting, "Stop that! Can't you see nobody's there!"

A man was beating on Aust's door with both fists. In Zillman's lantern light, the man's clothes appeared to be part uniform, his trousers army blue, but his shirt a regular work shirt. "Come out of there you no good runaway!"

A second man was holding one hand to his head and picking up a rock with the other hand.

Miksch was trying to tie the horse's reins to a post, but the horse kept pulling back.

Schmid leaned over the bending man and ordered, "Drop that rock!"

"You dad blasted Tory. Don't touch me or I'll report you to my Colonel," swore the soldier.

"If you don't put that rock, down, I'll do the reporting," Schmid retorted steely.

The man looked around at the several brothers, then dropped the rock. He rubbed his head with both hands.

Aust rushed up behind the man pounding on his door. "Stop that. I live here. There's no one in there."

The soldier reeled around. "Yeah. And there ain't no saints in heaven." He stumbled off the front step and crossed again to Schmid's house. "That fellow Schmid. He'd hide a deserter."

At that Schmid stepped forward. "I'm Schmid. What's this about hiding a deserter?"

"As if you didn't know. Jackson. That's who. Broke away from us right here. Look over there at my buddy. He's got a banged up head. Yeah. Jackson waited 'til we got here, then he upped and ran away."

The other soldier added in angry tones, "He wouldn't have run if you hadn't of swung at me for the flask. Made me fall. Now look at all the trouble we're in. We ain't got nobody to take in to enlist."

Bagge spoke up, trying to connect all the bits of the story. "You men say you were taking someone to enlist and that is when you *fell*," he spoke to the man holding his head, "after your partner swung at you, that this someone escaped, ran off?"

The door banger said, surly, "Sounds like a plan, don't it? Running away where there's a friend to hide him out."

Schmid said, "Well, let's go see if he's at my house. Zillman give us a light."

Holding his lantern to the side, Zillman walked around the knot of men in the middle of the street. At Schmid's front door, he stopped, lifted the lantern so Schmid could see to fit the key in the lock.

"Bagge, will you go with me to help these soldiers search for the man Jackson?" Schmid asked as he opened the door.

"Certainly," answered Bagge. He entered behind Schmid.

Almost immediately Schmid re-appeared at the door with a candle. "Zillman, give a light. If you soldiers will wait a moment, we'll be able to see."

The candle lit, Schmid went back inside. The soldiers stumbled into the house.

Meanwhile, Aust returned to his house and looked around all sides. Miksch joined him, having tied the horse to a fence post.

Brother Triebel pointed to the front of Schmid's house. "Look. Lot of damage to the windows."

Zillman walked across the front and held the lantern up. "Yes, lots of panes broken. That must have been the noise we heard like shots."

Aust and Miksch rejoined the men.

Aust said in his usual gruff voice, "What a mess. It's a good thing we came on up here. The pottery would have been next."

The soldiers came out of the house followed by Schmid and Bagge.

"Now, are you satisfied, he's not here?" asked Schmid.

"He ain't *now*. That ain't saying he wasn't here," blurted Tom.

"There're windows broken in my house. How do you men plan to fix them?" demanded Schmid.

"Ha, ha, ha. We're in the army, mister. We don't pay for nothin'," laughed Tom.

"We was doing our duty, bringing in our man. Let's look in the next house. Somebody open up this place," shouted the other soldier.

Aust pushed his way forward, muttering to himself. He thrust the key in the lock, flung open the door, and told Zillman to go in with his light.

"If you clumsy soldiers so much as break one clay pipe, I'll see you pay or you won't ever see your pay."

Either the gruffness of Aust or his threat must have sobered the drunken man because he was less noisy and steadier in his gait as he went into the pottery.

When the group returned to the street, Bagge asked, "Are you certain now that no one is giving refuge to your man?"

"We don't see him. Sorry we caused you people this trouble," the hurt soldier answered. Then to his buddy he suggested, "We better get on back to Bethabara."

"Yeah."

"My head is hurtin' somethin' bad. Where's the horse?"

Miksch said, "The horse is tied up over by the fence."

Both soldiers mounted the horse. As they started to leave, Schmid told them, "I'll be reporting this damage of my house."

The soldiers rode off without a rejoinder.

Bagge faced the men. "George, I'll be in touch with the Colonel tomorrow. Since your windows are out, do you want to stay here?"

"I'd better. Might be some looters in the woods who've heard all the commotion."

Bagge questioned in general, "Did anyone get the soldiers' names?"

Nobody answered. Each waited for the other to speak. Finally, Miksch said, "I've seen both men around before. They've been in for tobacco. Seems it was back in the summer, but they weren't in uniform. Fact is, I recall one of them mentioned he was working at Steiner's mill."

Bagge snapped, "That's something to go on. Let's get on back. Services have been held up long enough."

All the men except Zillman and Schmid retraced their path to the Gemeinhaus. Zillman continued his rounds. Schmid went inside to begin cleaning up the broken glass.

CHAPTER FIVE

The evening air was still with a touch of the early autumn chill; however, the crowded condition of the saal and the concern of the congregation boosted the temperature to a physical comfort, if not a mental one.

Services usually began promptly at the announced hour. Therefore, when ten, fifteen, thirty minutes passed, and Brother Reichel did not come into the saal, the men and women became restless and looked toward the door. The children began to wiggle on the backless benches. Their schoolmasters and mistresses gave them stern looks. The oldest members shifted positions a bit, hunching and straightening their backs.

Not one complained. No one asked questions directly. They had become accustomed to interruptions in their routine ever since the Revolutionary War started. Nonetheless, tonight was special to them, making the delay unwelcome. At long last, each of the settlements—Bethabara, Friedland and Bethania—would have its own pastor following tonight's ordination service. Graff would continue to serve Salem; and Marshall would be in charge of Unity affairs of the whole Wachovia area (a hundred thousand-acre tract), with headquarters in Salem.

Brother Marshall entered the saal and stood in the front of the room. The low murmurs stopped. Everyone was attentive.

"Brothers and Sisters, your patience is appreciated. I regret that our service is delayed tonight. Some of the brethren have gone to investigate a small disturbance in the north of town. We know they would like to be here, so we'll wait for them. Brother Heckewelder and Sister Miksch, if you will pass the hymnals, we will sing some selections. Brother Fredrich Peter has kindly consented to play for us."

The organ music and the familiar hymns had the effect of relaxing the congregation. They had just completed singing a fifth hymn when Bagge and the other men in a calm manner entered the room and found seats on the outside rows, except Bagge who strode up the center aisle to speak briefly with Marshall. Then he took a seat.

Marshall left the saal but returned in a few moments followed by Bishop Reichel, then Brothers John Heinzmann and Christian Fritz. Fredrich Peter joined them. Martha gazed in awe at Bishop Reichel as he stood in the front center of the room. She had never seen anyone so beautiful in all her life. He was dressed in his official robe of white, fine linen that hung full from a yoke.

Martha, enraptured, continued to watch his every movement. The brilliance of his white robe, even in the soft candlelight, outshone everything else in the saal. He appeared to her like the one big star shining between the darkened tree leaves outside her window at night. Both were scenes that she felt she could thrust out hands and touch; but she couldn't. It was a strangeness that she couldn't grasp. She was in the scene: the stars were real, the trees were, too, but she could not for all her stretching, touch them. She had the same yearning now to reach out and be a part of this scene. She couldn't in a physical sense.

Even the bishop's voice rang with a bright ethereal quality tonight as he called forth the Brothers Christian Fritz and Samuel Stolz, the Sisters Fritz, Elizabeth Culver and Maria Elizabeth Krause. They were received as Akoluthies. Each extended his right hand to the ministers and the minister's wives. Together the congregation sang: "They give their hands, oh Lord, Help them to Serve Thee."

The Akoluthies returned to their seats. Bishop Reichel called the name of Brother Heinzmann who came and knelt in front of him. The bishop placed his hands on Heinzmann's head and declared, "I ordain thee, John Heinzman to be a Deacon of the church of the Brethren, in the name of the Father, the Son and Holy Ghost. The Lord bless thee and keep thee and give thee peace."

Bishop Reichel raised the newly ordained Brother and kissed him. He ordained Brothers Fritz and Peter in the same manner. Following, the congregation all knelt.

Martha felt someone punch her in the side and she, too, quickly knelt. While the congregation sang the doxology, Martha could see down the aisle that the newly ordained ministers were prostrated on the floor. A feeling of joy and peace lay over the room. Martha felt a part of all that was taking place and her heart was full. What had happened touched her, not with hands, but in a spiritual way.

When Martha saw the deacons rise, she stood up as did the other members. She watched Bishop Reichel shake hands with the three men. Then Marshall and Graff shook their hands. Next, the married men and single brothers surged forward.

Martha couldn't see anything else up front. Anna was speaking to her. "Martha. What do you think happened? Isn't this an exciting night?"

Some mothers were looking for their daughters and Martha and Anna moved into the aisle so that the other girls could get out. Martha and Anna moved toward the back of the saal.

With awe, Martha whispered, "Wasn't it beautiful? Do you think the angels could be any more beautiful than Bishop Reichel?"

"His robe was glorious. Martha, do you think we could ever spin a thread so fine!"

"I couldn't. Maybe you could."

"And his red sash was so wide."

"Anna, we'd better hush. You know what teacher would say if she heard us talking about clothes."

"I know, but everybody looks so nice tonight."

Martha let her gaze skip over the women in their everyday dresses of dyes of madder root, onion skin, cochineal, indigo, apple bark, berries, roots and leaf combinations. From the back they did resemble a colorful quilt. Even the ends of apron sashes poking between bodice peplums and skirts reminded her of little strings that were left knotted and uncut on quilts. The men and boys' coats were more like thick wool blankets, heavy and solid. Their white shirts with full sleeves were tucked neatly in the waist of trousers that were secured below the knee. Everyone appeared neat and clean in their best clothing.

"Yes, Anna, they look nice," she agreed and added, "and they are nice. Isn't it great to be a Moravian?"

"Oh, yes. Papa says so. He goes everywhere. He sees lots of other people. He always says it's good to get home with the Moravians."

"My father says the same thing. So does mama. She doesn't travel now. She and father have been to Europe and England. My grandfather is a bishop."

"Oh, Martha, you are so fortunate."

Maria maneuvered through the crowd and found Martha. "We'll be heading home. It's late for you. Hello, Anna. I didn't see your mother. Did she come tonight?"

"No ma'am. She's at home with the boys. I'm waiting for my father. Bye, Martha."

Sister Schmidlt came up and thanked Maria for the supper.

"Won't you stay the night? We could put down some quilts," Maria offered.

"No. Thank you for asking. With things like they are, everybody wants to be home at night."

Brother Schmidt approached them. "Better be getting on now. We've a good little walk ahead."

Maria fretted a bit. "Wish you two could stay the night."

"Thank you, maybe some other time," he replied.

Sister Schmidt said, "Don't worry about us. There're several couples to go together." As they emerged from the Gemeinhaus, she looked up. "And look, Maria. See how He sent out the night lights to guide us. Take comfort: He'll go with us."

The two old friends clasped hands, and then Sister Schmidt took leave. She and her husband joined the other married couples who had come from Bethabara.

Martha, Matthew, and Maria walked home in silence, not even lighting the lantern Maria had brought. The joyful spell of the evening lingering with them. Inside their own house, Martha went to the kitchen and waited while Maria bent toward the fireplace, pushed back some ashes, found a small red hot coal, brought it forward and lit two candles. One she put in a little clay holder on the high kitchen mantel, the other she gave to Martha to take upstairs.

"Goodnight, dear," she said as she kissed her.

"Goodnight, Mama," Martha kissed her mother. She turned to her father who had entered the kitchen. "Goodnight, Father." They exchanged kisses.

"Father? Did you ever see grandfather in his bishop's robe?"

"Once."

"Was he as splendid as Brother Reichel?"

"As splendid? Well, Martha dear, if you mean did he look as impressive, yes. But then your grandfather has always been impressive, even in his everyday brown clothes."

"I wish I could see him. Father, Mama says I can write a letter to him. Could you ask Bishop Reichel to take it to him?"

"I'll ask him."

"Everything was so beautiful tonight. I didn't even mind the waiting, although I didn't know all those hymns we had to sing," she sighed.

Maria said, "Run along to bed now, child."

Martha gathered her full skirt in one hand and held her candle high with the other in order to cast a light ahead of her on the steep steps.

She was thinking about the candlelight and shadows in the saal, and the bishop's white robe and angels. Her thoughts shifted to Sister Reichel. She began to wonder how she had come to marry the bishop. She wondered about Sisters Graff and Marshall. How did their husbands pick them out?

Martha undressed in her room and spread her dress to air over the chair back and folded the apron over the chair seat. Her mind sleepy asked endless questions about marriages. She didn't know any of the answers. Slipping into bed, she was too tired to reason out any conclusions for herself. "They'll tell me soon. I know they will."

In this half wakefulness, a dream that was to haunt Martha for years was born. She experienced the desire to marry an important man. She could envision herself being a helpmate to a man who worked hard to serve the brethren and all mankind. The splendor of his service reflected on her and she, too, felt radiant.

As she drifted off to sleep, the stars continued to shine outside her window and to cast a path of light into the room.

CHAPTER SIX

The next morning dawned fair, clear, and cool. The fire, which had been uncomfortably hot all summer, felt pleasant to Maria this morning as she fried eggs and toasted yesterday's bread for breakfast. She brought the teapot to the hearth and added water to the rose hips. She left the teapot to steep and called Martha at the foot of the steps.

"Breakfast is almost ready."

She went to the back door, opened the top half and called Matthew to breakfast.

When they both came in, Maria dished up the eggs and set them on the table. She poured the herb tea into their mugs and they all sat down. Holding hands and bowing heads, they repeated, "Come Lord Jesus, our guest to be, and bless these gifts bestowed by thee. Amen."

"We're out of sugar, but use the honey for the tea," Maria said passing the honey pot to Matthew.

"Thank the Lord for bees," said Matthew.

"Father, do you think Brother Schmid's bees got their honey from the nursery?"

"I wouldn't be surprised."

"Then when we buy honey from him, it's like buying from ourselves."

Matthew chuckled, "Do I hear you thinking young lady that maybe George shouldn't charge us?"

"Well, maybe he should just charge us half price."

"Martha, what would happen to our nursery if the bees didn't come?"

"There wouldn't be so many flowers?"

"And without the flowers, we wouldn't have seed to sell for seasonings or new plants. Of course, that's for plants that are started from seeds."

"Does Brother Schmid own all the bees in Salem?"

"Bees are found everywhere. I'm not sure the bees we see come from his hives, but we do know that he has several of them. Did you know that George got those bees twenty years ago? Drove to the eastern part of Carolina and brought them back?"

"I wouldn't want to ride with a wagon load of bees. Mama, when are we going to make candles again? I love your candles; they smell so good."

Maria, finishing her tea, said, "Soon. They'll be killing more animals when it's colder, then we'll have plenty of tallow."

"And George should have a good supply of beeswax. See, Martha. We also need George's bees for candle making."

"Matthew, we better see about the molds. Did you put them upstairs in Martha's closet? And Martha, you can help me spin and get the wicks ready," Maria said as she stacked the dishes.

Matthew said, "Martha, get the Bible."

Maria continued with her candle making thoughts. "Can you ask George today about the beeswax? You know we've got to have enough candles for the saal and love feasts all year. How many did we use in the house last year? And how many did we sell in the shop . . ."

Matthew interrupted, "Hold on, Maria. You'll make us all tired before we start the day. This is the Sabbath, a day of rest; remember. Thanks, Martha," he said as she handed him the Bible.

He thumbed through the old Bible and winked sideways at Martha, "Do you think we ought to read the Martha story for your mother?"

"Aren't you going to read the text? What verse is it today?" Martha asked.

Matthew located the section he was looking for and Maria and Martha listened quietly as they sat at the table while he read.

On the Sabbath, Martha heard the Bible read from many times; usually twice at home, once at breakfast and just before bedtime. She heard it again at services morning and evening.

Walking home from services later that morning, Martha heard Maria ask Matthew if anymore had been heard from the soldiers who caused the disturbance last night.

He told her, "No, but Traugott sent a report to Colonel Armstrong by a messenger who was going that way. I expect we'll hear from him soon."

Martha enjoyed Sunday dinnertime. There weren't so many chores to do. Maria always started the dinner early and left it on the tripod on the hearth to stay hot. She pushed the coals far to the back when she was going to be out of the house for awhile. Now, she pulled the covered stew pot forward, removed the lid and spooned the vegetables and meat chunks onto the plates. While Martha went to the cellar for the butter and peach preserves, Maria sliced a loaf of bread and put the pieces in a basket on the table.

"Martha, after dinner would be a good time for you to start the letter to your Grandfather and Grandmother Spangenberg. You think about what to say first, so you won't waste paper," Maria said as they sat down to eat.

"May I ask you if I need help on some of the hard words?"

"Yes," she answered. Then she turned to Matthew. "When you unlock the desk, could you get a paper for her and leave out the quill and ink?"

"A fine dinner, Maria. Yes, I'll get the paper. I need to work on love feast accounts a bit," and he pushed back his bench, got up and stretched as he walked into the front room.

Maria looked over at the water bucket and said, "Martha. I need some water."

Martha picked it up and went out. This was one chore that didn't know Sundays. "If the springs stopped flowing, maybe there wouldn't be any water to carry," she moaned to herself on the way to the standpipe.

Just then the day dimmed. Martha glanced up and saw a dark cloud had covered the sun. Other dark clouds were forming. "Well, I guess there'll always be rain and Mama would probably have a rain barrel for me to fill the buckets from. I'm glad Father has a rain barrel in the nursery, or I'd be carrying water forever and ever."

She decided to be thankful for rain.

"Father," she said as she came into the front room and crossed to his desk where he was working, "does man really need so much water?"

"Why? Are the buckets too heavy?"

"No, I can even lift them as high as Mama's washing bucket."

"Yes, it's important. More important than food. Because water is so important to all of us, we give that job to you children. We want you to do important work—necessary work, so that you'll know we appreciate your having the water here and ready for all our needs. Now here's your paper. Go along and write your letter."

Martha took the paper to her bedroom. She took off her cap and apron and settled on her bed to think what to write. Soon she lay down. The excitement of last night and the late bedtime hour made her drowsy. Shortly, she was sound asleep and never heard her father close the front door or his footsteps on the street headed north to Brother Schmid's.

On the way Matthew noticed that the shops were all closed as customary. He felt comfortable about walking up to his old friend's house. Matthew wasn't going to buy or sell, but he might mention the beeswax. Might not be a bad idea to ask him to save us some honey, he thought.

The street was quiet: perhaps the overcast skies kept the people inside. Dust rose from the walkway where Matthew plodded along, welcoming prospects of rain to settle the dry particles.

At the front of Schmid's house, Matthew observed that glass was on the ground as it had been last night. Looking up at the windows, he saw papers stretched across where the panes had been broken. He knocked on the door. As Schmid opened it, horse hooves were heard striking the road to the north. Both men leaned to look. A single rider galloped past and a cloud of dust marked his trail.

"Somebody's in a hurry," surmised Schmid. "Did you recognize him?"

"No. A soldier though. Maybe one of Armstrong's men. Are you going to have any trouble getting your windows replaced?"

"Which way do you mean? By the soldiers or Triebel?"

"Well, if the store has any glass, I'd think Triebel ought to be able to get to it. You know Zillman moved out yesterday and there're no soldiers quartered with him now."

"Well, he's slow getting around to things."

"There hasn't been much building during the war. I expect he'd like the work."

Again, hoof beats pounded up the street. Schmid had walked out the door. He and Matthew stepped closer to the road.

"Sounds like more horses this time. Fact, it appears like three or four riders coming."

"George," Matthew said, "will you have enough beeswax for love feast candles this year?"

"Should. The hives were really full."

"I'll be needing some for shop candles, too. I'd appreciate your saving me honey for the crocks."

"I'll do what I can, but you know how hard it is to save. The army comes through like the plague, taking and eating everything in sight. If you want any honey, you'd better get it soon and hide it yourself."

Now the riders were nearing Schmid's house. Matthew was facing that direction. Quietly, he said to Schmid, "I believe two of the soldiers riding toward us are the two who caused the trouble last night. I don't recognize the two others."

The riders halted their horses at Schmid's house. Matthew

was right about two of the men. A third soldier was a corporal and a fourth was a sergeant.

The sergeant dismounted, keeping the reins in hand. He asked, "Is this George Schmid's house?"

"Yes. I'm George Schmid."

"These two men came back to camp late last night. They were sent to bring in a man named Jackson." The sergeant motioned to the two soldiers to dismount, then continued, "They say he escaped from them along about here. Were you home last night?"

Schmid addressed the sergeant. "I was at the Gemeinhaus when Brother Bagge called some of us out. Some other brothers had heard noises up this way. When we got here, we saw the two soldiers here. One was banging on the pottery door. Windows were broken on my house as you can see."

The sergeant quickly looked over the front of the house, then back to Schmid. "Did you see a third man?"

"No. These two soldiers searched my house and Brother Aust's next door."

At this point Matthew interjected, "Pardon me, sergeant. I'm Matthew Miksch. I live down the street."

"Yes?"

"Just before the commotion in front of this house last night, my family and I were leaving for services when we saw these two soldiers and there was a man walking with them."

"Did you see the man Jackson run away?"

"No. When our night watchman and I got up here, there were only these two men. One of them was throwing rocks at Brother Schmid's house."

"Can you tell which one?"

"No. It was quite dark at the time."

The sergeant walked over to the two soldiers. "Make your amends to the folks."

The one who had been riding last night mumbled, "Sorry 'bout the trouble, but we had to hunt for our man."

"I could of sworn he sneaked inside that house," said the other.

Schmid asked, "Which one of you is going to replace my window panes?"

The two soldiers looked at each other and shrugged their shoulders.

"And this glass has to be cleaned up, too," Schmid waved his arm toward the walkway at the front of his house.

Coming up the street, loomed Bagge with a paper in his hand. The group watched while he rapidly took the slope as if it were flat meadowland. Bagge with his great, determined stride was as threatening as the storm clouds that over hung the sky.

He waved his paper and announced forcefully, "Here's Colonel Armstrong's reply, brethren. A written Protection for the Store and the Tavern."

One of the disturbers muttered in a sarcastic manner, "This ain't no tavern or store."

Bagge caught the remark but went on speaking to the Moravian men. "And Brother Charles Holder has written authority to arrest any further disturbers of the peace. He can send them in as prisoners."

The brothers spoke to each other of their appreciation of Colonel Armstrong's actions.

Bagge asked Schmid, "Are these your visitors of last night?" Schmid nodded. "Thought so. Well, what's being done?"

The sergeant offered, "These men have said they are sorry to have caused any disturbance in your town."

"What about damages?"

"Our pay's spent," said one of the offenders.

"Yeah," agreed the other.

"Is that all you have to say?"

Again, the pair shrugged their shoulders.

The sergeant and corporal looked uncomfortable in this situation. Finally, the sergeant ordered everyone to mount. "Let's get on our way back to camp. Looks like a storm coming up."

The sergeant slapped the reins across the horse's neck, pulled around, and broke into a gallop with the other three riders falling right in line.

Bagge surveyed the house front with his eyes, "Sorry about your windows, but we do have some panes at the store."

Aust joining the group grunted, "Guess you'll want everybody to contribute, eh?"

"That's our agreement, Gottlieb. What one suffers, we'll all share," Matthew reminded him. "Maybe we should all start now with sharing in the clean-up."

Bagge waved his paper again, "I was on my way to Holder's to give him this authorization from Armstrong."

He turned and was off back down the street. Schmid started picking up glass.

Matthew spoke sardonically to Aust, "Gottlieb, don't you want us to dump this mess in your shards?"

"Umph, dig your own ditch and dump 'em in."

Schmid with his hands full said, "There's a trash pile down near the back fence."

Matthew suggested Schmid bring a barrel or bucket so they wouldn't have to walk back and forth.

"Leave it to you, Matthew, to save some steps," Aust said sharply.

"No need to waste time or energy. Over to the right, there's a big piece. Pile the pieces there till he gets back. Are you going to be turning any water pitchers soon? Maria's been wanting one to keep on the table in the bedroom—to save some steps to the kitchen bucket," he added humorously.

"With all the traffic at the tavern the wheels are mostly used for plates and mugs."

"I understand. The clay pipes go fast, too, in my shop. It's good to be so busy. All the customers like your pipes, brother. Your pottery sales surely bring in the business. Well, let me know if you throw a pitcher. Maria specially likes your yellow borders and designs."

As Schmid returned rolling a barrel, Aust grunted, "You were long enough. You can finish up." He retreated into his house.

The first bell for afternoon services rang. The two men quickly finished the clean up, and Matthew walked back home reflecting about the brethren and their different natures: gruff and kindly, leaders and followers, but all working together peacefully. Yes. It's a peaceful settlement, he concluded happily.

CHAPTER SEVEN

The next day rain clouds continued to hover over Salem. The air was sultry. Martha saw few strangers or soldiers in town as she hurried home after school. The war did not seem to exist for her except when she saw the uniformed men traveling through or trading in town, or when the adults talked about shortages of things because of the *war*.

She was in school from eight to eleven every weekday morning and one to five every afternoon except Saturdays. Sister Sehner never talked of the war.

Martha, like the girls in town, was shielded from contact with men outside her family. She listened to the brothers whenever she could on the street and in the saal because their talk was always interesting. Most of what she heard concerned congregation affairs. No Moravian men served in the army; therefore, none of the war talk centered on men who lived in any of the Moravian settlements. Sometimes, she was curious what the little boys talked about. Once she asked Anna what her brothers, Fredrich and Carl, talked of. Anna said, "Just things like we do. They like to pretend to be big and copy the older brothers. Papa told them not to play soldiers."

Today Martha was counting to herself all the boys in town. Which one might she marry? she wondered.

The air grew heavier and thunder rolled in the distance. Lightning flashed and Maria urged Martha to get into the house quickly.

Maria, shutting the door, exclaimed, "The rain's finally coming. I'm going down to the cellar. I need to bunch those turnips and stir the cucumbers. Soon as you rest a bit, start on the spinning."

"Oh, Mama. I wanted to finish my letter. I fell asleep yesterday."

"All right. When you finish the letter, see to the spinning and stir the soup." Maria changed from her white apron to an old checkered one she kept hanging by the cellar door. Takes less time to change than to wash was her motto.

Martha picked an apple from the bowl on the table and began to munch as she untied her cap. She took it off upstairs and hung it on the back of the chair.

She looked down at the table where she had left the half-written letter. She had thanked her grandparents for their letter that the bishop had brought from Germany, and she had told them about her studies in school and about helping bring in the water. Now, she wanted to tell them about how beautiful the bishop looked at the service and, of course, about her rosemary plant.

She wished she could go to the nursery to see it, but the rain was beginning to splash on the roof. She knew her father was taking care of it, so she sat down to commence writing. She worked slowly, carefully, making her letter neat. After finishing, she blew on the ink. When it looked dry, she folded the paper and took it with her downstairs.

"Did you stir the soup?" her mother called from the cellar.

"Right now," Martha pulled the crane toward her with a long handle ladle. With a long fork, she lifted the lid, then stirred the thick soup with the ladle. "Mama, when are you going to make gingerbread again?"

"When it's colder. The new molasses ought to be in soon."

"Why is everything going to be as soon as the weather is colder?"

"Like what?"

"Like molasses, and hog killing and moving plants and mulching and wool cleaning." Martha sat on the top step of the cellar to talk to her mother who was tying twine around the tops of some turnips.

"Everything has a season, dear. Molasses making comes after the sorghum or cane is harvested. It'll spoil in real hot weather. Meat doesn't keep long in the heat either."

"We surely do have to work a lot in the fall, don't we?" Martha said.

"And in the winter, spring and summer. It's good to have work to do. We must thank the Lord for this good harvest. While you're sitting there talking, seems to me you're not working much," Maria reminded her daughter in a pleasant voice.

"Mama, I'd rather do something else."

"Then set the table and put on the bread. I'll bring up the butter. You can do the spinning after supper."

As Martha placed the soup bowls and spoons on the table, she asked, "Where's father?"

"He's back in the bedroom, working on the book for Brother Bagge."

Martha saw that the door was closed, knocked and waited for him to say come in before she entered. Her father was seated at the table, bending over the leather volume, opening and closing the front cover.

"Are you through yet?"

"Almost." He turned the book over and tested the back cover.

"Father, that's the prettiest book I ever saw. The leather is so smooth. What do you have to do now?"

"Decide on the lettering style and which metal to use."

"Metal?"

"Yes. It really needs gold. That would last longest."

"Gold? Where would you get any?"

"Oh, I could file a coin, course that would lessen the coin's value. Or someone might trade in a piece of jewelry."

"What will Brother Bagge do with the book? I mean since he's read it, since he translated it. Will he give it away?"

"I don't know. He might want to keep this English version of our history. His visitors, the strangers coming to town, might want to read it."

"You're really nice to bind this for him. You've been working so long on it."

Matthew chuckled, "I'm sure Brother Bagge thinks too long. But I'm glad to do it."

"Father," Martha groped cautiously for the right words, "sometimes I think you and Brother Bagge are friends, but sometimes it seems as if you and he are — well, strange to each other."

Matthew put the book down, placed a sheet of paper in front of him with several types of script. He looked up at Martha with earnest eyes and a voice to match, "We are friends, Bagge and I. But we do not agree on all things. He has his way of doing business and I have mine. He speaks and does what he feels he should and so do I. We both hold to the beliefs of the Unity, and try to do the will of the Lord — and those things are bigger than our small differences of opinion."

"Well, I *don't envy* him, Father, but I sometimes wish our store was as big as his!"

"Now, Martha, that doesn't sound like you. Brother Bagge runs the store for the whole congregation, not just for himself. I used to do that in Bethabara when that was our major town. I retired. The small shop up front suits what we have to sell."

Martha gently ran her finger along the book edge, "Why don't you bind more books like you did in Germany?"

"Times aren't the same here, dear. This is a new country. People are busy clearing land, building roads, setting up governments, and starting trades. They haven't slowed down enough yet to spare the people to write books. Books take lots of paper and there's a lot more to binding them than just sewing. Besides to turn out many books you need a press and all that goes with it costs much money."

"If we had a press we wouldn't have to wait so long for our school books and texts to come from Europe or Pennsylvania."

"True. Someday Salem will probably have a paper mill and print shop."

"I hope so. And you can bind the books."

"Not me. I'll be too old."

"You'll never be old. Father, someday will you help me make a book?"

"And you can help your children make books. We'll have our own private apprentice arrangement. What kind of book would you like to start with?"

She wrinkled her forehead, tightened her lips, then spoke decidedly, "One about our nursery."

"Oh. You know of course Brother Reuter has written about all the flora and fauna of the Wachovia Area."

"Well, my book will be different. I'll write it for children."

"How will you make it different?"

"I'll draw pictures of all the plants, especially the herbs, and the flowers that smell good."

"Yours will be a fragrance book?"

"Yes. I'll press a real leaf or blossom on every page."

"But won't the flower dry and loose its fragrance?"

"Not for a long time. When that happens the people will just have to go into the garden and get another flower."

"Wonder what Comenius would have to say about your book?" he laughed merrily.

Maria poked her head around the corner. "Supper's on."

Matthew wrapped the book in paper and folded the script paper on top, and then he and Martha went in for the steaming soup.

The rain had stopped when Martha awoke the next morning. As soon as breakfast was over, she ran out to the nursery to inspect her plant.

"Father, it looks right again. See the stem is standing up like the others. May I take it to my room?"

"Um hum. How about helping me set out the other clumps when you get home from school. I'll work the beds this morning."

"I'd love to."

As she walked back up to the house, holding her pot in two hands when she could or clutching it tight against her when she had to open the gate and door, she realized that the air was cold.

"Mama, look. Look at my rosemary."

Maria was kneading dough so Martha held the pot over the table for her to see. Maria leaned sideways and sniffed.

"Rosemary for remembrance."

"Why did you say that?"

"That's what the people in England used to say. On days that were special to them, they'd give a sprig of rosemary away or carry one with 'em. Brides there would carry bouquets with rosemary tucked inside."

"That sounds nice."

"There are nice English people, Martha. Lord Granville sold us, the Unity that is, all this land. Some of our members are English born. But you had best not be going out from the house and speaking up for England in general. And you shouldn't talk against them either. Don't talk about them as individuals or as a country. That way you won't have to answer for yourself—or make explanations."

Martha didn't understand quite what her mother said. She wanted to go upstairs so she hurried on with her plant.

Since her little window faced north, Martha put the herb on the sill knowing the sunlight wouldn't be too strong. She took her cape from the hook in the closet, wrapped it around her, and fastened the one button at the throat.

At the doorway she bid her mother goodbye and was off to school.

On her return trip home at eleven o'clock, she had to stop before crossing the street. There were wagons and carts creaking up the hill and people walking by. There was no one she knew passing. The women wore white hats on the back of their heads but the material ended in a ruffle around their faces allowing a bit of hair to show in front. The older women must have had their hair tucked inside the cape for none showed in back. The young women, just like the little girls, left their hair long and flowing, some almost waist length.

Many of the people stopped at the town pump and drank thirstily. Others took buckets and stood in line at the pump.

Martha walked over to her house thinking how she, too, would be back to get water in a few minutes. Somehow she had never realized that if she got to take a trip one day, that she's still have to fill water buckets.

She sighed as she walked up the steps into her house. "Will I ever go on a trip? Anna has been out to Bethania and Bethabara with her family in the wagon, but I haven't been anywhere."

The smell of pork chops frying, apples stewing, and turnip greens boiling, greeted Martha and she immediately forgot about traveling.

The family ate heartily of the bountiful dinner. After chores, Martha headed again for school. Strangers still filed up the street. Martha quickly glanced at the faces of the men, walking singularly or in small groups: their expressions were serious; no one was laughing or talking.

Down the hill, she could see more people coming. She wondered where they were all going. She attempted twice to ask her teacher about the people, but each time Sister Sehner was preoccupied with helping someone with an arithmetic problem. Martha decided to wait and ask her father later. She put her book and slate away in a hurry when the sister announced class was over.

Her father was waiting at the square. She ran to him and they started down the street. A wagon stopped at the intersection. A heavyset man leaned over and struck the horse with a whip. The horse jerked and moved his feet in place. For all its struggle, the horse could not pull the wagon. The man angrily hollered back to some people straggling behind the wagon. "Come on. You young 'uns will have to tote a bag. Boys, come on! Help push!"

A woman who Martha thought must be the man's wife, gasped for breath as she reached the wagon. "Ezra, we're all so tired. I don't think we can go any further."

One of the young children cried, "I'm hungry."

The woman pleaded, "Let's stop for the night. There's water here," she said looking back to the pump.

Ezra furtively looked around the town. He spotted Matthew and asked anxiously, "Pardon me, mister. Is there any where around here that we can camp out for the night? My family's been walking all day."

Matthew responded politely, "There're woods on both ends of town. And good streams."

The woman spoke to her husband in anxious tones, "Woods? Are there any wild animals in these parts?"

Matthew heard the question, but his reply was directed toward Ezra. "We try to keep the underbrush cleared. That keeps the panthers away because there's not much small game."

The woman appeared relieved and again begged to stop for the night. Ezra agreed. Then he ordered his biggest boy to drive the horse and wagon on up the slope. He handed bundles from the wagon to the little children. He took two water buckets from the wagon and set them at the side of the street.

"I'll give you all a start. Walk on. I'll catch up soon." He gave a tremendous show of strength by putting his shoulder to the back of the wagon, pushing until his neck and face were swollen and red. The wagon moved forward, the horse lurched, and the small family caravan proceeded up Main Street.

Ezra straightened up, breathed deeply a few times, then bent over and picked up the buckets. "Could you tell me where I could get a bit of salt? We've been out for months."

Matthew pointed to the community store. "Where you folks from?"

Ezra answered, "Mecklenburg. The English are moving this way fast. Folks on the Catawba are fixing to move out, too. Excuse me. I need to be getting on."

He swung around toward the store.

Martha and Matthew stood another few minutes while a family passed. The father was pushing a cart loaded with quilts. A chair back was sticking up at one end. Some pots and a lantern were hooked onto the side. The mother balanced a child of about two years on her hip and half supported another of about five years with her other hand. The uphill climb was evidently hard for her as she was sweating. The family looked tired and dusty. The father paused a moment, stared at the hill still to climb.

"We'll rest at the top," he promised his family. Silently, they continued their trek.

Martha, too, was silent as she and Matthew walked home. She went straight upstairs. Hanging her good apron on the chair back, she saw her rosemary plant on the windowsill; and beyond it, she glimpsed through her window, more people struggling up the hill. She felt a strange uneasiness that crept from her heart to her stomach, to her knees and legs. She reached her hand to her bed for support and sank down on the quilt.

Staring ahead she vividly recalled the faces of the women and children, the strain of the man Ezra's neck muscles, the family struggling with the pushcart. Slowly, over those images emerged the shape of her tiny rosemary in its clay pot. What was it Maria had told her? Rosemary for remembrance. She had spoken of happy associations in England. Remembrance could be for other occasions, couldn't it? Her rosemary could remind her of two emotions: the upheaval of these families in wartime along with sadness she was feeling for them, as well as the joy she anticipated in watching her plant grow.

She put on her very oldest apron, the one that was too short, the one she saved to wear in the nursery.

Outside, Matthew showed her how to make the hole for the new rosemary plants and how to press the dirt firmly around the base of each. She worked without talking. When all the plants were in the bed, Matthew plunged a bucket in the rain barrel and drew it up full. He dipped a gourd into the bucket and poured some water around a plant. Then he let Martha wet the others as he watched. Again, his hands pressed the soil around each plant.

"Martha, you're quiet. Any special thoughts?"

"I was thinking about all those people going through town, Father. They're so sad looking."

"They're leaving their homes. It's not easy for some folks to do."

"Why do they *have* to leave? Why are the English running them away?"

"Different reasons. One man may not want to live under the British occupation with soldiers telling him what he can and can't do. Then some families live out on farms in isolated areas. It's hard to stand one against an army. Some hear stories about armies taking possessions, taking everything a family owns, even burning houses. They think it's safer to take all they can pack and they move on."

Martha was silent, watching the water run into the red soil. Then she asked apprehensively, "Father, if the British come here, will we have to move?"

Matthew looked directly into his daughter's eyes. He was touched by her serious, questioning gaze. "No, dear. We'll stay here."

"But, Father, won't *we* be afraid if the army comes?'

"No, not afraid. We built this town to be a home for our brethren and a place from where we can do the Lord's work. We must have faith in His protection."

A horseman galloping up the street drew Martha's attention. She stood up, looked toward the street and counted two, three, four more riders headed north—travelers, not soldiers.

"Father, where will they go?"

"Virginia probably."

"Maybe they can settle together. Build homes and make a new town."

"Martha, we should all be able to be at home anywhere in

God's world. You know, dear, we believe, when the Lord calls, we must be ready to serve wherever it is."

"Oh, Father, it's all so confusing. Staying, moving; knowing what to do. Didn't you and Mama have to move?"

"Yes, we did. Back in Herrnhut. She left first when the Unity began to sense opposition from others. I stayed two more years until we finally did have to move."

"Then how do you know we won't have to leave Salem?"

"In the Old Countries where the state religions had been powerful for so long, it was not easy to hold to different views or practices. Here in the colonies, religious freedom was promised. Besides, the Unity *bought* this land from Lord Granville. That's why we've all worked so hard to pay the purchase price of this Wachovia land."

"And Salem is all ours?" she asked hopefully.

"Yes. All Wachovia is. Only right now it's a little hard to prove."

"Why?"

"Because when Bishop Reichel was journeying to Salem, he carried the deed that transferred the title from England to Brother Marshall in his coffer. You've heard the coffer was stolen?'

"Oh," she slumped dejectedly.

"Cheer up. We can get a copy if the coffer isn't recovered."

"Won't that take a long time?"

"Yes. Some evil people who doubt us will settle as some already have started doing, on our boundaries. Have faith, little one. We have followed the Lord's will. He shall take care of us."

Martha felt relieved, "Father, I do believe you. I'm glad we don't have to move. I love our house, the nursery, and Salem. But," she looked again toward the street, "I'm sorry you and Mama had to run away like those people."

"Your caring is good, Martha. But there was a difference. We were not a sad group. Our conscience was clear, our lives were dedicated to the Lord—we were not afraid."

The bell tolled the dinner hour. Martha finished washing her hands in the rain barrel and shook them to dry.

Walking toward the house with her father's arm around her shoulder she said, "Tonight at Bible reading, let's pray for Jesus to walk with these people too."

Matthew squeezed her affectionately against him, "We will."

CHAPTER EIGHT

"The wheel is slowing down, Martha," Maria spoke without looking up from her knitting.

"Isn't this enough thread for the wicks?" Martha asked.

"How many spools have you done?"

"Ten. This makes eleven."

"That'll give us enough to start the candles. There is a lot of flax left. You could start a fine thread for your new dress."

"My new dress?"

"You're growing right out of that one. By next fall, you'll be needing a new one."

"That's so far away."

"At the rate you're spinning, you'll need that much time."

"Mama, can't we get the spinner in? Some of the girls at school say the spinner comes to their house and does all their flax and wool."

"We can't afford that extra help. You can be deciding which color you'd like for your dress. When the wool's all spun, you can help mix up the dye."

Matthew, who was sitting at the table tooling the letters onto the Bagge book, suggested, "How about dying the wool before spinning? I hear that gives the best results?"

"We could if she decides the color, and dye stuff is available, and the weather holds out."

"Mama, why does the weather have to be good?"

"I prefer dying outside. There's not much place to hang the

wet wool inside, and I don't care for the smell of it wet." Maria reached over into her yarn basket and picked up the end of a new ball and carefully knitted that end into the last of the ball she was finishing.

"Mama, why didn't you just tie a knot in the two ends?" Martha had stood up from her spinning and walked over to watch her mother knit.

"This way there's nothing to rub against your foot. The sock will be more comfortable. Take off your shoe a minute, I need to measure how long to make this. Your feet are growing, too."

"Turning the heel looks hard," Martha said as she examined the sock Maria was holding against her foot. "What will you do if my foot grows longer before you finish the other sock?"

"I'll just unravel the toe, add some rows, then taper off again. On the next one, I'll let you turn the heel. You might as well learn how. But right now, scoot on back to the spinning and start on the warping thread."

Reluctantly, Martha put an empty spool on the wheel and resumed spinning. Thoughts of a new dress made her feet turn the wheel faster.

"Matthew," Maria spoke up, "have you heard anymore about that new weaver's apprentice?"

"You mean that Hessian soldier?"

"Yes, are they going to let him stay? I hear he keeps asking to join the congregation."

"Matthaas Noting is his name. They decided today to take him into the weave-shed at the Brothers House on trial."

"I hope it works out for him. And that he is a good weaver," she said as she thought about having to get someone to weave the cloth for Martha's new dress.

"Father, if he's a Hessian soldier, what's he doing here?"

He answered, "He was with the English army, but he was captured by the Continentals at Charleston. Then they released him. I don't know, but I assume in his wandering about this was the first German speaking community he found. Anyway, he seems happy here and wants to stay."

Martha stopped spinning and went over to see her father's work.

"The letters are so neat. The gold is beautiful." Suddenly, an idea came to her. "Gold. That's the color I want my dress."

Maria startled, exclaimed. "Not real gold, Martha."

Martha laughed, "No. Gold colored."

Matthew laughed, too. "Hear that, Maria. Sounds like your daughter, liking the yellow and gold."

"Now I know we'll dye outside!"

"Why? What will we use?"

"Onion skins!"

"Phew."

From the street came the night watchman's conch blast. Matthew wiped his tools, saying, "Nine o'clock. Reading time."

Maria shivered. "We'll have to move into the front room at night. Putting her knitting back into the basket, she proposed, "How about a cup of rose hip tea to warm us up?"

"Fine," replied Matthew. "I'll take the Bible to the kitchen."

Maria took a candle from the stand and held it in front of her as she moved to the kitchen.

Martha following asked, "Can we have bread and honey, too?"

"Yes. The honey pot's on the table. Slice three pieces of bread."

The coals in the fireplace glowed and the family sat close to the hearth enjoying the warmth, good food and fellowship as Matthew read to them.

Two nights later, during the congregation meeting there was much cause for rejoicing.

First, Brother Marshall announced that the coffer stolen from the bishop had been found. The good news had been brought to him by Bader, the man who had taken letters in the spring to Pennsylvania for the brethren. He had heard of the coffer being returned with all the valuable papers inside—but minus the money.

Marshall planned to send a brother for it immediately. Bader had also brought private letters, for which the recipients were expected to pay, and the Wachricten newsletter, for which the congregation paid.

Bader reported to Marshall that all was quiet at the time these letters had been written in the Moravian congregations up North, a condition for which the Salem brethren were very thankful.

The second good news came during the singstunde, evening song service. Two young couples were betrothed. Reichel recommended the couples for remembrance of the congregation before the Savior.

At this news Martha again wondered whom she would marry. Shyly, her eyes darted over the row of young boys. She offered a brief prayer, "Please, not one of them."

The third bit of news was happily received by most of the congregation. Matthew was displeased. Martha felt mixed emotions. The news was that a location for the boys' school had been decided: Brother Triebel's house. The move would take place tomorrow morning. In the afternoon, the bishop and the brethren of the Aelsten Conferenz would conduct a love feast for the boys, their fathers, Brother Schrober who was their new school master, and Brother Martin Schneider who would assist in supervising the smallest boys.

The parents and older people were glad the boys would now be more in the center of town where they could keep a close watch on the school. Also with Triebel's house in use as a school, the soldiers could not be quartered again in the center of town.

Matthew's concern was for Martha. She'd be more exposed to the boys and the usual mischief young boys get into, and the procession of schoolmasters. He folded his plump arms across his broad chest and set his lips tightly together, knowing there was no use to complain. The decision had been made and that was that!

While Martha had a few minutes ago prayed she wouldn't have to marry any of the Salem boys, she felt a new excitement at knowing all those boys were going to be next door.

The following morning as she was leaving for school, Martha was surprised when her father put on his tricon hat and said he'd walk with her.

Outside, she noticed he had a package under his arm. He sensed her curiosity and said, "It's the book for Bagge. How'd you like to go with me to deliver it?"

"Now? To the store?"

"Yes. We're early. Maybe Anna can walk to school with you."

At this departure from routine, Martha's feet fairly skipped the full block to the store. It wasn't quite opening time, but there was a wagon at the entry. Brother Balzer Christman was sitting up front holding the reins for the team of horses.

Matthew stepped over to the wagon. "Where you're headed, Balzer?"

"Hillsborough."

"Are these the hides the army ordered?"

"Leather for uppers and soles."

Brother Gottlieb Strehle came out of the store. "Morning, Matthew."

"Morning, Gottlieb. Do you think the general is going to accept the leather?"

Strehle shook his head, "Let's hope so. We could never in a lifetime have made all the shoes the general ordered. Even Major Hartmann knew that. That's why he told us to supply the tanned hides instead."

As Strehle swung himself up on the seat beside the teamster, Matthew inquired, "You going along, too?"

"Yeah. We need some raw hides. This order has about depleted our supply."

Brothers Biwighaus and Bagge emerged from the store with the latter reminding the former, "Now keep strict accounts in the presence of one of their accountants of every hide they take and any new ones you select. Keep your travel expenses on a separate page."

Biwighaus tucked a small ledger in his coat pocket.

Strehle motioned, "Come on up. Might as well ride while you can. Going down hill."

Biwighaus jumped up front. Strehle flipped the reins, released the hand brake, and the team started off. Bagge and Miksch waved them on. Bagge re-entered the store with Matthew and Martha close behind.

"Need anything this early, Matthew," Bagge spoke quickly not even turning around.

"Not today. I brought you something."

"Um?" Bagge wheeled around surprised.

"Your book. It's finished." Matthew handed the brown paper wrapped package to him.

"You've had it so long, I'd forgotten it."

Bagge put the package on the counter and removed the paper in an instant. He took a long, hard look at the leather volume. He wiped his strong hands on his trousers before taking it up.

Miksch glowed inwardly at this compliment.

Bagge walked over to a window where he scrutinized the book.

Martha squeezed Matthew's hand and the two exchanged a happy look. He softly told Martha to go outside and to the Bagge private quarters' door and ask Anna if she were ready for school. Happily, Martha ran out.

Sister Bagge answered the door and stared at Martha as if she didn't recognize her.

Martha was a little embarrassed, but she spoke up. "I'm Martha Miksch. Can Anna walk to school with me and my father?"

The woman's eyes brightened somewhat. "Oh, yes, Martha, one of Anna's dear friends, do come in."

Martha followed her into the front room, noticing how Sister Bagge smelled strongly of a whole flower garden, not just a wisp of a fragrance like Anna. In fact, Martha pondered how a mama could smell like anything except bacon and coffee at breakfast time. Martha sniffed deeply then decided even the house didn't smell like breakfast had just been cooked. To satisfy her debating mind, she concluded that today must be an oatmeal day, which did not smell up the whole house.

Nobody in Salem was rich, Martha knew that, but she noticed that the Bagge's house had more furniture and nicer curtains than her house had, and their rag rug covered almost the whole floor, but what really caught her attention were the shelves of books.

"Oh, how I'd love to have some books. Father's book will be just perfect here," Martha said to herself but as Anna came in, she said aloud, "Anna, you must have more books than the school."

Anna, fastening her cape, tossed her head, "There're father's."

As they left the house, Martha asked, "Does he read them to you?"

"Sometimes. Every time he starts, he has to stop to go somewhere or somebody needs him. I think that's why he likes our school so much. So I *can read there*. Martha, aren't you excited about the boys' school next door to your house?"

"I don't know. Will you be walking your brothers to school?"

Anna giggled, "You know papa wouldn't allow that. You'll get to see the boys all the time. Why I bet you'll be the first one to get married."

Martha blushed, "But you're the prettiest. You'll be first."

Anna shook her golden curls. "You're the oldest. You'll be first. I'm always last, just like with the small pox."

Martha thought Anna was going to cry—just as she did last year when all the girls caught the pox and she was so long getting it; but if there was one thing Martha couldn't stand, it was seeing people cry so she turned away quickly and said they'd better go on.

Inside the store, Traugott completed the surveying of the bookbinding job. "Matthew, a fine piece of work. I always said you should be a craftsman."

Matthew smiled, pleased, "That kind of job takes time. I couldn't turn enough of them out to keep us in bread."

"How much do I owe you?"

"Not a shilling. I enjoyed doing it."

"See here, that's too much work. A book bound like that in Pennsylvania would be worth . . ."

"No, Traugott. This is a gift. You've done much for Martha. I'm glad I can do something in return."

"I appreciate it."

"The girls are waiting. Is it all right if Anna walks up with Martha?"

"Fine."

Matthew joined the girls outside and Traugott went to his home to put the book with his others.

All morning the boys aided by their school masters trudged up and down the street taking books, maps, globes, slates, and the like into Brother Triebel's. Matthew watched sulkily from the nursery. He couldn't see the Triebel house from his shop; therefore, he stayed inside all afternoon, away from the windows so he wouldn't have to wave to his friends as they passed going to the love feast at the new school location.

Maria, sensitive to her husband's moods and patient with his brooding, kept silent. However along about four thirty she knew it was time to speak up.

"Matthew, it'll work out. Have faith like you're always telling us. The thing is done. Now leave it to the Lord."

He sighed; he knew she was right, but his bullish nature didn't like to be rebuked.

"I'll leave it to Him. But don't you think He wants me to keep an eye open down here?" Matthew slumped in his chair and grumbled.

"Yes, and you know I'll help you. Matthew, you've done a good job with Martha. She's never been a minute's trouble."

"True."

"If she likes men, well, it's because she loves you so much. You've been good to her, spent time with her. It's been a good relationship. I don't think she'll let you down."

"She's a good girl," he spoke more softly.

Maria sensed the dark mood was ebbing. "How about a cup of tea. I have a stick of sassafras left."

"Yes, thanks. Put a spoonful of honey in," he called as she went into the kitchen.

When Maria returned with the steaming cup, he commented, "I think I'll go up to the Gemeinhaus tonight. The Conferenz is meeting."

Matthew's low mood had vanished by the time he reached the Gemeinhaus. He caught Brother Marshall's attention as he was entering the meeting room.

"Brother Marshall, may I speak before the Conferenz a few minutes? It's about the soldiers and the disturbance the night of the ordination."

"You're welcome to speak, Brother Miksch. We'll want to hear your views."

The two entered and took seats around a long wooden table, Marshall at the head and Matthew on the side near the door. Marshall called the meeting to order and Brother Graff opened with a prayer. Matthew noted that all the ministers and their wives as well as Bishop Reichel and his wife were in attendance. Brother Meyer, the tavern keeper, was sitting opposite Matthew.

Marshall announced that Brother Miksch wished to speak to the Conferenz.

Matthew leaned over closer to the table. "Thank you for letting me intrude upon your meeting. As we all know there was an unfortunate experience the other night that delayed our service. The soldiers who caused the trouble passed by my house as I was on the way to the service. One of the men appeared to be quite intoxicated and he was drinking on the street. I don't know where he got his whisky but he was coming from the direction of the tavern. Now Brother Meyer, I'm not saying he bought it at your place, but I am here to ask if such disturbances could be prevented in the future, if we did not sell whisky to the regular soldiers."

Marshall replied, "We have been thinking along the same lines, so we asked Brother Meyer here to discuss the problem. Brother Meyer, do you have any suggestions?"

Meyer nervously kept turning his hat in his hands, "I'd like nothing better than to quit selling to those foot soldiers, but when they come in demanding drink, 'specially a whole bunch of them, it's plumb hard to refuse."

"Do they usually have money to pay you?" Graff asked.

"Continental money."

"Could enlisted men be required to have their officer's permission to be served?"

Marshall said, "That sounds like a reasonable approach. After all, it's troublesome for them to have to be solving problems caused by their men's misconduct."

"If it's agreed, then we'll write out orders to the effect that Brother Meyer is not to sell to any soldier without the officer's approval and we'll notify officers when they come into the tavern," Graff suggested.

The bishop spoke, "Brother Graff, how is the wine supply for communion?"

"Very low. The brothers gathered what grapes they could find and made some wine, but the yield was poor last year. This year's harvest is better. It's not ready for serving yet."

"Brother Meyer, do you have wine in the tavern cellar?" the bishop asked.

"Yes, but not as much as usual."

"Brothers Marshall and Graff, what about taking the tavern wine and bringing it up here to use at communion?" Reichel asked. "That may help solve some of the intemperance at the tavern. Brother Meyer, please encourage moderation even among the officers."

"I'll try. Remember, the foot soldiers usually order beer. That's about all they can afford. I'll reserve a few bottles of wine for the gentlemen who stay in the tavern. Here is a collection for the poor box. Some of the soldiers left it with me. They seemed quite pleased that we took care of the poor." Meyer handed a sack to Marshall. "If that's all, I'll be getting back."

"Thank you for coming, brothers."

Matthew rose to leave too. The Conferenz began to talk about widows. Someone suggested that widows' pensions should come from the widows' society until they remarried.

Matthew closed the door and he and Meyer walked out into the cold night air, pulling their coats tightly around them. Meyer took a left turn at the corner and Matthew a right. As Matthew passed Triebel's house he was thankful that Martha's bedroom window faced north.

CHAPTER NINE

The following afternoon Bishop and Sister Reichel visited the Miksch shop. Sister Reichel ordered a dozen beeswax candles for their up coming trip.

Maria said, indicating the ones in the candle box, "These are a few months old. I'll be pouring some in the next few days. Matthew just brought down some fresh wax from George Schmid's. When are you leaving?"

"Around the fifth of next month, if we get our pass. I can wait for the candles if buying these will put you in short supply, although I don't mind the old ones."

Maria offered them a cup of herb tea, which they accepted.

"Sorry it can't be real tea or coffee. I believe that's one of the pleasures we miss the most during this war time," she apologized as she served them in the front room.

"There's something about the aroma of coffee that wakes up the drowsiness, morning or night, whereas a cup of tea seems to quiet a body," Matthew commented.

"Or cure an ill," added Sister Reichel.

"Well, we'll appreciate the coffee all the more when trading resumes someday," said the bishop.

Maria passed a plate of honey teacakes. "Meanwhile, I'm grateful for Matthew's herbs and roses. And thankful the Lord has sent a good growing season."

Matthew rose and walked to his desk, "Bishop, Martha has

written a letter to her grandparents Spangenburg. Can we trouble you to deliver it to him?"

"I'd be glad." He took the letter and put it inside his coat.

"What's the latest news from Germany?"

"Unlike the rest of the world, conditions there are extremely quiet. Germany is enjoying a calm, productive time. It's possible that the economy there will be strong enough that we can send some assistance later," Reichel spoke evenly.

"That is good news."

"I'll report your needs here on my return."

The front door opened and Colonel Armstrong came into the entry. Matthew walked across the room to meet him.

Armstrong said, "I went up to the Gemeinhaus looking for Bishop Reichel. They said he might be here."

"He is. Hang your hat," Matthew pointed toward the pegs in the hall, "and come on in."

Maria cleared the tea things and moved them into the kitchen.

"Good afternoon, bishop. I brought a pass for your return trip to Pennsylvania." The colonel held the signed paper.

"That's kind of you to bring it personally."

"Glad to. Just let me re-check the particulars. You're taking two teamsters, who'll return later with the wagon. And one brother will go up and will remain in Pennsylvania?"

"Correct. Brother and Sister Marshall will ride with us to the noon halt, but will return here immediately," the bishop said.

Armstrong handed him the pass. "There were signs of frost all along the country side this morning. I expect you'll want to get on your way as soon as possible."

"We plan to leave October fifth."

"I'm sure the congregation will miss you," the colonel said as he bid them goodbye.

Several days later and just two days before Reichel party's departure, the store wagon rolled into town from Hillsborough. Everyone had been awaiting news of the outcome of the trip. Many people crowded around the store soon after the wagon stopped.

They waited while Bagge read a letter from General Gates. The crowd learned from the teamsters that the wagon was full of new skins.

Bagge told the assembled group, "It's a friendly letter. He writes that they are satisfied with the leather. He sent part payment, and offers a ticket for the balance to be paid when the money comes in. He says they're willing to serve us in anyway."

Mixed reactions were voiced among the assembled townspeople. Some were relieved that the army accepted the tanned skins instead of the shoes that had originally been ordered. Others were disgruntled because the payments were delayed.

As Bagge folded the letter, he and Marshall went into the store. Bagge said tersely, "Another loss, Brother Marshall."

"In currency, yes. The people could well use the money. But it will be in our favor for the officials to know we try to comply with their needs and orders," Marshall reminded him.

"He enclosed a pass for me to go to Cross Creek to get salt."

"Good."

Brother Biwighaus entered the store. "Brothers, I heard some news from Major Penn while I was in Hillsborough."

"What was it?" asked Marshall.

"It's going to make the people mad, especially the tanner and everybody who worked so hard to get that big order ready—and everybody else who had to wait for their own leather needs."

"The news, Brother," Bagge urged.

"That leather we sent—it wasn't needed."

"What?" Bagge looked surprised.

"Nope. They just asked for it to test our sentiments to this state."

Before an explosive reaction could begin, Marshall calmly stated, "They have their answer and they are pleased. It was right we did the best we could. Surely things will go better for us. Give your team a rest, Bagge, then do what you can about getting salt. It'll be needed."

Bishop Reichel expressed pleasure at hearing the leather situation had been handled successfully and that the war news in general was quiet. He and his wife visited the choirs and as many families as they could before their departure.

October fifth turned out to be a favorable day for travel, cloudy with the wind out of the northeast. The Mikschs, along with many others from Salem, gathered around the Gemeinhaus as the Reichels boarded the wagon. Everyone wished them a safe conduct to Pennsylvania and on to Europe. As the wagon pulled around the square, Brother and Sister Marshall rode horseback beside them.

The adults returned to their homes or crafts and the children to school.

Martha was sad that the bishop had left. The past four months that he had been in Salem had made everyday events special. He had been so interested in everybody. Even the townspeople were friendlier than usual to each other.

Sister Sehner stopped by Martha's seat and asked if she were having trouble with her assignments.

"No, sister," she replied. She was embarrassed to be caught daydreaming so she put her mind to her schoolwork.

At the end of the day, her father was waiting at the corner for her. She ran down the short block to meet him.

Struggling up the main street hill, were several wagons, heavily loaded with household goods.

"Father, are these more families leaving home?"

"Yes. Folks have been passing through all morning. Most of these are from Salisbury."

"Is that far away?"

"Not far, not far."

Martha didn't ask anymore questions.

A man on horseback trotting north passed the wagons. He halted as he reached Matthew.

"Sir, is there a place to buy bread here?"

"Yes. There is a bakery." Matthew pointed down the hill to the building behind the Brothers House.

"Much obliged," and he spurred his horse down the side street.

Two other people asked Miksch about bread. "You men traveling far?" Miksch inquired of the walkers.

Martha went inside the house while Matthew paused to talk with the men.

"Going to Virginia," one man answered.

"Is that where most of these people are headed?"

"Reckon so. At least we're aiming to leave the English behind us."

"Is there any fighting in your area?" Matthew searched for news.

"The fighting is mostly south of Salisbury. That's where we're from. The militia are rounding up all the Tories, but they're taking them prisoners."

"You people going to stay if the English move in?" The second man asked anxiously.

"We're planning to stay. Maybe they won't march this way. We hear General Davidson is waiting for them. And General Gates may move down. The units usually around here have moved out," Matthew stated.

"The Continental army will need all the help it can get. We better be getting to that bakery. We want to cover a few more miles today."

The men turned toward the bakery and Matthew entered his house. He heard Martha telling Maria about the people in the street.

"Mama, what would it be like not to have any bread to eat? Even when wheat was scarce last winter, we always had cornbread."

"I hope you never have to go hungry, Martha."

"Mama, we don't plant wheat or corn, yet we always have some."

"That's the way our town is set up, dear. This is a craft center. We live by our handwork, our trades, but the leaders planned for the farm, and the dairy to take care of our food needs. Thus we could be free to do our work."

"We have our gardens."

"Yes, but they are small. They don't require the time and care of a big farm."

"I feel so sorry for all those people leaving their homes and moving on. Nobody looks happy."

"If you ever have to move, I pray it shall be a happy time. Now let's eat our dinner."

Martha just stood looking sad.

Maria spoke consolingly. "I understand you want to help, but now is not your time, dear. The best you can do for yourself and others is to eat and grow stronger and when you're called to serve, you'll be able to do so."

Suddenly, Martha threw her arms around Maria's neck. "I love you, Mama."

CHAPTER TEN

The battle of Kings Mountain October 7, in which the English Major Patrick Ferguson and his men were defeated, was a turning point in the war. However, other English troops began marching north. Militia continued rounding up Tories. Continental soldiers were constantly passing through Salem. Messengers were riding into town with orders for various officers who stopped often at the tavern.

The second week of the month, some Continental troops met in Salem and the men and horses had to be fed. The officers stayed in the tavern while enlisted men camped out in the open area behind the tavern. They built fires and cooked outside even in the heavy rain.

Martha came home from school one afternoon to find her mother bustling about, cooking turnips and grating cabbage. Martha was instantly put to work mixing a dressing for coleslaw.

"Mama, who's this food for?"

"The tavern. A number of officers are down there. The staff there can't take care of all the extra work. Some of the married sisters are helping out with the cooking."

Matthew was in the loft twisting more tobacco ropes. The soldiers had bought out his supply on the shelf.

"Martha," he shouted downstairs, "bring me up a piggin of molasses."

Maria nodded her head toward the cellar. "The new batch came in today. Open up the front barrel. Be sure to get the molasses piggin. And use the dipper. Try not to run it over the sides. It's a mess to clean up."

Martha took the lantern off its peg on the kitchen wall and opened the front latch. She took a twig from the bundle by the fireplace, stuck the twig in the fire until it caught, then lit the candle. She blew on the twig, closed the lantern door, and went down to the cellar.

The cellar was cold and damp on this rainy day. Her father had already loosened the top so she didn't have any trouble getting it off the barrel. The dark molasses smelled sweet as she dipped into the piggin.

"Mama, where can I put the dipper. It's sticky?"

"Bring it up in the piggin."

Martha came up to the top of the stairs and hooked the lantern over the door latch, then returned for the molasses. By the time she reappeared, Maria had a bowl for the dipper.

"We'll sop this with bread for supper."

"That'll be almost as good as gingerbread," Martha said, as she continued up to the loft with the molasses.

Matthew took the piggin and poured the thick syrup over the coils of tobacco set in a wooden trough, then handed it back to her.

The loft was crowded. There was tobacco hung to dry on the side next to a small outside door that was used only to hoist the new tobacco up so it didn't have to be carried through the house. There were troughs for holding the sweetening coils, platforms for the salting process, baskets for the stems, burlap hanging around the walls for covering the aging sweetened coils, and shelves with mortar and pestle for grinding the snuff. There were several extra buckets for storing clay pipes and reeds.

"Father, you're running out of room to put things," Martha declared, as she couldn't locate an empty spot to set the piggin.

"What we need is a tobacco manufactory. A building all by itself."

The rain beat steadily against the roof.

"Father, how are the soldiers going to get the turnips and slaw?"

"I suppose I'll have to carry the food down to the tavern."

"You'll get soaked."

"You all keep the fire up and I'll hang the clothes to dry when I get back."

He took the piggin from her and disappeared down the steps. Martha had gotten wet herself returning from school so she took off her skirt and hung it over her chair. She put on her old cotton skirt. When she heard the front door shut, she went out to the hall and picked her way to the head of the stairs where she stood on tiptoe to look out the window. She watched her father balancing the hot pot of turnips in one hand and the bucket of cole slaw in the other.

As if by some miracle, she discovered she didn't need to stand on tiptoe anymore. With her feet flat on the floor, she could see out the little window.

"I'm almost grown," she admitted to herself, and when she looked down again she gasped. She could see her whole foot and her ankle.

That night after supper, she volunteered to spin without being asked and she kept the pedal moving steadily much to her mother's surprise, until it was time for services.

So many of the brothers were involved with making temporary arrangements for the troops, that the service was shortened. As the congregation was getting ready to leave the saal, a soldier opened the door. Water dripped from his long blue cape onto the wide planked floorboards. His boots were muddy. He glanced hastily over the group assembled.

Quickly and quietly, Brother Charles Holder, who had been sitting on the end of a rear bench, approached him. "Can I help you?"

"We need a doctor out in the camp. Is your doctor here?" The soldier asked brusquely.

"Just a minute," Holder answered. He walked down the aisle and motioned to Dr. Bonn.

Bonn said excuse me as he squeezed by some brothers.

"Yes, soldier, what are your needs?"

"We have several wounded men in our camp. They need a doctor."

"What type of wounds, surface or puncture?" Bonn asked as the three men eased into the hallway.

The soldier thought then spoke. "They are not too deep, but the men need attention. Can you go with me?"

"I'm needed here now. There are some patients I shouldn't leave. But I can let my assistant go with you," Dr. Boon offered.

"We appreciate that."

Bonn asked Holder to get Dixson from the saal and to explain the situation to the ministers.

As soon as Dixson appeared, Dr. Bonn asked him to accompany the soldier; however, he instructed the younger brother to go to his rooms first to secure any items he needed because he might be away a few days. He asked Dixson to meet him and the soldier at the apothecary, which was located in the doctor's home.

The trio left. The congregation soon filed out behind them, each picking his way carefully in the street as the rain continued to pour and to run like little streams down the slope.

Three days passed before there was any word of Brother Dixson and the wounded men. And when the news came, it created a feeling of terror seldom experienced by the Moravians. Again news came at night, but this time it was before services started.

Martha and her parents were about to open the front door of the Gemeinhaus, when suddenly Martha felt herself being pushed roughly against the doorframe. She heard her father saying sternly, "Careful there."

Martha regained her balance and position and saw a soldier swiftly stepping through the doorway. She faintly heard him apologize, "Sorry" as he hurried on.

Maria spoke, concerned and surprised, "Are you all right? What could cause a man to act so rudely, to push a child about?"

As the Mikschs reached the saal, they heard the soldier demanding in a harsh voice to see the doctor.

"I know he's here. Which one is he?"

Marshall approached the soldier. He was not the one who had come three nights ago. This man was tougher looking and spoke forcefully and loudly.

Marshall politely reminded the soldier that they were in a room dedicated to worship and invited the stranger into the hall where he would try to be of assistance.

The soldier narrowed his eyes and uttered tersely, "I want your doctor to come with me, now. That assistant he sent says my officer's wounds are too serious for him to treat."

"Joseph Dixson is a capable assistant, however . . ."

"Listen here, sir. I've ridden all the way from the banks of Atkin [Yadkin] to get help for my superior. He's a good man. We don't aim to lose him. Your doctor returns with me *now*, or I'll come back here in three days with 150 Virginia soldiers and we'll *burn* this town to the ground!"

The soldier's rough voice had risen to such a volume that everyone in the saal had clearly heard his ultimatum. Dr. Bonn had heard also and was on his way to the hall.

Marshall breathed once deeply, keeping complete control of his temper. "If you would kindly let me finish. I was saying that however, I'm sure that Dr. Bonn will accompany you if the wounds are serious enough to need his expertise."

As he finished speaking, Bonn was beside him. "I'll go where I'm needed. Now come along, soldier. Tell me about your officer while I get my instruments."

Diplomatically, Bonn walked in front of the soldier, and out the door causing him to have to quit the saal and Gemeinhaus, too.

The violent threat caused a strange fear to creep into Martha's heart. The look of terror and helplessness in her eyes was mirrored in many other faces. Martha didn't want to sit with her teacher. She wanted to be near her father, to feel his large arm around her shoulder. She had just taken her usual seat, but she had the urge to beg the teacher to let her move. Her years of training kept her on the bench; no girl had ever sat with the men. Inwardly, Martha trembled. This was a new experience; never before had anyone threatened to burn their town: that meant the Gemeinhaus and her house—her dear yellow house. How can everyone just sit here—and wait?

Martha could not realize now during her moment of personal terror that the older brothers and sisters had experienced threats of one kind or another before in Germany, in Georgia, even in Bethabara. Threats were never easy to hear. Shock always followed unexpected threats to themselves or their homes, but previous experience had taught them to be patient and to use self-control as they absorbed new blows. Brother Marshall calmly and confidently marched up the aisle to the altar table.

He faced anxious people.

"Brethren, I'm aware the messenger in the hallway was speaking loudly. I would like to inform you of the present situation. One of the officers whom Joseph Dixson was sent to bandage had wounds deeper than Brother Dixson felt he could attend. So, a call was issued for Dr. Bonn to treat the officer. He has now gone with the soldier to the camp on the Yadkin. The soldier made a threat to burn our town if Dr. Bonn did not go with him. The threat was unnecessary. Dr. Bonn is always willing, as all of us are, to go wherever our services are needed. Remember, this town was built at the direction of our Lord. It is His town. It cannot be burned unless *He wills* it to be burned. Now, let us begin our service."

Most of the brothers and sisters relaxed in the trusting reassurance of Marshall's words. Martha's fears were quieted somewhat, too, but a trace of anxiety lay like a shadow over her all night and she kept wakening from her sleep. She was edgy all the next day.

In the evening after the family returned home from service, Martha asked permission to stay up and spin a while. Maria knew she had been apprehensive about the threats so she gave her consent.

"I'll help you carry the wheel into the front room near the stove."

Placing the wheel near the stove, Maria next lit a candle from hot coals in the kitchen and put it in a wooden stand that she moved near Martha's chair. Martha brought in the flax basket, took out a handful of the coarse fibers and sat down.

Maria spoke to Matthew, "How about a mug of cider?"

"Can you heat it?"

"Yes, it would be good hot. How about you, Martha?"

"Yes, Mama. I'd like mine hot, too," she said as she fingered the flax into a thin strand and joined it to the end of the thread on the spool on the wheel. She was absorbed in her task and hadn't heard the front door open. When she looked up and saw Dr. Bonn standing in the front room doorway, she let out a little cry.

"Pardon me, Martha, I didn't mean to frighten you." Dr. Bonn spoke kindly. "Evening Matthew, evening, Maria," he added as Maria came in quickly from the kitchen.

"Brother Jacob," Matthew greeted him warmly, shaking his hand firmly, "are we glad to see you."

"It's a blessing, you're back. Lord be praised, " Maria said as she clasped her hands together.

Martha still stunned by his sudden appearance blurted out anxiously, "Are they, are they going to burn Salem?"

Dr. Bonn strode over to her and placed a steady hand gently on her head, "No, dear girl, they aren't going to burn the town."

Martha was so relieved she almost cried, she covered her face with her hands a second, then dropped them to her lap.

Matthew, the ever genial host, said, "Jacob, we're about to have hot cider. Join us, please."

"No, thank you. I haven't been home yet. I just stopped to get some candles and to see if you have any sage and chamomile flower heads to spare."

"Yes, I have both herbs. Come now. Sit a moment. The cider 'll do you good after that long ride."

Maria said, "I've got some fresh gingerbread."

Dr. Bonn sank into the nearest chair. "Maria, that does it. I doubt there's a man alive who could say no to your gingerbread."

Matthew told Martha to get the sage and chamomile from the hooks in the kitchen, then he turned to Bonn and asked, "Now tell me about the trip to the camp."

"Matthew, I was a might worried going out there. I really believe that soldier would have taken some action against us, even if only out of desperation."

Martha rushed to get the bunches of herbs down. She wanted to hear all about the doctor's adventure. She didn't even offer to help her mother get the refreshments.

Martha quietly placed the herbs on the table and settled in her seat, not looking up and pretending to be engrossed in her spinning, hoping they would not notice her and would continue talking, which they did.

"Jacob, was the officer seriously wounded?"

"His wounds needed cleaning out all right, and draining, but they weren't dangerous at that point. He probably just didn't have enough confidence in Joseph."

"Well, I'm glad you could take care of him."

"I sat by during the night, while he slept, and when he woke this morning he was feeling better. He's really quite a nice man." As he saw Maria bringing in the cider, he smiled, "Now if he'd had some of Maria's cooking and service, he'd really feel peppy."

"How are things otherwise there?" Matthew inquired before tasting the hot cider.

Maria passed the gingerbread and both men took large pieces.

"There are some prisoners in the camp. They're going to leave them at Bethabara."

"Oh," uttered Maria, "who's going to guard them?"

"Can you believe this? The Continental Army was going to leave twenty soldiers—*twenty* to guard a few *wounded* men?"

"*Were* going to?" echoed Matthew.

"When I heard that, I talked to the officer I had treated. I suggested he might find a few guards enough in that peaceful village. The army needs its well men elsewhere."

"What did he say to that?"

"He ordered only three guards to remain behind," the doctor answered finishing his gingerbread.

Matthew nodded approval. "That'll be good for the Bethabara brothers. Feeding twenty soldiers could surely cut into their supplies."

Bonn said gravely, "Matthew, there's talk that Cornwallis is moving up this way. Nobody seems to know for sure what General Greene is going to do. It looks as if he's in retreat. We may see more troops through here soon, more than we've had before."

As he rose, Matthew handed him the herbs, and then walked over to the candle box. Bonn followed saying, "I'm glad you've got some herbs, I may have to call on you again if my medicinals run out. A spot of herb tea may make the patients feel they're better. Don't bother to wrap the candles."

"By the way, if there's any particular root you want, let me know. I will be going out to survey sometime next month with Meinung. The ground might be still soft enough to dig," Matthew informed Bonn.

"If you see any sassafras, bring me some. Everybody will be wanting it the first of spring. Goodnight all, thanks again for the gingerbread and cider, Maria. Martha, don't worry about the soldiers. They seemed quite friendly when I left them today." Bonn smiled kindly at her then left the house.

"Mama, isn't Dr. Bonn just wonderful?" Martha said in admiration.

"He's a very wise man," her mother responded as she gathered the mugs.

Matthew unhooked the tiebacks and closed the blue curtains over the windows. "You know Martha, lots of people besides the Moravians here have a high opinion of our good doctor. He's fair-minded. He was a justice for many years."

"But, Father, it is his doctoring that saved our town. I'm going to say a special prayer for him tonight," she stared dreamily.

"That reminds me that it's time for prayers and bed," Maria yawned. "Matthew, do you have a short reading tonight?'

"The Good Book has selections for all our needs and times," Matthew concluded with humorous tones.

Later, in her room alone, Martha repeated to herself Dr. Bonn's conversation. His words had quieted the fears that had lived with her the past twenty-four hours, but at the same time a new excitement was being born in her heart. Dr. Bonn all by himself had gone to the army camp, had treated the wounded officer, and had saved the town from being burned. He was a wonderful person. He was a doctor. And soon she was asleep with these happy thoughts.

CHAPTER ELEVEN

On October 9 Martha was getting ready for bed, her mind full of thoughts of tomorrow when she would be twelve years old. She knew she was changing physically; that she was larger than her classmates were. She liked being an older girl, and not having to go to school with the little ones. She was wondering how the cherry red ribbons or even pink ones like the Single Sisters wore, would look on her gold dress.

Her musings were interrupted by some unfamiliar noises from outside. She pressed close to the window to see what was going on. She didn't see anything unusual, but there again were sounds of laughter as if from a large group of people.

She hastened down the steps. She didn't need the candle because she could still see lights below.

"Father."

"Yes, Martha?" he looked up from the desk where he was working on accounts.

"Can you hear the noises?"

"No. Where are they coming from? What kind of noises?"

Maria came in from the kitchen.

"From up at Stockburger's, I think. Sounds like lots of laughing."

Matthew opened a window and they all listened.

Merry making noise drifted in.

Matthew deducted, "There was to be a corn-husking up at Stockburger's right after supper. Sounds like they're still at it."

"But Matthew," Maria uttered astonished, "it sounds like a social; not like a work task."

"It does indeed," he agreed as he pulled the window down.

"I declare, the bishop is scarcely out of town and the brothers have forgotten the seriousness of our mission," she continued perturbed. "Martha, run on back to bed."

Martha went back up to her room and changed to her nightgown. She heard the happy sounds off and on until she drifted into sleep.

Upon awakening, she felt the social must still be going on as she heard someone softly singing. As she sat up in bed, she recognized the sweet voice as belonging to her mother. Martha opened her door and listened to the verses of the hymn while she put on her old faded green woolen dress. She took out the braids, brushed her hair, and then braided it again carefully. She wanted to look as neat as possible on her birthday.

Before going down to breakfast, she poured a little water from her piggin onto the rosemary plant. "I wish you had leaves to spare, so I could pinch one off, then I'd smell good, but I'll have to wait till you grow some more."

In the kitchen she hugged her mother. "Mama, thank you for the birthday song."

As she sat down, she spied a neatly folded square of linen on her plate. "What's this?"

"Open it up," Maria said.

Martha unfolded the linen that had been evenly rolled and whipped at the edges with the tiniest stitches. In one corner the letters MEM were embroidered with a light pumpkin colored thread.

"Mama, a handkerchief for me. It's so pretty. Thank you."

Matthew entered the back door, "How's the birthday girl? October is a fine time for a birthday *except* that the garden doesn't produce bouquets for you."

Maria filled their mugs with hot tea, then heaped their plates with cornbread, sausage and apples.

Matthew, who had gone into the front room, returned and handed Martha a tiny brown paper package.

"Another gift?" she marveled.

Excitedly, she unfolded the paper until out rolled a metal thimble. She held up her right hand and placed the thimble on her third finger. The thimble was too large. She put it on her middle finger and the fit was snug.

With gratitude showing in her eyes, she thanked him.

At school, the girls and the teachers all wished her a happy birthday. Everyone was so nice she thought being twelve must be the nicest age ever.

During the day, several of the brothers came to the tobacco shop. The conversations of all of them included remarks about the socializing at Stockburgers the previous night.

One of the brothers told Matthew that news had already reached Marshall and Graff and their reactions had not been favorable. In fact, the feeling apparently was that although frivolity accompanied corn husking in some communities, it was not appropriate in Wachovia. This would be a good time for fathers to remember that they were responsible for everything that went on in their houses.

Brother Samson shook his head as he stumped his tobacco in his pipe. "I sure don't envy you, Matthew, having to raise Martha right here in the center of town, especially with the boys' school next door. Oh, the boys are mostly good, but they can get into mischief. My little Peter keeps wanting to play soldier no matter what I say to discourage him. It's hard to keep an eye on him and tend to my work. Bessie stays busy with the baby. It's colicky."

Another brother lamented that the Stockburgers affair might have the young brothers and sisters making up their own minds about whom to marry. This kind of frolic led to such things he had heard.

After the shop closed, Matthew strolled down to the square to meet Martha. She noticed that he was solemn on the walk. Following supper he asked her to come into the front room to sit with him.

"It's time we had a little talk about your future. You know your mother and I support the Unity in all its aspects that includes its marriage customs. We have both been happy together."

"Oh, yes, Father, I know."

"We hope you want to accept the Unity's rules for your own, too."

"Oh, I will—I do."

"Martha," asked Matthew, "do you really understand about the marriage arrangements?"

"I'm not sure. I know Moravians marry Moravians. I guess I'll marry a Moravian. But I don't know how it all comes about."

"When you're older, a single sister, and you've learned about housekeeping and caring for children and when you're ready for responsibilities of a family, then you may be selected as a helpmate, a wife, for a brother," Maria said as she joined them.

"And that means your mother and I will also have the right to approve or disapprove as well. So will the elders. Of course, we'll all want the lot's approval in such an important matter as marriage."

Maria reminded her daughter, "Yes, dear. They do have to approve, but parents are also consulted, as well as the girl. You—as a single sister—will have the right to refuse or accept."

"What about the brother?" Martha asked.

"In some cases, he is the one who initiates the marriage issue. When he is ready to marry, he will ask for a certain sister or he will ask the Conferenz to select a suitable sister," her father clarified.

"When is a brother ready?" Martha wanted to know.

"When he has finished his apprenticeship, has a job, is free of debts and can provide lodging and necessities for a wife," answered Matthew.

"For the brothers, like ministers and doctors, who really need a wife, the Elders will suggest someone," Maria added.

Martha showed her relief. "Then I don't have to think about it, Father. You and mother can think about it for me." She reflected a moment, then seriously she asked, "But will it be all right later when I'm older if I know someone I like a whole lot, can I tell you, so that you'll know?"

Matthew and Maria looked across her to each other and silently communicated approval.

Matthew replied, "Of course, you may. And Martha, we are the people you should tell. You know *not* to make any contacts with any young men yourself."

"Yes. You, and sister have told me so before," she said in her most grown-up manner.

Matthew chuckled, "I trust you will continue to look up to us for advice."

Martha smiled in answer to her father. To herself she mused happily, there is no boy in our town I know of that I want to make any *contact* with, at least not on any permanent basis.

CHAPTER TWELVE

Talk of the war echoed up and down Main Street. Every time a messenger rode in or a brother came from one of the western or southern villages, the townspeople waited eagerly for the news to be dispensed. Each related what he had heard. After the threat of burning the town and the news of a large number of soldiers and prisoners in Bethabara, the Salem brothers became more protective of their children. Parents accompanied children to school in the morning and the schoolmasters walked them home in late afternoon.

The Conferenz warned the school masters and fathers to be sure that each other knew where the boys were to be at all times. Contact with outsiders, especially the military, was to be minimized.

Even Martha's supervision tightened. If there were customers in the shop, Maria found jobs for Martha in the cellar or kitchen. If Maria had to leave the house on an errand or attend the Grosse Helfers Conferenz, Matthew gave Martha instruction in the use of scales, which he now had for weighing coins in the shop, or he took her to the nursery.

She began to ask more questions about the herbs.

"Father, what was Dr. Bonn going to use the chamomile for?"

"I can't say for sure, but I've heard it makes a good tea to cure nightmares."

Her blue eyes widened, "Does Dr. Bonn have nightmares?"

"Not he. Some of his patients."

He could see Martha was thinking this over. He put out his hand and covered hers. "Dear, he's probably just getting ready. In war times, men see and do some terrible things. Afterwards, sleep may come hard; it may be disturbed. Even bystanders, get fearful sometimes. They imagine that all the evil things are going to happen to them."

"Father, do Moravians ever get worried?"

"Do you, Martha?"

"Not much. I always know you and Mama are here."

"Who do you think your mother and I know is looking after us? Who do you think we put our faith in?"

"Jesus and God and the holy angels."

"Do you think they're looking after you, too?"

"Oh, yes. I know they are."

"Now, does knowing we are here, and God and Jesus are looking after you, does that help ease your worries when they come?"

"Yes."

"Martha, being a Moravian does not insure us that the problems of the world won't reach out and touch us, but it should help us to not be defeated or over burdened by those problems. Carry the love of the Lord in your heart and do God's will and you shall know a happiness that no problems will spoil."

"Father, we are God's helpers, aren't we?"

"I believe so."

"And God uses us and our talents to help others."

"Right."

"Do you think *I can* be a good wife someday, when I'm older, of course?"

"You have the makings of a fine helpmate."

"I said I wasn't going to ever worry about who would ask me, I'll trust you and Mama to say yes to the right person."

"I'm pleased to hear that. Your mother will be, too," he smiled.

"But would it be all right, if I told you, if I ever felt I knew a marriage would be right?"

He looked into her serious eyes and answered in the same

manner, "I'll be open always to hear your wishes. You don't already have someone in mind do you?" he inquired cautiously.

Quite definitely she assured him, "No, no. I won't be marrying a brother or older boy from here."

This sudden assertion caught Matthew quite by surprise. Martha opened her mouth to add, "Because I'm going to marry a doctor," but she decided to keep that decision to herself.

She returned to blowing the chaff from the seeds in the flat pan, then handed them to her father to sift in the strainer.

"Father, can you help me to learn about herbs?"

Matthew watching the seed fall through the large holes answered, "The best way to learn is to work with me. Help plant them, pinch back and harvest the seeds and the leaves."

"I'd like that. Can you tell me how to use them as medicines?"

"No. That's not my area. I'll teach you about growing and harvesting. Your mother can tell you about cooking with them. But medicines, you should leave the study of remedies to the doctor."

She watched him pour the cleansed seeds into a paper square then neatly fold it flat.

"Maybe someday, Dr. Bonn will teach us. After all, when I get married and have a family, I'll have to know how to make teas, and how to get everybody well if the doctor's away."

"Let's not be in too much of a hurry to learn," he admonished her. Matthew had immediately caught the change in her phraseology—for the first time she had not said *when I grow up or if I marry*.

"Martha, in the matter of marriage, the first steps are taken by the brother. Remember that."

Just as Dr. Bonn had predicated, Salem was seeing more soldiers. Those who were stationed in Bethabara came into Salem to shop. One day the militia came in along with both English and Tory prisoners.

The townspeople were surprised to see that the Tories were more closely guarded than the English soldiers were. The prisoners were allowed to walk about the town and to shop in all the craft houses. Since many of the brothers spoke English, the captives found their purchasing easier than expected in the predominately German area.

The children were excited when the news of "prisoners" in town reached them. Teachers reminded them there would be no stopping or talking with any strangers on the way home.

A few parents were waiting to escort their children, but they were also in a hurry to return to their homes and shops. Trade was bustling. Since the prisoners were to be in town only a few hours, shopkeepers shortened their lunchtime. The English didn't have paper currency. They had coins. And the craftsmen were anxious to have their trade.

The word prisoner was vague to Martha. She had a notion that a prisoner would be in ragged clothes, with his hands bound and a guard standing with a weapon at his back. So when she heard the front door open, she sneaked up to the closed kitchen door and opened it a little. She was astonished to see the red-coated men walk in by themselves and ask for snuff.

Matthew served them politely. He asked if they would like to buy a snuffbox or tobacco stamper. He was anxious to sell these more expensive items to the men with gold and silver coins. He spoke to a few of his customers about his own brief stay in England.

When it was time to return to school, customers were still in the shop, so Maria walked with Martha. At the corner they met Anna and Biwighaus. He offered to walk them both and Maria thanked him and hastened back home.

Martha and Anna exchanged impressions of the soldiers and prisoners. Anna'a apartment door didn't open into the shop so she hadn't seen or heard much, but she did find the English officer's uniform colorful, like a cardinal, she said.

It was about a month later that the girls saw the prisoners briefly again. About one hundred Tories who were being held in Bethabara were released to go home and wash their clothes. Many of the men were short of supplies so they journeyed into Salem. They went to the mill for provisions they would need the following day when they were to march to Salisbury. This time about twenty English officers were allowed to come into town.

Along with them came Mr. Brooks, an army commissary for the soldiers. He had been quartered in the midst of soldiers for so long, that he sought a quiet place in town to stay. He remembered Miksch's tobacco shop and straight away headed there.

"Brother Miksch," he heartily hailed the shopkeeper.

"Come in, Mr. Brooks. What brings you to town today?" Matthew asked genially.

Noticing that two English officers were selecting soap and snuff, Mr. Brooks replied, "A pipe. Oh, here they are." He bent down and rummaged through the pipe basket. He selected a smooth red clay pipe then found a reed that fit snugly into the stem end.

The Englishmen gave their items and money to Matthew. He wrapped the purchases, handed them over and bid them good day. They slipped the packages into their pockets and left the shop.

"Need any tobacco today?" Matthew inquired of Brooks.

"Yes, about this much," he said holding up a medium size twist.

"That's all made of mountain burly."

"You make a good tobacco, brother."

"Thank you. Anything else I can do to serve you?"

"Well, yes, there is. You have an upstairs room closed off, haven't you?"

"Yes."

"I'd like to rent it for a few days, while the troops are here."

"Mr. Brooks, I'd like to oblige you, but that's my daughter's room."

"Brother, I tell you going up and down the country side looking for food, then getting back to camp, has worn me out. I need a quiet place to sleep."

"The loft is full of tobacco. Most people really don't appreciate the smell through the night."

"Huh. Have you ever smelled an army of men at the end of the day? Tobacco would be a welcomed change. I surely would appreciate your letting me *rent* the room for a few days."

"We've never rented a room before," Matthew stated.

"I'll make it worth your while," Brooks urged.

"Well now, I don't quite know how to figure, the continental currency fluctuates so." Matthew drawled, considering the proposition.

"I have a little hard money, some Spanish coins; I can pay most in that."

"The same rate as the tavern for a single room?" Matthew proposed.

"The same, if I can have fresh water daily, brought up."

Matthew put out his hand, "All right, Mr. Brooks. I'm glad we can be of service to you."

Mr. Brooks eagerly shook his hand. "Thank you."

As he started out the door, Matthew cleared his throat, "Err, the pipe and tobacco."

Mr. Brooks started to say put it on his bill, but on second thought decided to keep the accounts separate. He could probably get his room expenses back from the government someday but not his tobacco. He gave Matthew an English coin.

"I'll have Martha move her things after school. You can come any time after six," Matthew said.

Brooks nodded and left.

Matthew opened the door to the kitchen and told Maria of the arrangement. As usual, she was agreeable with his decisions.

He said, "We'll make a quilt palette for Martha in our room. Let's not bring up any more foodstuffs from the cellar than we have to. Not even full molasses jars for the shop."

"I won't even mention food," she promised.

"That's probably a wise idea. Caution Martha to do the same. This cold weather here in early November makes me feel we're in for a long winter. I'm going up to the Gemeinhaus. I want to let them know about Brooks' coming."

"Matthew, we may not be able to go to services and leave the house open."

"I can go to any day time meetings. You and Martha could go at night if some others are passing by. I'll check with some of the married people up the street."

He put on his big wool coat and tricon hat and went out into the raw November weather. Already leaves had fallen from the trees except the big oaks, but the grass was still green in the backyards and town square.

The few nights for which Mr. Brooks had requested the room turned out to be a ten-night visit. Martha was beginning to get weary of sleeping on the cold floor. She missed her room.

"War changes our days and our nights," she fretted to herself. "It even comes right into our home and takes away my bed. Mama won't cook much food—and none of our favorite things and we can't go to services together. They both watch me so closely. Anybody would think the militia was going to take me away with the prisoners."

She decided war was evil. Everyday she grew more in understanding and appreciating of Moravian ways.

On the tenth day, while she was home for lunch, Mr. Brooks dashed in. He poked his head into the kitchen where the family was eating vegetable soup.

"Pardon me, Brother Miksch, for interrupting your lunch, but the English soldiers are being moved to Hillsborough. I came to get my things. Could you prepare my bill?"

"Certainly." Matthew wiped his mouth on his ample linen napkin. Putting the napkin on the table, he said softly, "Leave my soup. You can add some hot to it later. And bring up some cheese and bread and peach preserves from the cellar."

Maria smiled and Martha giggled.

Matthew had kept a running account of Mr. Brooks' room rental, half expecting a sudden departure. He made a copy from his ledger. Mr. Brooks set his satchel in the hall and entered the front room. Matthew handed him the bill. Mr. Brooks opened his purse and drew out several Spanish coins.

"Here are the Spanish coins I promised you. The remainder will have to be in Continental currency," he said as he counted several sheets of paper money. "Thank you for everything."

"You were welcome. Have a safe trip," he bid the commissary agent.

Matthew approached the kitchen table and showed Maria and Martha the gold coins.

Maria said gratefully, "It's good to have some money of value again. There are so many needs." She noticed the paper currency and asked, "Did he pay the paper?"

"Yes. We can't refuse to take it you know. He stayed longer than he had planned. Maybe he didn't have many coins left and he does have to travel a lot. Anyway, it's all clear profit. I'll find a safe place to keep it until we decide the best use. Now where's the hot soup?"

CHAPTER THIRTEEN

The cold weather limited Matthew's nursery activities but gave him time to accompany Brother Meinung, the congregation clerk and surveyor who lived in the two-story house, on some surveying trips. He was grateful for the chance to walk out in the countryside, to break his steady routine for a short time, and to earn a little extra money. He used the surveying trip to the Wach, below the mill, to gather some more reeds for pipe stems. The cattle had stripped the foliage leaving the stalks easier to cut.

Maria used the days he was away to thoroughly clean the shop: wash windows, scrub woodwork, polish the furniture and floors. After that was done, she baked bread and cookies, fruit and ginger, and sealed them in crocks for Christmas and winter eating.

"Mama, our house smells so good," Martha declared as she pushed the back door shut. She'd come to the back knowing her mother would have the front latched while her father was away.

On baking days, Maria always saved a cookie sample for Martha to have with a mug of milk when she came in.

Sitting on a tiny rug pulled in front of the hearth, Martha asked, "Did you save the cinnamon for me to grind or the lemon for me to grate?"

Maria always tried to leave these jobs for Martha because they were favorites.

"Yes. Why do you like to do these things?"

"They're fun. I like the smells," Martha admitted.

"Are you sure it isn't because you can do them sitting in front of the fire?" her mother teased.

"If we didn't have a tobacco shop, I wish we had a gingerbread shop. It smells just as good."

"Would you like to have gingerbread everyday?"

"Um, um."

The two were quiet for awhile. Only the crackle of the fire, the soft tread of Maria's house shoes on the floor as she moved around the kitchen and the gentle tapping of the grater against the bowl interrupted the agreeable silence.

Grinding the bits of cinnamon sticks, Martha asked, "What can I give Father for Christmas?"

"Let me think. You could learn some more Bible verses."

"I did that last year. What are you giving him?"

"Some wool gloves I'm knitting."

"I wish I could give him a book," Martha said wistfully remembering the shelves of books at the Bagges.

"What about a bookmark?" Maria said enthusiastically.

"Does he have one?" she asked skeptically.

"No. He would probably like one for his ledger."

"What kind would be best?"

"A thin one. A bit of leather or ribbon."

"How about a woven one? Sister Sehner has a small loom at school and she said we could use it."

"Martha, that sounds like a fine gift. You can take some of the flax you've spun."

The Miksches didn't have a great deal of family preparation at home for the Christmas season. Matthew had checked with Aust and found that he would have the pitcher ready for Christmas for Maria, so he ordered a smaller one for Martha. Maria was knitting a scarf for Martha. And Martha decided to weave a key tab for her Mother.

However, the tobacco shop was deluged with customers, as was every shop in town, especially on Saturday, December 23. The word must have spread like a brush fire throughout the nearby counties that the store wagon had returned on Friday, the twenty-second, with a load of salt, because the town was thronged with large crowds that day.

People were finishing their Christmas shopping. The tavern could scarcely serve all the strangers. The brothers' bakery sold out of its day's supply before the loaves had barely cooled on the shelves. The second baking had been reserved for love feast buns.

In the afternoon, Martha looked after the cooking in the kitchen, because her mother was helping the women customers while Matthew was serving the men. Martha kept the door ajar. Once in a while she would peep out. She was interested in watching the *other ladies* in their more elaborate dresses with designs woven into the fabric and with ruffled sleeves on their blouses and ruffled caps. Some ladies even had fur at the neck of their capes. The women were buying the new decorative ribbons, molasses, and pickles. A few bought the remaining snuffboxes as gifts for their husbands. Martha couldn't understand why the women and young girls had come to town. She and her mother never went anywhere to buy gifts, and they never went with their father on his trips. When Maria came into the kitchen to check on the stew, Martha whispered. "Why did the women come?"

Maria answered likewise softly as she stirred the stew. "Most of them live on farms. They don't have many chances to come to town."

While the crane and pot were pulled forward, Maria took the long handled shovel, scooped up some hot coals and threw them into the iron stove that was jammed up against the chimney wall in the front room. This was convenient for Maria for she didn't have to go through the front room with coal or ashes. The closed stove in the shop and front room kept the room cleaner and smoke free. She pushed the crane back to keep the stew bubbling.

"Martha, go out back and get some wood," she instructed just before returning to the shop.

The Miksches didn't have time to rest the following day, as it was Christmas Eve and the fourth Sunday in Advent. After attending morning and afternoon services, they had the major serving duties of the love feast for Matthew and Maria were diener and dienerin. The late afternoon love feast was planned for the children while the evening one was for adults.

Maria made hot chocolate in the kitchen of the saal for the children's service. Some of the women who were helping serve, filled the hand-woven straw baskets with large round buns.

For the first love feast service, Martha entered the saal with her teacher. Late afternoon light streamed in through the clear glass windows. This was Martha's favorite service. She savored every moment beginning with the band music prelude. Next, Brother Graff welcomed the thirty children. He asked them to stand and sing an ode, which was accompanied by instruments. Martha concentrated on the words of the lyrics as she sang joyfully with her friends. When they were seated again on the benches, Brother Graff told the wonderful story from St. Luke about Jesus' birth. He reminded them that there are Holy Angels who love and protect each of them.

Then, the dienerins came into the saal and passed the baskets of buns. Everyone took a bun and passed the basket down the row. A dienerin waited to receive the basket and start it down the next row. Martha placed her bun on the birthday handkerchief from her mother. Most children spread white napkins across their laps. After everyone was served, the dienerins left the saal, but returned in a few minutes, followed by the dieners who bore large wooden trays holding mugs of cocoa.

While the dieners held the trays, the women took a mug and passed it to the first person on the row, and it was passed on to the next person. When all children had mugs, the servers left the saal.

While the children ate and drank, the choir sang Christmas hymns.

Martha loved the warmth of the hot ceramic mug and the smoothness of its glazed surface. The aroma of chocolate wafting upwards in the steam was a pleasing fragrance she anticipated from year to year. The bun, too, released its fragrance of mace as she bit into it. Martha was always appreciative that Count Zinzendorff had started the love feast custom of sharing bread and drink in fellowship back in Herrnhut in 1727.

After the children finished drinking, the dieners and dienerins returned and collected the mugs. Again they exited the saal.

Now the children stood and sang more hymns. Before the last song, the sun had set and only the altar candlelights glowed in the room. The minister told that Jesus was the light of the world. Dieners and dienerins returned, the latter carrying a lighted taper and the former a tray with holes into which small beeswax tapers were set. A dienerin lit a candle on the tray then passed it down the row. As the candles were lit one by one, the room slowly became lighter and brighter. Children were shown how one candle, along with all the others, could light a room. This action was compared to the way their devotion and lives could shine brightly in the world. After a final hymn and benediction, the children, carrying their lighted candles and leaving the saal, were given a written bible verse.

Martha clutched her verse in her hand as she followed the other children into the cold, winter evening. The little light flickered but did not go out. She stood at the top of the steps and watched the children, met by their parents, walk home with their lights shining along the street. When she no longer could see any flickers of lights, she pivoted into the Gemeinhaus and on to the saal kitchen where her parents were helping wash up the mugs, drying and replacing them on the trays: all were ready for the evening service.

Matthew announced that he would make the coffee for the evening service. At the word *coffee* everyone looked up surprised.

Someone spoke. "Why, brother, you say that as if we really were going to have *coffee*."

"We are," he beamed.

"Why, where in the world did you come upon some coffee?"

He didn't answer, just continued to smile.

Someone else joked, "Well, I guess there are some advantages to housing a commissioner at your house."

Quickly Maria said, "It's the first I know of it. Wherever he happened upon it, he didn't bring it home."

"Matthew, this is one love feast we'll all remember. Hot coffee."

"We ought to make it early and open up all the doors and enjoy the smell as long as possible."

"And invite all the strangers passing through or camping below the tavern."

"Now, now. Let's not be letting the coffee overpower the message," Matthew warned good-naturedly.

"No fear of that brother. We'll be seeing you—about seven-thirty."

The servers left and Maria covered the buns with linen cloths. Matthew refilled the big kettle with water. "It should be hot by seven."

"Good. That'll give you time to come home for a quick supper," Maria said.

"No need. The bun and coffee will be enough. You've had a busy day. Don't trouble yourself with supper."

She responded, "I'll go home with Martha a few minutes to freshen up. Maybe we'll have some cold beef and cheese. I could bring you some back."

"No. I brought some nuts along. I'll crack those. Take care walking home."

"I'll light the way," Martha offered showing the small candle she still held.

Matthew laughed. "Dear, you two best be off. That candle is about burned down to the red ribbon."

Martha and Maria pulled their capes about them and headed home.

After they washed their faces, used the necessaries, and ate supper; they hurried back to the Gemeinhaus, this time Maria carrying a lighted lantern. Martha tried stepping on various shadows in the lantern light as her mother walked a step in front of her. The shadows constantly changed form on the uneven street, and Martha shifted her stride and position in accord until Maria finally urged her to stop lagging and to come on.

Martha liked being out at night with her parents. Most children stayed at home for this service while some adult or schoolmaster stayed with them. Martha didn't go into the saal. She stayed in the kitchen. The room was small and warm and the saal was unheated. She tried to stay out of the way while the servers were busy. She sat in a corner on a stool with her feet drawn up under her. She held the stub of her love feast candle and sniffed the beeswax and thought of honey and springtime.

One of the sisters watched her with the candle, then inquired, "Do you like the beeswax smell, Martha?"

"Oh, yes, ma'am. It's as pleasant as—as rosemary."

"That's a nice comparison for Christmas. When I was in London, waiting to come to the colonies, I heard a story about herbs being used in a Christmas crèche."

"Please, tell me," implored Martha.

"Let's see. First, you use thyme for Mary's bed, then creeping pennyroyal because legend says it bloomed at midnight when the Christ child was born. Then you add rosemary because rosemary recalls the Presence in the garden. It's for the memory of the Garden of Gesthsimene where rosemary grew under the olive trees."

"That's beautiful. Rosemary for remembrance." Martha thanked her. Secretly, Martha prayed that someday her plant would be big enough not only for leaves for a sachet but for a crèche.

In the saal the minister gave a special welcome to the large number of young people from Bethania and Friedburg who had come in to join them. Then he announced the arrival that afternoon of a packet form Pennsylvania containing the newsletter and the daily text for the first four months of the New Year. The congregation was excited and pleased.

When Matthew came back into the kitchen, Martha heard

him tell Maria he'd have to come to services early or either write the text out at home, so he could have it on the table for everyone to see each evening. The printed forms of the text had not come yet.

As the servers were cleaning up for the night, they told Matthew that everyone was surprised at tasting real coffee again.

Maria lamented having to pour out the once used coffee grounds. "I wonder if we could use them again?"

Matthew shook his head, "Maria, you know the grounds are only good once. It might spoil the pleasure of the treat tonight to have a bad brew tomorrow. Let's dump them out."

Reluctantly she consented.

They spread the remaining coals on the fireplace hearth. Matthew dunked them in water, cooling them quickly so they could be reused. Everything in good order, the Miksches trudged wearily, but happily, to their little yellow house.

CHAPTER FOURTEEN

The security Martha knew within the yellow house was rarely threatened. The faith of her parents and their general calmness in manner in carrying out the will of God for their lives gave Martha strength to rely on. More and more she was beginning to see how faith aided her parents and likewise her own faith increased.

However, having faith in God and trying to do good, Martha found out, did not mean a life void of problems. The month of January 1781 brought an abundance of demands that had her family and the town concerned for its physical safety.

The first indication of a new burden resulting from the war was when Mr. Glascock came into town. He announced to the leaders that he was there at command of General Greene to make arrangements for some men who needed a rest from war. The men coming were three officers and twenty sick cavalrymen. They would require quarters and provisions of grain and meal. Also, thirty or forty horses would need forage and shelter.

Marshall called the Ausfer Collegium members together and presented the demands to them. No one was happy about the unexpected arrival of so many men and horses, but they did not shirk their responsibilities and quickly got down to the central and immediate problem. First, where to house the men. Because of their sickness, everyone was in agreement to try to keep them out of private homes and preferable all together in one place. There was no vacant building available. Someone suggested the new night watchman house.

Matthew hastened to ask, "Then where would Brother Zillman go?"

"It would be easier to find one room for Zillman than a whole house for the soldiers."

"Remember all the trouble we had in July when the soldiers were at Triebel's. The crocks were broken, and water was put in the wine kegs after they drank the wine. I don't like having them nearby again," Matthew grumbled.

Marshall spoke directly to Matthew. "Brother, I dare say no one *likes* this imposition; if you can suggest a more appropriate place to house the sick men, we will all be glad to hear it."

As he waited, Matthew could think of no other place; he just folded his arms across his chest and lowered his chin and eyes.

Marshall continued to the group. "Now what about the horses?"

"Would the brickyards do? There're sheds there."

"Good idea."

"We really need that house we've been talking about at the tavern: the one for the travelers who can't afford the tavern."

"And it could be used for the soldiers."

"Yes, we do. But remember we couldn't raise the subscription."

"Let's hope Brother Herbst still has the peeled logs he offered to give us whenever we could get the work done."

"A fellow came into the shop saying folks outside Wachovia think we're going to build a house just for *troops.*"

"News like that won't be good for businesses."

Marshall thanked the brothers for the solutions to the problems at hand and asked them to serve the sick men as best they could if called upon.

On Sunday, January 7, Matthew was sitting at the kitchen table when he looked out the window and saw Zillman outside his little house, his arms loaded with bedding.

Matthew jumped up, got his coat from the hall peg, and rushed out the back door. "Zillman!" he shouted.

Zillman, almost to Triebel's yard, stopped.

Matthew hurried through the yard to the back of the nursery. "Are you moving again?"

The night watchman lifted his full arms. "Well, I'm not doing my laundry."

"Have you heard when the soldiers will arrive?"

"Today. Sorry I can't stand and talk. I have to get everything over to the Brothers House." Zillman moved on, his conch swinging by its strap from his arm.

During the afternoon, twenty-two cavalrymen rode into town. They had been told the location of the house where they were to be quartered. However, they rode up and down the street in front of Miksch's looking for a path to the log house. Matthew came out and showed them how to go around Triebel's and cross over the back lots. The soldiers, being ill, wanted to leave their personal bundles at the house before riding their horses to the brickyard. Two wagons brought baggage.

Martha watched the men come and go all afternoon. She felt sorry for them. Their clothes were not sufficient for the winter weather. Some did not even have boots. They slumped as they walked, seemingly too tired to go on. She wondered how so many men could fit into the little house.

Fact was, they couldn't.

Lieutenant Simmons, the officer in charge of bringing the men and supplies to town went up to the Gemeinhaus to say so to Brother Marshall.

"Sir, we have to have more room."

"Do you have some men who are not very sick? Perhaps we could quarter them up at Brother Yarrell's. It's not far. It's just a block north."

"The trumpeters. There're four of them. They're not so worn out."

"I'll send word to Brother Yarrell to expect you."

"In about two hours?"

"That'll be fine."

After settling the men, Simmons rode on leaving no one in charge of the soldiers. Within a short time disorder prevailed among them. Their demands and needs were primarily those of sick people, not rowdy soldiers on a merry-making leave.

Fortunately, Lieutenant Hughes and another officer arrived the following Friday. Hughes was to be in charge and he immediately set about to attend to any pressing needs. First, he realized the men were short of grain and he sent to the mill for some.

Next he surveyed the horse situation and decided to board up the sheds and use them for stables. He ordered boards from the sawmill and nails from the store.

The brothers who had supplies requisitioned began to complain to each other. Zillman didn't like being put out. Matthew didn't like the constant traffic across his back lot, the school master found it hard to keep the boys away from the windows when they were inside, or the back fence when they were out for exercise.

Finally Brother Marshall called the brothers together again. He stated that it was understandable that those who bore the heaviest burdens had a right to their complaints and he asked the patience of all. He suggested establishing a committee to handle all matters resulting from the war. Everyone was in agreement. Four brothers were selected: Bagge, Reuz, Stotz and Yarrell.

On Sunday, a week after the sick men first came, Mr. Brooks arrived to arrange for their support. Originally, the men were to have most of their own provisions. Brooks' arrangements had the town continuing to supply corn and grain.

Brooks was also the County Commissioner for the provision tax. He had to see that everyone paid a peck of corn per $100 value of taxable property. So the grain supply had already been heavily dipped into. Maria, like other housewives, tried to be conservative in her food preparation. She roasted more potatoes and boiled more turnips than she baked bread.

The community was hardly prepared for the problem that rolled into town on January 16.

A sergeant from General Greene's army drove up to the community store, got out, went inside and asked Bagge where he could find the Conductor of the Military Stores.

Bagge looked up. "There's no such officer here."

The sergeant replied shortly, "There must be. General Greene sent me here to deliver some things."

Irritated, Bagge asked, "What things?"

"Two loads of ammunitions."

Bagge walked briskly out the door. He looked right at two loaded wagons halted in front of the store. He also counted eleven more soldiers awaiting the sergeant.

"By all that's just, what does General Greene think Salem is— a big city?" he muttered half to himself.

"Biwighaus!" he called loudly back into the store. "Go fetch Brothers Reuz, Stotz and Yarrell. Then get Lieutenant Hughes down here."

He asked the sergeant to have his men wait while the proper people could assemble to handle the situation.

When Lieutenant Hughes arrived, the sergeant repeated that he had orders to deliver the wagons to the Conductor.

Hughes replied, "I'm in charge of the cavalrymen here."

"Can you take charge of the wagons or have your men guard them?"

The lieutenant drew himself up and tartly answered, "No. These men are sick. They're here to recuperate. Furthermore, they don't even have proper clothes or shoes to wear for any kind of duty."

Meanwhile inside the store, the committee of four hastily discussed the situation. They decided to send a letter to Colonel Joseph Winston apprising him of the delivery.

The new group of soldiers camped near the wagons.

Later that night Colonel Armstrong rode into town. He was delighted that some munitions were close at hand.

Needless to say, the townspeople did not share his joy. On the nineteenth, they finally breathed easier when they saw the wagons roll out of town and enjoyed a night of restful sleep.

The relief was short lived.

The next day the munitions wagons returned. They were followed by two more wagons plus thirty men who had been sent to Salem to recover their health.

When Martha heard the news at lunch time she exclaimed, "But, Mama, that's more soldiers here than we have men. How can we care for all those sick people?"

"This is a heavy burden. The committee is meeting now. Surely the Lord will tell them what to do," Maria acknowledged.

Just then Matthew opened the front door. Straightaway he came into the kitchen, taking off his heavy coat there. "Well, Maria, they're going to *make* munitions here."

Maria gasped.

Martha asked, "What do you mean, Father?"

"A conductor has been sent here with orders to make ammunition for the army from all that gunpowder the wagons brought," he replied, then took his coat to the bedroom and returned.

Maria recovering from the shocking news, asked, "Where will they make it?"

Sitting down at the table he said, "They want a laboratory and I think now that the town will have to build that log house behind the tavern."

"Thank the Lord, it'll be out of town," Maria said as she dished up some sweet potatoes and beans.

"Father, who's going to build this house?"

"The townspeople," he replied as he began to eat.

"Will you help?"

"I'll do what I can, dear. That means your mother will need more help from you."

"I'll do what I can, too."

Martha thought a minute then she asked puzzled, "The building will take a little while. Where will they keep the gunpowder? In the wagons?"

"No," he answered, not looking up.

"Where, then?" she prodded.

"The committee will help them find a place."

The three ate in silence, each thinking about these new burdens. Martha was sitting opposite the window and she glimpsed some soldiers moving along the back fence. She watched a few moments, then said, "There're a lot of soldiers walking around down there."

Maria and Matthew leaned over for a better view.

Maria exclaimed, "Surely no one is going to try to put any more sick men in the small house. They had to take some out already."

Martha commented, "It looks to me as if they are moving out."

Matthew rose, opened the top half of the back door, and gave a long look, "I believe they are. I'm going down to find out what is taking place."

Martha jumped up to follow him but her mother extended a restraining hand. "No, Martha. Your father will come back, tell us what we need to know. You are getting to be a young lady now. You must not run after him when he talks with the brothers or strangers like you sometimes did when you were little."

Martha sat down again, but she felt she was missing something important. She wished she could hear the conversation for herself and not have to wait to be told. She watched her father as he talked to two or three men. As he turned up the path, she could tell by his rapid walk and the firmness of his mouth and jaw that he was not pleased.

Matthew stamped up the back steps, flung the door opened, and shut.

Maria anxiously asked, "Matthew?"

"Do you know they are going to store the gunpowder in the watchman's house!"

"Oh, no," shuttered Maria.

"But the sick soldiers?" despaired Martha.

"They're all being moved to Yarrell's," he informed them.

"Father, the town is going to need another house for soldiers soon."

"The brothers will meet after services tonight, to organize all the work that has to be done."

Maria tried to be cheerful, "Well, let's be thankful that all this extra care comes when the craft trade is lowest and after the harvest and before the spring planting."

Matthew smiled, "It's good to have you around, Maria."

She blushed while clearing the table. "Martha, if the men are going to organize, we best do the same. The cooking, washing, ironing—have to go on. The men's needs will be different with the building going on."

Martha hinted hopefully, "Maybe I won't have to spin at night."

"Whether there's a war or not, you'll need that dress. And there's not but one way I know of for you to have it. If the sick keep moving in here, we may be requisitioned for our sheets and cloth. No, the spinning wheel has got to turn."

"All right. Now, I'll go get the water." Maria stood at the front window and watched Martha.

Martha could see the end of a wagon pulled between Triebel's and the Brothers House waiting to be unloaded. She noticed the pipe stand had been wrapped in cloths and she could faintly smell the manure underneath the fabric. Well, the water won't freeze, she concluded while twitching her nose at the unpleasant odor.

Lingering for some men to pass by on the street, she gazed at the Brothers House. She remembered when there was a gun displayed outside to let shoppers know that guns were made there. Matthew told her when it was taken down that there had been a decision not to make guns during the wartime. Moravians did not take up arms with or against either side. They were peaceful men.

Martha's young mind couldn't make any logical sense about what was happening now in her town. If the men were not going to bear arms or fight, why did soldiers come here so often? Why did they leave their sick, their troops in Salem or other Wachovia towns? Why did they demand so much grain, so many favors? Why don't they let us alone?

When the street cleared, she crossed over to her house, carrying her bucket of water.

CHAPTER FIFTEEN

The next day as Martha was changing the pails at the pipe stand, she saw two more wagons draw up to the corner and turn down the side street.

Upon re-entering the house, she stated, "If it takes gun powder to end the war, then, Cornwallis may just as well stop now. There's enough here to . . . to . . . to . . ."

"Kill everybody," her father finished for her. "Dear, let's hope the war will be over soon, and they'll never have to use it."

Maria said, "I hear our gunsmith has even closed his shop."

"For gun making yes, but he's making traps and locks."

"I'm glad he can stay busy. A man needs his work."

Work was certainly the order of the day for all families, as well as the single sisters and brothers. The children continued school every day. The girls' school being located a block away from the Main Street was isolated from the activity. Home tasks increased and kept children too busy to know all that was going on in town. Being intuitive as children are though, they sensed the danger of the gunpowder stored in the center of town, the diligence of their men in building the log laboratory for making the munitions, the double responsibilities of their parents at home and in the shops. The children reacted with high spirits. The wisest parents put this new energy to good use; others became irritable.

On January 24, the brothers finished the twenty-four by thirty foot log house in the rain. It wasn't until February 2 that the difficult job of transferring the ammunition could be undertaken.

Colonel White came to help. Everyone walked on tiptoe and spoke in whispers while the gunpowder and munitions were reloaded on the wagons and transferred to the new house. At the end of the day, there was rejoicing and thanksgiving that no one had been injured putting up the house or moving the gunpowder.

The brethren felt a new unity of heart as they shared a common burden. There was a close tie among the people in the services and on the streets. Martha experienced a growing kinship with the community and her happiness at being in a congregation town increased.

There in the midst of this peace-loving town (a town whose name in Hebrew meant *peace*) where the men were exempt from military service because of their religious beliefs, where men never made weapons for war purposes: here the men raised a building in less than a week for the Continental Army to make munitions for military use. Would there be an end to the tests of Moravian loyalty to their country, their state, and their fellow man?

The military men proceeded with their duties. The last thirty soldiers that arrived acted as guards of the ammunition as soon as they recovered their health in the quiet community.

The brothers returned to their normal schedules as much as possible.

The Mikschs offered a special prayer of thankfulness when the ammunition was removed from their back yard: Martha asked her father why there were so many fast horses in town during the afternoon.

"I hear there were express messages for the officers. Something must be brewing. They are pressing all wagons around here, too!"

"Why?"

"To move the ammunition out."

"That is good news," Maria exclaimed.

However, the first outside news the family heard the next morning was not good.

Mid-morning, Dr. Bonn appeared at the shop. "Maria, could I trouble you for some help?"

"Certainly, Dr. Bonn."

"Could I put you in charge of gathering any old linens, sheets, towels, aprons that the married ladies can spare? And can you get someone to clean them. Boil them if possible?"

"Yes," she said willingly, but puzzled.

"We're going to set up a hospital."

"What?"

"For the Continental Army. A surgeon's mate is in town to set it up."

Matthew asked, "Where will it be?"

"In the two-story house."

"More people to move," Miksch said sympathetically.

"Yes. Everybody seems to have a share in these upheavals."

Maria questioned the doctor, "If the army is setting up a hospital, and the ammunition is being moved out, does that mean there is going to be a battle near here?"

He spoke kindly, "We don't know any war strategies, Maria, but what we hear from people coming in from all directions, I'd say General Greene is just north or northeast and Cornwallis is near the Yadkin."

"And we're in between," she said soberly.

"Keep faith, you two. Maria, when you get the linens ready, bring them up to my house. My wife will keep them until they are needed. We'll let the army use what they have first."

"All right," she said.

Bonn started to leave then stopped. "Too bad it's not summer and the native herbs are up—to heal the wounds. Matthew, if they run short of fever medicine, I may ask you to show them where to get some holly?"

"Be glad to help. Take care of yourself, Jacob."

After Bonn closed the door, Matthew said sadly, "He's going too hard. These sick men have added greatly to his concerns."

"He's a good man. Everybody loves and respects him."

Martha was excited about her mother's part in helping with the hospital. She begged to help. Maria told her there would be plenty she could do. The women were all going to bring the linens and white cotton cloths to the Miksch house and they would all wash the material in one pot and hang then over the fence to dry.

"We won't tear them until they're needed. If they aren't used, the women can get them back."

When Martha came home from school on washing day, she helped stir the last batch of cloths in the big iron pot over the fire in the backyard. The women helping stayed for lunch. Maria had made a pot of soup. She set out applesauce with cinnamon and some of her gingerbread. Along with herb tea it was a delightful meal.

Martha longed to be of more help to Dr. Bonn. She wished she could make bandages, mix his medicines—even take him water. But it wasn't her time to serve in this way. So she trudged back to school to learn how to convert fractions into percentages. "Always preparing," she argued with herself. "When will I ever do something really of service!"

CHAPTER SIXTEEN

On February 9, a messenger rode in hard from the west. He told everybody that Cornwallis had crossed the Shallow Ford on the Yadkin. The following day, another rider galloped in with the news that Cornwallis' troops were camped in Bethania and were pillaging everything. They were killing all the cattle they could find, stripping fences for firewood, raiding the stillhouse, and threatening the residents.

The Salem people hurt inside because their brethren were being tormented. Martha grieved, too. She prayed Brother and Sister Schmidt in Bethabara would be spared terrible treatment. She even hoped that the old apothecary garden and the parent rosemary plant, from which her thriving young plant came, were not dug up or trampled.

The following day, another messenger brought news more fearful for the Salemites: Cornwallis was headed toward Salem and would probably camp out in their area.

The war committee and the ministers conferred. There was no panic, but precautions were taken. Residents were informed of the British approach and were warned to say inside until needed and sent for. Meals were sent to the schools so the children could be kept inside until the army passed through or settled for the evening.

Marshall elected to remain at the store with Bagge where he could talk with Cornwallis if he marched straight down Main Street, the most likely route.

From the exterior of the houses, no trace of recent munitions processing could be detected. And no signs of the number of soldiers who had stayed in town so recently were detectable either. Townspeople busied themselves surveying their own yards and streets, the tavern, the watchman's house, the magazine, the two-story house for any remaining evidence of the Continental Army. The sick men had evacuated south as the British were approaching from the northwest. The munitions had been hauled away a few days ago, but the townspeople were not certain where and in cases like this, the less information they had, the better.

But the Lord works in mysterious ways and on this day, the rains poured over Salem all day and all night.

Around ten o'clock the following morning when Lord Cornwallis appeared at the top of Main Street slope, it was a muddy path all the way down hill. Accompanying him were other generals and the royal governor, Josiah Martin. They proceeded into Salem. As they came abreast the community store, they halted. Bagge and Marshall walked out to greet them. The generals and Governor Martin dismounted and went inside the store.

When the soldiers entered town, they were given a short rest. During this break they demanded much—brandy, oxen, foods, grains—and the brothers came forth to fulfill the demands. For water the soldiers were directed to the spring in back of the Brothers House. During the passing, laundry that was hanging on the line behind the Brothers House was stolen.

Fortunately, the rest stops were short, but there were many men, approximately 3,000 to march through the town. Therefore the passing took until four o'clock in the afternoon.

The British generals and the governor talked with Bagge and Marshall for about an hour and a half, and then they proceeded on to Friedland where they set up camp for the night.

Lingering longest in Salem were some German soldiers who were well behaved. They appreciated a chance to talk to some people in their native tongue, and to visit with men from their own country.

When the children were finally allowed to go home from school, they bombarded their parents with questions. The teachers had not been able to tell them anything because they had been inside and away from the activities. For the most part, the parents were drained from the worry of the day and exhausted from trying to accommodate the demands of the thousands of men. They were too tired and too busy to fully answer many questions. So, it was the results of the British march that left impressions on the children.

And during the coming days, they caught snatches of conversations: pillage at Friedland, Cornwallis pursing General Greene's northern forces, General Greene's stand at Guilford Courthouse, the battle there. Some heard that Cornwallis won the field; others heard that Greene had killed so many British that the army was reduced to two thousand. News reached them that Greene turned back south and that Cornwallis did not follow but went to Hillsborough where he stayed a few weeks before going to Wilmington to seek reinforcements and supplies. Greene recaptured South Carolina and Georgia for the Continental armies.

Martha's attention was more closely focused on the night watchman's house where once again soldiers were staying, only this time it held wounded men.

Martha often saw out her windows, Dr. Bonn cutting across the backyard to the log house.

On February 14 as he wearily left the house, Miksch, who was pruning roses in the nursery, hailed him. "How're the patients?"

"Not well, Matthew." He paused by the fence, leaning upon the top rail.

Matthew, compassionate of the doctor's long hours, suggested, "Jacob, come on in. A sassafras brew will do us both good."

"That, Matthew, is perhaps the easiest sell you ever made," and he climbed over the rail fence and followed Matthew up the path.

Inside the kitchen, Matthew asked Maria to drop a few sticks of sassafras into the hot water kettle. She poured some hot water into a pot and let the sassafras steep.

While Matthew washed his hands in the bedroom, Bonn settled into the one large armchair, laid his head back and immediately fell asleep.

Upon entering the room, Matthew saw Jacob asleep and quietly crossed to the kitchen. "Maria, do you have any of those good rolls left from lunch?"

"A few I was saving for supper."

"How about serving them to Jacob? He may not have stopped for lunch."

"Certainly, and I'll whip up some honey in butter right quick."

Dr. Bonn woke up instantly when he heard Matthew walk back into the room. "Well, that was a good catnap." He stretched his arms out.

Matthew sat in the desk chair near his friend. "I always enjoy a few winks myself. Maria's bringing in the tea."

"Matthew, you know since these last men were sent here, I've had to oversee their care."

"Yes."

"Well, now it's come to the point, I also am having to act as nurse." He yawned and stretched his arms then took a deep breath. "I can't get to see our congregation patients like this."

"I have noticed you down at the watchman's house often."

"I'm planning to ask the Salem families for some help. Maybe the families could take turns with the nursing duties. What do you think the reaction would be?"

"They'll be glad to help out. Everybody's been mighty good about this sort of thing."

"It would surely be a blessing to me."

Maria brought in the steaming mugs of sassafras and the plate of buns she had just warmed up and a small pot of golden honey butter.

Dr. Bonn buttered two buns, savored a bite from one, then said, "Maria, if you ever go into business, I hope it'll be baking."

To Matthew, he continued with his former ideas. "I'm going up tonight to ask Brother Marshall to talk to the congregation."

"I'll volunteer for tonight, Jacob. Just tell me what needs to be done."

"Matthew, you're an answer to a prayer. I need to get home and attend to some matters."

Maria asked, "Dr. Bonn, would nourishment be any help if I made a pot of soup sometime for Matthew to take to the watchman's house?"

"It surely would. The men would appreciate it, and so would I." He rose saying, "And thank you, too, for the refreshments. I'll be on my way."

The nursing plan was put into effect immediately. The wounded men remained in Salem until April. Many a steaming pot of soup, fresh loaf of bread, and stewed fruit was handed across the Mikschs' back lot to the log house. Dr. Bonn continued to check on the patients daily and to leave instructions for the brother who assisted in their care.

Matthew furnished herbs for teas. At suppertime, Martha begged to grind the dried herbs. She would always ask, "What is this one for? Or how does this help?"

Sometimes she was allowed to add the herbs to the pot and pour boiling water in. But she was never allowed to take the tea to the back lot. In fact her father did not let her help him in the nursery these days. Even though the season was winter and there was not much to do, he was out occasionally and she always wanted to go.

Under all the good care, the wounded men recovered before leaving Salem in spring.

The townspeople continued to help each other with all the extra demands that the war put upon them. One of the lingering problems they had to bear was a repercussion from Cornwallis's march through Salem. That was the ill-treatment they received from their neighbors and some men of the militia who accused the Moravians in Salem of being friendly with the British and because of this friendliness the enemy did not pillage the town as it did Bethania and Dobson's Crossroads. Militiamen were rowdy when they came to town. They made harsh accusations. For the most part, the Moravians remained polite in the face of the attacks. Occasionally, however, someone would utter a sentiment that appeared to show sympathy toward England.

Marshall cautioned the people to use the uttermost discretion in their conversations, especially when talking with strangers. For his part, whenever he heard any accusations concerning the Cornwallis' passage through town, he countered with the information that Cornwallis had not stopped for the night here, that it was raining that day and therefore their losses had been less than those in some other settlements.

Slowly, good words about the Wachovia Moravians began to circulate, especially in official places. The Virginia men whom Dr. Bonn had treated wrote how pleased they were with his care and treatment; the officers involved in the leather deal attested to their loyalty to the state, and General Greene wrote how well his troops had been treated.

There were many assembly men who passed through Salem, and they offered to help the Moravians whenever possible in the legislature.

And the Moravians were reminded of one of their prime reasons for having come to America – to do mission work among the Indians – a mission, which as yet had not been fulfilled in North Carolina. For there had been the French and Indian War, then this current Revolutionary War. They were reminded of this mission when in late spring one hundred Catawba Indians, their wives and children, passed through Salem. They came quietly. They camped peacefully in the woods. The group was returning to their land on the Waxhaws.

There were other people who camped near-by who were not peaceful. Men who feared being drafted had run to the woods to hide. They often robbed travelers. Marauders also hid in woods throughout the county. Traveling became dangerous. When it was necessary to go to other towns, people went in groups.

The townspeople were careful to keep weeds cut and lots cleared. They burned leaf piles. They eliminated all possible hiding places.

In spite of the time and energy these outside problems took, the congregation continued its religious practices of services, lovefeasts, and choir meetings. People continued to marry. In May Single Brother Carl Opiz of Bethania was betrothed to Single Sister Christina Jorde of Salem. They were married a week later. New members were invited into the church in August and Martha was surprised at being asked to join the congregation.

She exclaimed to her parents, "Oh, I'm so happy."

Maria, excited also, said, "And you're so young in years, my dear. How well I remember my own reception. I was fifteen."

"And I was seventeen when I was received," Matthew said. "But I whole-heartily agree that you're ready. This year you've grown greatly in accord with the Unity's beliefs.

Martha had grown physically, too. No longer did she have the body of a child. At twelve, almost thirteen years she had the form of a young lady. Maria was very much aware of this as she began to measure her daughter for her new dress.

"Martha, I can't believe the changes in you in so short a time. I even have to *look up* to you now."

Happily, Martha laughed, "Mama, do you think we dyed enough wool? When will the weaver be through?"

Adjusting the paper pattern, Maria commented to the first question, "I don't know." To the second, she replied, "I'll ask your father to hurry him along."

"Do you think you could finish the dress by reception time?"

"If I get the cloth in a few days. But Martha, the wool will be so hot. Hadn't you rather wait till January when you will take your first communion?"

"Mama, I've grown so much and you said so yourself. I just can't wear *this* dress. It's too little. It was even too short last year. Remember?"

"Yes. Well, we'll try to finish it. But Martha, you know what this means don't you?"

Martha looked puzzled a minute, then caught her mother's glance at the spinning wheel. She sighed. "More spinning for a summer dress."

Shaking her head affirmative, Maria added, "We'll take care of this pattern. I believe you're as tall as you're ever going to be."

"Then I'll spin cotton for the summer dress, not flax."

"Flax will last longer."

"Cotton will be cooler."

"If you spin the flax first, then later, when you're ready for a change, you can spin the cotton. That would give you two dresses."

Martha thought, "Two dresses, I'd be like Anna."

Martha helped around the house, cooking and cleaning as much as she could to free her mother to hand sew the dress. Although Maria was handy with a needle, the sewing was tedious. There were many panels to join to make the full pleated skirt, a number of pieces to set accurately together in the bodice, and several holes to whip stitch for lacing.

Martha's help was also needed because Maria was one the sisters on call as a nurse for the married ladies whenever they were sick. In the springtime, Dr. Bonn had organized the married women so they could serve each other as nurses. When Maria had to be away from home, usually in the daytime, her own chores would have to be done when she returned.

The Single Brothers House had a room where the men and apprentices stayed when they were ill, and the single sisters had a similar arrangement. Thus, they could take care of their own.

Dr. Bonn was greatly respected for this nursing organization and it proved to be a blessing because on the evening of October 31, 1781, he had a heart attack and passed quietly to his heavenly home. The community grieved at the loss of a beloved friend and doctor. People throughout the county and the area whom he had attended as a physician or had known at court offered their condolences. Outsiders who came to his funeral were impressed with the orderliness and dignity of the service. His memorabilia was read, odes were sung, and music was played by the trombone choir. The brothers, followed by the sisters, walked behind the casket, born up the avenue to the graveyard. Dr. Bonn was laid to rest in the married brothers' section.

Strangers found the choir system an unusual burial plan. Families were not buried together. Instead, plots were laid out with the men being buried right of a center aisle and women, left. Married men were in a section nearest the gate, single men and young boys next. The same pattern was followed for the women. All gravestones were alike, flat and square, with the deceased name, date of birth; on some stones, the place and the date of death were chiseled on top.

With the death of a husband or wife, the family's situation often changed. Since most shops were in homes, if there was no son to step right into the shop, it was usually sold as soon as possible and the widow moved into smaller quarters. If a brother's wife died, he often remarried within a short time.

Dr. Bonn's death left the community without a doctor. Martha asked her father, "Will Brother Dixson become our doctor?"

"No. He's not qualified. He only helped Jacob. A man needs much education and special training to become a doctor," her father pointed out.

She was so relieved she blurted out, "Well, I'm glad to know. The Virginia soldiers didn't think he'd get them well. Wasn't it great that Dr. Bonn cured the men and saved our town from burning?"

Maria questioned her husband. "What will Jo Dixson do now?"

"He'll probably move into the Single Brothers House. Help out in some trade. He'd really like to study medicine someday."

"That would be costly."

"Father, what will we do for a doctor?"

"Marshall will write to Pennsylvania. Maybe they can send someone to us."

"Meanwhile," Maria added, "we'll try to stay healthy. Do the things Dr. Bonn taught us."

"If anything serious comes up, we can go to the nearest town that has a doctor."

CHAPTER SEVENTEEN

The news of Cornwallis' surrender at Yorktown reached Salem and everyone held hopes that the war would soon be over. But they were instead soon to be receivers of another burden – the North Carolina Assembly decided to meet in Salem.

Immediately upon hearing this news, the leaders met to discuss how to handle the situation. The tavern was not large enough to house all the men who would be coming. This was settled by asking families to take in guests. The families would also have to serve some meals.

Where to permit them to meet, was a big problem. The people did not favor the political gathering in their saal. They voted to ask the assembly men to meet in a conference room at the Gemeinhaus.

After a check with the tavern stack of dishware, a need for more bowls and mugs was apparent. Brother Aust was requested to start on this order as soon as possible.

There wasn't a family that wasn't involved in readying the town for the visitors who were scheduled to arrive in late January.

Martha was chagrinned at having to give up the flax she had spun so that it could be woven into a new sheet and a pillowslip. Bandages needed for the wounded soldiers the year before had depleted most families' supplies of extra linens. But Martha recovered her good spirits quickly because she felt her spinning had been helpful. She was going to miss her little room. Her family was taking in one assemblyman. However her thoughts dwelt more on her first communion which would be January 29, than on the assembly. This event was usually a highlight in the church life of the Moravians and Martha had long looked forward to participating in it.

On January 25, 1782, Governor Alexander Martin, whose home was near by on the Dan River, and a few other leaders arrived in town. The congregation decided to open all their services to the public. Martha felt shaky at knowing that many outsiders might be in the saal on communion night.

When the twenty-ninth arrived with a cold wind, she truly hoped the visitors would stay away. She stated as such to her father.

He admonished her. "Would you ever have the people stay away from God's House?"

"No, Father. I was thinking of myself," she hung her head slightly.

"We're thinking of you, too, Martha, dear. All Salem congregation knows it's your first communion; but you won't be singled out, you understand, like at reception."

"That will make it easier."

"Yes. Situations will not always be easy for us. But never despair or fall back for that reason. The Lord will give you help."

"Father, you always know the things to say to make me feel better."

That evening as they walked to the church, a cold, strong wind lashed out at them from the northwest, making the uphill climb difficult.

Arriving inside the saal early, Martha saw no strangers and she relaxed as she took her usual seat. The room was cold and she kept her old cape drawn closely, covering all but the lower hem of her gold dress. Her mother had finished the dress in time for her reception and she had worn it everyday since. The old cape was narrow, prompting her to wonder how many skeins of thread and how many turns on the knitty-knotty it would take to get a new one?

As other girls sat beside her, her mind came back to the current situation. Services tonight would begin with singing so that visitors could take part. Salem, unlike most Wachovia settlements, had some services in English.

Martha did not turn around to see if there were any spectators or outsiders in the back pews. She kept her eyes ahead. When communion bread and wine were passed, she stood with the others and partook of hers in the true spirit of humility and repentance.

The assemblyman lodged with the Mikschs told them that there were not enough members to form a full house. A few men who did not like the Moravians and their pacifist ways had found rooms in homes outside Wachovia; however, they daily came to Salem joining the other men to discuss various issues.

On Saturday, the attending members again took a count and still a majority was not present. They decided to adjourn. The following morning the assemblymen left town. The townspeople were so busy assisting the visitors that they could not hold morning services.

The guests thanked the townspeople for their kind treatment. They promised that they would try to hold the Assembly in Salem again in a few months.

And they did. The results were the same: there was not a sufficient number who could make the trip to form a majority. The Moravians had spent untold hours preparing and serving the two groups. Many had come the last time who had not come the first – and some men who came in January did not return, so in effect, almost two different groups of state leaders had come and witnessed the spirit of helpfulness of the Moravians. This was to be of benefit to them later in legislative matters.

Some outsiders had been impressed with Traugott Bagge and had asked him to run as a commoner, which he did in March and won that election.

In April Marshall and Bagge traveled to Hillsborough, where the assembly was meeting, to present a petition to protect the Brethren from the Confiscation Act.

With these two leaders taking care of legal issues, the British troops withdrawing to the coast and finally only seen in Charleston, and the Continental soldiers concentrated in other areas, the Salem people could began to resume their normal duties. The shops were more peaceful and the men pursued their handcrafts. The children continued their studies in school. The housewives returned to their primary responsibilities that of preparing meals, cleaning house, looking after babies, making candles, spinning and weaving.

There were still bands of marauders round about so the townspeople traveled only when necessary. The tavern was usually full as other travelers sought a safe place to stay.

One thing everybody had in common was the lack of money. The Continental currency had fallen so low in value it was almost worthless. Hard money was almost never seen. The Moravians continued to use script among themselves. A few times, craftsmen had to be reminded not to offer for sale, items they had taken in exchange for goods, especially if an item was sold by another brother.

Townspeople were hard up for funds to buy goods for themselves. Outsiders seemed to have only foodstuffs to barter, and the tradesmen could take only a limited quantity because they lacked proper storage for large quantities.

The Mikschs mulled over numerous ways to increase their own income. Matthew believed he could profit more by concentrating on tobacco. He felt men would continue to buy small quantities of twist and snuff and he wanted to have a good stock. He needed to expand and to design a better arrangement for manufacturing his tobacco.

One spring evening as he stood in his backyard smoking his pipe, he looked beyond his nursery to the watchman's house, which stood empty at the moment.

"That's it," he exclaimed.

Maria standing at the backdoor heard him and asked, "What's that, Matthew?"

"The night watchman's house. It's empty. It'd be just the place for my tobacco processing."

"Do you think the Collegium would agree?" she asked.

"Well, I won't know 'til I ask?"

Martha peered over her mother's shoulder as she dried a plate. "Father, you mean I won't have all that good tobacco to smell anymore?"

Matthew chuckled and knocked the ashes from his pipe. "Martha, I doubt if the tobacco smell will ever leave these walls. Generations from now my grandchildren, your grandchildren will be saying, 'My forefathers cured tobacco in this loft.' Even if no records were left of what we did, the fragrance of the tobacco will linger in the wooden beams to tell our history."

Matthew received permission on a temporary basis to use the watchman's house. He set about at once to study the floor plan of the log house, mentally picturing how best to arrange his equipment. One warm evening Maria and Martha walked down to the house with him.

Maria looking over the interior said, "It's small for a house, but it's large compared to our loft space."

"I think I'll work in the smallest area that's comfortable – determine exactly how much space I'll need," he remarked.

Martha spoke with interest. "Need for what?"

Matthew replied, "This move is temporary, you know. I've been wanting to build a manufacturing building for a long time. This is a good time. Lots of people need work. There's been no building during the war. I'm sure the town will get underway soon some of the buildings it has planned to construct for years."

"Oh, Father. How exciting! But, where will you get the money?"

"I've been putting away all the hard money I could during the war. Those extras like lodgings for Mr. Brooks and surveying, all went into a building fund."

Maria asked, "Have you decided where you'll put the new building?"

"Yes. Up near the house. I'll show you as we go back."

The three climbed between the fence rails and up the nursery path. On the other side of the fence, in the backyard, Matthew pointed out a place to the back and left. "Right there. It'll be convenient to the house, but it won't block the breezes through the front and back door, and it won't block the view from the house to the nursery. I'll put in a walk along the side of the house for deliveries. It'll be a straight line from the street."

Maria observed, "Matthew, you really think of everything."

"Father, has the Collegium given permission to build the manufactory?"

"I think there will be no objections, but I'll wait awhile before inquiring. Well, do you two ladies feel like moving day tomorrow?"

Maria and Martha laughed as they all went inside. Darkness had rapidly descended.

CHAPTER EIGHTEEN

Martha was especially delighted that her father was in the watchman's house because once again she had the freedom of going into the nursery. She was almost fourteen and like most young people her age, restrictions or space limitations were hard to live with.

Now when she came home from school, it was her father who had the most chores for her to do. Often he would ask if she would spread a layer of mulch around the plants, or pick the beetles off the roses or tie up the cucumber vines.

One noontime after dinner while Maria was making pickles, she asked Martha to gather some more cucumbers. Martha picked up the empty willow basket and went out right behind Matthew who had some tobacco leaves to salt down in the watchman's house.

Martha stopped in the garden, dropped her basket on the path and began to pick the cucumbers. She half filled her basket when she heard someone say, "Hello."

She glanced up. No one was in the nursery or backyard. She knew she hadn't imagined the voice, so she continued to search with her eyes. Her back had been turned to the Triebel yard. Slowly, she turned around and there just beyond the fence was one of the older boys leaning on the top rail. The hollyhocks planted near the fence were so tall and thick, she could hardly see him. During a long, second look, she realized this must be a new boy, from one of the other Wachovia towns, because she didn't recognize him.

"Hello," he said again, pushing a hollyhock aside.

Two different impulses tumbled against each other in her mind: I shouldn't talk to a single brother, but I have talked to Brother Triebel and Brother Zillman. They are neighbors.

The boy stood up and separated two stalks of hollyhock. Martha thought he's the tallest older boy I've ever seen. His hair was reddish brown and his skin bore a healthy tan.

"Excuse me, but I dropped my twine over your fence," he said with a grin.

Martha lifted her skirts carefully and held the ample folds close to her while she squeezed between the vines and hollyhocks.

"Do you see it?" he asked teasingly.

"Yes."

"Could you hand it to me?"

Martha bent down and picked up the ball of twine. When she straightened up, she was rewinding the loose end. She sensed he was staring at her.

"Peter says you're real nice."

"Peter?"

"Peter Sampson. Your name is Martha isn't it?"

"Yes."

"Oh, I hear Brother Schrober coming." Instantly he let go the hollyhocks and was lost from view.

The next day at noon she had been asked to pinch off the tallest mint stalks. She was absorbed in her task, enjoying the pleasant smells, when again she heard a friendly hello.

This time she looked directly over to the hollyhocks. There was the same reddish-brown head.

"Excuse me, but I dropped the twine again. Could you, please, retrieve it for me?"

Martha couldn't hide her smile as she stood up and walked toward the fence. Matthew, walking through the backyard, noticed Martha leave the mint bed and walk to the fence. He saw her stoop and pick up something. Then he saw the boy standing in Triebel's yard. Matthew headed in that direction.

"Martha!"

She spun around, startled.

The boy ducked from view.

"Boy! Boy!" Matthew called.

Embarrassed and flushed, the boy slowly reappeared.

"What's this all about?"

"Sorry, sir. I . . . I . . . uh just dropped my twine."

"Father, I was going to hand it back to him. See, I'm just rewinding it," she admitted, holding the ball up for him to see.

"Well, that's a neighborly deed. You go along back to the mint now," he said gently and she scooted away. Matthew held the ball a minute, while scrutinizing the boy. "You have the gardening chores for the school?"

"No, sir, I mean, I help out some. Brother Triebel says the garden has gotten too big for him to tend alone. Brothers Schrober and Dixson are real busy with the younger boys."

"Oh? Well, here's your twine. Keep a good tight hand on it."

"Yes, sir. Thank you, sir."

That night, Matthew announced on the way home from services that he was going to stop off to see Triebel.

Maria and Martha walked on home. Martha asked her mother why was her father going to see Brother Triebel.

"I don't know, dear. He'll tell us if we need to know."

Martha felt uneasy. She wondered if the boy was going to be in trouble for talking to her. She hoped not. "Maybe he's new and doesn't know our rules. But *I* know. Oh, I wish I had pretended not to see him. But he needed help. Father said that I did a neighborly deed. No. I will not fret myself like this. I told father I'd let him worry about me and I will. If I ever again *have to speak* to a boy or brother, *I will but I won't worry like this*. It makes me more tired than spinning."

With the giving up of her burden, she fell immediately into a peaceful sleep.

At breakfast the next morning as Maria poured tea and Martha put toast in front of the fire, Matthew announced, "Well, beginning today I take on a new job."

"What's that, dear?" Maria asked as she put the teapot on the table and sat down.

"I'm going to tend the garden at Treibel's."

"Is that what you went to see about last night?" Maria inquired helping herself to a fried egg.

Martha didn't look up; she watched the bread carefully to be sure it didn't burn. She turned the iron toaster a half circle to toast the other side. She listened closely as Matthew continued.

"I heard the garden was too much for him. I suppose those big boys over at the school eat large quantities of vegetables. This is the busiest growing season, you know."

"Can't the boys help in the garden?" Maria wanted to know.

"Oh, yes. They can help. But I'll direct their chores."

Martha lifted the bread from the toaster with a fork and placed it in a rush basket. She put a piece on her plate, then put the basket on the table.

"Martha."

"Yes, Father?" She responded buttering her toast with downcast eyes.

"If I'm going to do Triebel's garden, I'll be needing your help more here. Course we're not planting just now. Most of the work will be routine with some harvesting."

"I'll be glad to help."

"Matthew, is Brother Triebel to pay you for this work?" Maria inquired as she spread preserves on her toast.

"We're trying to work something out. With money so scarce, I think I'll exchange him some labor."

"Oh, you mean for the new manufactory?"

"That's what I'm thinking. I'm going up to talk with Brother Graff about love feast accounts. I'll talk all this over with him and Marshall. I'll need to start getting materials lined up. Martha, I'll walk to school with you this morning," he said as he rose.

At the Gemeinhaus, Martha walked up the steps at the left to the door that led to the sisters quarters and the schoolroom.

Matthew climbed the steps that led to the saal and ministers' quarters. Bishop Graff had been ill lately and Matthew observed today that the older man did not look well. Matthew greeted him cheerfully.

"Good morning, dear Brother Graff."

"Morning, Matthew," Graff replied weakly.

"I brought the love feast ledger. Most of the accounts are paid up. If money stays as scarce as it is now, it is going to be hard for people though. The few whose accounts are in arrears are noted with a check," he explained, passing the ledger over to the bishop.

After reading the figures, Graff asked about expenses. Matthew indicated, "The other marker. Yes, that's the page. One list is for communicant love feasts; one is for congregation love feasts."

"Yes, I see. Very detailed records."

"Notice we're using a quarter pound of tea at each communicant love feast. When there's no tea, I'll supply herbs from the nursery."

"How's the coffee supply?"

"We have none. When the store sends a wagon to the coast, I hope some is available."

"Whenever the store gets any, we'll have them send the first to you to put in the love feast supply cabinet." Graff nodded slightly.

"The brothers gathered lots of chestnuts last year. You know, we could prepare those instead of coffee, if any are left."

"In the fall, remind the families to pick up all they can. It may be awhile before sea trade returns to normal."

"With the British still holding Charlestown, we won't get many shipments from there."

Bishop Graff handed the ledger back to Matthew. "Good job. Just continue to be sure people get what they pay for. Be sure the buns remain a proper weight."

"I'll be going on. I want to see Brother Marshall. Take care."

Matthew went out and closed the door. He walked on down the hall and located Brother Marshall.

"I was just in to see Brother Graff. He doesn't appear too well."

"No, he doesn't."

"I have some plans I want to talk over. Do you have a few minutes?"

"Yes," Marshall replied cordially.

"I'm manufacturing my tobacco products in the night watchman's house now on a temporary basis. I'm going to need a building soon. And I'd like to build a log structure on my lot. It seems like this fall might be a good time to start it. There's no building going on right now."

"No, but we anticipate the community can undertake some of its planned projects soon. Do you think you can manage this manufactory financially?"

"Yes. I've put some aside for a start. And I just last night talked to Triebel about doing work for him, tending the garden for the boys' school, in exchange for some joiner work later. Of course, I'll speak to the Collegium, although I'm not adding any new products for sale."

"It's wise to keep them apprised of all business changes," agreed Marshall. "I'm pleased you can undertake this."

Over in the schoolroom, Martha heard of some building plans herself; rather she overheard two sisters talking about a building. Martha had been busy writing on her slate when the teacher approached her and asked if she'd please gather all the rags used to clean the slates and take them outside and shake them. So Martha collected the soft white cloths from both the older and younger girls' classrooms. She walked out the back door and dropped the dusty rags onto the top step. She took up one and shook it vigorously, then another. A window was open to the right of her and she heard two sisters inside talking.

"Don't you think it's time we talked to Brother Marshall?"

"I do. We need our own choir house. There's just not enough space to keep taking sisters in."

"And we should. All the girls in Wachovia should have the chance to live in a choir house."

"Did you realize that since this choir started in Salem in 1772, we have had sixteen single girls to get married?"

"There is always another single sister ready to move in. We've only had one to go home and one to leave Salem, isn't that right?"

"Yes. Oh, I do hope we can have a larger house soon. How much do you think it will cost?"

"More than we have now. But we need to start planning."

"Brother Marshall can probably give us some suggestions."

"Yes. Is there any other way we can earn more money? Are there any services or other handcrafts we can do?"

"I don't know what the people would pay with. Oh, did you hear that the last time we sent gloves to the store, that Brother Bagge seemed reluctant to take them?"

An astonished voice said, "No!"

A definitive voice answered. "That's what I heard."

About this time, Martha sneezed from the dust shaken from the dozen or so cloths.

The voices inside stopped a moment, then resumed in lower tones; thus, Martha, even though quietly folding the cloths into neat squares, could not overhear the conversation. As she returned down the hallway to class, she wondered when she would come to live in the Single Sisters House. She had always known that was a custom of the Moravians – at around eighteen years of age girls moved into the choir house if there was room. "That's in four years," she estimated. The thought of leaving home, of leaving her mother and father, created an uneasy feeling in her stomach. She wasn't sure she would like that part of being a Moravian.

"But that's a whole four years away," her debating mind changed the emphasis and secretly she thought "maybe they won't get the house built or maybe there won't be a room for me."

She handed the stack of cloths to the teacher who thanked her and suggested she read her history lesson.

"I've finished the book, sister."

"Then would you listen to Rebecca read?" the teacher asked.

"Yes, sister." Martha sought out the younger girl who was struggling with her book and sat down next to her.

The teacher drew her eyebrows together as she wrestled with

the problem of what to teach Martha. "She has been through all the books we have. I wish we'd receive some from Pennsylvania or Europe. Maybe I can find some English books in the house that she can start. She might copy some songs for the younger girls."

She saw that Martha was getting Rebecca to say her words carefully. Rebecca was responding eagerly, something that she did not usually do. "Martha has a way with these younger girls."

Matthew had his way with the Ausfer Collegium about the manufactory construction, too, but not without a little rebuttal from Bagge. When Matthew presented his plans to the Collegium, he stayed long enough to answer their questions concerning the project, such as: why build now when money was so scarce? His answer was because the time is ripe.

"Will men be buying tobacco when they can hardly get hold of money for other things?"

"I think so. In hard times, men still enjoy their moments of relaxation and pleasure. A smoke enjoyed in good company provides this opportunity for many men."

"Would you have to raise your prices?"

"I don't plan to. Tobacco twist or snuff – finished, is cheap: a man can buy what he wants; as much or as little as he can afford. If a man can come to town knowing there'll always be a good supply of tobacco, perhaps he'll trade at the other shops, too. I'll help the tavern by having tobacco for travelers and the pottery by selling the pipes. It'll keep the staff from having to stop work to see to these small items."

However, after Matthew left the meeting, Bagge reasserted his long held views. "I don't like the way Miksch stores his tobacco."

"The new arrangement will provide him better storage facilities."

"He should stick to earning his living with his handcrafts. He's a good craftsman," Bagge stated.

Another brother replied, "Manufacturing the tobacco is his present handcraft."

"Expansion, operating a manufactory, goes into bigger business," shot back Bagge.

"Miksch seems to view this as a better physical arrangement for his already established business."

The request to build the manufactory was put to a vote and consent was given.

Next, Bagge stated, "I'm not planning to handle the sale of leather gloves for the sisters any more."

"The sisters will be disappointed. Those sales are important to them, especially as they want to build a choir house of their own." Marshall emphasized.

"Can they afford to do that?" one of the brothers questioned.

"No, not immediately. Probably not on their own later. They have been frugal. Their accounts are in good order. However, the truth is that they need more space."

"Can the gloves be sold at the tailor shop?"

"It isn't the most appropriate place," the tailor spoke up. "Women can't come into the Brothers House to try them on."

"They need to be sold in a really clean place, where they won't get dirty or anything spilled on them."

Bagge said, "The gloves are marked high because of the soft, good quality leather and the difficulty in stitching. Ladies don't have money for expensive items. I don't like to keep the community store inventory high, our taxes being as they are."

Marshall thanked Bagge for his concern and suggested the Collegium think seriously about another market place for the sisters' gloves.

As if by inspiration, one brother popped up a solution. "Why not ask Miksch to handle the gloves? His shop is always neat. Maria can collect the gloves from the sisters and turn over any sales money."

The tailor added, "She could also serve the ladies, help them get the right size."

Marshall asked the brothers for a vote. "All right. I'll inform

Brother Miksch that he can go ahead with the construction plans, and I'll ask him whether or not he can handle the glove sales."

Soon after Matthew was notified of the approval of his building plans, he proceeded to gather the necessary materials and line-up the people who would be needed. He bought the side logs, had them squared and notched on the ends for a dovetail construction. He arranged through one of his customers to bring him a load of lime from the Dan River on his next trip to town to buy supplies. He asked various brothers in town whenever they were going out with a wagon and returning empty, to bring back any large stones they saw and had time to stop and load. The manufactory would have a stone floor. He also planned stone paving from the street to the manufactory door.

Brother Triebel was making the windows, doors, and a new press. Gottlieb Krause was to erect the manufactory. Krause suggested putting a necessary on the left side of the building – with the door to the back (facing the nursery). All the Mikschs favored this new plan; Matthew especially liked having the two facilities under one roof, Maria and Martha looked forward to having fewer "potties" to empty.

Maria also anticipated a small candle room in the manufactory. Matthew had decided to put in a central chimney with the fireplace in a small room, that Maria repeatedly called the candle room. The door could be left open in cold weather to heat the manufacturing room. In summer the door would be closed if a fire were going to help cure the tobacco which would be stored in the loft. Two outside doors – directly opposite each other – one on the south and one the north side would provide cross ventilation and permit prevailing southerly winds to pass through in hot weather.

With plans so well prepared in advance, construction of the building moved orderly and quickly once it was undertaken.

Martha and Maria again helped Matthew move his equipment. They both hoped this would be the last time, not because they were weary, but because they wanted the manufactory to be as satisfactory as he planned it to be. And it was.

One mid-fall day as Maria went out to inspect the new operations, she heard a wagon rattling along the newly laid stone cart way.

"Matthew, I hear a wagon coming." Looking out a window, she saw a mountaineer who had been in town previously. "I think it's the old man from the other side of Pilot Mountain."

Matthew walked to the door, "I bet he has a barrel of molasses."

"I declare. I've been wanting to make some gingerbread."

Matthew opened the door, waited for the driver to halt the horse and stop the wagon. "Good day, Amos."

"Howdy, Matthew," the thin, gray-headed man called back.

"Are you bringing some of your good sorghum?"

"Sho 'nuff. A big crop of cane this year. I heard in Bethabara about your new building. This is mighty fine."

Matthew urged, "Come in. Look around. You remember my wife, don't you, Amos?"

Maria stepped back to let Amos in, giving him a nod of recognition.

He nodded, then said to Matthew, "Yes, sir, mighty fine. Are you going to keep your molasses supply in here?"

"Yes, let me show you." Matthew walked toward the back door and indicated a small niche. "Could stack a couple of barrels here."

While the men dickered over the price, Maria peered through the window and her gaze rested on the wagon. She saw three molasses barrels. Suddenly, an idea sprang forth. If she could get that other barrel, maybe she could make gingerbread to sell in the shop. Quickly, she mentally scavenged her resources for something she could trade: preserves, herbs, turnips, pickled cucumbers – no his family would have all that. Then she remembered the flax thread. She had a number of bobbins already spun.

She turned toward the men who were settling on a fair price. When they finished, she bravely asked, "Amos, Matthew is taking two barrels. I see one more in your wagon."

"Yes'm."

"Would you like to trade it to me?"

"What you hankering to trade?"

She took a deep breath. "I've got some very fine flax thread spun. It's already on bobbins. I was planning some fine linens with it." Amos appeared interested so Maria continued. "I'll let you have them for the barrel of molasses."

Matthew listened with surprise. He never knew of Maria to initiate a trade on her own, but he respected her judgement and did not interfere.

"Well, I might do that. My missus has been helping out with the molasses making. She hadn't much spinning time. She might be needing some warping thread to go along with that."

Maria hadn't planned to include that thread also. She decided to try for a compromise. "I have some thread for the warping. Had you rather have that instead of the fine thread?"

Matthew rather enjoyed seeing his wife's bargaining prowess. He waited while Amos considered this alternative.

Amos was a seasoned trader and did not want to be out done. "How about some of each?"

"If that's what you want, I'd be glad to oblige. One fine to two warps threads. After you unload the molasses barrels, come into the house. Matthew, I'll make some tea. Amos, could you join us?"

"Thank you. I'd like some. It's a long ride back up the mountain."

"Good. Oh, can you roll *my barrel* on into the kitchen. Matthew, can we store mine where you used to store the shop's barrel?" She asked over her shoulder as she walked out of the manufactory.

"That'll be fine," he chuckled, realizing that he was now committed to putting this into the cellar.

Later that evening as the family was eating molasses and biscuits at dinner, Maria told Matthew and Martha of the plan that had been forming in her mind all day. "For sometime it has bothered me Matthew that I couldn't be of more help to you," she began.

He interrupted. "Why, Maria, you are always helpful."

"I mean in helping you bring in money."

"But Mama," Martha broke in, "you pickle the cucumbers and bunch the turnips and mould candles."

"Yes, dear. I know all this. But you see this is all doing in part. You and your father work in the nursery, your father does all the tobacco, certainly most all of it by himself."

Matthew asked interested, "What are you getting at, Maria?"

"I want to do something all my own to help out. I think I know what it can be."

"Does it have anything to so with the molasses you bought – er – bargained for today?"

"Yes. I want to make gingerbread to sell in the shop," she said anxiously watching for Matthew's reaction.

She heard Martha's first. "How grand! Everybody loves your gingerbread."

Matthew walked slowly over to the fireplace, put in a large twist of paper, watched it ignite then lit his pipe. He blew out the flame on the paper, pinched the burned section off, and replaced the twist on the mantle. He drew on his pipe as he slowly sat down again.

Maria waited, as she knew he was carefully thinking over all the complications. In a few minutes he asked, "Where would you do a quantity of baking?"

"I'd need an oven in the backyard. You said the brickyard had some culls. They ought to come cheap. Could we get the mason who did the manufactory chimney to do it?"

"I'm not sure we can pay him?"

"Maybe we could make arrangements to pay him a little at a time out of the profits from the gingerbread?"

"Maybe. I'll have to go back to the Collegium, you know."

"Yes. I realize that. Matthew, we might as well ask for exclusive rights to make and sell gingerbread as long as we're going into this."

"Since the brothers bakery never makes it, we probably could get the rights. Maria, I hope you've given this careful consideration. Once you enter an item for sale, people come to expect it. You'll have to be the total supplier. Baking is out of my domain."

"I have. I've decided I want to do it."

"Then I'll present the request to the Collegium for you. But first I want you to write your needs, your expenses for one baking, and write down the size of squares or weights you plan to sell and how much each will cost. Then figure how much profit you can expect to realize. Don't forget to include the cost of wood for the oven heating."

"Mama, can you get molasses in the summer for gingerbread?"

"Usually we run out in spring."

"Could you buy more when the men make it in the fall?" Martha asked.

"Probably, but if the summer's hot, it could spoil. Gingerbread is more a cold weather treat. Perhaps we could just offer it in cool seasons. Then I could have a break. I'll need the summer anyway for all those helpful things I do," she laughed.

The other two joined in merrily with her.

Maria gained consent for her enterprise easily. Her reputation for gingerbread baking was well known and the people looked forward to the completion of the oven.

In school Martha painted a small picture of a steaming square of gingerbread on a crisp white linen napkin. In one corner of the napkin, she lettered in vivid, goldenrod yellow (her mother's favorite color) the initials *MM*. She so much wanted a frame for the painting that she did a very bold thing. One evening after school and before supper, she went to the nursery. When she saw Brother Triebel go into the manufactory to see her father, she waited 'til he came out, then she hurried through the gate.

"Brother Triebel," she whispered. He turned, surprised to hear Martha calling.

"Yes?"

"I want to make a frame for a picture I painted for Mama for Christmas. Do you have any old scraps of wood? Nothing fancy. Just four plain strips?"

"About how big, Martha?"

"The picture is this big," she showed him the size with her hands.

"I'll see what I can find."

"Brother Triebel I don't have any money. Mama and Father would not like me to beg. How can I pay you?"

"Let me think on that. I'll let you know when I find the scraps," he whispered.

"Thank you so much," she smiled, turned and ran into her house.

A few days before Christmas, Brother Triebel watched for Martha to come down the street at noon. When he spotted her rounding the corner, he put on his coat and walked outside. As she approached his house, he blocked her path, smiled pleasantly and handed her a package.

Surprised, she looked up at him.

"Your order."

"Oh, thank you. How can I pay you?"

"Your father says you have some pots of rosemary. When the season's right, dry some leaves. A mug of rosemary tea helps my thinking."

"I will," she beamed with shining eyes. As she hurried home, she thought how nice he was to let her give him something that really was hers to give.

Inside the house, she dashed up the stairs before going to the kitchen, calling to her mother that she needed to wash her hands.

She unfolded the brown paper. There in the center of it lay a smooth, finely sanded and beautifully stained cherry wood frame. This was more than she dared hope for—not scraps, but a real frame, and finished by the best of joiners. She jumped up from the bed and opened her clothes press. She felt for the painting in the back under her summer gown. She withdrew it carefully, walked over to the bed, sat down and put the picture on the frame. With a little trimming it would fit perfectly. She cut some brown paper for a backing. She was so excited about having such a lovely gift for her mother. She enjoyed thinking about it and inspecting it secretly for two whole days before she re-wrapped it in the brown paper and tied it with some yellow knitting yarn. In the center of the small bow she tucked in a sprig of holly and a few red berries that she had found earlier that day in the street.

Maria's expression of pleasure on opening the package pleased Martha.

"Look, Matthew," she said, "a picture. Martha, did you paint it? I see an MM in the corner."

"Yes, I did, but the M M is for you. Maria Miksch is the gingerbread maker."

"Matthew, why can't I use this as my trade sign? When the gingerbread is ready each day, I can place the picture toward the window. When we don't have any, I can turn the picture toward the room."

"It's all right with me. Martha, that is a beautiful frame. Did you make that, too?" He asked incredulously.

"I'm glad you like it. No. I bought it."

"Bought it?" Maria expressed shock.

"Well, bartered it, for some of my rosemary," she confessed.

"Now there are two business women in my house."

And so the year 1782 ended on a progressive note for the Miksch family. Times had been hard and were still hard, but the family was active, in good spirits, and happy.

The following year went swiftly for Martha. Matthew spent most of his days in the manufactory. Maria was involved in the baking business and Martha divided her time during the after school hours between household chores, spinning, dying, and nursery chores. Her schoolwork took less of her time as she had already covered all the books the teachers had available for her. The sisters encouraged Martha to busy her hands with needlework; Martha did, though without interest. She was always having to take out her stitches. Often times as she sat sewing near Anna Bagge, Anna would laugh good-naturedly at Martha's work, saying her flowers resembled cabbages or her birds, the chickens. Then she would snip out the stitches and deftly rework them. And Martha would meanwhile pick up Anna's history book and read to her. Other times as Anna practiced scales or songs on the clavichord, Martha would hum or sing along. But that was as far as Martha's musical talents went.

One day Martha lamented, "Anna, how will I ever fit into the Sisters Choir? I just don't do anything well. My sewing is terrible; my instrumental playing even worse?"

Anna tossed her golden curls as she looked up from the keyboard. "Don't despair, Martha. There'll be a job for you. You know God has work for all of us."

"Yes. But what is mine?"

Anna reflected a moment, then said gaily, "You work very nicely with the little children. Your work may be taking care of the little ones. You might even marry and have lots of babies. Wouldn't that be fun? I could play them a lullaby."

Martha blushed and quickly changed the subject. "Anna, when do you think the sisters will start their choir house?"

"Father says it'll probably be the first of next year before all the materials are on hand."

"Wasn't it generous of the sisters in Germany to send them money to help start the building?"

"Martha, are you going to wait to move in after they finish the new building?"

"I don't know. Nobody has said anything to me. I do know they don't have any vacant rooms here now. When will you go into the house?"

"I don't know either. I may have to stay home with mama. She's not well. If poppa ever gets a sister who can stay and look after her, I can go, especially now that the boys are staying in the home school. Maybe you and I could have a room together someday," Anna said hopefully.

Talk of the preparations to build the sister's house filled the girls' conversation while another "moving procedure" was also of concern to the congregation. This concern was about the large number of people who were leaving the area and moving to Kentucky. Many of the people owed money to the Moravians. Some had bought lands and turned them into well-cultivated farms. Now those people were leaving their farms.

The economics were currently crushing many people. Paper money was worthless. No one had hard money to buy needed goods. Commerce was nil along the North Carolina coast. The British had only evacuated Charlestown in December 1782, and trade there had not recovered yet.

Men had no place to sell their farm produce or their handcrafts. Therefore some men who had purchased land considered it more feasible to pick up and move their families west and start all over. Many even drove all the cattle they found in the woods, cattle rightfully belonging to the Moravians, west with them.

Marshall, as Wachovia administrator, had to attend to the reclaiming of the lands. Buildings not inhabited, farms not plowed quickly degenerated into a rather worthless condition.

Even the spirit of unity among the Moravians, so strong during the war years, was weakening. The older boys, apprentices and journeyman were restless. They just couldn't clearly see the purpose of unity or the pressure to produce when the products had no market.

Thus, the ministers had the additional tough job of keeping up the spirits of the congregation. They recognized the need for real work for the men. Building projects seemed to be an answer so that is why the sisters were going to begin their choir house. Also, plans were fermenting for an addition to the Brothers House.

During the night watch reading of the memorabilia of Salem, December 1783, Martha heard the recounting of some events that had brought joy to the congregation.

At the time of happening each event had seemed a single entity to her, but now hearing them in sequence, she realized how one naturally followed the other and read like a brief saga – "The aftermath of war" – still dotted with soldiers – or men who were soldiers no more – but discharged men on the long march home without the power of officers or organization to supply their needs en route. In a flash, images of hundreds of men on horseback, followed by others on foot in the rawness of short February days marched past her inner eye. Their haggard appearance, their pleas for food were etched deep in her memory.

On April 30, the congregation had heard the news of the cessation of arms on land and sea by Proclamation of Congress.

The North Carolina Assembly had voted for a day of public Thanksgiving and they had instructed Governor Alexander Martin to proclaim July 4 as such.

Upon hearing this, the congregation began planning for the special day. Little did they know that they would be the only group of people taking up the suggestion. They showed their heartfelt joy at the return of peace with four special gatherings and the composition of new music for the July 4 occasion. First, the people were awakened on July 4 by the trombonists. Next, at the preaching service, *Te Deum* was sung along with the trombones, and Brother Bengien used Psalm 46 as his text. Third, at two o'clock in the afternoon there was a love feast with the *New Psalm of Joy*. Finally, at eight o'clock, the congregation met in the saal, where the choir sang. Then the congregation formed a circle in front of the Gemeinhaus. From there they walked around the square to the music of antiphonal choirs. The street had been illuminated for the night event. The circle was reformed at the Gemeinhaus. The people were dismissed with a blessing of the Lord.

The full Treaty of Peace had not been signed until September 3 in Paris. It was not until December 4 that George Washington was able to leave his offices in New York.

With the coming of peace and the signing of the treaty with the Indians on the Halston, the Unity was allowed again to send a brother forth to investigate mission possibilities.

CHAPTER NINETEEN

Early in 1784, Salem did have an event, which brought the people together again in a spirit of unity and cooperation. It was a tragic event.

Late during the last night of January, a fire broke out in the tavern. As soon as the fire was detected, an alarm was shouted. The bell in the square was rung. Every able-bodied brother and sister donned boots and heavy clothing, grabbed an empty bucket and ran to the square. As soon as they learned the location of the fire, the strongest men raced on to the tavern to help save whatever they could.

The fire wardens instructed the other people to form two lines from the square pump down to the tavern. Martha lined up with the girls and women on the left. They spaced themselves so that they could cover the long block to the tavern. The men were opposite them on the right. A brother vigorously worked the pump handle. When a bucket was filled, it was handed to the first man in line who in turn handed it the next man. The last man flung the water on the burning building. The empty bucket was passed to the first woman in the return line.

This was Martha's initiation to the bucket brigade and she was clumsy with the first few buckets passed to her. She kept telling herself to be calm. In a few minutes she worked out a hand pattern, receiving on the left, passing to her own right hand before giving it to the next girl. She glimpsed her father up near the pump. Splashing water darkened his clothes. She couldn't see her mother. Martha thought she, too, must be near the pump. The fire burned brightly, lighting the whole block. Martha wondered if the barn in back would catch fire. She could see the flames leaping straight upward; there was no wind to send them fanning to nearby out buildings. Yet she could hear someone shouting to the brothers who were stationed back of the tavern to keep dashing water over the barn and to continue stamping out any flying sparks.

The Tavern guests, shaken but unharmed, were hustled to the Reuter house on the corner. The Meyers' belongings and some of the furniture from the main floor tavern rooms were hauled across the street.

Martha's arms ached. She knew she must have passed a thousand buckets. Her neck and shoulder muscles throbbed and she wanted to rest. She looked around and saw everyone else still handing buckets, leather ones, wooden ones, anything that would hold water. "No, I won't stop!" she told her aching hands and arms. She saw her father had relieved the brother at the pump. Later, she looked down again and saw another brother pumping water.

The night was bitterly cold, but Martha in constant movement did not notice. Only, when news from down the line reached her "no more buckets" and she stopped, did she become aware her feet were numb. As she stumbled up the street for a closer look at the remains of the smoldering tavern, she felt she was walking on stumps instead of feet. She kept stamping her boots as she gazed at the stone foundations, about all that was left of the half-timbered building. The circulation was returning in her feet about the time she felt her mother come up and put an arm around her.

"Come on home, dear. Your father is wet through," Maria said.

Martha turned and followed her. At the pump, Martha stopped to find her bucket. From habit, she filled the empty bucket. Maria and Matthew waited for Martha, then they trudged homeward.

While Matthew changed into dry clothes, Maria filled the water kettle, then put some thyme in a teapot. Martha poked up the fire that had been banked earlier for the night. Maria pulled a bench near the fireplace and spread Matthew's wet clothes to dry.

"Martha," she directed, "get the bricks from my bedroom and the cloths. We'll get them warm for the beds. Oh, Matthew, I hope you don't catch cold."

He did come down with a cold and didn't feel up to going to services the following evening. Maria and Martha went. Upon their return, Matthew who was seated in the living room near the jamb stove sipping thyme tea asked what the news was.

Maria, taking off her cape and gloves, answered, "We all gave thanks to the Lord upon hearing no one was injured or killed last night. Well, the congregation voted to rebuild the tavern right away."

"That's logical. But it will take time," he sniffed.

"Not very long, Father. The town is going to use the materials the sisters had ready to start their house."

"What?"

"Yes, Father. This morning late, Brother Marshall asked the sisters if they would discuss it. They met and voted to let the congregation have the materials. They really are rather sad."

"I'm sure they are. I'm glad they can be so generous," he said.

While warming her hands over the stovetop, Maria said, "It's really necessary for Salem to have a tavern. Without one, the trade would be at a standstill."

Matthew asked, "Did anyone say where the Meyers will live?"

"They are going to fix up the log house. The one where munitions were made. It has two rooms, you remember. They'll use one side for their residence and one side to accommodate guests. And townspeople can take in any overflow if there's a pressing need. But we'll try to stay away from that."

The rebuilding of the tavern provided much-needed jobs for men in the area. Some of the women had opportunities to prepare and serve meals for the workmen and travelers. The craftsmen were busy making furnishings for the interior.

Meanwhile, the log house was moved from back of the old

Tavern to the lot just opposite it on Main Street. Again the parents were more protective of their daughters, because a number of outside men were working as day laborers in town.

For Martha, though, it was a long year. The other girls enjoyed progressing to fine embroidery and designing pictures. They chattered constantly whenever the teacher left them alone so that she could work with the younger girls. Martha grew weary of sitting. She wasn't excited about long and short stitches or perfect X's in cross work so she didn't jump up and peer over the other girls' handwork, as most of them seemed to be constantly doing.

Next year started with the same pattern. Other girls her age were excited about making linens, aprons, and getting things ready for their move into the Sisters Choir House. After the tavern was completed, the congregation promised to help the sisters collect materials to build their choir house. Most of the girls knew that when the house was finished next year, there would be room for them.

Martha did her spinning at night, more from long years of habit than pleasure. And she certainly found no joy in talking about it. The community was full of things happening: she wanted to be out sharing in the events. She wanted to serve, not to sit and spin or talk.

She wanted in winter to grind herbs to help relieve people with sore throats, in spring she longed to be on her knees in the nursery putting tiny seeds in the earth or dividing mature plants, in summer she begged to dig stock for customers. She had the urge to run down the street with the little girls: and, yes, she hungered to gather berries and nuts with the little boys who climbed trees and harvested such.

One day at noon her mother was feeling low, not sick, but tired. Since Matthew had gone out in the woods for the day, she just decided to rest a bit. When Martha came in, Maria asked her to go the bakery for some bread, as she hadn't baked.

Martha was happy to have an outside errand. She swung her basket freely over her hand as she walked during the unusually warm late winter day. She hadn't been asked to go the brothers' bakery, which was just behind the Brothers House, since she was a little girl. Because her mama had the outside oven now, she baked her own bread. She pushed the heavy oak door open and walked into the front sales room. It faced west but was still rather dim inside. The walls were white washed and the floors were scrubbed red tile. The odor of burned oak logs mingled with the freshly baked bread and lingered tantalizingly in the air.

Martha was inhaling the aroma appreciatively when someone appeared suddenly at the little window to the room that she gathered to be the baking area.

"Can I help you?" An apprentice in his teens inquired.

"Mama wants a loaf of whole wheat." She glanced at him briefly, then lowered her gaze.

He disappeared a moment then came through the doorway carrying a round loaf on a napkin. "It's still warm."

"It smells delicious." Instantly, she was embarrassed at having spoken more than was necessary. She handed him the money, careful to let it drop in his palm without touching him.

"I'll wrap it for you," he offered. He laid the brown round loaf on a square of paper and neatly folded the edges together then tucked them under. Before handing it back to her he said, "We'll have some herb bread tomorrow."

"Oh," she was surprised. "I didn't know you made it. What do you use?"

"Mostly dill seed. You like to work in herbs, don't you?"

"How did you know?" She was puzzled because she never talked to anyone about her nursery work. She looked up and noticed he had keen, brown eyes.

"I've seen you, there through the back, sometimes when the weeds are down or the greenery is trimmed."

"May I have the bread? Mama needs it for lunch?" She knew she shouldn't be chatting.

He handed it to her and she dropped it into her basket and left the building. All the way back home she wondered if baking would be fun day after day. Her mother did it, but she did a number of other things, too.

The following day, Matthew was in the manufactory when she returned home. She asked her mother directly, even before removing her cape, "Mama, can I go to the bakery for bread?"

"I have gingerbread, dear."

"But, Mama, they are making herb bread today. I've never had any. Please, let's try a loaf," she begged.

Martha rarely asked for anything. "All right, it might be a nice change. Your father will wonder at our extravagance, bought bread two days in a row."

This time she didn't take the basket since the baker had wrapped the bread yesterday. She almost skipped to the bakery. Once inside, she only had to wait a half-second before the young baker looked through the window. He smiled and said, "I'll be right out."

Martha had time to realize there was a tangy odor today, and that the baker had his hair combed neatly and wore a clean apron.

He carried a large white loaf and held it up for her inspection. "I cut one earlier. It's really good. I hope you'll like it."

"I'm sure we will," she answered. "How much?"

"The same as the whole wheat." As he wrapped it, he glanced over the table at her. "No basket today?"

She shook her head and laid the money down. She waited till he moved his hands, then she took the bread and went out the door. As she turned to pull the door closed, she noticed he was still watching her. She blushed and hoped the brothers coming down the street would think it was because of the warm weather. He was a pleasant boy like the one who dropped the twine.

At the dinner table, Matthew took a bite of the herb bread and looked up. "What's this kind of bread?"

"It's a new one from the baker, do you like it? Martha just picked it up."

"Martha," he said, brows drawn together, "were you down at the brothers' bakery?"

"Yes, Father."

Maria left the table to go to the backyard oven to see about the last batch of gingerbread.

"You know I don't like for you to go down there especially without me," he spoke sternly.

"Mother needed bread yesterday. She didn't feel well so I went."

"And again today?"

"The baker said they were trying a new bread today."

"Oh, so you had a conversation with him."

"Just about the bread. Do you like it?"

"It's a good loaf. Martha, I know you conducted yourself admirably. You always do."

"Thank you."

"But it's these chance encounters, especially if they are allowed to be repeated often, that can lead to more serious consequences."

"I'm sorry if the trips to the bakery upset you, Father. What do other families do for bread when they need it and there are only girls to go? Shouldn't there be some way for them to get it?"

"Yes, there should be. But let's not dodge the issue. Martha, I want people to think well of you, and I'm sure they do. However, you must be careful of the kind of impression you make upon the single brothers. It will not be long before you will be an age when a brother can ask for you as a wife."

"Father, that will be years from now!"

"Not so many. Tell me, have you thought about what you'd like to do?"

"A little. I'm not very gifted, you know in music or with a needle or in any way like the other sisters. But Father, I do so want to be of real service – of active service. I'd like to do something with plants like you."

"Do you want to marry?"

"Yes, Father. And please listen—don't scold me for my sinful thinking – but I want to marry a great man and be his helper."

"Martha, I do not know where the sin would lie? In your idea of great, or in your thinking you have a rightful place beside greatness, or in the wish to make your own marital plans."

"I will not make my own plans. From the first day we talked about this, I promised I would not worry and I haven't and I won't. I can't explain to you or to Him. There is a longing in a corner of my heart. I don't understand it, but I accept it."

Maria thrust open the back door and brought in a pan of sweet smelling gingerbread. "I had to rake the coals out. Martha, can you take this up to the Gemeinhaus? Sister Marshall wants to serve it to some guests this afternoon."

Maria covered the pan with a clean towel. "Take it in the pan. It'll keep warmer."

"All right, Mama." Martha pushed the bench back, put on her cape and left carrying the covered pan.

"Maria," Matthew said sipping his coffee, "do the married women or single sisters ever have to go to the bakery for bread?"

"Certainly if they don't have an oven. The single sisters who work in service for families often have to go."

"This doesn't sound like a good practice."

"Well, how else can they buy it?"

"It could be sold somewhere else. A place where the women could go."

"Um. Um!"

"How about if we offered to sell it here? Just as a convenience. No profit."

"It sounds reasonable. It shouldn't hurt the gingerbread sales. We could always try it, if the Collegium and brothers approve."

Soon after Martha's seventeenth birthday a big change occurred in her life. It all started when the teacher of the little girls was betrothed and therefore had to resign her job. Sister Sehner, the senior teacher, conferred with the pflegerin of the single sisters choir as to a possible replacement. The two could not come up with a candidate so they asked for an appointment to talk with Brother and Sister Marshall.

When they arrived at the conference room, the sister in service to the Marshalls, opened the door and invited them in. She finished stacking some books and took them out with her, saying the Marshalls would be in soon.

As they entered, Sister Sehner immediately stated the problem saying, "I don't intend to be abrupt but I need to get back to the classroom."

Marshall commented, "I understand. Your concern for your students has always been appreciated."

Sister Marshall inquired, "Who takes charge of the girls when you have to be out of the room?"

"I call a sister from the choir house."

"And what if the other teacher is away?"

"I usually ask Martha Miksch to watch them if I am in my room."

Marshall quietly asked, "And how does Martha handle the children?"

"Quite well."

"Do the little girls like her? Respect her?" he further inquired.

"Yes. She brings out responses in some shy girls that we teachers seldom succeed with."

The pflegerin asked, "What about Martha's studies? Has she completed them?"

With slight embarrassment Sister Sehner confessed, "She finished all the books we have to teach from over a year ago. Since then we've encouraged her in handwork, but she doesn't have much interest in this area."

Brother Marshall asked the teacher directly, "In your opinion, is Martha as well qualified to become teacher of the little girls, as any of your other older students?"

With only a slight pause, she answered. "Yes. She is the best student, and the most adept at handling young children, which is rather unusual since she is an only child. And, I might add, I believe it will be good for Martha to have the responsibility. She needs work that she enjoys to keep her busy."

"Is that agreeable with you?" he turned to the pflegerin.

"I respect Sister Sehner's judgment. One point though, Martha is still living at home. As a teacher, choir house living might be preferable. I understand she has a lot of work to do at home. She's very devoted to her parents. It would be difficult for her to continue those duties and at the same time prepare for the students."

"I agree. The change would be necessary," Marshall stated.

"Sisters," Mrs. Marshall interjected, "you will give her all the assistance she needs for the adjustment. This will truly mean two large steps for Martha. Her first time away from home, and her first occupation. She is still quite young, seventeen, isn't it?"

"We will help her as we do all the girls. But remember, many of us have left our homes at earlier ages and journeyed to unknown areas," the pflegerin replied a trifle put out.

"I did not mean to favor Martha, just to make her transition as smooth as possible," Sister Marshall said kindly.

Sister Sehner asked, "Who should inform Martha?"

Marshall said, "You may do that; today if you like. However, if you would want me to, I'll talk to the family this evening before services about her moving into the choir house."

"Yes, thank you. I'd appreciate that," Sister Sehner said and rose and took her leave along with the pflegerin who was instructed to make any necessary arrangement.

As they left, Brother Marshall said sympathetically, "This will go hard for Matthew and Maria, the first parting with their child."

Sister Sehner asked Martha to remain for a few minutes after the other girls left school. Once alone she began, "Martha, you realize one of the teachers is leaving us? Brother Marshall, the pflegerin and I would like to offer you the opportunity to become the new teacher for little girls."

Martha was stunned. She immediately sat down on the nearest chair. She stared at the teacher. "Me?"

"Yes, Martha. Do you think you'd like the position?"

Recovering her poise, Martha murmured, "Yes, yes."

"The pay is not much. However, if you're thrifty, it should be sufficient for your needs."

"Yes, I'm sure." Martha thought to herself. Money. Paid to teach, to do the things I've been helping with for so long.

"Thank you, sister. Oh, can I tell my parents?"

"Of course. You will have to start in a few days."

Martha grabbed her cape, flung it around her shoulders, dashed down the front stairs, and almost flew home.

"Mama! Father!" She shouted breathlessly as she threw open the Dutch door and slammed it behind her.

"Martha, what is it?"

"Quick, where's Father. I have to tell you both something."

"Why, he went to meet you, dear. Didn't you see him?"

"No."

Just then the door opened and Matthew appeared. He also was breathing hard. "Martha, I was talking to Brother Bagge in the square. You were moving so fast, I couldn't catch up with you."

"Oh, Father. Mother. I've been asked to take the position of teacher of the little girls!"

"Why, Martha, that's an honor," said Maria.

"Yes, indeed," echoed Matthew.

The three Mikschs laughed and talked and cried in their joy and excitement.

So as it turned out, that Martha who had done the least planning and preparation, talked the least about moving, was the first of her group to move into the sisters apartment.

As soon as she accepted the teaching job, she ceased being a student. She was given a few days to pack and to learn the job from the sister who was leaving.

Martha for the first time felt conflicting emotions developing inside her. She was joyful at being asked to teach and anxious to start, but she was reluctant to leave her parents. In spite of their congratulations and their efforts at smiling, their eyes were almost tearful.

She assured them, "I'll only be up the street. You can always come to see me, or I can run down after class and pump water for you."

And they laughed with her. In their memories, they knew better; they too had been teachers. They knew the insatiable nature of little children. They knew, too, the stamina demanded of teachers; the need for a good night's rest; the nightly selection of the right materials to start each day; the energy and ability to discipline needed to carry through with the well-laid plans. To discipline called for a maturity gained only from countless situations, unexpectedly arising every day as students tested teachers. As students changed and grew, they employed new tactics. The teaching skills and maturity would all come. Everything would fall in place – but not immediately.

Matthew and Maria accepted that Martha's energy and time must move from the little yellow house and them. They had always known that she would someday go to the sisters house according to Moravian rules, but the move had come before they expected it. They did not talk about Martha's leaving. Each one dealt with the separation in his own heart.

CHAPTER TWENTY

Martha found hundreds of things to do in the few days between being a student and a teacher. First, she had to decide which articles to take to the sisters house. She ran up and down the stairs asking Maria if she would need this or that. Maria tried to remember back to her own single choir days.

"Martha, do take an extra blanket in case your room isn't warm. Take plenty of soap. Try to keep up with your laundry or you may find you'll have to pay someone to do it."

"But Mama, you've always done it."

"Keep the spots tended to and you won't have much to do."

Martha asked her father questions about handling money.

"Be sure to keep your account in order. Try not to get into debt. Pay your rent and board, and other bills you incur during the month, as soon as you receive your salary. If you can, save a little. No matter how small it seems to you, save some amount every time you are paid."

She didn't have many clothes to pack. She was still wearing the gold dress Maria had made when was twelve. She had one linen and one cotton dress, both for warm weather. Fortunately, she was soon to have a new cape. She had finished the spinning and dying of the wool and it was with the weaver.

"We'll still have the weaver's fee. We planned to pay for it. I'll make the cape when the cloth comes back. I'll send you a message when it's ready to fit. It can be a going away gift," Maria stated in a matter-of-fact manner.

If Martha wasn't packing, she was at the school talking to the teachers. She checked over the supplies and copied a list of her new duties.

On moving day, she took a pot from the windowsill. The once small rosemary plant had thrived under her care. It now filled the pot like a good-size bush. Martha had made a sachet for herself, dried leaves for Brother Triebel, clipped branches of the evergreen for crèches at Christmas, snipped fine needles to drop into the stews or on a chicken to be baked, and brewed tea from the fragrant leaves when her mother or father had a cold. She had always felt special when she could serve or bring pleasure to someone with her own plant.

Today she gently carried the pot out to the nursery. She placed it on the potting shed shelf. She remembered it's fresh fragrance when she accidentally crushed it against her father. Very carefully, she pushed a sharp knife into the pot a few inches from the edge and cut a wedge of stem, root and soil. She wiggled it slowly from side to side and extracted the cut section. This she laid beside the pot. She reached under the shelf into a sack of potting soil her father kept there, retrieved a handful and dropped it into the rosemary pot, filling the empty space.

Next she took a trowel from the shelf and the wedge of rosemary and walked over to the bedding area – not where Matthew grew his rosemary for sale but over near the edge where the parsley grew. In a newly cleared small plot, she scooped some red earth previously mixed with humus. She tenderly placed the green rosemary in the earth and with her hands filled the dirt in all around it, packing it firmly. She got a dipper full of water and sprinkled it around the cutting.

Unbeknownst to her, Matthew had watched her from the manufactory. He waited until she finished before going out. She so seldom wanted to be alone, and he sensed she needed those few minutes.

As she heard his steps on the path, she turned her head. "Father, I hope you don't mind my using the new bedding spot."

"I don't."

"I wanted to leave a little rosemary for remembrance."

"Not for selling?"

"Not for selling."

Fondly, father and daughter embraced each other. If there were any tears in their hearts, their eyes did not let them escape.

Brother Triebel came to the rail fence to ask if they were ready for him to help take the trunks up.

"Yes. Bring the cart around to the front, thank you."

As they slowly walked up the path, arm in arm, Martha said, "Does Brother Triebel really like living in his little house?"

"He doesn't complain. He's fixed up the small building real comfortable."

"I can remember when he lived in the big house by himself. And then the night watchman stayed with him, and the soldiers during the war. The school boys have really taken it all over for themselves now, haven't they?"

"They needed the room, especially when it became a home school."

"Father, why can't the brothers stay teachers after they marry?"

"It's our rules. Single brothers are teachers."

"Is that why Brother Jo Dixson hasn't married? He likes teaching?"

"I heard Brother Dixson still has his heart set on being a doctor."

"Well, I guess he'd be as good as Dr. Lewis."

"Dr. Lewis has his problems. Well, tell your mother goodbye then come out the front. I'll load the cart."

Martha placed the clay pot, saucer underneath, in the windowsill of the room she was to share with Sister Elizabeth. There were two single beds, hers was to be the one nearest the window, two straight chairs and one table. The single chest belonged to Sister Elizabeth. There was a shelf over Martha's bed and two hooks near the door for her use. Martha therefore left her linens except what went on the bed and extra clothes in her trunk, the same one her mother had brought to Bethabara and later to Salem. It was old, of heavy wood with cracking leather hinges, but it was sturdy. The second trunk, that she had packed her blankets, spread and pillow in, belonged to her father. He was to pick it up after the evening service so she shoved it into the hall and to the top of the stairs.

Soon Elizabeth came into the room. "Is there anything I can help you do to get settled?"

"No, thank you. I was getting ready to make the bed."

"Let me help you," she volunteered and walked to the opposite side and caught the ends of the sheets as Martha flipped them open. "I hear you are the new teacher."

"Yes. Do all the sisters have jobs?"

"Of course. We all work."

"I mean outside the house?"

"Teaching isn't exactly outside."

"I meant, well. . . ."

"Besides housekeeping." Elizabeth snapped the spread in place on her side. "We each do according to our talents or whatever work we can get. We've been taught all work is honorable."

"It is," Martha reaffirmed, but she felt somehow she was not off to an agreeable relationship with her roommate. She looked toward the window trying to think of something else to talk about. "I hope you didn't mind my putting the rosemary in the sill?"

Elizabeth walked to the window, peered at the plant. "Did you grow it?"

"Yes. It started from a single sprig."

Elizabeth wheeled around and faced Martha. "Maybe you'd like to help work in the garden in the spring."

"Oh, yes, I'd love to," she said enthusiastically. "Maybe we could make a pot of tea some night."

"Do you have a pot? I don't."

"No."

"Oh, well, this stove doesn't get too hot. We try not to use much wood. We all share wood expense. Would you like to bring in the wood morning or evening?"

"Either time. What do you want to do?" Martha was struggling with negotiating skills.

"I've been doing it in the evening."

"Then I'll bring it up in the morning."

"And start up the fire?"

"Yes."

The bell rang for church services so the girls put on their capes and blew out the candle.

Elizabeth took a key from her pocket and locked the door. "The pflegerin probably has a key for you."

They went out the front door and down their choir apartment steps and over to the Gemeinhaus steps. Martha started to follow Elizabeth down the saal aisle. Elizabeth said over her shoulder, "I'm in the sisters choir. I sit with them."

Martha hung back then slid onto a bench used by the older girls. She had been so rushed with the move, she was thinking of herself as a single sister, although she was quite aware the sisters didn't take in new girls until they were eighteen.

She was eager to know more about Elizabeth. What her job was. Where she was from. She knew she wasn't from Salem.

Someone sat down beside her. She turned and saw it was Anna. "Hello," she whispered.

"How is the sisters house?"

"Different."

"Who's your roommate?"

Martha pointed to Elizabeth.

Anna said, "Elizabeth. She's from Bethania."

"You know her?"

"She comes to the store sometimes."

"What does she do?"

"She makes gloves."

"Oh."

The minister Brother Koehler stood in front of the group so the girls opened their songbooks.

After the service Anna left with her father. Matthew and Maria waited outside for Martha and walked to the sisters steps to pick up the trunk.

Maria gave Martha a quick hug. "We'll miss you and remember you at prayers."

"I'll pray for you, too, Mama."

The pflegerin came up. "Good evening, Brother and Sister Miksch. Rather cold for an October night. Martha, if you'll come with me, I'll give you a key to your room."

Martha squeezed her mother's hand and hurried up the steps. She held the door open for the pflegerin and then followed her inside.

Martha woke up with the rising bell, instantly puzzled as to why it sounded so loudly. The room was dark. She opened her eyes and realized she was in her new room and the bell was outside this building. The room was cold as she threw the covers back. Shivering, she inched over to the small iron stove. Putting her hand lightly to the side she felt it was warm. She felt for the wood bucket and locating it, her hand reached inside. Empty.

She had to go for wood, which meant she had to dress. She always bathed first at home because the water kettle stayed hot on her old tile stove. There was no kettle or warm water here. She groped toward the table and found the water pitcher. The water was cold. She cupped one hand and poured a little water and splashed it on her face. She blindly stepped toward the door for her towel. After drying her face, she took her clothes off the other hook and quietly dressed. All this had been done in darkness. She debated whether or not to wake Elizabeth.

Why didn't she rise with the bell Martha wondered? Will lighting a candle wake her? Martha decided to light it, so that she could locate the bucket and get out the door. First, she quietly opened the stove door, raked the ashes off a hot ember and ignited a paper twist to light the candle.

When she closed her room door, she set the candleholder on a high wall shelf in the hall. This illuminated the hall enough for her to see. She remembered the woodpile was outside the back door. She crept down the hall softly so as not to disturb the others; she could hear faint sounds behind bedroom doors. While filling the bucket outside, she trembled from the early morning cold and the strangeness at being alone in the dark out-of-doors.

Back inside, she was grateful for the candle she had left burning in the hall. In her room, she found that the live coals she had seen a short time ago were no longer in evidence. She had thought they wouldn't die out if left uncovered briefly. Frantically, she pushed gray ashes aside with the poker. Way in the back, a few red coals glinted. She poked the smallest pieces of wood from the basket into the stove opening. She sat on the straight chair waiting for them to catch.

Elizabeth hadn't moved. Martha began to be concerned. To her the bell had been loud enough to wake the soundest sleeper in town. How did Elizabeth wake up? Surely, breakfast would be soon. She decided to rouse the sleeping girl and boldly called, "Elizabeth. Elizabeth."

The covers moved slightly.

Martha stood up and moved near the bed. "Elizabeth, the rising bell has rung."

"Um," her roommate answered.

"The bell has rung," Martha repeated.

"All right." Sleepily, she rubbed her eyes and sat up. Pulling the covers tightly about her. "Is the fire going?"

"I put some wood on."

"Good." She jumped out of bed landing her slender white feet on her little rag rug. She scooted along on it, stopping close to the stove. "It doesn't feel hot."

"It didn't catch good."

Elizabeth reached over to the other chair where she had folded her clothes. She pulled her arms out of her nightgown, using it sort of like a tent, she dressed inside thus keeping out of the early morning cold and giving some privacy.

Martha was undoing her braids and brushing her thick hair. She leaned to one side and smoothly put the three strands back into a braid and repeated the procedure with the other side. She adjusted the cap, covering all her hair except the two braids, which now hung, evenly down her back.

Elizabeth brushed her hair, pulled it all together, gave a quick twist or two and produced a neat bun that she secured with two pins on the top of her head.

Putting on her cap, she announced, "We usually have time for the beds before the next bell."

The girls aired the sheets with several up and down flips. When she finished, Martha checked the stove again. Peering inside she saw the new wood beginning to smoke. She added one more piece and closed the door.

The bell for breakfast rang.

"The dining room won't be warm yet. You may need a shawl or your cape, although it's hard to eat with the cape on."

"Thank you. I'll take my cape." Martha didn't have a shawl, but she considered she should learn to knit one.

At breakfast Martha missed the fragrance of her mother's kitchen, as well as the warmth. The meal of oatmeal with cream, bread and butter and stewed apples was filling for the hard work the sisters had before them during the morning; however, Martha did not have much appetite.

An older sister, named Agnes, watched Martha eat small portions. Kindly she reached out and patted Martha's hand. "This is a big day for you, isn't it? Your first day at your first job?"

Martha nodded her head.

"We'll all say a word of prayer for you this morning. I remember the first day I started in the laundry here. I was so nervous pushing that stick around in the big boiling pot. I thought I'd poke holes all through the brothers' shirts. When I wasn't worrying about that, I was inspecting my skirt and apron, so concerned they were going to catch on fire."

Martha gazed into the kindly eyes of the older face, noticing that it was crinkled with laugh lines more than wrinkled with worry ones. She relaxed and her own face contoured into a smile.

Morning devotions followed breakfast, right in the dining room. This morning Martha's new friend Agnes stood and read the daily text. Next she led the prayer and asked each of them to pray the Lord's blessing to be on Martha as she began a new role in her life. Agnes reminded them each of their commitment to serve, and thus to help Martha in anyway they could. Martha was touched by the prayer and in her own mind she reaffirmed her desire to help and to be of service to the sisters and the little girls.

Upon leaving the dining hall, Martha went to the use the necessary out back before going to the classroom.

Arriving in the little girls' classroom, she walked directly to her desk on top of which she saw a small ivy plant in a little clay pot that had been glazed a warm brown and fired to a satin smoothness. Beside the pot was a folded note addressed to her. Her fingers deftly lifted the flap and opened the note. She read: To Martha Miksch, May your teaching days be a joy to you and your students. Sincerely, Sister Marshall.

How kind everyone is. I hope I shall not disappoint these dear sisters, Martha wished then slipped the note inside her apron pocket.

She took up the stack of slates and walked over to the two tables where she placed a slate down where each of the ten girls would sit. Next, she put at the places, chalk and a wiping cloth. Finally, she put a copy of the manuscript alphabet they were to use in the center of the table.

Standing there looking around the room, she realized how tidy it appeared. The books were straight on the shelf, the puzzles neat on the tray, the tiny animals all inside the small Noah's Ark, the miniature tea set with forks and knives in the reed basket, and the linen squares, needles and yarn in the straw basket.

Sister Sehner entered her classroom, then came to the door

that stood open between hers and Martha's classrooms. "Good morning, Martha. How nice the room looks."

"Thank you. It's the first time I've ever seen it this way without the girls and all so tidy."

"Well, as soon as they arrive, it will look lived in right away. Is it warm enough?"

"Yes. Comfortable." Martha thought a moment, "Who takes care of the stove in here?"

"After today, you will. I take care of my own, too."

"But. . . ?"

"I started your fire today. I usually come in before breakfast. I bring live coals from my bedroom. I don't bank this one after classes. If I have hot coals, I carry them to my room."

"I appreciate your sharing all this. I'll try to get these new duties straight soon."

"You will, Martha. You're a good student . . . and I anticipate you'll be a good teacher." She turned and went back into her own room.

Martha did justify the faith placed in her as a teacher. The little girls responded well to her instruction, but not without testing her discipline methods. On the first day, the girls complained that they couldn't see the sample alphabet sheet, saying it was turned to only one person. Martha suggested they take turns and pass it around. This method resulted in four of them having nothing do while one copied. Next, Martha raced around and wrote a few letters on each slate for them to copy. Soon she felt she was going in circles. Then she took up the sheets and called out the letters and let them write from memory. She saw that some girls wrote quickly, others had to take time to recall the letters and labored over the writing. Finally, she decided to let the children write at one table, keeping both manuscript samples there, one turned toward each side of the rectangular table. With the other group, she read a story, and then the groups were reversed.

While they walked home for lunch, she cleaned the slates and cloths for the next day before she went to the sisters' dining room.

At the close of school, she remembered Sister Sehner's procedure about the coals. She looked for a covered ember pan but couldn't find one so she took the shovel and cautiously scooped up the red coals. Carefully, she walked down the hall, to her room. She fumbled for her key in her apron pocket. Inserting the key into the lock, she couldn't open the door with one hand. She hastily set the shovel on the floor, fearful an ember would fall and scorch the wooden flooring. Finally, she unlocked and opened the door.

She was surprised to see Elizabeth sitting in the room sewing. "What's that?" Elizabeth asked.

"Hot coals for the fire."

"The fire's going good. Where are they from?"

"The schoolroom."

"Oh." Elizabeth continued sewing.

Martha stood a moment debating what to do. To her the only sensible solution was to put them in the stove, so she did. Then she looked at Elizabeth's work.

"Your gloves are neat."

"Sewing on leather is not easy."

"How many sisters make gloves?"

"Several. But the number varies. In planting and harvest time more of them have to work outside. But I do this mainly. I do help with the fall and spring-cleaning. I'm on kitchen rotation duties."

Martha was so thirsty for a cup of tea. "What time is supper?"

"With the sun going down so early, it'll be soon, around five forty-five."

Martha lifted her pitcher and found it empty. "What are the water arrangements?"

"We all share the cost. It's going to be nice in our new house to have a well."

"But you'll have to pump. Anyway, I meant what are the arrangements for you and me to have water?"

"We get our own downstairs."

"Do we take turns?"

"That seems fair."

Martha wished Elizabeth would be more helpful, but she continued with patience. "Do we both bring it once a day like the wood, or you one day and me another?"

"Depends on how much water you use."

Exasperated, Martha grabbed her small yellow pitcher and exited. One day away and she missed the peacefulness of her own room and the harmony of her parents' home. While filling the pitcher at the tap, she reflected that Elizabeth might not have had all that peacefulness at her house. I'll do some nice things for her, perhaps then she'll see how much happier our room can be. She glanced around the kitchen for something to take Elizabeth water in. She spotted a piggin and filled it.

Back in the bedroom, Martha set her own pitcher in her red bowl on the table. She lifted the piggin to pour water into Elizabeth's larger blue pitcher. She saw it was almost full, still she added fresh water to the top.

Elizabeth watched her curiously.

Martha felt the gaze and said, "I thought you might need some water, too." She reached for her mug from the shelf over her bed poured water into it. "May I pour you a drink of water."

"Yes."

Martha filled Elizabeth's mug. Her roommate remained seated, still sewing. Martha handed it to her.

The cool water refreshed Martha. After talking all day she was thirstier than she realized. She poured water into her bowl and washed her face and hands.

"I'll take the piggin back down," she commented and left the room.

Approaching the kitchen, she heard the cook expounding. "Where's that piggin? Need something, and it's not there." Her helpers begin scurrying around in a search.

The cook turned and spied Martha with a piggin in her hand. "Now don't tell me. It's my piggin?

"I borrowed this a few minutes ago to take some water upstairs. I'm sorry if I inconvenienced you."

"Didn't your Mama tell you not to take things without asking?"

"There was no one here. It was only gone a few minutes. I won't use it again," she promised.

"Well, it's back now," softening her tone she added, "I like to know where things are."

"My Mama does, too, that's why I brought it right back. I'm sure the sisters appreciate your keeping check on the equipment."

The cook looked almost fondly on the gentle girl. "I hope so."

Martha detoured by the woodpile and picked up a few sticks of wood so she wouldn't have to go out in the cold in the morning.

That night after services while Martha prepared for bed, Elizabeth changed quickly and was between her sheets in a jiffy. She asked, "Are you ready to blow out the candle?"

"Not yet. But I'll light one of mine. You can put out your light." Martha took a sheet of paper from her shelf, ink and quill pen. She sat at the table.

"You're going to write a letter? After your long day?"

"Yes."

"Aren't you tired?"

"No. I'm too excited to sleep. I want to tell my grandparents all my good news. I wonder how long it will take a letter to get to Germany?"

"Depends on when it leaves. Do your grandparents live in Germany?"

"Yes. I'll send it by the first person going north. Have you heard of Bishop Spangenberg?" She asked as she wrote.

"Of course."

"He's my grandfather," she commented casually.

"Well, aren't you lucky?" Elizabeth spoke sarcastically.

Martha turned her head toward Elizabeth puzzled by the tone and the comment, but Elizabeth turned over in bed with her back toward Martha.

Martha resumed writing of her happiness and joy at being chosen to teach and of her desire to please and to serve.

The next morning Martha was surprised upon feeling in the wood bucket that all the sticks were gone. Thus she had to go out. After she got the room fire started, she took a few coals to the classroom and built a fire there.

Martha's generous nature soon had her trapped into bringing wood morning and night and drawing water for the blue pitcher as well as her yellow one. She rationalized that this way, she always had a warm room to come to in the evening, and since she didn't like to sit still long, this gave her excuses to stay busy and not have to sew.

On the first payday, Martha was amazed to hold so much money all her own. Before paying her bills, she ran home, right after class to show the money to her parents.

She waited patiently for her mother to wrap a loaf of white bread for a customer. The shop now retailed bread for the brothers. However, Martha noticed that several loaves were left at this late hour in the day, while all the gingerbread was gone. Her father came tramping in the back door, carrying some snuff jars. She went to close the door behind him. Her mother bid goodbye to the sister leaving through the front door.

"Mama, Father, I have to show this to you. I earned it all by myself. Father, I'm going to pay my bills like you said."

"Good."

"With what's left over, I'm going to buy a kettle."

"Isn't there one in the room?"

"No. I've had to wash my face with cold water every day. Oh, how I've wanted a cup of hot tea after class."

"Martha," said Matthew, "let's count out if you have enough."

Together they figured her expenses. "Not enough at today's prices for even a tin water kettle," he surmised.

"Matthew," Maria asked, "isn't there an old one down in the cellar?"

"It leaks."

"Can't it be repaired?"

"The tinsmith might do it for a small fee," Matthew answered.

"Father, can you take it and ask him?"

"I'll do it today. I'll close the shop and walk up."

"Can you have tea with me, Martha?" Maria asked with a hopeful tone.

"I have so many chores in my room, but I'll stay anyway."

"Good."

Martha sipped the hot brew with simple enjoyment. She ate a piece of gingerbread and expected it had been put aside for supper. As she was leaving, Maria wrapped a small piece in a napkin for her to take back to her room.

Maria watched her daughter flee down the hill as she had done since a little girl, never walking sedately unless she was reminded, always eagerly rushing to the next task.

CHAPTER TWENTY-ONE

Martha began sitting with the little girls at services whenever any of them came. In the opposite row were the little boys with their master Jo Dixson. Once Martha's attention was drawn to their row as a little boy fell off the bench and Jo assisted him back on. Her eyes met Jo's as he settled the boy. After a couple seconds' gaze, Martha looked down and turned her head toward the minister again, but she kept thinking of Jo. Why hadn't he married, why hadn't he gone on to study medicine; were his problems with the little boys similar to hers with the girls? She often wished to talk to someone else who taught children. All the sisters who had been teachers had married and lived in their own homes and she did not have opportunities to talk with them.

Will I ever get married she wondered. Now though instead of wondering who will ask for me, she began to steal glances at the apprentices and single brothers thinking, whom would I accept, if the lot approved, she always added. The girls rarely talked about the single brothers because almost always there was an older unmarried sister nearby who would frown in disapproval. But girls did talk about their families, brothers included, and some tradesmen; thus a little was known about the brothers' personalities and characters.

The girls knew about each other in their own choir. As they rotated duties in the house, pursued crafts, and rendered services; like the pflegerin, they soon realized what each did best. The pflegerin tried to know the girls as they went about their daily and seasonal duties, then whenever a request for a suggestion of a wife was made, she was prepared to recommend someone.

She was quick at analyzing Martha's industry and Elizabeth's languor. In this case, Martha's virtue was not helping Elizabeth's vice. The pflegerin was recommending different room arrangements when everyone moved into the sisters new house. Before the move she had an opportunity to help balance the present inequities.

The house was under construction and a solicitation was made among the sisters for some furnishings for their saal. When Martha was approached, she admitted unhappily, "I don't have any money."

"Martha, is your salary covering your meals?" The pflegerin asked directly.

"Yes, sister. But there's no money left over. Father wants me to try to save a little every month, even if it's only a farthing."

"That's good advice. I'll talk to the ministers about your situation."

When she discussed the matter with them, they suggested that Martha learn to do something with her hands, something that she could do while she watched over the girls in school.

"Martha doesn't excel in fine needlework."

"Has she tried glove making?"

"I'll talk with her about that," she replied with a secret thought.

Sister Marshal doubted that the people talking were aware of Martha's active class. The girls were not rowdy, but they were often not silent for she could hear them from her apartment.

The pflegerin pondered how best to present the glove making idea. When she believed she had a workable plan, she knocked on the bedroom door one night; and Martha, as she expected, opened it. Closing the door against the coldness of the unheated hall, she sniffed, detecting an unusual aroma.

Martha aware of the detection hospitably responded. "We're having a cup of rosemary tea. Won't you please join us?"

"Thank you, I will," and she took the chair near the stove that Martha offered.

Martha gave the pflegerin her cup saying, "It has a little honey for sweetening."

She poured herself some tea into a saucer from her yellow pitcher that also served as a teapot.

"I see you have a kettle."

"Yes. It's Mama's old one. The tinsmith repaired it. It's so nice to have hot water."

"I'm sure it is, don't you agree, Elizabeth?"

Elizabeth, who had only nodded to the pflegerin, admitted, "Yes. I was used to cold water, but this is very pleasant," and resumed drinking from her mug.

"Elizabeth, I've come to ask a favor of you."

"Yes?"

"To be a teacher of our teacher. A volunteer that is. I want you to share your special skill and knowledge with her. I want you to teach Martha how to make gloves."

"Of course."

"You do such expert work."

"Thank you."

"Perhaps you could show her a few steps here, then she could practice them while her students are busy writing."

Martha opened her mouth to comment that that was so seldom, but she caught a quick refraining glance from the pflegerin and remained silent.

"The light tan leather could dirty quickly around children," Elizabeth exclaimed.

"She could begin on black leather, couldn't she?"

"I suppose so."

Martha said, "I could never turn out gloves as finely stitched as Elizabeth."

"Martha, we can't all excel at every task, but that shouldn't stop us. I'm sure Elizabeth will be patient while you master the techniques. She won't judge your work by hers, only by your own improvements."

Elizabeth brightened under the praise. "It's not that difficult, Martha, once you learn how to handle the leather, where to ease, when not to over stretch."

"And Martha," said the pflegerin, "you could help Elizabeth by taking the gloves to your family's shop for sale. That would relieve the sister who now has that responsibility."

Martha tried to conceal the excitement of a chance to go home even on official visits.

So Martha became a pupil at a craft task she didn't relish; however, the reward of visiting her parents spurred her to work more than the small amount of extra money.

All single sisters spent most mealtimes talking about the house and how the building was coming along. Eagerly, every day they walked out front to see how far the brick course reached, or gaze at the neatly laid red tile shingles. Every time the carpenters threw out scrap wood, some of the sisters would dash over, collect and bring the scraps back in their folded-over aprons.

One day the ministers observed the girls in the gleaning process and immediately sent word for the pflegerin to meet them in the conference room.

Martha heard about it at supper.

"Pflegerin was quite upset to be sent for on this matter."

"She had given permission for us to pick up the scraps for kindling."

"Now we have to wait until after their quitting time."

"It's so exciting to be building your own house. I don't want to miss a day seeing what's being done."

"Can the married ladies watch their houses being built?"

"How should we know?"

Everybody laughed.

"Seems I remember my mother being able to go places and speak to men."

"Perhaps when we get married, we get special privileges."

Again the women giggled.

During a week in late February, the weather turned from very cold to warm within a few days, then cold again. Several of the residents in town developed sore throats and colds that settled in their chests. Elizabeth was one of the first victims. She was very short-tempered during the early stage. Martha knew illness affected people like this sometimes, because she had heard her mother remark so after sitting with sick sisters.

Once Elizabeth asked in her now squeaky voice, "Why haven't you caught this cold?"

Martha replied, "I don't know. I never get colds."

"Haven't you been sick?"

"No, except for the small pox."

Martha now had Elizabeth's duties as well as her own. So many sisters were ill that the few well ones took turns waiting on the others. Martha brought Elizabeth's meals to the room, emptied her chamber pot, tidied her bed daily, swept, and dusted the room. She kept the kettle on the stove so Elizabeth could have hot teas whenever she wanted them.

One night after service, Maria caught up with Martha as she was leaving. "Martha, are you all right? You haven't taken sick?"

"No, Mama."

"You look tired."

"Elizabeth's still in bed. I've been helping out more in the house."

"Don't overdo. You look a bit down, like you've lost weight." She slipped her hand into a pocket then put a small paper wrapped package into her daughter's pocket.

Back in the room, Martha drew out the package, unwrapped the paper and there lay some ginger cookies. "Elizabeth, look at the surprise for us from Mama. Let's have some tea. How about a thyme to clear your head?"

"Martha, you are too good."

Surprised at this kind remark, Martha responded with astonishment. "Why, it's nothing more than you'd do for me."

"You really believe that, don't you?"

"Of course I do. Doesn't this tea smell like summer in the

garden? Let's ask if we can plant thyme along the walks back of the new house?"

Elizabeth tried to laugh but started coughing. After the seizure abated, she sipped the hot liquid. "Martha, anywhere you go will always be bright and light and summery."

Embarrassed, Martha bent her head over her cup and drank the tea. Inwardly she felt a warmth at having had her first words of friendship from her roommate.

In April, the Sisters House was consecrated. The women moved in with the help of fathers and brothers of their families, and of some other married brethren. Martha was surprised when her father came in carrying a small chest. Her mother was bringing in two empty drawers. After he set the chest down, Maria fitted in the drawers.

"There are two more at the house," panted Maria.

"And a chair, too," added Matthew as he dropped on the bed to rest a minute.

"Where did the furniture come from? I don't remember these pieces?"

"A family was leaving for Pennsylvania and didn't have room to take their furnishings."

"We bought these at an auction for you." Matthew said, recovering his breath. He rose and took a key from his pocket. "You can unlock this section. Pull the top down and use it like a table."

Martha ran her fingers over the smooth finish. "It's lovely. My own desk." She admired every detail. "I know the family didn't want to part with it. I shall take care of it."

Maria smiled. "We're glad you like it. Now, let's go back and get the other two drawers and chair."

Martha spoke. "I'll go with you."

She noticed suddenly how short of breath her parents were. They looked older than she had ever seen them. To herself she wondered have I been away so long? No, only a half-year. I must remember not to be so busy that I forget to pay attention to them.

The furniture in her room in the choir apartment belonged to either Elizabeth or the sister's diaconie. Whatever she used of the diaconie's, she had to rent.

While they walked to the yellow house, Martha said, "As soon as I save a little more money, I want to buy a bed."

"I wish you could have your old one, but we're going to rent your room, dear," her mother announced.

"I'm glad you're going to have someone with you. Who is it?"

"A Bethabara girl just entering the older girl's choir. She's coming in to start school next week."

"The new group of sisters and older girls who're going to live in the Sisters Choir House will be coming in next week, too."

While at the yellow house Martha packed a basket with soap, candles, dried herbs, a bottle of ink, and a loaf of bread. "Mama, I shouldn't take all these things without paying you. The other sisters have to buy these kind of supplies."

Matthew said, "We're glad to give them to you. I expect the other sisters receive gifts of some kind from their families."

"Didn't you say Elizabeth's bed, table and chairs were made by her father?" Maria asked as she sliced a wedge of cheese for the basket.

"Yes. Mama, could I ask for something else?"

"What?"

"Do you have an extra mug? If I'm having tea and someone comes in, I use the saucer, but I'd like a mug for guests."

Maria reached up on the shelf. "Here, take this blue one. It's an odd one. I never use it. How about a spoon?" She put the mug and spoon into the full basket.

Martha hugged her mother, then her father. "You are both so good to me."

They walked up the hill around the square to the beautiful new brick Sisters House, which stood one building lot below the Gemeinhaus. The warmth of the sun on their backs, the peace of the moment cast a comfortable spell on the threesome and they were reluctant to part. To spare them the trip upstairs again, Martha offered to take the drawers and chair upstairs.

The sleeping floor was divided into two sections. Martha and Elizabeth were in separate sections. Martha checked in on Elizabeth, who had not regained her health yet. She was sitting by a window that overlooked the front. The girl who was to have the bed next to Elizabeth had not arrived from Bethania.

"How're you feeling?"

"Better, but tired," Elizabeth responded weakly.

"Are you going down for supper?"

"I'll try."

"Good. We can go together."

Even after the new roommate came, Martha continued to check on them – to be of help to the new girl as well as to boost Elizabeth's low spirits after her illness. Martha often brought her gloves for Elizabeth to help with the fine turning stitches.

Martha enjoyed her new room although she was seldom in it. She did find it difficult to get used to living with so many people, and at tea time after school, someone was always down at her end of the room.

The sisters kept her filled in with local news such as the brothers house addition, the wagons departing and returning, and so forth. Usually Martha smiled and listened, rarely commenting. When she did, her words never stirred up a controversy, thus before long she was known as a pleasant person to take tea with, and her teas were always unusual and delicious – and quite often she had some of Maria's gingerbread to serve.

Maria's gingerbread was so popular that loaf bread sales in Miksch Tobacco Shop began to decline, a fact the brothers were not happy about. Their solution was one that Martha learned of in an unusual way.

At eleven as the little girls left for lunch, Martha was watching them from the steps when she saw a cart being pushed up the street. As it neared, she saw the baker with whom she had talked when she purchased the dill bread pushed it. On the cart she read the word bread. He rang a small hand bell. He called out, she guessed to her as no other person was nearby on the street.

"Bread, white, whole wheat, sugar cake. Fresh."

Martha merely shook her head and turned to go in. The girl in service at the Marshalls darted down the steps to buy a loaf.

At lunch Martha overheard two sisters whispering about the baker. "He's a journeyman now."

"I heard he's going to Bethabara tavern to bake. He wants to farm, too."

"Then he'll need a wife."

As they giggled, Martha wondered who the girl would be.

The pflegerin matter-of-factly told the whisperers that it was not wise to discuss such matters. Marriage arrangements were best left to elders and parents.

Martha did breathe a slight sigh of relief when the minister announced the betrothal of the baker to a sister in Bethabara. As much as she longed to work out-of-doors again, she knew that was only for a small part of her life. She couldn't see herself committed to a farm or a kitchen life. She thanked her Lord from the depth of her heart that she had not been called to make such a decision.

Martha was now eighteen and was formerly invited into the Single Sisters Choir. She joined them in her first love feast as a single sister on March 31, 1787, and enjoyed the happy event commemorating the laying of the cornerstone of their choir house two years ago. Martha thought this is truly a church that remembers – the happy as well as the tragic times – or maybe more than the tragic times.

Life continued in a rather set pattern for Martha, with most of her time being devoted to the care of the little girls.

The challenge of adjustments had been made. She felt in command of the schoolroom and life in the choir house went smoothly. As often happens with young persons, she began to feel restless, not quite fulfilled. There were so few materials to work with in the school. She had presented all she knew to the girls for their age. For the older ones she was attempting to stretch the lessons until the girls moved up.

One day, through the open door, she noticed Anna piddling

over her needlework with saddened eyes. Martha's students were quiet so she tiptoed into the other room to ask the teacher if Anna could help her for awhile and introduce some new stitches to her girls. Consent was given. As she and Anna selected some linen from the workbasket, Martha asked if there was any bad news.

"No. Only today Carl and Benjamin are leaving for Pennsylvania."

"Why are your brothers going up there?"

"Papa's sending them to Nazareth Hall to enter the boys' school."

"Who's taking them?"

"Brother Biwighaus."

"Anna, I know you'll miss them, and they'll miss you, but they'll be happy there."

Martha called a few girls to Anna for instruction, then she gathered the others in a circle around her to paint small pictures on the edge of their paper work. Martha felt happy that Anna smiled.

On May 5 when Brother Schober returned from Pennsylvania he brought the Nachricaten and some letters to various people in the congregation. He left the letters with Marshall, who in turn handed them over to the addressees.

The following evening, he signaled to Martha to wait after the services, which she did.

"Martha, I have a letter for you."

"For me?" she was shocked.

"Yes. From Germany."

"Oh, is it from my grandparents? How much do I owe you or whoever brought the letter?" She remembered that her father always had to pay for letters sent to him.

When he told her the small fee, she said, "I'll go to my room to get it."

"You many take the letter and bring the fee tomorrow."

"Thank you," she said and held the letter tightly in her hands as she hurried from the building. There was a haze around the moon she noticed, indicating rain tomorrow.

In her room, she lit a candle, settled on her chair and placed the letter on the desk. Very carefully she slit the envelope open, almost like a ceremony, so unusual and so special to her was receiving a letter. She unfolded the long sheet of paper and recognized her grandfather Spangenberg's script. He congratulated her on receiving the teacher's post and reminded her of the importance of the care and education of little ones. He suggested that this was a time during which she could learn the hymns of the Unity.

She stopped reading to reflect. "Yes, I can. It will be good for me to continue learning. I can start with one a week – learn the words and the melody. The simplest ones I can teach to the little girls. If I can't play an instrument, I can at least praise the Lord with singing."

Returning to the letter, she read that her grandmother was not too well. He asked to be remembered to her parents.

I wish it weren't so late, I want to tell them about the letter. I'll go down right after class tomorrow, she promised herself.

Before retiring she thumbed through her small hymnal seeking one to learn first. She couldn't make up her mind so she closed the book and read a chapter from her Bible.

Rain threatened all the following day and finally poured in mid-afternoon. At the close of classes, Martha walked out with the little girls. The rain had stopped but the air was still oppressive and hot. She walked quickly to the yellow house. A customer was leaving and said hello to Martha in passing.

Martha opened the Dutch door, closed it behind her and went into the shop. Her father was counting money.

"Good afternoon, Father."

He turned. "This is a surprise."

"Is Mama in the kitchen?" she asked going toward the doorway.

"She just went upstairs to take something to the girl's room."

Footsteps were heard from the stairs. Martha called, "Mama, come in here. I want to show you and Father something."

"I'm coming. I declare, I do have to check on that girl. She goes off and forgets to take her laundry up."

"I received a letter. Guess who from?"

Matthew said, "Since you came to share it, I'd say your grandparents."

"Oh, Father, you know everything," she pretended dismay.

The three sat down to tea, Martha read the letter aloud. As she finished, she remarked, "I'm taking his advice about the hymns. My mind has been unsettled lately. I seem at loose ends."

"Is the work at school going well?" Maria asked.

"It's all right. I feel there's more I should teach the girls but I don't know what."

"Are you a bit restless?" her father asked.

"Maybe." The air was close, oppressive. Martha, sitting between her parents, got up and walked to the doorway. The door was opened and she stood there looking out at the sky, which was partly blue, partly gray.

Matthew and Maria exchanged concerned glances.

Martha stood in the opening, her back to them, meditating.

Without warning, a flash of lightning appeared and thundered through the sky, struck the yellow house, shaking the entire frame and knocking bricks from one of the kitchen walls onto the middle of the floor. Streaks of fire darted across the room, one going out by the window over the table, one out the back door.

As soon as the room was quiet and still again, Matthew and Maria, having dropped their heads on the table, looked up at each other. Seeing they were both all right, their immediate concern was for Martha. She was no longer standing in the doorway. They saw her lying in a heap on the floor. Maria screamed. Matthew struggled to push back the bench. In his haste, the bench legs wouldn't move. He didn't want to thrust it backwards for Martha lay close behind him. Finally, he stepped backwards over the seat.

He knelt on one side of Martha; Maria bent down on the other side.

Martha didn't move.

Maria lifted Martha's head gently and cradled it in her arms, softly calling, "Martha, Martha!"

"She's breathing," Matthew announced anxiously.

The front door swung open. Jo Dixson and some schoolboys rushed into the shop. Jo shouted, "We heard the thunderbolt. Is everybody okay?"

"Help us! Martha. Oh Martha!" Maria bent her head over the unconscious girl.

Jo Dixson strode into the kitchen. Matthew moved aside for him to look at her.

"Was she struck?" Jo asked.

"I don't know. Everything happened so fast." Matthew sounded helpless.

One of the fire marshals hurried in. "Did anything catch fire?"

"Fire?" Maria's face turned ashen.

Jo Dixson ordered, "Miksch, let's take her next door. The marshal can check the house."

"Surely," Matthew agreed.

"Sister Miksch, permit me to carry Martha," Jo spoke gently to her. He reached down and put one arm under Martha's shoulders and slid the other under her legs. As he stood, Martha's head rolled back.

"Oh," Maria cried in alarm.

"Matthew, go first. Get the boys off the steps."

Matthew jumped at the command. He waved the gathering crowd aside. He moved quickly next door to the school. The boys had left the door open so he waited for Jo to pass.

"Watch her head," Matthew shouted.

Jo turned sideways as he passed through the narrow entrance. "The second door on the left, Matthew. Open it."

Matthew edged around Jo to push the door inward. Jo entered, easily laid Martha on the single bed.

Maria and Matthew stood together, staring down at the still figure of Martha.

"Is she all right?" Maria moaned.

"Sister Miksch," Jo spoke, "will you loosen the ribbons on the bodice?"

Relieved to do something, Maria untied the pink ribbons.

Jo meanwhile dipped a clean cloth into a solution. He wrung the cloth then patted it on her face and wrists.

Martha opened her eyes briefly. The three stared down at her. She opened them again and looked from Maria to Matthew to Jo and back to her parents.

"Why is Jo Dixson here?" She appeared bewildered.

"We're at the school, dear," her mother spoke soothingly.

"Why are we here?" Her face showed puzzlement.

"Lightning struck our house," answered Matthew.

"Lightning?"

"Yes, dear, don't you remember?" asked Maria.

Jo peered at Martha. "How do you feel, Martha?"

"I feel fine," she answered as she raised up on an elbow. "Why is my bodice unlaced? Where is my cap? My shoes are off." She appeared befuddled at her disarray.

Jo stepped back. Maria sat on the bed. Martha laced her bodice over the white blouse.

"We were so worried. We thought the lightning had struck you."

"What?"

"Yes. You were standing in the open doorway when the bolt hit."

"You were unconscious. We brought you over here while the marshal checked for fire."

Martha tried to jump, but Jo put a hand on her shoulder. She stopped her motion but still asked, "Is our house on fire?"

Matthew answered. "We haven't been back to see. We wanted to be sure you were not hurt."

"Father, please go back. I'm all right."

Matthew left the school to check on his house. Brother Koehler was coming up the street. He hailed Matthew.

"Was there any damage?"

"I'm going over to the house to check. Martha was knocked unconscious so we brought her here. She's awake now."

"I'll go in and speak to her," Koehler said. He bounded up the steps, saw Jo in the hall and inquired about Martha.

"She appears to be in perfect shape. The Lord was protecting her."

Koehler entered the room. "Martha, I hear you've had a narrow escape."

"Brother Koehler, I don't remember anything. I was looking out the kitchen door at the sky and thinking how half of it was blue with sunlight and half of it was gray, darkened by clouds. The next thing I knew, I was in here."

"There're no burns, no pains?" he asked.

"None."

"The Lord has spared you, Martha Miksch. Let us offer a prayer of thanksgiving."

Each bowed his head while Koehler thanked God for watching over one of his servants. He prayed that her life be re-committed to doing His Will.

One of the brothers knocked at the doorway. "Sister Miksch? Matthew asked me to tell you that there is no fire in the house."

"Thank you, brother. Was there much damage?"

"Some plaster was knocked off the wall between the kitchen and the front room. About a dozen bricks were shaken from the fireplace surround. God be praised those dropped on the hearth. A few roof tiles were broken and some roof timbers were split."

"Oh, Mama."

Maria reached over and laid a hand on Martha's arm. "Where did the bolt hit?"

"Best we can tell, it struck near the chimney, then split or divided with part going down the partition wall. The other part probably traveled by the open door then out the window. There's a hole burned in a pane."

Maria gasped, "Martha had been sitting at the table in front of the window."

Footsteps resounded outside in the hall. Bursting into the room was Dr. Lewis. "I heard Martha was hit by lightning."

He stopped short. He gaped at Martha sitting on the edge of the bed.

Maria said, "Thank you for coming. She seems to be unharmed."

"Were you hit, Martha?"

"I don't recall anything. I didn't hear the thunder or see a flash."

"You're so composed?"

"There was nothing to frighten me."

"Well, if there's nothing I can do . . . I'll go back. If you need me later, do send someone."

"Yes, I will. Mama, let's go see the house?"

"Are you sure you feel like walking?"

"Yes. Thank you Brother Dixson for your help."

He nodded.

"We shall always be grateful for your quick aid," Maria assured him.

Several people outside the school spoke to Maria and Martha, expressing concern for their safety.

The fire marshals were leaving the house. One spoke to Maria, "It looks safe. We couldn't find any sparks."

"Thank you brethren for inspecting for us. We'll keep checking, too."

"Glad to help. It's good to know no one was injured."

The women passed into the yellow house. Martha stepped over the hunks of plaster and fallen bricks and reached for a broom.

"Why, Martha, I'll sweep this mess up. You sit down," Maria took the broom and began sweeping.

Martha heard Matthew in the loft so she climbed the familiar steps. Her father ran his hands over the split timbers.

"Father, will they have to be replaced?"

"I think not, if we can get some new roof tiles on soon. I wouldn't want water to get in the big splits. But I'll have Krause check them over."

"Can he get someone to fix the plaster and put the bricks back in place?"

"I'm going to ask him."

"I'm glad no one was upstairs," Martha said.

"We were very fortunate."

"Well, Father, I'd better be getting back to the choir house."

As they descended, Matthew said, "This would be quite an event to write about in your next letter. Maria, I'll walk part way back with Martha."

She came to the door and kissed Martha. "I know the Lord's looking after you. He must have important work for you to do."

CHAPTER TWENTY-TWO

In her narrow bed, Martha lay still and sleepless. Darkness surrounded her but she was not afraid. "Why was I spared?" she asked of herself, of the Lord. No answer pierced the quietness. "Is there something I must do? Something that I'm not doing now? Is there some new calling for me?" Martha ceased questioning and listened. No revelation came.

After awhile she said to herself I must stay with the duties for which I have been already called. A new calmness and sense of purpose enveloped her. "Thank you, Lord, for the blessing of service." She drifted into an untroubled sleep.

The next morning Martha set about her daily schedule with a new burst of energy. She swept her braids onto the top of her head, pinned them securely and pulled her cap on firmly. She didn't want to be hampered with braids flopping down today. There was too much to do with the little girls. Spring was in her steps as it was in the air.

At breakfast, she paused and spoke to each sister. She heaped double portions of eggs, bacon and bread onto her plate.

"There's no need for a schoolroom fire, so let me draw your water," she gaily volunteered to the pflegerin, who handed her the bucket willingly, but surprised.

To the cook she offered to pick radishes and carrots. In the garden she stooped to pull stray weeds. "What a glorious day!"

Her feet fairly skipped along the walk to school and her arms swung freely. Without realizing it she began to hum as she set out paper and charcoal for the girls. She eagerly awaited their arrival.

As soon as everyone was assembled, she rang a little bell, signaling the girls to come to attention. "Girls, this is a beautiful day. Sun, green grass, trees in foliage, flowers perfuming the fresh air. These are all gifts of God. Let us go and enjoy them!"

The girls jumped up and down clapping their hands and squealing with glee.

Sister Sehner poked her head in the door.

Martha smiled, "Sister, we're going out to observe the beauties of the world. Girls, take your papers and charcoal. We are going to draw some of the things we see."

Martha led them through the hall, out the door and down the steps. "Girls, look at all the different greens we see in the grass and on the leaves – light, dark, yellow green. If you see a fallen leaf, pick it up. We'll take the collection back to the classroom later.

The group walked, stopped, and walked again up toward the graveyard. At the crown of the hill, Martha suggested they all sit upon the ground.

"Look around. All around. Do houses and streets look difference when you're at the top?"

"Yes, the school almost hides the Sisters House."

"They look smaller."

"I can hardly see the Brothers House through the trees."

"I can see the graveyard. And the fence."

Martha directed, "Find the view you like best and draw what you see."

As their little fingers sketched, Martha ambled among them. She would drop to her knees and bend to discuss their work. When they finished, each girl showed her drawing and talked about it.

Exuberance ran through her. The children were enthusiastic about their artwork. Their drawings and attitude delighted Martha.

The following morning Martha pinched a few leaves from her thriving rosemary plant. In class she handed each girl a thin, needle-like leaf. She instructed, "Look at the leaf. Tell me everything you can about it, learning through your eyes."

When their vocabulary was exhausted, she said, "Now close your eyes and gently stroke the leaf with one finger. How does it feel to your touch?"

Next, she urged, "Bruise the leaf. Rub it between two fingers. Do you like the aroma? Does it remind you of anything else you have smelled? Would you like to taste it?"

Two girls giggled and stole shy glances at one another. "You may taste it, if you want to. Remember that you must not go around nibbling on every plant you see. Always ask sister or your parents if you're not absolutely sure what the plant is."

Martha began to anticipate each school day. Finding new adventures in learning was no longer a problem. Suddenly everything she saw seemed to be a page for her textbook.

In the late afternoons she scampered down to the yellow house as often as possible. Her mother moved slower these days, but she pursued her baking and kept the house clean and tidy. Martha noticed the nursery was not tidy, so she made excuses to pick an herb but tarried long enough to weed a bed or two or water a drooping plant.

She also looked after the herbs and helped cultivate the vegetables in the sisters' garden. Her housekeeping in her choir room consumed very little time. She kept up with her personal washing daily and took bed linens to the sisters' wash house where she enjoyed listening to the sisters talk while ironing on the back porch.

Whenever she was alone, she worked on memorizing a new hymn or sang one already learned. Sometimes she was singing softly as she walked down the choir house halls and was unaware she had passed a sister.

The sisters, who were all busy themselves, were amazed at her energy, her diversity, her constant willingness to help, and her concentration. They thought this latter trait was why she occasionally didn't speak.

Martha taught the easiest hymns to her girls. Soon they were heard singing in the saal at services and the congregation noticed and listened approvingly at the clear voices. The girls sang on their trips outside and on the way home from school.

One afternoon Brother Koehler came in as she dismissed her class. "Martha, we've had a request from a Mr. Winegardner. He wants us to take his little girl into our school."

Martha remained silent, listening.

"The school has had requests in the past, I've heard. The war and lack of teachers prevented this taking in of outsiders at the time. Conditions appear to be more stable now. This man sounds in earnest. He wants a good education for his daughter. Do you have any comments?"

"Brother Koehler, I'll be happy to do whatever the Conferenz wishes."

"Would you object to having an outsider?"

"No sir. I have not had much experience with other people, but I will do the best I can."

"Then we will take her on trial. We will expect her to show good behavior and to stay clean – free of lice and itch. Each Monday, the payment for her week's schooling will be due. If any one of these points is not observed, she is to be sent home. We'll have a thorough understanding with the parents."

"Yes sir."

"Oh, when you and the girls are out walking, if you come across any stones, have the girls pick them up and carry them down to the creek. The bridge support washed away and needs rebuilding."

"They will be delighted to help."

"Pile the stones up on the bank. The brothers will use them as needed."

Martha was right. The girls had fun collecting the stones. They begged to wade in the creek. They had heard that the boys got to wade, even fish some times when they were out in the late afternoon. Martha was not swayed by their pleas.

As they walked solemnly back up the long hill one-day, Martha said, "If you girls want to do something with water, I'll take you around back to the well, and we'll fill buckets and water the new plants behind the school. Excitedly, they squealed and doubled their walking pace.

Upon reaching the corner, one girl in back of the group, shrieked. Martha stopped instantly and turned to see the cause of alarm. Racing up the hill were two horses. They were headed toward the girls at a full gallop.

"Quick, girls, up here!" she gathered them close to her and ran along Main Street to the yellow house. She shoved the girls inside the fenced area. She darted in after the last girl and let the gate slam shut.

Huddled together, the girls held their breath as the pair of horses sped past the fence.

Martha leaned against the pickets and peered down the street. Two, three brothers charged up the hill, carrying ropes. Seeing the girls protected by the fence, the men continued the chase.

She said reassuringly to the girls, "The brothers will soon catch the horses."

"Is it safe to go out? Are they all gone?" The girls shivered and sought further assurance.

"Come to the fence and look." Martha motioned them forward, her hand and arm extended.

"Where did the horses come from?" Cautiously, they moved toward her and the fence.

"Probably the brothers farm on down the hill. Do you think they wanted to get out and run, like we did? It's such a pretty day." After they had time to see the road was empty, Martha stated, "Come along now. We must get back to school." She urged the girls as she gently herded them out of the yard.

After school, she related the run-away horse incident to Sister Sehner. "The horses really frightened the girls. I wish we didn't have to have them in town."

"I hear Brother Bagge's horse jumps the fence and runs loose, too."

"Well, I hope the Collegium sets up some posts along the street north of father's house. You can hardly tell the walking path from the street. Posts do offer some protection."

"I heard that the brothers are going out searching for post oaks soon. Did you know that some families are to use the open field between the square and God's Acre for an orchard?"

"No. Father may have some fruit trees."

Walking to their rooms, Sister Sehner added, "They've decided to plant sycamores in the square. They grow rapidly. I believe we're getting those from Brother Herbst."

One event in September 1788 caused Martha as well as the congregation a touch of sadness. It was the departure of Dr. Lewis and his wife. The doctor had a weakness for alcohol and could not carry on his medical practice adequately. Brother Dixson was asked to assist the people in town with his medical knowledge; however, he could not go elsewhere, because of his duties in the school. Dixson was given temporary charge of the apothecary shop.

The congregation desired a fully certified physician and surgeon in their community. They made their needs and wishes known to the Brethren of the Unity of Elders Conference. They specified a doctor who knew English or at least a man who would be willing to learn the language.

On the same day that the Lewises left, another but happier departure took place. Brother Christian Ludwig Benzien left for Europe as a delegate to the Synod. Brother Benzien was presently serving as an assistant to Brother Marshall, who deemed it wise that someone else knew the congregation's affairs. Benzien carried with him some private papers to be opened before the Synod convened, in order that the proper people could know of the needs of Wachovia. Marshall had written that it would be convenient for Wachovia to have a resident bishop again. As it stood now, a brother had to make a long trip to Pennsylvania in order to be ordained. Such trips were costly.

Thus in this day there had been situations bringing joy and sadness. Martha thought no matter what small conflict or difference in opinion arose during the workday, in the evening, each became less significant compared to the overall unity of spirit as everyone lifted his or her voice in praise and song.

Also during September, the Single Sisters conducted a choir communion at which time they thanked God for his blessing on their material affairs. The sisters had all their needs provided. Six girls were taken into the choir. Among the new sisters was Anna Bagge. Four girls moved into the choir house at this time, but Anna was not one of them. She was still needed at home.

The following May, Anna undertook her first long trip. She accompanied her parents to Bethlehem, Pennsylvania. Sister Maria Hauser went with them. The single sisters chatted excitedly about the trip and helped Sister Maria with her preparations. Whenever Anna was in the choir house, they questioned her about travel plans. Martha, outwardly, was happy for both girls, and offered to help with some of Maria's chores while she was away. She told Anna that she would miss her, not that she often saw her during the day, but they frequently sat together at nightly services. Martha had no wish to travel; having never been out of Salem, she had no knowledge of what the outside world was like. She was content in the busy niche selected for her.

Nevertheless, for a fleeting instant she would have liked to jump up on the wagon beside Anna and to bounce off in a friendly adventure.

She stood with a few other sisters in front of the community store and waved to the people in the wagon until they were out of sight. The sisters started back to the house. Martha said she was going to see her parents.

Slowly, Martha walked up the street. She took deep breaths of the fragrance of the spring day. Honeysuckle filled the air, masking the late pollens and freshly cut grasses. Sunlight trickled down the hill between shadows of buildings and trees. Ahead the little yellow house shone like a comforting beacon.

As she walked on, she realized how lucky she was to have a mother she could talk to; someone she could count on to be strong, a real helper in times of need. Poor Anna had never had such a pleasure. Martha tried not to sound prideful – but she would rather be herself going home to tea with her mother than off on a jaunt to a faraway state.

At tea, Martha learned the roomer was leaving. Maria said, "The girls complain about the tobacco smell."

Martha replied, "I hope you find another roomer soon. You need the help."

"They all think the work's too hard."

Before leaving, Martha kissed her mother.

"Martha, I'll walk as far as the Gemeinhaus with you," Matthew stated.

She waited as he took his key, unlocked the desk, and withdrew the love feast account book. He locked the desktop.

"Are you going over the accounts?" She inquired as they walked together.

"I'm turning the books over."

"Aren't you going to handle them anymore?"

"It's time another brother takes over."

"Father, you have done them as long as I remember."

"Now someone else can have the opportunity. It has been a pleasure, my dear."

Martha swallowed hard. Sensing her eyes would tear; she turned her head quickly, as if she could turn aside the thought that her father might be aging. That he, the strongest, most reliable person she knew, might need to give up any duties. She rarely knew him to need rest and even then it would be for a brief time. Yes, he was slower when summer came, but so were most people here; still they kept on working until jobs were done.

During the hot summer, she often went to the nursery to help him with chores before services. Sometimes during the day she would march the little girls around the square and down to the nursery where she passed along her knowledge and love of growing plants. She taught them the difference between weeds and plants and thus they kept beds weeded. They carefully divided clumps of rosemary, sage and mint. Matthew offered each girl a plant to take home. They were just as excited as Martha remembered having been with her first plant. Martha allowed the class to assist her in preparing a bed in the sisters' kitchen garden. She told them when the plants were large, that they could pick some leaves and make a tea. Thus, the girls had a continuing interest in *their plants.*

One afternoon in September, the class was checking on the plants. They were intent.on pinching back dead leaves following a very hot, dry spell.

"Sister Martha, can we draw water from the well yet?" asked Rebecca Sampson, indicating the new well that had been dug the previous week.

"No. It won't be long before the workmen have it ready for us," she replied.

"Why haven't they finished?"

"They have wells to finish at the store, tavern, Brothers House and the pottery," she informed them.

Rebecca said with youthful perplexity, "If the sisters already have a well, and we have a water system in town, why do we need so many new wells?"

Martha sat down beside her little redheaded student and patiently explained. "At times our water flow is slow, especially during a dry season like this year. Our water comes from a big spring underground. When it doesn't rain, the big trees and bushes and grasses absorb more water from deeper in the soil. People have to water their gardens where plants have shallow roots, the animals need water when the creeks dry up."

Rebecca interrupted. "Are you saying we need more water and we're digging way, way down to get it?"

Martha smiled. "Yes. Now put a little more mulch around the parsley. She watched Rebecca go to the old clippings pile, gather a handful of dried grass, carry it over to the low growing border of mossy-leafed parsley. How like her brother Peter, she thought, when he was a little boy.

"Martha," a soft voice spoke behind her. It was Anna.
"Why, Anna, when did you get back?" cried Martha.
"Just now."
"How was your trip?" Martha asked rising to her feet.
"Martha, I'll tell you all about it later. It was so exciting. But now – please, go to your parents' house?"
Martha's eyes registered surprise. She tried to keep her voice calm, knowing the little girls were listening. "Is anything wrong? Who will stay with the girls?"
"They can go back inside. Sister Sehner can get an older girl to stay with them. Go along."
Martha called the little girls together. "Girls, wash your hands then go inside. Sister Sehner will tell you what to do."
Martha hastily washed her own hands and rushed to the yellow house.
Opening the door, she could see into the front room. There standing in the middle of the room, hands behind his back, was Traugot Bagge. She had never seen him in her father's house before. Her eyes sought her parents. Matthew was seated in the chair at his desk. Her mother was standing beside him with a hand on his shoulder.
"Mama? Father?" Martha called as she entered the room
Bagge turned. "Good afternoon, Sister Martha."
Maria left Matthew and walked over to Martha, putting an arm around her waist. "Martha, Brother Bagge has brought us unexpected news. Your Grandmother Spangenberg has gone home. She's with the Lord now."
"Grandmother?"
Maria nodded.
Martha hugged her mother then moved to her father.
Bagge spoke to Maria. "I'm sorry to have returned with this news, but I thought you'd want to know first. I'll inform Brothers Marshall and Koehler. I expect they will announce it at services."
"Thank you for your kindness," Maria said.

As Bagge neared the door, Matthew lifted his voice in broken tones. "We're thankful the Lord gave you and your family a safe journey back."

Bagge waved his hand and left.

"Matthew, I know Brother Joseph will miss her. She was a good helpmate."

"I haven't seen her in so many years, but memories bring vivid pictures," he spoke in a low voice.

Martha stayed and listened to her father talk of his childhood. When he went into the bedroom to be alone a few minutes, she offered to lay out a cold supper for the family.

A short time later Brethren Marshall and Koehler came. Martha washed up the dishes while they talked with her parents.

A change took place at the Sisters House. A sister married and left. Anna Bagge moved in. She was on the same floor with Martha except in a different room. Anna filled her space with handsome, finely crafted wooden pieces including a three-quarter bed, a clothes press, a desk, table and chair.

The afternoon of Anna's arrival, Martha stopped by after class.

She knocked on the door. When Anna opened it, Martha inquired, "Can I help you get settled?"

Anna pulled her into the room. "Oh, yes. I need to hang these curtains." She was holding a rod with the curtains run through the top and the ends draped over her arm. "How do you get them over the hook?"

"Do you mind if I stand on the chair?"

"No."

Martha slid the chair over to the window and stepped on the seat. "Now hand them to me. This end on the left fits into this hole, then down. The other end sits up on this bent iron nail."

"Thank you for showing me and hanging the curtain."

Martha held the back of the chair and stepped to the floor. She returned the chair to the table. She admired the already cozy look of Anna's part of the room. "Your curtains are beautiful. Your needlework is lovely. And the fringe . . . when did you learn this?"

Anna laughed. "While you were teaching, I was working on this." She took a pillow from the clothes press and placed it on the chair, next an appliqued quilt top for her bed.

Martha observed, "It really looks like a home, all in one day. You're here to stay."

Anna didn't reply.

"If there's nothing else, I'll go on," Martha said.

"Nothing else, but thank you."

On impulse, Martha asked, "Would you like to come down to my room for tea?"

Anna brightened. "Yes, I would." She closed her door and they walked down the hall, Anna chattering about the big houses in Pennsylvania and the really nice schools.

Martha unlocked her door and let Anna enter first.

Martha saw her room in a new light after having been in Anna's. Her area was sparsely furnished. Its appearance had suited her, but she realized it was barren and dull compared to the room she had just left.

Anna scanned the room then walked to the window. "What a nice view of the garden."

Tea was a few mint leaves crushed in room temperature water she had brought up that morning. She offered honey for sweetening. Anna politely drank a few sips before resuming talk about the trip north and all the inns where they had stopped.

"Did you hear whether any doctor there could come down here? We really need one. Wasn't it terrible Brother Aust had to go up there to have the cancer on his face treated? We were sad to hear he died there."

"I wonder if the candles being used in the saal came from Sister Aust? They said she's making them of tallow taken in at the pottery. They certainly do smoke a lot. I hope they go back to the nice beeswax ones they used to burn."

Martha didn't answer since she knew her father previously supplied the saal candles. However, other people must have complained because a diener was told that wax tapers were to be used and that they should be obtained from Miksch.

Martha's school and choir duties kept her very busy. She did not have as much time to visit her parents.

Anna employed herself in the choir house learning the finer details of needlework and the intricacies of housekeeping.

Martha did go by Anna's room one winter afternoon for tea. Anna served pekoe tea brought back from Charleston by her father. When Martha admired the tea service, Anna replied, "It was one I liked so much in Pennsylvania, Papa bought it for me."

"I hear it's about time Brother Johann Krause returned from Pennsylvania," Martha commented.

"It's taking a lot of brothers traveling up there to get Brother Shrober's paper mill started."

"Well, Brother Shrober who went to learn paper making, wrote back that someone should go up to see how the operation works so it could be built right!"

"You'll be glad when there's lots of paper here, won't you?"

"For the schools – yes. Then the children will be able to keep more samples of their work."

Currently in the classroom, Martha was teaching the little girls how to wind knitting yarn into balls so that the string could be pulled from the center of the ball. If the ball were to be dropped, the yarn could not unravel. The little girls had been inside for several weeks due to very cold winter weather. Now in late February the winds continued whipping over the mountains in the northwest and crossing Salem with a chilling force.

Rebecca kept jumping up from her seat and wandering around the room, her red braids swinging and her blue yarn ball rolling across the floor.

"Rebecca, come let me show you again," Martha said in her patient manner. However, after the fourth attempt even Martha's endurance was wearing thin. She realized she too needed some out-of-door exercise. She decided at that point to visit her parents that afternoon.

At four o'clock, she wrapped her scarf at her neck and put her cape over her shoulders and accompanied the girls to the steps. One by one they were called for. They headed home, the wind lashing at them, tossing capes back like little flags. Martha spotted a wagon across the square; it pulled up in front of the store. Martha was chilly waiting with Rebecca for someone to come for her. She wished she had on gloves. She tucked her hands into her apron pocket but the wind whipped open her cape. Rebecca jumped up and down the steps to stay warm. Finally, Martha suggested they walk toward Rebecca's house. Rebecca was delighted at the extra attention. She skipped on ahead.

Martha called her back. "Look out! There are horses on the Main Street."

Rebecca waited at the corner beside the fence on the square. She watched a couple of horses with riders trot up Main Street until her attention was drawn to a leaf sailing close pass her. Up and down it swirled with the wind gusts. Suddenly, she had a keen urge to see if her yarn ball would go up and down, too. She took it out of her pocket and threw it as high as she could. As it fell, she ran after it.

Martha was caught by surprise at Rebecca's quick action. She started off after the laughing running child. She didn't want to run down Main Street, especially in front of the Brothers House, but she had no choice. Rebecca was her responsibility and she was aware a wagon was in the street.

When the yarn ball landed, it rolled down the street leaving a long blue trail, not having been wound correctly. In chasing the ball, Rebecca accidentally kicked it, sending it further away. When she looked to see how far it had gone, she spotted her mother waving from the next block down.

Rebecca yelled goodbye back to Martha and ran on toward her home. The wind caught the words and Martha never heard them. Her scarf came loose at the neck as she drew her cape tighter. The scarf ends fluttered and flipped over her face. For a few moments, she could not see anything. She let go her cape, lifted wide her arms to catch the scarf. She kept moving forward and while her arms were outstretched, she ran straight into something solid. She stumbled. She felt someone grab her arms and slowly steady her. Her heart was pressed against another person she was sure. Against a very sturdy chest. She could hear a pounding heart, not her own. She inched her hand up and over and drew the woolen scarf down.

She stared up into a stranger's face. A handsome, squared face with a firm jaw, a warm sensitive mouth, and eyes that said a dozen things to her. In one short minute she read more in his expression than she had seen in any man's eyes in her twenty-two years of life. And she knew she looked back at him: she did not drop her eyes, as she knew was proper. She was no longer cold. Where his hands grasped her arms, was a pleasing fire. His breath warmed her face until she felt she were standing directly in the sun. Was she giddy? Or was she dazed from the collision? She did not know.

The stranger leaned back, his grasp still tight. He surveyed her critically. "Are you all right?"

"Yes, I'm sorry I bumped into you." He dropped his hands. "One of my students was running down the street. I wanted to stop her . . . the horses," she finished weakly. He continued examining her.

She peered around his shoulder. "She's with her mother now." Again, her eyes engaged his.

He started to speak again but closed his mouth. Scrutiny over, he swung around to the wagon.

Martha reluctantly turned toward the yellow house. She noticed the ball of yarn on the ground. She stooped and recovered it. She rewound the yarn as she walked to her parents' house. Every muscle in her ached to turn back to see the stranger again, but they obeyed her will to go forward.

At the shop door, she stole a sideways glance back to the community store. The stranger was carrying something inside.

In the shop front room, her father was talking to Johann

Gottlob Krause. Martha moved on to the kitchen. Maria was stirring a pot of stew.

Her father was in a jovial mood, welcoming an old friend home.

"Matthew, your tobacco is the best between here and Pennsylvania."

"Thank you, brother."

"By the way, our new doctor came back in the wagon with us."

"I didn't know one had agreed to come from Pennsylvania," Matthew remarked.

"He's not from Pennsylvania. He's from Europe."

"What part?"

Martha listened closely now to the conversation, pretending to warm herself at the edge of the fireplace and leaning toward the open doorway to the front room.

"Silesia."

"A Moravian?"

"Yes indeed. A real committed young man. His family was Lutheran. He was baptized one, too. But he leaned toward the Moravians while studying medicine in Berlin."

"Is he a single brother?"

"Yes. This is his first call. He is eager to serve. I'll be getting on home now. Good day."

"Good to have you back."

Martha came into the front room as Krause left. Matthew had never seen her so radiant, eyes all aglow, skin flushed.

Maria came in with a pot of coffee.

Matthew commented on the good smell. "It's a pleasure to have coffee again. I hear we're going to have it at love feast too."

The three talked about various community topics. Matthew was curious about Martha's glow. Maria went back to the kitchen to see about supper. She decided she needed more turnips from the cellar.

Martha stayed upstairs. She tried to word what she wanted to say carefully. She didn't know how to be clever or subtle with her father. Thus in the end she started with, "Father, remember I told you a long time ago that I would leave the arrangement of a marriage up to you and the lot."

"Yes, I recall that," he said calmly to her. Silently, he thought so it's come to this.

"Father, there is someone I would marry. Or should I say there is someone whom I would accept."

"Who, Martha?"

"The new doctor."

Matthew almost dropped the pipe he was smoking. "Have you met him"

"No. I mean yes. I ran into him accidentally," she blushed as she spoke.

"Did he introduce himself?"

"No."

"Did he tell you his name?"

"No."

"How do you know, he's the doctor?"

"I just do."

"Martha?" He started to form a question but she continued.

"Father, don't ask me how I know. It was he. I am not trying to arrange my affairs. I feel God has arranged them."

"Martha. This is very sudden. The brother has only arrived an hour ago. And he didn't speak to you."

"Yes, he did. He inquired if I were all right. He looked at me to be certain. Like a doctor should. But in his eyes I knew."

"Martha?" Matthew furrowed his thick eyebrows.

"And Father, I may have been unseemly, but I explained to him that I was running after my student. I was concerned about her safety. It was the first time I have spoken with a brother on the street." She stopped, unready to reveal her reactions to the encounter. Being young and innocent of interfaces with brethren, she was unaware of her radiance; he perceived her emotions had been bestirred.

"Martha, I will pray about it."

"Thank you, Father. I'm going now. I'll see you at services."

After she left, he sat for a long time and thought. His only child—the daughter close to his heart and his helpmate and companion in the nursery—had grown in another direction within an hour. It was the first interest she had shown in a brother as a man. That brief running-into she called their meeting, had had a physical impact on her strong enough for her to come to him with marriage on her mind. This was an issue he could not ignore.

CHAPTER TWENTY-THREE

After Martha went up the street, Dr. Samuel Benjamin Vierling reached into the wagon and withdrew a large black musical instrument case. He set it on the walkway. Next, he yanked out a black travel trunk and placed it beside the first case. He stood a moment taking in the town of Salem.

"So this is the place my Lord has called me to. I trust my service will do him honor."

He thought how unlike Rudelstadt, Berlin and Zeist this was. Salem was more rural. His observant eye took in the pump across the street, the fenced square, and the new brick house that he supposed to be the Sisters House from what Brother Krause had told him on the way down. He saw the Gemeinhaus and remembered that the girls' school was conducted there.

"What kind of congregation town is this where sisters run in the streets after children? Such forward sisters, speaking directly to strangers."

Vierling strode confidently into the community store. Several outsiders were buying supplies. Brother Biwighaus was taking care of their orders. Toward the back, Vierling spotted an impressive looking, serious-faced man tallying some figures. He passed the outsiders and walked directly to the man.

"Pardon me, sir, but are you Traugott Bagge?"

Bagge glanced up, holding his thumb on his place. "Yes."

The young doctor removed his hat, thrust his hand forward

and spoke warmly. "I am Brother Samuel Vierling. I'm the new congregation physician. Johann Krause came down in the wagon with me. He suggested I stop in first to see you. He said you could tell me where to find the people I need to see."

Bagge was obviously impressed by the doctor's straightforward manner. "It's good you're here. How was your trip?"

"A splendid ocean voyage – excellent company. We arrived in New York the day after Christmas. The trip to Pennsylvania took only a few days."

"Did you have the opportunity to see our congregation town there?"

"I was there only a short time. I was impressed with the work of the Brethren."

"Let's go over to my apartment for coffee before walking up to talk with Brother Marshall." Bagge pointed to the front door and Vierling retraced his steps. Bagge called Biwighaus aside and told him to send a boy to tell Marshall that he and Vierling would soon be along.

Bagge saw Vierling's baggage on the walkway. "These yours?"

"Yes."

"Let's put them inside my doorway for now." He helped Vierling move the large bag inside.

The Bagge living room was warm and cozily furnished Vierling noticed.

"Have a seat, I'll get the coffee."

Vierling walked over to the bookcase and scanned the titles of the books. He picked up "History of the Brethren" translated by Bagge. He was admiring the binding when Bagge re-entered carrying two steaming mugs. "I see I'm the guest of an author."

Behind Bagge, tottered his wife.

"Why Traugott, you should let me serve our company," she said in a slightly chiding voice.

"I didn't wish to disturb you. Dr. Vierling, this is my wife." Bagge answered handing a mug to Vierling.

"Cream or sugar, brother," she asked.

"Cream, thank you, Sister Bagge."

"Now, Traugott, don't worry about me. I'll get it," she said petulantly and left the room.

As her mother exited the room from the back, Anna was about to come in the front door. She heard the strange man's voice and paused. He sounded young and her father called him doctor. She smoothed her apron, checked the outline of her cap to be sure all the stray ends of hair were in place, and straightened her pink bows. When she heard her mother returning, she smiled and entered, too.

Deliberately, she sought her mother's presence and in a most solicitous manner, she gracefully glided over to her. "Here, Mother, let me help you."

"Why, Anna, dear, how thoughtful of you to come visit me," her mother replied as she presented a cheek for Anna to kiss. Anna obliged her and helped her to sit in a chair.

"May I do anything for you?" Anna spoke softly.

"Anna," Traugott said.

"Yes, Papa?" She acted surprised he was in the room.

"We have a guest."

Anna turned and saw Dr. Vierling. She smiled demurely and lowered her gaze immediately after they exchanged a glance. "I'm sorry Papa. I didn't know."

"This is our new doctor, Brother Samuel Vierling."

"Oh, Mama, may I bring you some coffee?"

"Yes, dear. But first could you serve the doctor some cream?"

Anna picked up the pitcher with the handle protruded toward him making sure their hands did not touch. Samuel took in every graceful act she performed. He observed her lovely slender hands, her small feminine body as she stood close to him. "Such a lovely, gentle sister," he said to himself, "so unlike the hurricane on the street."

Anna brought coffee for her mother and herself. Except for

kindly comments to her mother, Anna was quiet unless asked a question.

Bagge stated bluntly, "One of your cases looks as if you brought a musical instrument."

Vierling replied, "My cello. I didn't know if I could get a good one here so I brought it. I understand you have several musicians in Salem."

"Our band is good. Anna plays the clavichord. She especially enjoyed the tones of one she played in Pennsylvania," Bagge commented.

"Did she go to school there?" Samuel did not look toward Anna.

"No. We have a good girls' school here. We went up last summer to see my sons. They're both in school in Lititz."

Anna said, "Papa, excuse me now. I must return to the Sisters House. I came to check on mama."

She pulled her cape around her and put on her fine smooth leather gloves. With downcast eyes and merest flutter of an upward glance, she said, "I'm pleased to have met you, Dr. Vierling. I pray God's blessing on you in your calling here."

Samuel's eyes followed her smooth exit. To himself he compared her to a breath of spring on a gray winter day. A beauty to see and a joy to hear.

Bagge quickly perceived Samuel's lingering stare and he did not disapprove. Anna was twenty and he had hoped a worthy brother would come along for her. "Yes," he thought, "this young man has the look of good character. Well, we shall soon see how he goes about his profession."

The two men walked to the Gemeinhaus against the blowing wind. Neither clutched at their hats or great coats.

Frederich Marhall received them in his living room. After a pleasant chat about mutual friends in Germany, Marshall suggested that Vierling dine with his wife and him. Following evening services, Samuel could move into the Brothers House temporarily.

Bagge excused himself and returned to the store.

"At present, Brother Jo Dixson has the key to the apothecary shop. He has helped us during the interim we've been without a physician. After he's had a chance to move his personal belongings, you can inventory the stock. Then you may move your instruments in."

"My instruments? I did not bring them," Vierling stated in genuine concern. "I was told you had everything needed here."

Marshall obviously disappointed remarked, "No. There are very few here. I thought my letters were clear on that point."

"The information I had was to the contrary. I sold all my instruments, even the surgical ones in Berlin, thinking they would be extra baggage." Suddenly, he laughed.

Marshall appeared puzzled. Vierling explained. "But I brought a cello. Maybe I can play for the patients until I can get some things sent down from Pennsylvania."

Marshall smiled, too, thinking it was good to have a doctor with a sense of humor – and who planned to take care of problems promptly.

At the early evening service, Koehler heartily welcomed home Krause. He introduced the new community doctor. "Brother Vierling studied anatomy in Berlin where he gained practical experience in surgery. He was granted permission by the Unity's Elders Conference to live in a congregation settlement. Before leaving Europe, he visited Herrnhut and Zeist. At the latter he was received into the Unity of the Brethren. He sailed from Amersterdam in the company of many of our brethren. In that group were Brother Ettwein, known to many of you, and Brother and Sister Benzein. Benzien will be coming here soon as associate pastor in Wachovia."

During the introduction, many in the congregation looked to the brothers' benches. The younger single sisters seeing him seated in the single brothers' section, sat up straighter. Each one was aware of some vibrations from the girls next to her. Anna and Martha, seated together, retained their composure. Later, as they walked together back to the choir house, neither admitted they had already met the handsome brother.

Maria was anxious to get home. The evening was cold, as was the saal, so Matthew left with her. Bagge lingered, while many brothers shook hands with Samuel and welcomed him into the fellowship. When he could get away, he joined Bagge.

Out in the evening air, Samuel told Bagge of the unexpected news of lack of instruments. "I'm thankful my needs in traveling were few. I saved the money from the set I sold. When will a wagon be coming down again?"

"There's no regular delivery from Pennsylvania. When we need something for the store, I send a wagon up."

The two were silent a minute. "Make out your list. I'll have a wagon going soon," Bagge offered.

"I'll get to it as soon as I can check on supplies here. I left some barrels in Pennsylvania with books and things to be sent later."

Bagge helped Vierling move his cello and trunk into the Brothers House. Vierling spent his first days talking with the brothers, learning names, walking the streets, stopping in at shops and becoming acquainted with the physical layout of the town. He visited the boys' school and struck up an immediate friendship with the School Inspector Brother Kramsch. He also took an instant liking to Brother Daniel Koehler.

He did not visit the Miksch house although he passed it frequently.

"Well," Matthew decided, "if he won't come here then I must seek him out."

As soon as he heard from Dixson that Vierling had taken over the apothecary stock, he put on his old black tricon and told Maria he was going out.

Upon reaching the apothecary, he knocked on the door. A large voice called out, "Come in," so Matthew pushed the latch down and walked in. The room was unheated and chilly; however, he noticed Dr. Vierling had his great coat off and his shirtsleeves rolled up. His arms were lost inside a barrel. Vierling looked over to his visitor.

"Good morning, brother. Do you come in good health or do you need my services, medical?"

"Good health."

"Fine, then I'll proceed with the unpacking." He extracted glass beakers, one in each hand and placed them on a high shelf. "I'm glad to find these were packed away carefully."

"I heard you came over with Brother Ettwein and his daughter. My wife and I were fortunate to make our trip to Bethabara in '64 with him and his wife. A fine man. We were sorry to see him leave."

"He's done some outstanding work for the Unity. I was fascinated with his accounts of work among the Indians."

"The Indian work here has been a disappointment." Because Vierling looked up questioningly, Matthew added, "Not from lack of interest on the brothers' part. Various situations prevented our going out among them. There are not any large tribes in our immediate area."

"Oh." Finished with the barrel, he rolled it easily to the back of the room.

Matthew asked. "What shape have you found the apothecary garden in?"

"This time of year, it's hard to tell. It looks not extensive, but I trust it's adequate."

"I have a little nursery down the street; I keep a few herbs. If you need any, drop by. I have some herbs dried," Matthew extended his hand. "I'm Matthew Miksch."

Vierling accepted the hand and shook it firmly. "Everyone is being most helpful."

"Remember the yellow house if you need anything. If I'm not in, or the sign's not out, just take the side path around to the tobacco manufactory. Go through it or the gate to the nursery."

"Thank you."

Matthew left the doctor checking the stock against the inventory list. He thought about the man on his way home. He asked himself some serious questions about whether or not Samuel Vierling would be a good husband for Martha. When he reached his house, he trotted right on by and turned toward the Gemeinhaus. "Whom could I talk with?" The current ministers were relatively recent arrivals. He wished at this time for his old friends. They not being available, he decided on Marshall.

Matthew wanted to say: You realize of course that Martha is twenty-two years of age now. She's had three solid years of experience with the little girls. We're all grateful for the trust and responsibility the congregation has placed in her. Her interest in people, young and old is genuine. You know she devotes much of her time to nursing in the choir house. She's been a big help to me in the garden in the past; she has a good knowledge of growing herbs. I expect soon the Altesten Conferenz will be thinking about a marriage for our new doctor. If in the discussion, Martha's name should come up, I'd like for you to know that I would have no objections.

Matthew couldn't say any of these thoughts. The Conferenz would make its own decisions. So after general conversation, he said. "Well, I best be getting back to the shop. I trust you're enjoying good health this winter?"

"Yes. After the long illness last year, it's a pleasure to be able to say so. Are you and Maria faring well?"

"We have our good days and poorly ones. We're not as young as we once were, eh, Brother?"

"No. But the Lord's work must go on."

During the next couple of days, Marshall observed that the single sisters were arriving quite early for services and were taking their leave more slowly. Every time Sister Marshall raised her front window to pull the bell (the cord having been strung from the bell tower to her room so that she did not have to go outside to ring it) she noticed one or two sisters out walking. She stood awhile to watch the direction they were taking. Finally, she resolved to discuss the "promenades" with her husband.

"Frederich, if the weather were better I might not be suspicious. Do you suppose the sisters are visiting Dr. Vierling? Surely, so many couldn't have suddenly developed ailments?"

"I'll go speak to the pflegerin," Marshall answered.

After hearing the sisters were seeking medical advice from the doctor, Marshall went to Koehler's rooms. A member of the Friedburg congregation was speaking with him.

"We expect her home going is near."

Daniel Koehler saw Marshall and urged him to enter. "There is distressing news. Sister Magdalene Kraus' time has come to deliver her child. The worst is feared."

"I'm sorry to hear the news. Is the minister there?"

"Yes, sir. We had word that the new doctor had arrived. Is that true?"

"He's here."

"He may not be of any help, but where can I find him?"

Koehler offered to go with the brother to find Vierling. On second thought, he said to Marshall. "I'll go to Friedburg with Dr. Vierling. He won't be able to find the way back easily. He may need some comfort if his first case goes home."

"Thank you. We shall all pray tonight for a safe delivery and recovery." Marshall said. He decided to put off the marriage discussion until Koehler returned.

The town waited half-expecting to hear the trombone choir's music announcing a married sister's home going. Instead, they received the news that the new doctor had brought Sister Kraus safely through the birth of a stillborn child. Individually, the members of the congregation were relieved and appreciative at knowing that their doctor was a capable physician.

As the adulation of the doctor grew, Marshall felt the matter of a marriage should be settled quickly. He called the Conferenz together. He asked for suggestions for a suitable mate, emphasizing some of the qualities the sister should have. The members considered the matter in silence, each going over the names of sisters in Salem and Wachovia.

Sister Marshall was the first to speak. "I would like to suggest Martha Miksch, our teacher of little girls. She's proven herself responsible, always conducting herself in a modest fashion and she appears very strong and healthy."

The pflegerin's opinion was solicited. "She would be a good helpmate. Might I also add that she is very patient with sick sisters. She frequently asks for sickroom shifts."

Brother Marshall invited other members to comment. No other name was supported. He said, "Brother Koehler shall we put it to the lot?"

Koehler wrote the questions and inserted them into the small hollow reeds. A single reed was drawn from the bowl. It was *ja*, the German word for yes.

Marshall commissioned Koehler with a question. "Would you like the pleasure of informing Brother Vierling of the name approved by the lot?"

"I'll tell him tomorrow."

Early the next day Koehler hiked down to the apothecary shop. He rapped on the door. Vierling opened it with one hand, his other hand carrying a split log.

"Come in," he hailed Koehler cheerfully. "This fireplace is about to get its first fire or at least my first attempt at building one."

"Did you find wood out back?"

"A few logs. I split them. I need some hot water to wash the stored glass."

"Do you like this shop?" Koehler asked as he surveyed the room.

"The location is good. The arrangement is satisfactory. Another room for operations would be nice. I'm thinking of buying it."

"Dr. Bonn's heirs will most likely be happy to sell. Brother Marshall can help you with details."

"Daniel, I never dreamed when I gave my heart and life to the Lord that I'd ever leave Germany. But I was glad to follow his guidance. Now here I am in a new country, meeting new friends, and making new fires. Come on back to the kitchen."

As Daniel followed Samuel, he tried to state why he had come. "Now that you've decided to buy this house, I have some news for you."

"What's that?" asked Samuel as he bent to light the paper and kindling in the open fireplace.

"The Conferenz has met concerning a possible marriage for you. The lot has approved. She's Martha Miksch."

"No. I don't want to marry her!" His words exploded in the air as he thrust the log forcefully onto the grate.

Daniel stepped back. He was startled by Samuel's negative outburst. Before he could speak, the doctor jumped up and blurted bluntly. "I want to marry Anna Bagge. Single Sister Anna Bagge, Traugott's daughter."

"I'll give your answer to the Conferenz. I'll talk with you again later."

"Do that." Vierling knelt again to light a fire.

Daniel took his leave. He shook his head as he walked up the street. Hadn't he understood a few minutes ago that Samuel was happy to do the will of the Lord? That very definitely didn't include the Lord's approval of a wife. But tradition did allow for parties involved not to accept the drawing of the lot, be it yes or no.

Straightaway, Daniel reported to Marshall, Vierling's strong negative reaction to Martha as a wife. Neither man could explain this empathic rejection. However, they were both pleased he had a name to offer, that he had a preference. A second time the Conferenz assembled to consider the matter of a helpmate for the doctor. The members submitted Anna Elizabeth Bagge's name to the lot. Again, the positive *ja* was drawn.

As Vierling had already made his wishes known, Daniel this time went to the store to consult Brother and Sister Bagge about the marriage. Both immediately gave their approval. Daniel stated that he would ask the pflegerin to discuss the proposal with Anna.

The pflegerin had not spoken against Anna as a suitable candidate when names were mentioned, but she had some reservations. Anna had not shown herself a strong girl as far as work was concerned in the few months she had been in the choir house. A doctor's wife had a demanding job. However, since the lot approved, the pflegerin trusted the girl would be equal to the task.

When she put the question of marriage to Anna, she responded enthusiastically. The pflegerin related Anna's consent to Marshall, who in turn told Vierling.

At supper Anna hoped to sit beside Martha to whisper the good news to her friend. Seats on either side of Martha were already occupied so she moved on down to another table in the dining hall. After the meal was over, she waited for Martha outside the door.

She called to her, "Martha, I want to talk with you."

Martha smiled at Anna. "Anna, I'm sorry I've been so busy lately. And I have to go to Mama's now. She's been down with a cold, I need to check on her."

Anna sighed a bit dejected like a little girl.

Martha put a gentle hand on Anna's arm, "Please, save the news for me. I'll sit with you at services, and then we'll walk back to the house and talk as long as you want to. I promise."

Anna forced a weak smile of understanding. As soon as Martha left, Anna's face turned fretful. She had wanted to tell Martha first. Two sisters passed her in the hall. She caught a sentence or two of their conversation.

"Isn't Dr. Vierling the handsomest brother you ever saw?"

"Do you think he'll choose a wife soon?"

Anna's head jerked up as they moved out of hearing distance. I won't tell anybody! I'll let them be surprised, she pledged with a slightly triumphant air. Immediately, she realized that was not a good Moravian trait and lowered her gaze.

Martha washed the dishes for Maria. She pulled the spinning wheel into the front room and spun quickly while her mother sat near the stove in a chair with a quilt about her legs and a shawl around her shoulders.

When the bell rang announcing services, Martha pushed the wheel back into the bedroom. Putting on her cape, she asked, "Father, are you coming tonight?"

"I think I'll stay home with your mother tonight. The weather's raw. My bones ache on nights like this," he said.

She kissed them both. Descending the steps outside, she almost collided in the darkened street with Dr. Vierling. Both of them stopped short.

Staring at him, she gulped, "Excuse me, again."

"Do you always run into people?"

"Not usually."

Immediately, both were embarrassed to be breaking congregation rules forbidding single brothers and sisters talking together. They turned and began walking in the same direction. Simultaneously, they realized they were in step side by side. Martha slowed down, planning to walk a pace behind him, at the same moment he had the identical idea. Next, both speeded their steps, with the same result.

As they reached the corner, Brother and Sister Bagge approached from the other side. Together Martha and Samuel spoke. "Good evening."

Martha scooted beside Sister Bagge, saying "We have missed you at services lately."

"Thank you, Martha. You are always so thoughtful. Isn't this a happy night?"

Samuel fell in next to Traugott who informed the doctor that the wagon would be ready to leave in a few days to get the remainder of his things. He stated, "My sons will be returning with the wagon."

"Excellent news! I appreciate the expediency, sir."

The foursome entered the saal and broke up as each found a seat in his or her own choir area. Martha sat on the end of a bench beside Anna.

Martha sang the hymns with unusual joy. She hardly noticed the radiant eyes of her friend so close to her side. During Koehler's readings, Martha's mind wandered to the walk up the hill. She was alternately distraught and ecstatic that she had run into Dr. Vierling for a second time. She admitted he was somewhat exasperated by the suddenness of an encounter, a physical bumping into her. In both instances he had stopped. He had not brushed her aside nor pretended they had not touched each other. With that thought she instinctively felt she had blushed and lifted her hand to her face as if to push aside a slight annoyance such as a single hair might cause. Thus if her skin were rosy it would appear from the brushing of her own hand.

Furthermore, he had not tightened his lips and brusquely chided her with only a frown. No, he had faced her and spoken. *Spoken. Conversed for each had said sentences.* He had asked a question. Surely, he expected an answer. Sitting straight and proper here in this assembly, her body retained the memory of their turning in perfect union and walking not a hand width apart up the street. Sensing the naturalness of this as not appropriate, both commenced to defer to the other's leading and slowed their pace. To be so in tune with another person when attempting to alter an action—the two were in concord. Ah, she breathed deeply.

She knew without turning her head that his eyes frequently were focused toward the row she was sitting on. She forced herself with great effort to retain a forward countenance.

Some sounds pricked her concentration. Words Koehler was speaking cut into her revelry. Did she hear the word *betrothal*? Now her eyes widened, her whole being became alert. Her attention pinpointed, waiting for Koehler's next words. They came slowly, distinctively: "Brother Samuel Benjamin Vierling and Anna Elizabeth Bagge."

The words stunned Martha. She wanted not to believe them. Never had she desired to hear any sister's name in the betrothal pair than her own. Oh, God, have I sinned to wish this union for myself?

She never heard Koehler praying the benediction. Slowly, she became aware someone was elbowing her. A soft nudging at her arm.

In a daze she pivoted her head, Anna was now jabbing her. Anna's voice came through like a whisper, "I'm so happy. I wanted to tell you first, Martha." Anna turned to accept some good wishes. When she turned to Martha again, she chided her life-long friend. "But you were in a hurry."

Martha sensed rather than saw, many sisters standing in the aisle impatient to speak to Anna. Martha murmured something vague to Anna and slid off the seat and stepped into the aisle.

She determined to exchange glances with no one. For once she maintained a downward gaze easily. She never lifted her eyes until she reached her room. Not one to cry in public, she wasn't going to start tonight. No candle was needed to light her dark room. She knew every inch in darkness or in light. And the blackness suited her mood. Only once in her life had she had a desire to marry and only to marry one man. Now that desire was not to be fulfilled. She quivered inside. Her composure broke. She gave in to the memory of his strong hands holding her arms, of her heart racing as her body pressed against his. Oh, God – no more. I'll never know the feel of his heart beating against me. I'll never experience it again. And the tears came. Standing in the middle of the room, she let them wash down her face and drip onto her clutched hands. And when the tears stopped, she dropped to her knees, her head bent over to the floor. After a long while, she raised her head and straightened her back, and sat quietly on the floor. Her mind formed words that she forced her lips to speak aloud. "Thy will, not mine, God. Thy will be done. I shall continue in the calling you have given me. Forgive my sinful desires."

Habit alone at this time, forced her to stand up, remove her clothes, give herself a bath, and put on her gown. She crawled into bed. As the other sisters entered the room, she wondered if someone spoke her name. She wasn't sure. This night Martha had no strength to answer.

CHAPTER TWENTY-FOUR

Matthew had not attended the preceding evening service and his reaction upon hearing the betrothal news from a craftsman in the store, was one of surprise.

Triebel, who had informed him, said, "Everybody was a bit surprised, too. Shouldn't have been. Brother Bagge's daughter is of age. A doctor needs a lot of help getting started. He'll have it now."

Matthew brought his display of emotions under quick control. "Brother Vierling is a good doctor, I hear. His first few cases have been highly successful."

"Yes, I know. But even a good doctor's got to eat and have a house. He won't be able to count on time to tend to those little chores that save money. He can't close up shop like you and me when there's a repair to make. And he's got to be ready to go at every knock." Triebel stopped, thought and added, "Someone has to be there to take his messages. Maybe hand out some remedy from the apothecary."

Other customers entered for gingerbread, and Triebel left.

Matthew had no time to think about the betrothal until lunch when the shop was quiet. He had been so certain that Marshall would favor the idea of Martha as a wife for Dr. Vierling. What had happened? Did the Conferenz suggest Anna? Was the lot the ultimate decider? He felt he would never know because the Conferenz members were not the types to talk freely and Matthew himself was above begging, snooping or conniving for information. He admitted inwardly that he was deeply hurt. He knew Martha would make an excellent helpmate for any doctor. The ache was most severe for he could not help her attain the only real wish she had ever voiced. His years of training and faith brought him to a conclusion similar to Martha's: It must have been the Lord's will. Help me Lord to wish Vierling and Anna, health and happiness.

He did not reveal these thoughts to Maria, believing that she was not aware of Martha's statement to him of the matter.

A few evenings later, all the Miksch family attended evening service at the end of which Samuel and Anna were married. Matthew glanced once at his daughter. She was composed. Even he could not read her thoughts, so he was assured no one else would detect any deep feelings on her part.

Martha set her eyes on the north windows and kept her gaze steady. She could not look upon the couple as they stood together. Following the services, however, she made herself go forward to speak to Anna.

"May your happiness be double blest now, Anna." To Samuel she said, "Anna has been a good friend. Take care of her. She will be a good wife."

Matthew standing near-by heard his daughter's words, after which Martha hastily exited the saal. He caught up with her outside. "Martha," he said in a low voice, "those were nice things you just said."

"Thank you, Father. Anna is a friend; she was in no way responsible for or aware of my other feelings. It is best if we not speak of things in the past."

"Martha, don't close your heart in bitterness."

"No, Father, there is none. Only acceptance."

"Then will you greet me with a smile next time I see you?"

Martha immediately turned the corners of her mouth up, but her eyes lacked their usual sparkle. "I shall not forget."

Anna moved with Samuel into First House. She was no longer a member of the Single Sisters Choir, and she in all probability would be invited into the married choir at their next meeting. People going to their house came away talking about the attractive furnishings. Everyone in the congregation, who chanced to see the young couple together, commented on their happy appearance. Anna, always pretty in the past, was radiant as a bride.

One afternoon, Triebel and Holder were in the tobacco shop. They noticed the couple pass outside in the doctor's new wagon. Holder observed. "Look at them. Happy as two new spring lambs."

Triebel commented. "The old saying must be true. Courtship comes after marriage."

"From what I heard, he had an eye for her from the first."

"Have you heard that her brother, Fredrich is now in the apothecary shop?"

"No, but I've seen him up there often. What's Carl doing?"

"Helping in the store."

Anna continued to ride with Samuel on his calls to patients in the nearby Moravian towns. Her daily life except for services differed from Martha's so they seldom encountered each other.

Once, Martha accompanied Matthew to Schmid's for beeswax. As they walked leisurely up the street, they heard strains of music. It was not until they were almost in front of the apothecary that both of them realized the harmonious sounds were from the cello and the clavichord. They listened silently, a trifle self-conscious as they passed the apothecary.

Martha worried about her father and mother. Both seemed to have aged so much in the past year. Not only did they perform all their duties more slowly, but also neither seemed cheerful. She wished a young girl boarder could live with them. Each time she mentioned the possibility, they reminded her that they had tried several girls over the past years and none had worked out.

After one of those replies, Martha countered, "But you mustn't expect the girls to be like me. They're all different – just like my students are different from each other."

"They don't work well like you did," grumbled Maria.

"I remember your calling me whenever I was slow coming

with water or reluctant to dry dishes. You'll have to keep telling them."

Maria retorted. "It takes awhile Martha to train people to do things your way. Then first thing you know, they've decided to go back home or move into the choir house."

"Oh, Mama," Martha reminded, "aren't all of us supposed to help with raising the young girls and boys?"

"We can do so in different ways. Let's not talk about it. I don't need any help."

Martha bit her tongue in order not to argue with her mother.

At school Martha worked diligently with her students preparing them in all possible ways for the older girls' class. She often conferred with Sister Sehner about lesson plans or student behavior.

Her school hours, including looking after the classroom and preparing lesson plans and assembling materials, were long. Except during meals she saw little of other sisters. She did her garden work in the early evening whereas the others finished their chores during the day. She enjoyed the contact with the other sisters but after talking all day, she was more of a listener in their company. The single sisters came to view Martha as quiet. Since she was not around them and showed little enthusiasm for their light gossip, they took it that she wasn't interested in all aspects of the choir.

On the way to services one evening she overheard someone saying to Sister Elizabeth, "Why is Martha so stand-offish? She's not interested in any of the things we like?"

Elizabeth answered, "She's very busy."

"Ump! I do my share! Every time I mention anything that I think is funny, she just gives me one of those sweet smiles and doesn't say a thing."

"Well, if you ever get sick, you'll appreciate having her around. She was really good to me."

"Oh, I pray if I ever have to go to the sickroom, she won't be on nursing duty."

"Don't be hard on her; you could do worst."

Martha dropped several paces behind as they neared the Gemeinhaus entrance. She allowed two sisters back of her to pass so that Elizabeth and her companion wouldn't think Martha could have overheard them if they spotted her as they turned on entering the building.

Services had become the only uncomfortable part of her day every since the betrothal announcement. Anna and Samuel didn't sit together but Martha could not help seeing how fondly they looked at each other. In the past, services had been a pleasurable part of her daily schedule; now she tried to think of something to take their place. In her head rambled the conversation she had heard on the way to the Gemeinhaus tonight. "You'll appreciate her if you're sick."

That was her solution!

Back in the choir house, she sought the pflegerin. "Sister, who stays in the sickroom during the evening service?"

"The nurses and I take turns."

"Could I volunteer for this shift?"

"Is there any special reason for this time, Martha?"

"I realized tonight that someone has to be around the sick rooms all the time. I could read from my Bible then, perhaps read to the sick sisters, if they felt up to listening."

"And perhaps sing to them?"

Martha lowered her eyes in embarrassment.

"No, I'm not making fun of you. We've all noticed how you sing in the halls and the garden."

"The hymns are comforting. It was Grandfather Spangenberg who suggested I learn them."

"They should comfort the ailing sisters, too. I'll discuss your request with Sister Anna, the one who is in charge of the sickroom."

"Thank you," Martha said and went to her room

When the request was relayed to Sister Anna, she replied, "This should help Martha."

The pflegerin inquired what she meant.

"Her eyes have been sad lately. Service to those in need is a good way to lighten a heart."

The pflegerin dared not question this wise sister further, but she couldn't help wondering if the news of Vierling's refusal to marry Martha had leaked out. "If Martha has looked sad, does she know the truth? No, I don't believe she does. Not any of us would have talked about this. It must be the very hot weather or concern about her parents."

Sister Anna showed Martha where all supplies were kept and gave her some general rules to follow. Martha had sat with sisters in the sickroom previously and had been instructed according to procedures the sisters had been given by Dr. Bonn years ago. The first time Martha stayed during the evening service, Sister Anna informed her that when there was a sick sister under the doctor's care, he checked in either just before or after services. Martha thus made it a habit to arrive and leave on time.

As Sister Anna had predicted, the regular nursing duty did lighten Martha's heart. She felt useful in a new area. The room was quiet and peaceful. The sisters enjoyed hearing her read and sing to them. They relaxed as she softly hummed hymns to herself while she tidied their beds before leaving.

One hot evening as Dr. Vierling checked on a patient, he commented to Sister Anna, "In the past few weeks there's been a change in the sickroom."

"How do you mean, sir?"

"The atmosphere is different. The sisters seem so calm. Of course as a whole they always have been, but now it's even more so."

"It must be Sister Martha."

Now it was Vierling's turn to be surprised. "How's that?"

"She's volunteering now, regularly during the evening service. She reads and sings to them. Sister Miksch is a good nurse." The older sister spoke the name slowly and watched the doctor.

"Oh," was all he said.

Martha had expected her life to go on indefinitely in this routine of teaching and living in the choir house, but a plea from her parents ended the pattern. They needed help at home and they wanted Martha. They would not be content with a stranger or a congregation member.

Matthew requested the Conferenz to release Martha from her teaching duties saying he and Maria could no longer dispense with her services. The request was granted.

With mixed emotions Martha packed her few belongings back into the old trunks. She watched them being wheeled around the square to her parents' house. Something about the move registered so final. She sensed she would not be coming back to the choir house to live. It was difficult for her to leave the classroom full of little girls that she had taught for five years. The girls who had gone over to Sister Sehner's class came in to tell her goodbye. Giving up the satisfying duties and the paying position were not easy, but she could never have refused her parents. She affirmed: they would not have asked this, if there had been a suitable alternative.

Her life at home resumed as it had been in years past, only now there was no school to dash off to. She remained a single sister and therefore not allowed to talk with the men who came to the shop or manufactory. Her father waited on the male customers and her mother served the women.

Cooking was something Martha had done very little of in the past. She found there was much to learn about preparing foods, adding flavorings, sautéing and frying, stewing, making good coffee, mixing a cake, whipping cream and such. Her mother was often near-by to give directions when necessary, but she left most of the doing to Martha. She didn't know whether it was the warmth of the open fire or the sudden release from the very tight schedule the past five years, but whatever it was Martha experienced her muscles loosening and her normal rapid pace decreasing in tempo as she moved around the kitchen.

Maria had developed gout and didn't move about so easily any more. She still made her gingerbread almost daily during cold weather. Those days, she let Martha go outside to build the fire in the oven, but she always checked it later. While the bread baked, Maria would visit with Matthew in the manufactory. There were no steps to climb there. Sometimes when he had the fire going and beeswax melted in the big pot, she'd dip a few candles for their own use.

When there were daytime services, Martha accompanied her parents. They didn't always go out at night in the wintertime; however, Martha continued to go to the Sisters House sickroom during the evening services. She joined her choir sisters for lovefeasts and festival days and took them the money for gloves and ribbons sold in the tobacco shop.

While nursing one of the sisters, Martha heard that a married sister who was in the doctor's care had died. There was much sickness among the brothers and sisters for the next three months. Most of them developed chest trouble and high fevers with the length of the illnesses varying. Martha spent many of her shifts sponging the feverish patients. During this time Martha also heard of the tragedy of Johannes Ackermann in Bethabara who fell from a wagon and broke his neck; then of the home going of Brother Valentine Beck who had been ill several months. On the heels of these unhappy announcements came the sad news of Sister Steiner's death while giving birth to twins. She had only been married a year.

The brethren were understandably upset by all the deaths, but this was not the end of their grief. The next accidents involved two of the area's promising young people. One, a child fell into a spring near Friedland and died. The other, a thirteen-year-old youth was killed by a falling tree.

Especially close to her own family was the sudden death of the widowed George Schmid. He had suddenly choked one day and his life was over before anyone could reach him.

One of the town's oldest residents, Sister Utley, the eight-four year old widow of Pastor Richard Utley, also went home.

The deaths touched each family.

Dr. Vierling rushed back and forth taking care of the numerous patients in town and drove out to tend those in the villages. Anna became pregnant early in the year and did not travel with him so often. While riding alone, Vierling wondered about the high rate of accidents and illnesses. Everything had gone so well his first few weeks in Salem. Why this sudden reversal?

In early spring, Martha helped the sisters plant their garden and reworked the herb beds.

Matthew decided he must let some of the nursery work go. Martha was disappointed.

"Father, I'll have more time to help you this year," Martha reminded him.

"It's time I started slowing down, Martha. The manufactory and shop are about enough."

"Where will people buy their herbs and bedding plants?"

"The shops are doing better now. The craftsmen's trades will support them soon. They won't be needing their gardens."

"They'll always need their herbs."

"Most folks now have their own herbs for their kitchen uses. The doctor can provide them with the medicines."

"I don't want to see the nursery grow up in weeds," she responded sadly.

"We can grow what we'll need. And we'll have a few vegetables and cucumbers for pickles if you think you can put them up."

"I'll try. Should we grass the beds we aren't going to use?"

"This year let's sell the perennials that come up and mulch where we take out. Later we'll think about grass or ground covers."

"Maybe the honeysuckle will creep over the fence and do the job itself," she laughed.

Matthew was pleased to hear her merry again. He had worried about her overly serious manner lately.

As the local illnesses and nursing duties subsided, Maria suggested that Martha should spin again while she had some free time in the early afternoon and evenings. "Martha, you may be asked to marry someday soon. What linens would you have to take to a new home? You need a dress. Why truly dear, you need everything. I'll dye and bleach things for you."

So for awhile, the days and nights continued in a full but not rushed manner.

Early in May 1791, the entire congregation responded happily to the news that President George Washington would visit Salem at the end of the month. Every resident busied himself cleaning up his house or shop.

It was a welcomed relief for the people to have something to talk about besides illness when they met.

The news had spread that General Washington always showed an interest in farms and in any unusual procedures successfully used on them. Upon hearing this, Matthew renewed his efforts in the nursery, realizing his place might be noticed if the President's company went up to the Stockburger farm.

At the tavern, the front room on the second floor was put in its best order for his lodging.

The musicians rehearsed with more enthusiasm than they had shown in several months. When a rider galloped into town, shouting, "He's on his way!" the Brethren Marshall, Benzien and Koehler rode out to meet the President. The musicians welcomed him to town with appropriate musical selections.

Residents from Salem and other Wachovia settlements lined the streets to see the leader of their country.

Everyone was pleased with the friendliness he exhibited during his two-day stay. President Washington did tour the town and he saw various craft shops and the waterworks system. He attended a singstunde in the saal. North Carolina Governor Alexandar Martin came from his residence on the Dan River to visit with the President. He, too, attended the singstunde service.

Martha was pleased to see that so many of the little girls were attending the service with their teacher. Everyone noticed that the President looked fondly upon all the children.

Later that evening, the townspeople could hear the musicians as they played near the tavern. The following morning, very early, around four o'clock the President, his secretary, his servants and Governor Martin left town. Brethren Marshall and Benzien rode with them to the border of the Wachovia lands.

The excitement of the President's visit was just subsiding when the weather turned from hot to cold, suddenly. Consequently, many people in Salem became ill. Sister Koehler lay very sick for many days. Brother Koehler also became ill. Dr. Vierling again wondered about the large number of illnesses at this time of the year.

While sickness continued to plague the community, there were some events around which the congregation's spirits could rally in good cheer. One of these events was the first sheets to come from Schober's paper mill. Because a local brother started the paper mill, another brother built it and another ran its operation, the enterprise was viewed with special interest.

Another event of considerable interest was the installation of the town clock, which had been made for them in Europe and had been eagerly awaited. Installation completed, the clock was struck on July 18. The congregation members gladly contributed to a free will offering to finish paying for the clock and the repairs that had been made on the tower.

As the year progressed, the town realized the best business and profits it had ever known. Marshall commented on the prosperity in his end of year report to the Unity's Administrative Board. He also reported on the continued land disputes he had to attend to, sometimes in courts. In the area of the congregation's business enterprises, he was concerned about the tanyard for the upcoming year. It had not been able to purchase new hides to replace those that had been sold. Another of Marshall's concerns was the lack of master masons and carpenters. The town was going to need some new buildings soon. As he thought over the situations, he wrote: It's the Savior's business and only He can direct and lead it . . .

The last day of July along about twilight, Martha sat at the spinning wheel longer than usual. Maria asked, "Martha, aren't you going to the sick room tonight?"

"No, Mama. I'm going to the evening service."

"Oh. Something special?"

"Don't you remember? Sister Catherine Sehner, my teacher and co-worker, is to be married tonight?" answered Martha as she pulled the fluff of wool into a fine strand.

"Yes. I forgot it was tonight. I'm glad you can go. She was always nice to you. It's good you've learned to spin so fast. Maybe you'll be next to change ribbons."

"Mama, please, don't say that."

"And why not? You're a nice looking girl. You are a good worker. Trust the elders, dear. They'll approve when the most suitable brother is ready. Be patient. Have faith. I've never been sorry a day that your father was chosen for me."

Martha did not answer. She ceased spinning and pushed the wheel against the wall.

Maria studied her daughter. "You're not disheartened because you haven't been asked yet, are you?"

Martha merely shrugged her shoulders, an unusual gesture for her.

Maria thought a moment before speaking. "Perhaps seeing the other girls marry has you asking yourself questions. Remember Anna was younger than you were, but Sister Sehner is much older. I'd venture to say Catherine will be as happy as Anna. Your time will come, too. Continue to enjoy your single choir. You'll be with your friends again someday, in the married choir. Don't go rushing this matter of marriage. Service and patience have their own rewards."

Martha found she had missed the girls she had known well in her early years. She sighed, thinking maybe it was best that she was at home now.

In the early fall she was walking one morning to the Sisters House when she saw a number of people trudging up the slope of Main Street. She considered by the clusters they moved in that they were several families traveling on foot together. Out of curiosity, she stopped by the fence at the square as they drew nearer. The people proceeded as if they were very tired. Many collapsed near the water pump. Others pumped water, drank from a cup, then pumped again for those too exhausted to get up. Two or three men left the group and straggled over to the store. In a short time they reappeared on the street. Bagge was with them. He pointed past the square over to Schrober's house. "So they're beggars," she said to herself.

Brother and Sister Koehler came out of the store and started up the street. Martha decided to wait for them. She noticed that the sister seemed recovered from her illness. Like the other Moravians in Wachovia, Martha was happy that Koehler had been made a bishop last year in Pennsylvania. Now the local men could be ordained without having to make the expensive trip to Bethlehem.

"Good morning," she said as they crossed the street.

"Good morning."

"I am always sad to see so many people having to leave their homes. Do you know where they are going?" Martha indicated the strangers at the pump.

Sister Koehler answered as the threesome continued up the hill. "I heard they are going to Cumberland."

"I wish they could have stayed at their homes and helped each other out. It must be hard on those little children to travel so far," Martha said sympathetically.

"Speaking of little children," Sister Koehler said with a sudden brightness, "have you heard that Anna Bagge was delivered of a little girl this morning?"

"No. I hope she – that is Anna and the baby are all right?"

"The baby appears in excellent condition. Anna is weak. You know, she's quite frail and the labor was long," answered Sister Koehler.

Brother Koehler said as they reached the Gemeinhaus, "Dr. Vierling will probably bring the baby for baptism tonight."

"Please, give Anna my love," Martha said as she left them and continued to the Sisters House. Her mind jumped back to the days when she and Anna talked eagerly about the house before it was built, then to the days they shared in it as mutual single sisters. Now Anna was a family woman.

On this glowing fall morning, neither Martha nor anyone else had any forewarning of the sadness that was to prevail the town, especially this Sisters House, the following January.

It all started when little Friedrich Christ, only eight years old, became quite ill during the night of the twenty-eighth. He complained of a painful throat. The next day he was no better. Dr. Vierling was summoned to check on him. Immediately, he knew the child had scarlet fever. He administered medicines and tried to make the boy as comfortable as possible. In spite of his efforts, Fredrich died at nine o'clock the morning of January 30.

Single Sister Maria Hauser helped to lay out the boy. The following day, she came down with the same throat disease. She, too, complained of sudden pain and later became delirious. As her end was evident, the sisters gathered around her bed and sang favorite hymns. She went home February 3.

The disease spread in epidemic proportions throughout the town, especially striking single sisters. Martha worked many hours in the sickroom and was often there when Dr. Vierling checked on the patients. When he was in the room, she moved quietly among the beds and often stayed beside a bed while a sister was delirious and tried to calm her.

Martha witnessed five young sisters and one older girl, all her friends, go home during the epidemic. Sister Anna lamented that in all the years of the Wachovia single sisters' choir there had only been one other home going and that had been fourteen years ago.

Weary from many hours of nursing, Martha was totally unprepared for the news she received late in the afternoon in the middle of March as she walked into the yellow house.

"Martha," her mother called to her, "here in the front room." Martha seeing no customers in the shop dropped into a chair. Maria asked, "How about a cup tea?"

"Mama, that's just what I need." She took the cup and pinched off a little sugar from the cane with tongs and dropped the lump into her cup. As she stirred, her mother passed her a plate of gingerbread.

"Mama, it's good to be waited on for a change." She relaxed, ate and drank with pleasure. As she finished, her mother's expression was strange. "Is something wrong?"

"There's been another death, dear . . . in the married choir."

"Oh, no. One of your close friends?"

"No. One of yours."

"Who, Mama?" The words hung suspended on a deep breath.

"Anna. Anna Bagge Vierling."

"But, Mama," she stopped. She wanted to shout: Anna can't be dead. She's too young, too happy. She has a baby. But she couldn't say that. Younger girls than Anna had died and they had not yet had a chance for the kind of happiness Anna had enjoyed. Martha tried to remember that all these friends would be together in a greater joy now in the presence of the Lord.

Thus, she swallowed before asking, "When?"

"Today."

"The baby?"

"She's all right. No signs of illness yet."

"Who'll take care of her?"

"One of our choir for awhile."

"So many people are suffering, Mama. It's so hard to stand by and watch and not be able to help them more. Why? Why, is this dreadful disease attacking us so, why?"

"Dear, we can not question these mysteries."

"But can we question ourselves? Are *we* doing something to displease God?"

"Are you, Martha?"

"I don't think so. If I am, I don't know what it is."

"Is the town as a whole displeasing our Lord?"

"Not that I see, Mama. We try to do His Will."

"My own physical strength is failing slowly these days, too, but I do not question my Lord about it."

"Where is father?"

"He went up to the Vierlings, to First House. He's a member of his choir. He wanted to see if he could help out. He took some extra candles."

The sickness raged on and the doctor was needed not only in Salem but also in all corners of Wachovia. His workload was heavier in the apothecary because Fredrich Bagge had died. The strain showed in his face, the sadness in his eyes. Koehler suggested to Vierling that he might like to call in Dr. Cox from Rockingham to consult with him about the epidemic. Vierling welcomed the suggestion and a messenger was dispatched at once.

As soon as Dr. Cox arrived, Vierling apprised him of the extent of the situation. The two set out to visit the sick. Upon completion of the rounds, Dr. Cox advised giving less strong medicine and more fresh air to the patients. He also recommended that funerals be conducted as soon as possible after deaths.

Vierling was grateful for the older doctor's concern and assistance. Medically speaking he was a big help. As for Samuel's own heart and conscience, they remained weighted under a heavy burden.

Losing Anna was like losing the music of life. The score had been too short. The days now moved like a fast march, but the nights alone in First House were as mournful as a dirge.

At one of Vierling's lowest ebbs, Koehler happened by for a visit. "Sam, is your grief still so heavy?"

"Daniel. If only I hadn't married her. Maybe she'd still be alive today."

"The Lord's Will be done."

"But did I follow the Lord's Will? Didn't you come here yourself and tell me the Conferenz wanted and the *lot* approved Martha Miksch for my wife?"

"You had a right to make your own decision. And the Lord did approve of Anna. You must not torment yourself."

"I did love her. And our baby. Our beautiful little girl. Who'll mother her now?"

"Yes, you will have to make plans for her."

"I'll think about it later."

During the summer, the epidemic ended in Salem although it continued in some of the villages. Koehler talked with the Conferenz about Vierling's situation, especially the need of a mother for the baby. No one could propose a suitable sister for a wife for him. Marshall remembered Vierling's outburst at the suggestion of Martha's name two years ago; therefore, he could not suggest her again to the doctor, although he stated to the Conferenz she would still be well qualified for his wife.

Koehler asked if they should send to Bethlehem for a sister to marry Vierling. The Conferenz agreed that this would be the best solution, but they decided to wait until the epidemic was under control throughout Wachovia.

Meanwhile, Vierling attended to his patients in the daytime and worked in the apothecary shop at night. One evening as he finished checking the patients in the sisters and brothers houses, he realized he needed some thyme and decided to stop at Miksch's nursery on his way home. The evening was warm and still fairly light.

Reaching Miksch's fence, he recalled that Matthew had told him once that he could go in the back to get what he needed. He was reluctant to go into the shop, being it was past business hours, so he pushed the yard gate open and went in. He walked on back to the nursery and opened that gate also. He closed it rather than letting it slam shut.

The doctor stood a moment taking in the neat garden plots and herb beds. Well-tended he thought.

Above the green, grape arbor and the honeysuckle-covered fence, the sky blazed as if it were a symphony of color: clear blue overall with a fiery red center and rays of lavender dotted with pink clouds like notes.

He had not seen a view so breathtaking since leaving Germany. His heart was flooded with a sense of awe at the beauty. He stood still for a long time, admiring the spectacular sight, which in itself began to pierce his taut muscles, soothe the heavy heart and unlock a guarded mind.

Slowly, he became aware of sounds from the potting shed. He called, "Matthew?" and strode down the path.

"He's not here," answered a feminine voice.

Vierling slowed his steps. He saw Martha standing in the shed. "I'm sorry. I thought Matthew might be back here. I came to get some thyme."

"He left early for service. I'll get it for you. Did you want plants or . . ."

"No. Only cuttings."

She took a paper and shears from the shelf and walked over to the thyme bed. She knelt in the path, laid the paper beside her, then leaned over to cut some sprigs.

"Does your father keep this by himself?"

"Mostly. I help when I can."

"Do you like this work?"

"Yes. When I was little it used to be my favorite place to come." She paused a moment and said almost wistfully, "It still is."

Samuel knelt beside her; he placed his hand on the thyme cuttings. She added another sprig to the group.

Glancing up at him, she asked softly, "Is that enough?"

"Yes."

"I never had an opportunity to say this before, but I was so saddened about Anna."

Their hands were close over the thyme, but neither moved.

"Oh, Martha, if only I could tell you. Tell you of my sin," he spoke with anguish. "My heart carries such a heavy burden."

"She was happy. You gave her so much."

"No, no, you don't understand. I have sinned. Can you forgive me?"

She reached over the short span that separated them and covered his hand with hers. Quietly, she asked, "Has God forgiven you?"

Amazed and instantly relieved, he declared, "Yes."

"Then I can, too." She was not sure what there was to forgive, but she was pleased to see that he appeared happier. She lifted her hand from his.

He stood up, then inquired with apparent interest. "Do you miss the schoolwork?"

"I miss the children and I really enjoyed teaching." She rose, too, and handed him the thyme.

"Tell your father I'll settle with him later." He spun around and walked rapidly up the path.

Martha returned the shears to the shed, tied a few long stems of mint together and hung them from the roof. The sun was close to the horizon, soon to sink from view. She knew she'd be late for service if she didn't hurry. Inside the house, Maria was ready. Martha washed her hands and changed aprons quickly.

"It's good there are no sick sisters," Martha commented.

Throughout the service, Martha kept going over the conversation with Dr. Vierling in the garden, and wondering what he meant by his sin and asking her forgiveness. No matter how hard she searched her memory, no revelations came to her.

A few evenings later, Dr. Vierling was driving home from Bethania after seeing some patients, he hoped the last of those with scarlet fever. The disease certainly seemed to be on the wane. He had wanted to get back to town early enough to stop by to see his daughter, Maria Rosina. Now it would be too late. She would be asleep and he didn't like to disturb her rest. She would be a year old next month. The idea rather startled him. Somehow he always thought of her as his six-month old daughter, the age she was when Anna died. No, he wouldn't see Maria tonight. He'd go on home. Home. The word rang about as empty as the house sounded these days. He thought how nice it would be to be returning to light and laughter, fresh cooked food and a sweet wife and a warm touch.

The memory of Martha's hand comfortingly on his rushed to the surface. Had Martha changed? She seemed so kind, so soft in the nursery. And in the Sisters House, she had worked miracles at calming patients. She did care for children. Why hadn't he seen that the first day in Salem when she was running after the little redheaded girl? She would make a good mother.

By Jove, that was his answer! He sat up straight, clicked to his horse, which broke into a trot. Sam hummed as he bounced all the way to Salem.

CHAPTER TWENTY-FIVE

The next morning after a hastily prepared breakfast, Sam Vierling mixed a few medicines in the apothecary, then he headed for the Gemeinhaus at nine o'clock, the time he knew the weekly Altestan Conferenz would be in session.

The conference room door was closed; he knocked, a voice replied "enter" and he did.

Bishop Koehler, sitting at the head of the table, spoke. "Welcome, brother. I hope you bear good news that the epidemic is about to come to an end."

"I think I can safely say that. There are still a few cases in Bethania and Friedland, but I've heard of no new ones yesterday or today."

The Conferenz members murmured appreciatively to each other.

"I came about another matter."

"Yes?"

"I would like to ask for one of the single sisters to be my wife."

"Whom did you wish to suggest?"

"Martha Miksch."

The uttered name for an instant froze the members; it was completely unexpected.

Marshall recovered first. "Has this been mentioned to anyone else?"

"No, sir. I decided last evening that I need a wife and my daughter needs a mother."

"Brother Vierling, we'll discuss this and will contact you later about the decision," Koehler said.

"Thank you. I'll be in the apothecary all morning unless someone calls me elsewhere." His manner and his statement precluded any doubt of the doctor's expectation that the discussion and process would be immediately on their agenda. With a nod, he left the room.

Sister Marshall spoke up. "This is certainly a surprise, but a pleasant one."

"Yes indeed. It will save his having to go to Pennsylvania for a bride," remarked Benzien.

Koehler offered, "Since this was put to the lot two years ago, I do not see a need to resort to it again. Do any of you?"

Everyone agreed to let the previous answer of the lot stand.

Sister Benzien said solemnly, "The Lord's Will, is to be carried out after all."

Marshall held his thoughts private. "Matthew and Traugott, strange mates for grandfathers of the same child. Never were there two men so at odds in business – both so determined and so dogged. Two personalities that never sought to harmonize – two minds that never traveled the same route, and Martha in the middle. It will not be an easy road. What a testing of her raising it will be – to weave together all these cross threads and make a smooth fabric. My prayers will be with you Martha Miksch. Martha Miksch Vierling he added, because he felt certain she would say *ja* as had the drawn lot reed.

After Conferenz meeting adjourned, Koehler once again made his way to First House.

"Sam, the Conferenz has approved your proposal to marry Martha Miksch."

"Fine."

"I'll go now to talk with Matthew and Maria."

"Thank you, Daniel. I'll wait for the answer." His firm voice and direct stare into Daniel's eyes were indicative of one who expects to hear results quickly.

Koehler deduced as he walked the block to Miksch's shop that Samuel Vierling was a man of few words when he had definite plans in mind. He never heard a man state a case or issue a plea so concisely, conveying all the urgency of a fire marshal at a major burning. He wondered if it was the personality of the man or the force of his energy or only the nature of the request, which always loomed major that stirred others to action.

How would Martha react to this strong personality, to this very confident man? Koehler knew women liked Vierling, especially the single sisters. He was a committed Moravian, which everyone in the Wachovia area related to, well educated that elicited confidence in his professional services, a good musician that bespoke a man of artistic dimension, healthy and strong in physical aspects coupled with gentleness when called for and surprising good humor except during the recent severe epidemic and personal lost.

At this mental delving into Samuel traits, Koehler pondered could any of the single sisters stand up to this commanding type of individual day in and day out? Vierling had been tender with Anna . . . her frailness had called for that. But Martha? – her heartiness doesn't require a light touch. Ah well, he trusted that her years of discipline in the choirs would be balanced by the years of command as a teacher and that she could fill the demanding job that was to be hers, if she agreed to the marriage.

Entering the yellow house, Koehler could see Maria and Martha shredding cabbage for kraut in the kitchen. The late morning was hot and the door had been left open.

"Good morning, sisters."

Maria wiped her hands as she rose from the bench. "Good day. What can we do for you?"

"I came to talk to you, Maria, and to Matthew about an important matter. Is he at home?"

"He's in the manufactory. Martha, can you run get him? And then, dear, you can pull some onions from the garden while you're outside."

Martha put down the kraut cutter, cleaned her hands and went out the back door.

Matthew joined Koehler and Maria in the front room within a few minutes. They were seated so Matthew sat down, too.

"Martha said you had an important matter to discuss, Bishop."

"Yes. Martha's name has been proposed for marriage by Brother Vierling."

"And the elders and the lot approved," Maria said more than asked.

"Yes, Sister Maria."

Maria looked at Matthew and nodded yes. Matthew gave her his customary approving nod in return. To Koehler, he said, "Her mother and I also give our approval." He did not wish to appear eager, so he added, "Of course, we'll need to ask Martha."

"Matthew, since she's not living at the choir house currently, I feel it would be in order for you to discuss this with her." Koehler decided.

"Thank you, I'll be giving you an answer soon."

"Good. I hope you two are enjoying better health these days?"

"We're slowing down, but we still manage to get along all right."

"Will you have to make other plans, if Martha leaves?"

"She's helped us catch up things around here. But we'll see how it goes later," Maria answered.

"Well, take care of yourselves," Koehler said before bidding them goodbye.

Maria asked, "Do you want us to ask her together? Now?"

Matthew stroked his chin, meditating a moment. "Yes. She should be back in with those onions soon."

"It'll be hard to lose her again. This leaving should be different, for awhile anyway. She won't be restricted to a schedule as rigid as the school position. A married daughter! Why do you realize, Matthew, that she will be in my choir?"

"Yes. You'll get to see more of her, even sit with her at services. As we get older, it might be nice to have a doctor in the family."

"And Matthew, you could help him with the gardening."

"Remember, I've been letting some of that go. If it comes to a decision between herbs and vegetables, which do you think we should stick to?"

Maria leaned over the arm of the chair, listening. "I believe she's coming in."

Martha entered the kitchen and dropped an apron load of onions into a basket by the door.

"Martha, come in here a minute," Matthew called.

She walked in, shaking out her apron. "Well, I guess I'll smell like onions the rest of the day."

Maria reached out and patted her daughter's hand. "Martha, we want to talk with you. Sit down."

Martha looked at her parents and sat in a straight chair.

Matthew put his fingers together over his rotund stomach. "Bishop Koehler came to bring us a proposal of marriage to you from Dr. Vierling."

Martha's mouth dropped, her eyes widened. She tried to answer, but couldn't.

Maria said, "This comes as a surprise, doesn't it?"

All Martha could manage was a nod.

Her mother continued, "Do you think you could be happy with Dr. Vierling? He seems to be a fine man. He's a good doctor, quite self-confident, that helps his patients. I've never heard anyone speak unkindly of him."

As her mother talked, Martha regained her poise. She glanced at her father. He showed no emotion. They had not spoken of Dr. Vierling for two years and he was not going to bring up the past now. More than ever she appreciated his keeping her confidences.

"Mama, I promised you and father a long time ago that I would let you arrange this for me." Then she quickly added, "And if you approve, I will accept."

"I have faith in the ministers' decisions and the lot. Your work in the sick room and your experience in the garden, both should be helpful to you as a doctor's wife," Maria surmised.

Matthew peered intently at Martha and spoke carefully. "Your years as a teacher should be helpful in raising children. You realize you'll be starting out as a wife and a mother?"

"Why she will!" Maria ejected. "Let's see, the baby should be about a year old."

Somehow Martha hadn't reckoned with that thought, that idea or that future. That immediate future. Now she was pensive. Maria Rosina would be there. Every day. Every evening. She was familiar only with girls a few years older than one year. A child took time to raise to be the obedient student that teachers were rewarded to have in class. There would be so much for her to learn. How to dress and bathe a one year old? What to feed her? Not to speak of how does a single sister transpose herself after a few words, sacred words, that joined her before the congregation and the world to a brother, a married brother? In her case she would be joined to a previously married brother.

What did she know about taking care of a husband? Trying to be rational, she admitted she was aware of what her mother did for her father: laundry, mending, cleaning, keeping the shop tidy and well stocked. But what was she to do about relating otherwise to a man as a wife? Her duties to him were completely mysterious. How would she learn those? Just the mental questions had her fearful she was blushing and she deliberately tucked her chin close to her bodice.

Maria rustled her apron and skirts and stood up. Her steps toward the kitchen were audible, as were the scrapings of chair legs as Matthew rose and shuffled his hard-soled shoes across the wooden floor after her. They were permitting her freedom of space to coincide with her liberty of choice.

Martha had accepted that she would be told what she was to do and only the topics her parents, teachers and ministers considered proper for her to learn were introduced. Vaguely, she knew about women and babies, but she had an inkling that there was more to be known. The single sisters, especially those who grew up as she had as an only child, were innocent of male behavior at any age. Their school and work experience, as well as the seating in the saal, was separate. She had known no other way of life. She accepted whole-heartily the Moravian customs.

A small sigh escaped the narrow space between her lips. Her thumbs rubbed across the tips of her fingers. She was a person who touched, who had to experience learning with the sense of feeling through her hands. Only this rubbing was flesh to flesh and produced strange sensations as she tried to envision life with Samuel. She stopped the motions, uncurled her fingers, shot them straight, erect, and then laid them on her apron. They were restless fingers that began to cross her apron, back and forth, side to side until she was massaging her thighs. To control her movements she brought one hand on top of the other and willed them to rest.

She as much thought as experienced another strong sense of gathering information; it smelled. Sniffing, her mouth turned up in a chiding smile. Now my hands and apron bear the scent of onions. Two hands, one on the other. What image coupled with that? The nursery and Dr. Vierling and her hand on his. He had not objected. He had not remained silent. And the thyme? Surely, that fragrance was stronger than onion. It had been on both their hands. He had begged her forgiveness and she experienced the moment his conscience cleared.

Why, worrying was not needful! Each day, every encounter would offer an opportunity to respond to him and he to her. Learning how to be a wife would be her life. Together they would understand their roles in each other's space and calling. She may still bump into him as she carried out her duties and he would be forgiving. And she knew she would have the patience to adjust to his expectations and needs.

She sighed again; this time with her face relaxed, her lips were more fully parted. The sound brought Maria and Matthew into the room. As she remained seated, they took their former chairs. Her eyes remained on her hands in her lap, but her chin was lifted. Martha allowed a short space of time to absorb her precious revelations rising from the hands, thyme and nursery exchange. The warmth of happiness she had experienced when she first met Samuel and the surety of wanting to live her life with him which she made known immediately to her father – all that enveloped her and she knew she was blessed. She had her answer now.

"Father," she looked directly at him, "if it's the Lord's Will that I marry Dr. Vierling, then it must be the Lord's Will I raise his daughter. I accept those responsibilities."

Matthew scrutinized her expression. He saw the rosy complexion, sparkling eye, positive demeanor that he had seen when she told him her wish two years ago. He smiled at her and clasped the arms of his chair saying, "Then I'll tell the Bishop tonight. Now I'll go back to the manufactory. I suppose you two have much to talk about."

Maria with a slight scowl declared, "Why wait, Matthew? It's not noon yet."

Matthew said as he walked to Martha. "Right, you are. Why delay?" He bent and hugged Martha. She stood up and gave him an affectionate hug.

Maria said, "We may as well finish the cabbage while we talk."

Matthew chuckled as he stepped toward the back door. His nose twitched. "Don't forget to fix those onions!"

The women laughed happily.

And happy is the only word to describe the Miksch family in the days that followed. The betrothal was announced the day after Martha accepted the proposal. Martha and Maria were busy with well wishers and with putting Martha's things in order. For the first time Martha appreciated her mother's insistence that she spin while she could. The linens had been woven and now they spent long hours cutting out and sewing undergarments, a gown, an apron, a haube and pillow slips. With winter coming Maria wanted Martha to make a new dress, but Martha decided to save the wool to determine if it were needed around First House.

"Mama, what about the blue ribbons?"

"I have some new ones – put away for this day." From the bottom of her old trunk Maria produced a card wrapped many times with the married sister's blue cording and ribbon.

Martha unwound the ribbon. "I'll press it. Are we going to have anything special like a love feast, or people to supper when I get married?"

"It would be nice to have the people who've helped us in the saal all these years."

"And the single sisters."

"Of course, we'd have to invite all our old friends from town and Bethabara. They've known you all of your life."

"What about the musicians that Dr. Vierling plays with?"

"Yes, my dear, and he probably has many other close contacts we don't know about."

"That's too many people isn't it?"

"I believe it is. Anyway they will all be there to see you married."

Dr. Vierling walked home from service one night with the Mikschs and Matthew invited him in. Vierling accepted. Maria prepared a cool mint drink and set out a plate of sugar cake. She asked if there was any thing he especially needed in his house that Martha could bring.

"Thank you, nothing I know of right now. I'm sure she'll see things, but I'll let her take care of that."

"Then we'll wait until she asks before sending any items except her clothes and linens. We could send them the day after the wedding," Matthew responded.

"Good," Samuel said. "By the way, Martha, Brother and Sister Koehler have invited us for breakfast on the ninth. I trust it was agreeable that I accepted."

"Yes, of course."

"A sister is cleaning the house tomorrow while I go to Bethania. I trust you will find it to your liking."

"I'm sure I will."

"Dr. Vierling," Matthew started, but Vierling interrupted. "My family always called me Sam."

"Sam," Matthew resumed, "Maria and I would like to give you something for your marriage. Our material means are limited, but we would like for Martha to have our house, the manufactory or the profit from both and of course, lot improvements, when our need for them is over. We would appreciate your handling this for her, for the both of you."

"That's generous. I'll do the best I can with it," he said as he visually surveyed the house.

"It's not large, but it's well built. The location is good for a trade," Maria pointed out. "It's old, but it's comfortable."

Sam laughed as he stretched and stood up. "It's not as old as First House, is it?"

Matthew chuckled, "Not quite."

Sam turned to Martha. "I may not see you before the service of the ninth. I'm riding to the villages to check on all the patients, then perhaps I won't be called away that day," he said with a warm smile. He left and walked up the street to his house.

On the morning of the wedding, Martha washed her long blond hair and rinsed it in rosemary water. Though the herb was generally used by brunettes, she preferred its fragrance, and the sentiment of remembrance. Surely one's wedding day was one to be remembered.

She sat on the back steps in the warm August sunshine and combed the damp locks. Maria paused in the doorway and watched.

"Martha, I gather that you'll go straight to Sam's house after the service."

"He didn't say, but if it's all cleaned up, I reckon so. How will I get my night gown up there?" she suddenly asked.

"Um. Let's see? I know. Some of the married choir are taking food up there, so you won't have to cook much for a couple of days. I'll take your gown to someone with my own basket of things."

"Mama, could you please put my linen dress in, too? I'd rather not wear the white one to the breakfast with the Koehlers tomorrow."

"Yes."

"Thank you for that and everything else." She sighed and looked past the apple tree to the nursery.

"Not having any doubts, are you, dear?"

"No. I was thinking how happy I have been here. I thought I'd be sad at leaving, but I'm not. It's strange, for I really don't feel like I'm leaving for good. I anticipate the yellow house and the nursery will always be here for me to come back to."

Maria sniffed the air then cried out. "I forgot the meat while I was talking on and on." She grabbed a poker, pulled the big pot away from the fire and pushed the lid ajar. After investigating the beef roast she exclaimed, "Well, it didn't burn, but almost!"

She lifted the meat onto a platter to cool. Later, she cut the roast in half: one part for their lunch and supper; the other, to go to First House. The half to go she packed in a new basket (one of her small gifts to Martha); then added a crock of pickles, several apples, buns and a wedge of cheese. She covered the basket with a new linen hand towel on which she had embroidered MMV.

About that time, Matthew came into the kitchen and offered to take the basket up the street.

"Thank you, dear," she said gratefully. "I didn't know it would be so heavy."

He started out the back door. She was curious why he didn't go out the front way. She watched him as he stopped at the manufactory door, reach in, get something, wedge it into the basket and proceed around the side of the house.

Maria fixed an early cold supper. She was thankful not to have to stand over a hot fire on such a warm evening. They ate as usual in the kitchen. They were silent, as each realized this would be the last meal together as this close family of three.

Martha started to help clear up, but Maria stopped her saying she'd do it.

Martha ran upstairs. She took her time washing up, then put on the borrowed white dress, and her own new apron and haube. She tied the pink ribbons in the neatest bows possible. Tomorrow, she would change to the blue ribbons.

Her parents walked with her to the saal; each took a seat in his own choir section. Martha found it difficult to keep her mind on the minister's text. Finally he finished and the congregation stood and sang. After they were re-seated, Bishop Koehler called Martha and Sam to the front. He united them in a service of marriage and asked the congregation to remember them in their prayers. Following the benediction, many people came forward to speak to Martha and Sam.

Though the scene was a blur to Martha, somehow she vaguely felt somebody was missing. Her eyes scanned the saal. She realized who was missing – the Bagge family. She wondered if Brother Bagge was away on a business trip.

However Martha's happiness was of such magnitude she did not dwell on the absence, or on anything other than the thought, "I'm married Sister Martha Vierling. It's really happening to me."

As the crowd dwindled, Sam turned and shook hands with Daniel. The latter said, "We'll be looking forward to seeing you in the morning at eight o'clock."

"We'll be here," Sam replied and faced Martha who was waiting at this side. "Shall we go?"

Together they walked out of the saal and up the street. Martha noticed Sam took the street toward the graveyard, thus they would not pass her parents' home. Reaching the crown of the hill, Sam stopped.

"This is about the highest place in town. Do you like the view from here?" he asked abruptly.

Somewhat startled, she answered, "Yes, when the leaves are off the trees, you can see most of Salem."

"I like that. I like to live on a high place. This is where we'll build our house someday."

Martha looked around in the dark of night. She could vaguely make out the outline of the fruit trees in Yarrell's orchard. "A house in an orchard. How nice that would be with so many fragrances, and so very practical."

"That's a long way, away. First House will serve us for many years. But someday, we'll live here."

Martha trembled inside. Something about his vibrant self-confidence caused an excitement to flow through her. "What fun it's going to be to learn the various qualities of this man!" she mused to herself.

Sam took her arm and guided her down the steep hill to Main Street and First House. He unlocked the front door, entered first and lit a candle with a spark from a tender box. He returned to the front door and lighted the way to the left for Martha. She had never been here before, but in the dimness she could see that it was cozy with simple, but nice furnishings.

"This is your new home, Sister Vierling," Sam proclaimed then laughed. "Well, hardly new, but anyway home."

He opened the door leading to a room directly beyond. It was the bedroom. Martha recognized the curtains with the handmade embroidery immediately. She turned her head quickly, determined not to think of Anna just yet. On the foot of the double bed she saw her linen dress on top of which were the smoothly pressed blue ribbons. And her nightgown.

He held the lantern high as he walked further backward to the kitchen. The table was neatly covered with baskets and food containers.

"Look at all the gifts, Sam," she marveled and drew closer to inspect. "People surely have been cooking for days."

He moved to the door that led to the front of the house. "And this," he said grandly, "is my work room."

"The apothecary?" she guessed.

"Indeed." He set the candle down on a stool and stood back for her surveillance.

Her face glowed with excitement as she examined the rows of bottles, the table with scales and apparatus for measuring medicines, the glass beakers gleaming on the high shelves.

"Sam, it's so fascinating: everything is shining." She knew that he was most proud of the shop. She asked as if to get procedures straight from the beginning. "Am I to be allowed in this room?"

"No place in your home should be off limits. Come in when you need something or whenever you like."

He was leaning back on one of the high worktables, looking at her intently. When she was aware of his gaze, she lowered her eyes and felt her skin turn hot, knowing, too, it must be red.

"I never thought I'd see you blush. You are feminine after all."

She raised her eyes.

"Remember the first day I saw you, my first day in Salem? You came colliding into me? I thought then, you were not like any sister I'd seen before. The ones in Europe had been so calm, so reserved. And here you ran flying down the street. You also spoke right up to a stranger."

Martha's heart pounded inside her tight white bodice.

Sam pushed himself effortlessly away from the table and in a few steps stood directly in front of her. "What do you look like with your cap off, Martha?"

Nervously, she reached up and untied the ribbon ends, pulled them from the loops and put the ribbon in her pocket. She caught the haube from the front and pulled backwards slowly, and off. The two heavy braids fell to her back.

"How does your hair look unbraided?"

She pulled a braid forward, untied the cloth strip at the end and with practiced graceful movements unbraided her long blonde hair. It tumbled in waves over and around a shoulder and almost reached her waist. Likewise, she freed the other braid. With both sides loose and shimmering in the candlelight, she stood still, looking at him, waiting for him to speak.

He was silent while appraising this new image. She said, "I usually sleep with it braided so it won't be tangled in the morning."

"Not tonight. Leave it loose. Martha, you're beautiful," he spoke tenderly as he reached out and ran his hands through the long locks and down the long waves. He bent his head and kissed her hair. She tilted her head back and he kissed her forehead and then her mouth. First, softly, then eagerly and forcefully. Her response equaled his ardor. He swooped her up in his arms as if she were a treasure to hold close to his heart, light in weight but solid in value. Effortlessly he leaned over and blew out the candle. He needed no light to make his way to the bedroom.

The next morning, Martha awoke around six o'clock. Sam was still asleep. She lay without moving in the bed for some time, looking at Sam and the room. After awhile she crawled out of bed. She was noiseless as she tiptoed over to the chair where her clothes were.

She dropped her gown to the floor then put on her camisole, her drawers, her white stockings, her full slip that hung from her waist to her ankles. Next she donned her white cotton blouse before stepping into her linen skirt and pulling on her bodice which had been dyed in the same batch of pokeberry so they matched perfectly. She laced the blue narrow cord up the front of the bodice. She looked about for the haube. Upon realizing it must be in the apothecary, she padded softly in her stocking feet to the door, eased it open, and closed it carefully behind her.

She picked up the cap from the floor and threaded the new blue ribbon through one loop. She carried it to the kitchen with her, all the while shaking her hair. She smoothed it as best she could with her hands.

At the food-laden table, she stopped to inspect what was on hand. Moving a tall basket in the center, she uncovered a clay pot with a small plant. Before even touching a needle or taking a sniff, she knew it to be rosemary – and from her father. Intuition told her, too, it was from his nursery. "How thoughtful he was to select this," she smiled. "I'll keep it here on the table until spring, then I'll plant it outside."

She realized that she was hungry and breakfast would be late. She found some butter in a crock and her mother's buns. As she ate, she decided she'd have to ask Sam if there was a place in the cellar for butter and other food storage.

Just as she was finishing her bun, Sam opened the bedroom door. He was dressed and looked fully awake.

"Morning. Are you having breakfast?" he inquired.

"A sampling. Can I get you something?"

"Any preserves for those rolls?"

"Surely there must be. There's everything else," she said while searching under the napkins. "Here's some peach, and some grape and pear preserves. Which do you prefer?"

"Pear."

While she spread the preserves, she asked, "Are there arrangements in the cellar for food storage?"

"Yes. Come along and I'll show you now." He opened a door she hadn't seen before.

She handed him the roll. "Wait a minute. Let's take the butter." She picked up a crock and followed him down the steep steps, holding her skirt and the crock with one hand and the stair rail with the other.

"What a large cellar. It's almost half filled."

"It is. I don't care for cellars; they're too damp. Try not to store anymore than necessary down here."

He opened the back door to the outside. "Come along. The horse may need some oats."

She walked beside him down the deep lot. She had to hold her skirt because of the early morning dew. She took a deep breath when they stopped.

"Doesn't it smell deliciously fragrant early in the morning? The world is so fresh. Why you could almost see father's back lot if it weren't for the few trees," she vowed as she stood on her toes and looked down the slope.

Sam opened the door to the small stable and let the horse out. He got some oats from a big bin and threw them in the feed box in the stall.

"I thought horses ate the meadow grass," she said.

"Oh, they eat that, but they need some grain also. But you're a town girl and don't know about such things," he teased.

"I never had a chance to ride a horse growing up. By the time I joined the sisters choir, the Conferenz had decided to sell the sidesaddle. The opinion was that the sisters rode too often. Really though, I'm a little afraid of them. They're so big."

"Likely as not, if you run after her to catch her, she'll run from you." Sam nodded toward the horse.

Pointing to a small building a few paces from the stable, she asked, "That was Dr. Bonn's old laboratory, wasn't it?"

"I hear it was. It hasn't been used for so long that it's not in good condition now."

"Are you going to repair it?"

"No. I can do my work in the shop."

"Sam, how did you come to Salem?"

"Wachovia needed a doctor and I was called."

"How did you decide to be a doctor?"

"My mother and father wanted all of their children to work in some field of service to people. As we delved into the requirements for many professions, and as I advanced in school, we agreed that medicine would be my field."

"Did you want to leave Germany?"

"I never had any thoughts of leaving Germany. I loved my family, my friends, my life. I would have been happy to have stayed there."

"Then why. . . ?"

"Why? Because this is where I'm needed. You've been a Moravian longer than I have, Martha. Surely you realize that we must be ready to go wherever there's work to be done."

"Yes, I know. Both mother and father came from Germany, too. And they've stayed. But some of the early people – even the ministers now – move around."

"Well, doctors usually stay in one place."

"Is Berlin a big city?"

"Very large. Martha, I'm here now, that is all in my past. Let's not talk further about it."

She looked into his eyes and read that this statement was uttered in his direct manner and carried no emotional overtones.

With this understanding of the man she married, she accepted with an open heart that the present was their time and their life. There was no baggage to transport into these days or their relationship. He held her gaze and witnessed his message had been received, accepted and appreciated. In return his expression portrayed *thank you*, warmth, and the seed of love. The latter attribute she could not name, she had not met it before. Her eyes sparkled, her face softened and mouth opened in a smile.

He thrust a hand toward her. As she instantly placed a hand in his palm, he closed his fingers tightly around it. His long forearm pulled her close to his side, as close as customary and permitted in the community.

"Do you think it's time we should get ready for the Gemeinhaus breakfast?" She spoke with excitement.

"Yes."

Martha, who always walked fast, had to almost run to match Sam's long strides up the sloping meadow. She struggled to keep with one free hand her long skirts above the high, damp grass.

Inside, she cleaned off her shoes and shook a few clinging dewdrops from her dress. Suddenly she put her hands to her head and giggled.

"What?" asked Sam.

"I was remembering how Mama never let me go out without a cap."

"You're so pretty without it, I hope you won't wear it in the house or backyard."

He moved closer and stroked her hair and quickly bent and kissed her.

Caught off balance, she reeled slightly and his arms caught her around the waist. Instinctively she put her arms around his neck and lifted her face. She enjoyed the close embrace so much she was reluctant to be released or to leave the house. After several minutes, they separated and she went into the bedroom to braid her hair and put her cap and apron on.

Breakfast with the Koehlers proved to be an enjoyable meal

and the first one at which Martha ever remembered having a serving girl present. She was one of the single sisters that Martha recognized and spoke to genially.

As the four partook a leisurely second cup of coffee, Daniel and Sam began to discuss some new church music, which had recently arrived from Europe. Sister Koehler used the opportunity to talk about the married choir with Martha.

"You'll find a few changes now, Sister Vierling." The name was used to allow Martha's hearing it in the smaller grouping before it would be called out among a number of people. She watched Martha's expression and approved the composed countenance while the new name registered with her. "For instance, you can walk up Main Street. You don't have to take Church Street to and from shops."

At this statement, Sister Koehler noticed the young guest's slight smile. Her puzzled look prompted Martha to say, "I've always lived on Main Street so I've traveled it more often than not. But it's pleasing to know I can walk it again."

"You can also go into the shops unescorted, though of course discretion will always be expected of all our sisters. I understand you did not assist your parents in the tobacco shop?"

"No."

"There will probably be times when your husband will be away and people may come into the apothecary; and you'll have to converse with them. This will be proper."

"I'll serve those who come to us in anyway I can," Martha promised.

"Martha, life as a doctor's wife will not be as routine or uneventful as that of say, some of the tradesmen. Your meals, your sleep, your household work are all subject to interruption. He may be busy healing people when you wish he were repairing something in the house."

"Thank you for pointing all of this out to me." After a moment, she asked, "Isn't a pastor's wife like this, too?"

"How perceptive you are. Yes, very much."

"Then might I ask one more question?"

"Yes."

"Have you found any helpful guidelines?"

"First, we look forward to serving others and whenever possible to serving together. We try not to let delays of time or materials discourage us from our ultimate goals."

The men had finished their conversation and were standing. Sister Koehler turned to them. "Is there anything else you would like? More coffee?"

Sam responded quickly. "Nothing, thank you. A delicious breakfast. Martha, are you ready? We should be going now."

Martha rose and thanked her host and hostess for their hospitality.

Outside the Gemeinhaus, Martha asked Sam, "Could we walk by Mama's house to ask someone to send up my trunk?"

"We can."

At the yellow house, they found Maria dusting the shop shelves. She smiled. "Well, look who's first in the shop today."

"Not customers though," Martha said. She greeted her mother with a hug and kiss.

"Good morning, Sam. How was the breakfast?"

"Fine. I hope Martha proves as good a cook."

"Is Father here? I wanted to have my trunk sent up."

"He's in the manufactory."

"Does he have Brother Triebel's old handcart?"

"I think so."

"If he has, I can manage the trunk," Sam injected. "I'll go check with him."

After Sam left, Martha asked, "Did you bring it downstairs?"

"We did. It's in the kitchen by the side wall."

"Mama, thanks for the meat. I had a roll and butter this morning early. Shall I return the basket?"

Sam reentered by the back door. He grabbed one end of the old trunk and pulled it across the floor and into the hall. Martha hastened to open the front door. Matthew was just stopping the handcart outside. Sam pushed the trunk onto the cart and Matthew rolled it away from the door so they could come down the steps.

Maria walked out into the walkway with them.

Martha turned to her parents and said, "We'll manage it. Please, you two come to see us and the house soon."

Maria nodded. "We'll give you time to unpack."

Martha looked fondly at them. "How about tomorrow afternoon for tea? We have so much food to share."

Matthew accepted for them both.

As Sam pushed the cart easily up the street, Martha marveled at her husband's strength. She was so proud to be walking with him. After Sam heaved the trunk into First House, he left Martha to unpack in the bedroom and he went into the apothecary.

She hummed a few of her favorite hymns as she took out her linens and clothing and folded them to fit on the two empty shelves in the clothes press. Her kettle and mugs from her choir room she set on the table in the kitchen.

She returned to the bedroom and sat down in the rocker. As she slowly surveyed the room, she began to realize something was missing. "What is it," she kept repeating to herself? "What is it?" As she rocked, she sought an answer to the question.

It may have been the rhythm of the rocking for in an instant it came to her . . . the baby. Maria Rosina was missing. Sam hadn't mentioned her. Oh, how grateful she was that he let her have one night as a bride without being a mother. Oh, God, I pray it's not a sin to want many nights like that with my husband. Now she debated whether or not she should go right in to ask Sam about the baby, or should she wait until he said something? Maybe he was waiting for her to say something. No, it was his baby. His relationship had priority. But now, she was his wedded helpmate and that meant to her responsibilities.

After much inward discussion, she resolved to make her willingness known, yet leave the decision to him. She pushed the empty trunk near the door and entered the apothecary. He was absorbed in reading a book.

She waited silently until he came to a stopping place before she said, "Sam, I don't see any of the baby's things around?"

"No, they're where she staying."

"Whenever you want to bring her home, Sam, we can go for her."

He closed his book with a snap of a hand and slapped his knee with the other hand. "By Jove! What a jewel. A bride one day and ready for family duties the next."

He jumped up and gave her a resounding kiss. "Let's go get her now!"

"Now?"

"Yes." He led her out of the house. "Let's take the handcart." He pushed it cheerfully in front of him as they walked down the street to the Sampson's house.

Inside the house, Sister Sampson was alone with the baby. All of her children were in school or had gone into apprenticeships.

"Well, I never expected you so soon after the service. Didn't you want a day or two to get settled, Martha?" Sister Sampson peered curiously at Martha.

Before Martha could reply, Sam spoke. "Sister Sampson, we've really appreciated your excellent care of Maria Rosina, but there's an empty spot in our house waiting for her."

Maria Rosina was crawling around on the floor, circling Sister Sampson's skirts.

Martha spoke softly to the baby, but refrained from trying to pick her up, deciding it would be best to wait until they were home.

"I was about to feed her," the redheaded sister said. "I'll show you her things. While you load up, I'll feed her so you won't have to do that at home as soon as she gets in."

"A sound idea," Sam agreed and followed her into another room.

Martha thought, "I never dreamed he'd act so quickly on my offer. What will I do with her? My little girls at school were at least three years old." Her eyes turned toward the low burning fire in the open fireplace. Fright filled Martha as she wondered how one keeps a baby out of the fireplace.

Her frightened expression drew an immediately response from Sister Sampson as she re-entered the kitchen. "What is it, Martha?"

"The fireplace – the fire! How do you keep a baby from crawling right in?"

"From the first day a baby gets down on the floor, you have to be almost heartless and really let her know that it is off-limits."

"You mean spank a baby?"

Sister Sampson laughed good-naturedly as she scooped up Maria Rosina and sat down in a chair with the little one on her lap. "If necessary, yes. You can take no chance that she'll learn about the danger of fire from experience."

Martha watched as the older sister skillfully fed the baby. It was a pleasure to see that this girl was a happy little one, who appeared to have a good appetite.

"There's much I need to learn," Martha admitted.

"You'll catch on quickly. You surely did well with my girls in school."

"Thank you."

"Any time you need help, ask any of the married sisters, or call on your mother. If you like, I'll drop by on my way to the shops. But Martha, come to think of it, that may not be wise at first. This little honey knows me well. She might not want me to leave. I've tried to get her to call me sister. But she's heard the other children call me mama, so she tries to say that too."

Sister Sampson wiped Maria Rosina's mouth and put a cup to her lips. After the milk was finished, the mouth was dried again.

"Let me change her. She'll be ready to go down for a nap soon after you're back home." She carried the wiggling armful over to a wooden bench and laid her quickly but gently down.

Martha was amazed at how fast she removed the wet diaper

and put on a dry one. "I'll bring her other clothes to you after I've done the washing."

To the baby she said playfully, "Here we go little one, let's brush the dust off your dress. I'll miss you. And methinks you'll miss me too for awhile. Martha, doesn't she look like Dr. Vierling?"

Martha observed the baby closely. Yes, she thought, she does have Sam's healthy color and keen eyes. Her brown hair hung straight, not a hint of Anna's beautiful blonde curls.

"Yes, she does. She's quite a jolly Polly, isn't she?"

Sam popped back into the kitchen. "Who's a jolly Polly?" He covered the small room in a few steps and picked up his daughter who let out a gleeful sound.

Martha confessed. "I said the baby is quite a jolly Polly."

He tickled the baby and she laughed. "Yes, you are. You like the name? Well, Polly we will call you."

Martha said, "Thank you again, sister, for all you've done."

"It was a pleasure to be of service."

Sam carried the baby out the door and the women followed. He asked Polly, "Would you like to ride in the cart, Polly?"

"Oh, Sam, you do you think it's safe?" Martha asked anxiously.

"If you hold on to her hand as I push."

As the three Vierlings traveled up Main Street that sunny August morning, Sister Sampson said softly, "Good fortune to you, Martha. You'll have fun raising the child, but my prayers will be that you'll soon know the trob of your own baby."

CHAPTER TWENTY-SIX

Martha never anticipated problems. She pretty much took life as it came, as she had witnessed her father do. After a few days in First House, she never saw raising Polly as a problem or even adjusting to marriage as anything traumatic. She dealt with each small situation as it appeared, doing the best she could. Thus, she slept well at night. When a new day dawned, yesterday and its problems were past and not thought about again.

This approach to life continued concerning Sam's refusal to talk about his personal past. He clammed up when conversations drifted into inquiry in that direction, not because his history was one of shame, but believing those days had been lived and were over. She accepted his silence in this matter, and appreciated that traditional festal days appealed to Sam. He never missed the observance of any of them in a calendar year unless an emergency medical situation arose.

Martha learned these traits, as well as many more, about Sam that first year of her marriage. She had been raised under such frugal financial conditions that her new status loomed one of luxury; though it was far from that condition. Sam had a steady medical and apothecary practice and people paid as best they could. By continuing a careful watch on her spending habits and wasting nothing, and because Sam was thrifty in his personal accounts, they never were pressed financially.

The day when they brought Polly back to First House, Sam sent Martha to the dairy for fresh milk. He insisted that whenever possible the family should eat fresh foods including milk, fruit, vegetables and meat.

She soon learned that Sam could never turn down a call for help or never turn away a patient even though these patients had no place to go following treatment. When a patient was from another town or county, Sam found a place to lodge him. If all the usual lodging places were unavailable, Martha made a pallet on the floor of her front room.

When Martha became pregnant about seven months after her marriage, she was especially glad to have Sam around to explain every symptom and body change to her. She had never been around any pregnant women and was quite ignorant about the condition.

So on the eleventh of December, when she awoke in the early morning and experienced her first labor pain, she reached over and gently shook Sam. Instantly he opened his eyes.

"Sam, I just had a pain."

"Good. Are you all right otherwise?"

"I feel fine. What do you want for breakfast?"

"Make it something light. I don't want you to get too tired today."

Martha felt a warm glow at Sam's obvious concern for her. Although he was never uncaring or cold toward her, he had little sympathy for minor aches and pains. She understood without having discussed the safety of pregnancy with him that after Anna delivered and did not regain her strength and died of scarlet fever a few months later that he would have a deep personal interest in this childbirth.

During breakfast she had another pain. He watched her face as the muscles tensed, then relaxed.

"Martha, this could go on for several hours being it's your first baby. I'll stay around here as much as possible."

Martha cleared away the dishes. While she was dressing Polly, she had to stop twice due to labor pains.

"Mommy, put shoe on," Polly insisted as she stuck her chubby little foot out.

Finally, Martha got both shoes on Polly, who immediately ran over to her chair and yanked her doll up. "Mommy, dress the doll."

"Polly, dress the doll," Martha answered.

"No. Mommy do it," Polly sulked contrarily.

Martha shook her head. She thought how like a little cherub you are. I want to hold you and hug you. However, another hard pain tightened her abdomen.

"Put doll's coat on. We go out," Polly pleaded.

Martha decided that might be a good idea. "Polly, would you like to go to Grandmama's?"

"Yes, yes!" She jumped up and down and clapped her hands.

"You get your cape and I'll put it on you," Martha directed.

As Polly ran to the bedroom, Martha sought Sam in the apothecary. "Sam, the pains are coming more frequently. I'm going to walk Polly to Mama's. She can spend the day."

"Good thinking. You want me to walk with you?"

"No. I'll be right back."

Martha returned to the kitchen as Polly waddled in dragging her cape and little cap. Martha buttoned the former and tied the latter on Polly.

"Wrap the quilt around your doll. I'll get my cape. You kiss daddy goodbye."

Martha took a few moments to sweep her braids across the top of her head and pull her cap over them. She fastened her old cape and went to the front door. Sam and Polly met her in the little hall. He opened the door for them.

"Walk carefully," he cautioned her.

Polly heeded not the word walk. She ran a few steps, stopped to investigate the steps at the two-story house, ran again and paused to peer through fence pickets.

At the yellow house, Polly climbed the few steps and knocked on the lower half of the Dutch door. As Martha reached the steps, she was stabbed with another pain. Maria opened the front door. Maria pretended not to see Polly and searched over the little girl's head. "Now what could that noise have been? I thought I heard a knock."

Maria glanced down and smiled. "So it was. Come in." She stood aside and Polly scampered past her. Maria now looked upon her daughter who remained standing in the walkway. "Won't you come on in, too?"

"I need to go right back. Mama, I think it's my time."

Maria called inside. "Matthew watch Polly for me." She closed the door and slowly descended the steps.

"Have you been in labor long?"

"A couple of hours."

"Want me to come up?"

"I'll send for you when I need you. It would really help me most right now if you could keep Polly for the day. She's got so much energy."

"We'll be glad to."

"Mama, go back in. You'll catch cold out here with no cape. I promised Sam I'd be right back. Let's not worry him."

"Martha, let me know how the labor progresses today."

"All right, Mama."

Martha retraced her steps, thinking she really should go by the dairy, but she didn't have her jug. Back at home, she had scarcely hung her cape when she groaned with a long, hard contraction. "Sam," she called. He came swiftly with an anxious frown.

"Martha?"

"I think it won't be long."

She eased down to the edge of the bed. "Oh Sam, it hurts to sit."

He helped her to lie down on her side. "Tell me when another contraction starts."

In a few minutes she said weakly, "Now."

He placed his hand on her abdomen, leaving it there until her muscles relaxed. "You're right. This may be a short labor. Can you undress – get your gown on?"

She nodded.

"I'll go get some things. Where's your gown?"

She pointed to the clothes press.

He found it and put it on the bed beside her. "The new blankets – sheeting for the baby?"

"Top shelf," she said, again indicating the clothes press.

"Call if you need me. I'll leave the doors open."

After that, time divided between pain and no pain. Her mind was shrouding her body's intense pains so that she was not fully aware of all that was happening.

She heard Sam repeating over and over: when the contraction starts, push, push hard.

Then in a flash, she felt her lower body being split wide open and she cried out. "Oh, oh, help me!"

"The head's out. Once more, now."

A wet weight was laid across her abdomen. "Sam?"

"It's your daughter, Martha. Let her rest there. I'm going to tie the cord, then cut it."

"A little girl," Martha murmured sleepily.

She didn't hear anything else for awhile. When she roused again, she knew that she was expelling something.

Sam saw Martha opening her eyes. He pronounced, "Afterbirth."

She dozed again. Awakening, she moved her hands to her abdomen. It was flat. She mused that it wasn't a dream. The baby had come. Aloud she called, "Sam."

From the direction of the kitchen she heard his answer. "Coming."

He walked into the bedroom holding a white blanket. He crossed to the bed and sat down next to Martha.

"Are you ready to see your new daughter?"

"Can I hold her?"

"As your doctor, I'd say that's in order." He placed the blanket-wrapped infant into her arms.

She pulled the covering away from the tiny head. "She's so small."

"Most newborn babies are."

"And so red."

"Normal."

"What color are her eyes?"

"Blue. I expect all our babies will have blue eyes."

"All? Oh, Sam, can we have some more?"

"I'd like to fill up the house with such dear little ones."

"That won't be hard," she murmured looking around at the already crowded bedroom.

"We'll add rooms in the loft," he raised his arms high.

"Sam, dear Sam."

"And if that isn't enough room, we'll build a big house two stories high up there..."

"On the crown of the hill."

"Yes, my love. And you'll stand on your front stoop or back stoop and see the children any direction they go."

"I love you so much," she whispered with brimming eyes.

He leaned over and kissed her tenderly. "But Martha, my very dear, Martha, you must tell me when you've had enough children. We will take care of your health." A strange look, almost of fear, came into his eyes. For a rare moment she felt him go tense, as he insisted, "Promise you'll tell me."

Although he was so close physically, she sensed a part of him was far away.

"Yes, Sam. I promise."

He relaxed and returned spiritually to the present. He kissed her hand that encircled the baby. "I'll leave you two alone and clean up a bit. As soon as someone comes by, I'll have him go give the news to the Koehlers."

"And Mama."

"Of course."

Martha dozed off and on, always waking to check if the baby was still in her arms.

In the middle of the afternoon, her drowsiness had passed and she moved her arm only to discover the baby was not there.

"Sam," she called.

Shuffling steps sounded on the kitchen floor, then in her room. Somehow she was surprised to see her mother.

"Well, my dear. You certainly surprised all of us with that quick delivery. Sam says you got along fine."

"Mama, where's the baby?"

"In the cradle."

"Where?"

"In the kitchen. It's warmer in there. I was fixing you something to eat. You feel like anything yet?"

"Yes. I'm hungry."

"Here's another pillow. Prop up there. I'll be right back."

Martha eased herself up in the bed to a semi-reclining position and smoothed the bed covers.

Maria returned shuffling and bearing a wooden tray. She placed it on Martha's legs, took a large linen napkin and tucked it in the neck of the gown and spread it out.

"Want me to feed you?"

"I can manage. Mama, please, bring the cradle in so I can see the baby. Get Sam to help you. It's heavy."

"I'll drag it. Sam's not here."

"Not here?"

"He went up to the Gemeinhaus. He's been gone sometime." As she struggled with the cradle, she added, "He should be back soon."

"The chicken is delicious, Mama."

"Tell me. Have you decided on a name yet? You know she ought to be baptized tonight."

"Yes. It's a beautiful name."

"Is it Martha or Elizabeth?"

"No. Those were your favorite names for a girl."

The front door opened letting in a blast of chilly December air. Sam closed the big door behind him and stuck his head into the bedroom.

"You awake?"

"I am."

"Feeling perky?" In the process of removing his great coat, he looked in the doorway again.

"Grand."

"Like walking out tonight?" He called out.

"Sam?"

He walked in and stood at the end of the bed, eyes gleaming. "I mean it."

Incredulous, she demanded, "Where?"

"Down the saal aisle!"

"You mean for the baptismal service?"

"Yes. Martha the new baptismal service order has just arrived. Daniel has already read it and likes it. He wants to use it tonight." Sam walked to the cradle, knelt down and put a finger toward the baby. "What do you say little one? Do you want to be the first Moravian baby in Wachovia to use the new service?"

The baby yawned. Sam laughed. "May we take that for a yes?"

Martha said, "Sam, do you think I can make it to the saal tonight? That's a long walk."

"My dear, you won't have to walk. I will carry you!"

"Who'll carry the baby?"

Maria proposed, "Any of the brothers or sisters around here will be happy to carry her. And light your way with lanterns, too."

Martha was hesitant. "Do you suppose we could go for the end of the service so I wouldn't have to sit so long?"

"I'm certain that can be arranged," he answered decisively.

Maria leaned over the bed and whispered. "All the mothers will understand. About the sitting."

Martha blushed and dropped her gaze. After the blush subsided, she asked, "Mama, what about Polly? Won't you have to go to the saal early?"

"I'll take her along. She's sleeping now down at the house. She'll be awake tonight."

Martha spoke softly. "I've been here in Salem, almost since it's beginning. I've been among the first at various events, but I've never been first. Sam, now our baby, my first baby has a chance to be first at something on her very first day of life. Do you think it's a good omen?"

He teased her good-naturedly, "I didn't know we looked for signs, sister."

"No, but, well, I think it'll be special for her. Mama, do you have the baptismal dress ready?"

"Yes. It was washed and pressed last week. It had yellowed since you wore it, so I sunned it outside."

"I'm surprised you didn't leave it yellow."

The front door swung open. When it was firmly closed, they could see Traugott Bagge standing in the entry. He held a large package. Sam stood up. Maria hastened as if to close the bedroom door that Sam had left open. Martha motioned for her to stop.

Martha projected her voice, "Brother Bagge, come in to see our newest daughter."

Bagge appeared surprised. "I didn't know about the birth."

Sam extended his hands for the package, saying, "Just this morning."

Bagge briskly approached the cradle, took a quick glance and offered congratulations to Martha. To Sam he stated, "Here's the order from Pennsylvania."

"Thank you for bringing it up."

"No trouble. Is Polly about?"

Sam replied, "No. We took her down to Maria's for the day."

Bagge's eyes darted a quick hard look at Maria. "I see Sister Miksch is here."

Maria informed him politely, "She was asleep when I came up to be with Martha a few minutes. Matthew is at home with Polly."

"Umph," Bagge grunted. "Martha, I believe you'll be ready to send Polly to the little girls' school now."

"Oh, no," Martha gasped. "She's only two."

"Her mother was only two and a half when she started," Bagge snapped.

Maria quietly left the room. Her face was not quiet.

"I remember," Martha said, "but I like having Polly around. And she'll like having a little sister. Polly will enjoy watching her grow and later playing with her."

Bagge rejoined somewhat harshly, "I want to see her get a good education."

Sam stepped between the visual line of the two. "We do also, sir. We'll send her when the time is best. We will decide."

At this statement Bagge turned and left the room and the house. Sam had followed him to the door.

Maria got Sam's eye and beckoned him near. "If that brother had to be so harsh, God be praised it was here in private. And let us pray, that upper handed confrontation didn't sour her milk!"

"She's too sensible and too healthy for that."

Maria returned to the kitchen to gather her possessions and Sam moved into the bedroom, this time closing the door to the hall.

He caressed Martha's hair. "Better rest now then we'll see if you can stand and walk a few steps. I'll be nearby." He peered at the baby before leaving the room.

Martha slid back down in the bed. She realized she was tired. She moved the second pillow over to Sam's side of the bed. Slowly, she turned over to lie on her stomach, something she hadn't done in many months. "Oh, how good it feels," she purred.

CHAPTER TWENTY-SEVEN

The baptismal service was as lovely as Brother Koehler had led Sam to believe it would be. Martha had forgotten that she had not told Maria the baby's name earlier. When Koehler put his hands on the child's head and said, "I baptize you, Henrietta Frederika Vierling," Martha heard her mother utter a slight audible gasp of surprise. Maria Henreitta Patterman Miksch now had her own namesake.

Quite clearly, Maria showed a fondness for her namesake. On afternoons when she felt able to walk, she visited the Vierlings for afternoon tea, often times bringing gingerbread. When her gout bothered her, Maria stayed at home and Martha and the girls came to see her. Maria and Martha worked out a signal. If Maria wasn't at First House when the town clock struck four in the afternoon, Martha knew she wasn't coming. Only the severest cold or rain prevented the daily visits. Sometimes Martha during visits with her mother would leave Henrietta with her parents and walk Polly to the community store. This arrangement gave her a chance for a few minutes alone with Polly and afforded Polly a bit of time with her Grandfather Bagge. Occasionally, Bagge would mention the need of school and Martha learned to say "before long" and change the topic, usually asking if supplies Sam had ordered had come in.

Twice a month, Martha and Polly would walk on to the post office to collect their mail when a rider was due. Sam was becoming well known. Often, he had inquires from people outside Wachovia concerning their own illnesses or the possibilities of his performing surgery for some other family member. In some cases people consulted him about their slaves' medical problems.

In springtime, Martha took the girls while she tended the garden or did the wash. Liking outside as she did, Martha made as quick work as possible of indoor chores. In good weather the three of them could be out much of the day. Often the Mikschs' kept the girls and Martha rode with Sam to see patients in the nearby Moravian settlements. Sam enjoyed company on his trips and it pleased Martha that he wanted her to go along. Being a companion was one of the happiest aspects of being a helpmate – a fact thoroughly engrained in her training.

Martha wondered as she sat beside Sam, why no one had ever told her during her girlhood *that merely being with your husband would give you immense satisfaction?*

In fact, Martha enjoyed so much her whole new family life that she was almost ecstatic when she realized a few months after Henrietta's first birthday that she was pregnant again.

"Oh, Sam" she whispered quietly in her husband's ear one morning, "we have been blessed again."

He rolled over, instantly awake as usual. "What?"

"I'm sure, well almost, that we're going to have another baby."

"When?"

"September."

"The harvest season."

As Martha predicted, the baby came in September. Martha was a little disappointed she had not had a son. However, she and Sam were both so pleased that the baby was strong and healthy that they had no time for negative thoughts. This girl was baptized Carolina Juliana and called Carolina.

And in just two more years on October 13, 1797, Martha gave birth to her third daughter, Johanna Eleonora.

Sam scrutinized their bedroom and asked, "Where are we going to put another bed, Martha? Really it's time to finish the loft."

"They're so young to sleep way up there," she replied.

"Polly is six, Henrietta, four. Surely they are old enough to take care of themselves. We can leave the door to the hall open at night. Why even Carolina at two would be all right with rails around a bed."

"If only the town would build a hospital, we could give the girls the front room."

"Martha, if you give up your front room, you'll feel like a pioneer. Any guests would have to go through the house or apothecary back to the kitchen, in order to sit down."

She laughed. "In case you haven't noticed, that's where I am most of the time anyway."

He gave her one of his most charming smiles. "I'm going to talk to Brother Krause today to determine when he can finish the loft into two rooms."

"Two? My good doctor, what a large house we'll have then. The congregation will think you're planning a large family."

He relished the lightness of converse she was acquiring; the cheerful, teasing humor added an appropriate ambience to their home. They had a growing partnership in speech as well as in family. He smiled tenderly and squatted beside the cradle. "They are dear, aren't they?"

Martha's heartbeat quickened at this tenderness and gentleness in her strong, manly husband. How could anyone not be swayed by him or his needs? She moved and stood beside him and placed her hand on his head, caressed his thick hair. He turned his head and buried it briefly into the folds of her gown.

"Do you think the Conferenz will ever build a hospital?" she asked.

He stood. "Not in town."

"Is it because they don't want so many strangers to come?"

"That could be a reason. When we get a hospital, I want it to be a proper place, a healthy facility."

Both were silent, deep in thought.

Martha spoke first. "Sam, if you continue getting more patients from outside that have to stay here, won't the girls be more exposed to outsiders and brothers? It's hard now to keep them in the kitchen."

"Your father often had customers in the tobacco shop? How did your mother take care of you?"

"She didn't let me in the shop when customers were there. I believe it was easier to maintain control with one child."

"Do you want to send them to school younger? When they are two and a half?"

"No. I like having the girls around. They have a time to form a relationship, while the older ones are in school. Don't worry. I'll work out the problem."

"I'm certain you will. I am concerned about the salvation of their souls. I want them to have the right education."

He had no time to comment further. There was a knock on the front door. He moved quickly, dressed and hastened to answer.

The loft was divided into two good-sized rooms, and the Vierlings were pleased with the results. On moving day, Martha took the baby and Carolina to her parents' house, then she returned home to begin the chore of transferring the girls' things upstairs.

Young Brother Frederich Meinung from next door volunteered to help Sam carry beds and chests up the stairs. Frederich was one of the more talented young brothers in Salem. Brother Marshall had shown particular interest in the boy and had kept a sharp eye on his progress in the boys' school. He had recommended advanced course of study and had even undertaken to teach him about design and building. Frederich had watched the building procedures at the Vierlings the past month and was curious to see the completed results.

After they had successfully negotiated the little bed up the steep steps, Frederich walked around the two rooms.

"This looks well built. Brother Krause made good use of all the space."

"He did. By the way, have you heard Brother Marshall say how the church is coming along?"

"He's started on the plans. He has some new ideas for details."

"He's not well, you know. Help him all you can. Brother Marshall is a wise man, knows how to take care of himself, but nevertheless if you see him getting tired, suggest a tea break – anything to get him to rest."

"I will sir," Frederich swelled with pride at being taken into the doctor's confidence and at being asked to assume this responsibility.

After the young brother departed and Martha was sorting some of the clothing to take upstairs, she asked Sam. "Do you think they'll use the old organ in the new church?"

"I trust not. A new one is truly needed. This one doesn't have much range."

"What could they do with the old one?"

"Put it in one of the smaller saals. Maybe the Brothers House or one of the villages might want to buy it."

"It'll be nice to have a saal big enough to seat everybody again. I can remember when about all of Wachovia could fit into the saal when it was new. Now many people have to stand on festal days."

Martha was surprised at how much she did enjoy the extra space in her bedroom. Only the baby remained downstairs, and she seemed to sleep more peacefully now that the room was quieter. In fact, Martha soon discovered she, too, rested better after she adjusted to the change. Previously, she was up at every sound from the children. Sam had trained himself to sleep through the children's noises, but he always awoke immediately when his name was called or if someone spoke directly to him. A trait he retained till the end of his life.

A good night's sleep helped both Sam and Martha to face the endless duties before them each day. Martha began having difficulty finding time to teach the youngest girls all the things she had managed to teach to Polly and Henrietta. Even with only two little ones at home, the cooking and washing chores had doubled. The house was larger so there was twice as much to keep straight.

Fortunately, she didn't have to answer the door any longer for the shop customers, patients or people seeking Sam. Everyone by now knew to come in the front door and go directly into the apothecary shop. Sam always told Martha if he were going out. If people didn't see him in the shop, they rang a bell on a table and Martha came in.

Members of the congregation noticed though that the shop was always neat and clean. In fact, everything and everybody in First House were neat and clean. It appeared no matter how many responsibilities Martha added to her schedule, she stayed on top of it all. The rooms even kept the fresh scent of spring year round. That was due to her keeping herbs in pots in the apothecary and the kitchen. Her father often teased her saying, "If you can't be outside, you'll bring a bit of nature in with you." Martha liked the fresh smell; she knew Sam did also.

One morning when she heard the bell, she had been reading a book to the girls. She put in a marker and went into the shop. A woman, not of the congregation, Martha could tell by her clothes, asked if the doctor was in.

"No. Could I serve you?"

"I need some medicine," she spoke after a hesitation.

Carolina came into the room, curious to see who was there. She left the door open and Eleonora toddled in after her. Both little girls stayed close to Martha.

The woman viewed the girls with surprise. "Are they yours?"

"Yes. This is Carolina and this is Eleonora," she said indicating each child.

"How nice they are. Such well-behaved little girls."

"Thank you. I'm sorry my husband is out, but I'll be happy to get the medicine for you if it's one we have in stock."

"Oh yes." The woman brought her attention back to her purpose. "My husband and I are taking our daughter to school in Pennsylvania, to your Moravian Boarding School. I left my medicine at home. I may need some on the trip."

She told Martha what she needed and Martha moved to a shelf and took a bottle down. "This is it. How much do you want?'

"An ounce. You knew right where to find it. Do you help your husband in here often?"

"Only when he's out."

"Mama, read now," Carolina said.

"Later, dear," Martha answered quietly.

"My, they're young for books. What age do you start young girls in school here in Salem?" She asked as she opened her drawstring bag to pay Martha.

"My oldest started at three. My other one started this year at five."

"I didn't know you had a school for very young girls. How far does it go?" The woman was quite interested.

"To age eighteen."

"Do you take outsiders?"

"No."

"I wish you did. It would be nice not to have our daughter so far from home. If they ever open the school to other people, I have some neighbors who would most certainly send their daughters."

The outer door opened and closed. Maria entered the shop. The little girls rushed to their grandmother and she bent to hug them.

Martha said to the customer as she finished wrapping the medicine bottle, "If you would like to visit the school and talk with the teachers or headmaster, I'm sure they would be delighted to see you. It's the half-timbered building on the other side of the square."

"Thank you kindly," she smiled at the girls as she left.

"Mama," Martha said, "come back to the kitchen."

As they all made their way, Martha lamented. "Mama, every time I sit down to read to the girls or try to teach them anything, something else has to be done."

"Do you think Sam needs anybody to help him in the shop?"

"I don't mind getting medicines for people. I really enjoy helping Sam out."

"Well, what's the problem?" her mother asked as she settled in a straight chair by the fireplace.

"Finding uninterrupted time for the girls."

"How much time?"

"Long enough to finish a book!"

"Dear, that's hard to do in the morning. Why not do that at night? Take little bits of time between chores if you must teach them in the morning."

"But at night the older girls are home."

"That's all right. Give a little time to them, a little to these." She hugged the two who were standing at her knees.

"And services and . . ."

"Hold on, Martha. This sounds like a complaint. That's not like you. Are you debating something in that head of yours?"

Martha was caught by surprise. A guilty expression crossed her face. "I suppose I am. Do you think it would be terrible if I sent the little girls to school earlier than I did Henrietta? There, they would have a more organized day."

"You know what Comenius wrote: A mother's school for the first six years."

Martha broke into a grin. "Yes, but I bet he didn't have to teach his children."

Maria snapped back. "He was a wise man. He saw results of various educations."

"I'm sorry, Mama. I didn't intend to demean his ideas. I know, you didn't send me early. And I kept Henrietta home until she was five, but I had more time then."

Shaking her head, Maria noted, "There have always been twenty-four hours a day."

"Mama, you always make me be so exact. All right, my time was more mine to use then. Or there seemed to be less to do."

"Yes, I'm sure that's true. But you'll get faster at everything, Martha. You accomplish a great deal in a day now, " Maria acknowledged as she gave a sweeping survey of the room.

"Thank you."

"This problem of when to begin school is all up to you. Think and pray about it, then do what you think is best. But for heaven's sake don't worry. That consumes more energy and time than peeling potatoes, or bringing in wood or teaching these babies. And besides, worry doesn't get anything done."

Carolina had been eyeing her grandmother's basket and could contain her curiosity no longer. "Grandmother, what's in your basket?"

Maria beamed. "A little surprise for us all. Ask your mommy if she has any milk for you to drink and coffee for me and herself."

Martha took the coffeepot from the hearth and poured thick black liquid into two mugs and filled smaller mugs with milk from a large pitcher.

Maria uncovered her basket and handed a sugared orange peel to Carolina and a small lump of sugar to Eleonora. Then she gave each a ginger cookie. They smiled as they took the treats and sat on the woven rag rug, a safe distance from the fireplace.

Martha settled near her mother who handed her a still warm square of gingerbread. She bit into it and recognized a new taste and fragrance. "Mama, you used orange."

"Yes. I was out of lemon peel. I had the orange so I tried it."

"It's delicious."

"Well, I hope the customers won't mind the change until the store gets more lemons."

The shop bell rang sharply, several times. Martha jumped up. She quickly put her mug on the table.

She was out of the room only a few seconds, when she raced back in. "Mama, can you stay with the girls? There's been an accident out on the Friedberg Road. I need to find Sam."

Martha jerked her cape from the wall peg.

"Sure, I'll stay. Martha is it anyone we know?"

Martha shook her head as she hastily disappeared.

Maria picked up the book Martha had not had time to finish, gathered the girls around the chair and read to them.

About fifteen minutes later, the front door opened and Maria heard several people enter the shop. She roused herself from the chair, walked to the door and stood there, keeping the girls behind her.

A stranger was speaking to Sam. "We took him back home. It was closer than here. The horses had run away; the wagon was broken."

Sam asked, "Was he bleeding? Slight? Extensively?"

"Yes. A good amount. We tied some clean rags around the wounds."

"Right. Martha get some antiseptic," Sam spoke as he opened a bag and put some instruments inside.

Martha, who had been standing out of sight, appeared. She put the bottle inside the open bag. Sam snapped it shut.

"I'll saddle the horse. It'll be quicker than the wagon. I should be back mid-or late afternoon."

"Sam, take care," Martha said.

He left by the front. The stranger followed. From the window Martha watched Sam go through the gate and down back to the barn. She was glad the horse was still in the stall; he wouldn't have to waste time with a chase.

Within a few minutes she saw him cantering up beside the house. The stranger unlatched the gate for Sam and closed it. Sam glanced toward the house, spotted Martha at the window and exchanged hand waves. The stranger, having untied his own horse, mounted and he and Sam rode down Main Street.

Martha returned to the kitchen; however, before she could say a word to her mother, someone else was in the shop ringing the bell. Martha retraced her steps.

Daniel Koehler, standing near the front table, was bending over to smell the thyme plant. "Delightful," he spoke, smiling.

"Good morning."

"Is Sam in or was that he that galloped down the street a few moments ago?"

"That was probably Sam. He was called to see an elderly man who was injured in a horse-wagon accident. Not a brother, but a neighbor of one, from what I understand."

"I see. Well, I'll stop back late this afternoon."

"I'll tell him."

After the bishop left there was a succession of customers and patients. Following each one Martha made an entry in a ledger of the person's name, what he wanted, any medicine he bought and whether he paid for it or put it on account. When she heard the clock strike twelve, she gasped and folded the ledger.

She hurried to the kitchen. "Mama, I forgot all about lunch. I know you needed to get home!"

"Martha, you surely stay busy. It's a good thing you had that gingerbread."

"If I hadn't had that, I might have gotten hungry and thought of lunch earlier. Truly, Mama, I've never been so remiss before. Anyway Sam won't be here."

"What about Polly and Henrietta?'

"Mama, can you stay a few minutes longer? I'll run down for them?" Again she grabbed her cape and paused a second for Maria's answer.

"Yes. I'll wait."

Martha started out, spun around, "Why don't I stop on the way back and ask father to come up here for lunch since you haven't been home to prepare any."

"He'll like that. I'll see what you have to put on the table beside that stew pot boiling there."

Martha moved her feet as fast as she thought respectable, maybe a little faster. Rounding the corner of Main Street at the square, she saw the teacher coming toward her with the girls. Martha waved. Polly and Henrietta ran to her. The sister headed back to the Gemeinhaus.

As the trio approached the yellow house, Martha told them she was going to stop and ask their grandfather to lunch with them. They clapped their hands with joy.

Martha noticed the old gingerbread sign that she had painted for her mother was not in the window, however the tobacco shop sign was out.

Martha opened the door and called inside. "Father!"

"That you, Martha?"

"Yes."

He came to the door.

"Father come have lunch with us. Sam's away. I was so busy with customers that Mama didn't get back."

"All right. Hand me the sign. I'll get my hat."

Martha handed over the little model of a boy with a snuff box and tobacco leaf that was his advertising sign nowadays. "Better put a coat on. There's still a chill in this early spring air."

She let the girls run ahead home while she walked slowly with Matthew.

"Have you finished planting?

"Now you know I couldn't finish without you," he jested.

"How about my stopping on my way back from taking the girls to school tomorrow morning? We could do it then."

"Fine. Have you finished yours?"

"Almost."

"Maybe I can help you then this afternoon. No need to hurry back. The gingerbread is sold out."

After dinner was eaten and the dishes cleared away, Maria put the little girls down for a nap, and Martha walked the others back to school. When she returned to the house, she entered the yard through the gate and walked around back. She opened the cellar door and exchanged her white apron for the gingham one she kept there for gardening.

Matthew was looking over the garden rows. "Are you going to sow the corn over here like last year?"

"I planned to. I like to keep the tall crops on the outside, but not too close to the fence. The horse will lean over and eat all he can reach."

"He'll get a stomach ache if he does."

"We can't take that chance. We have to keep that horse as healthy as ourselves. Sam never knows when he'll get a call."

"Shame we can't get another doctor. It would be good to have another one, perhaps in Bethania, then Sam wouldn't have to go in so many directions."

"The Conferenz knows the situation."

"Martha, what are you going to put over here?" Matthew asked as he came to the end of his row.

"The winter garden. Sam insists we eat fresh food as long as possible."

They worked until late afternoon when Maria called to them. "Tea time. Someone will need to meet the girls shortly."

Martha untied her apron and shook the dirt off. She cleaned the mud from her shoe soles with a stick, then scraped her shoes on the grass. Matthew offered to put the tools away and Martha went in through the cellar and up the steps.

She washed her hands in the kitchen. While drying them, she heard horse hooves in the backyard and peered out the window.

"Sam's home, Mama, put out another mug. Better slice a thick piece of the cheddar for him."

In a few minutes Sam and Matthew stamped up the cellar steps. The little girls ran to hug Sam. He knelt and gave each an appreciative kiss.

Martha asked, "Sam, are you hungry? We're getting ready for tea."

"The bread and cheese will be welcomed with the tea. Folks out there brought in lunch."

"How's the patient?" Martha inquired.

"He'll be all right. He had some head injuries and cuts and bruises on his arm."

"What happened?" Maria asked as she passed the mugs.

"The same thing we see so often of horses shying. Bolting. This time the old man was caught off balance. The horse ran under a low limb. The man was hit in the head and fell to the ground. They said he was unconscious for a short time, but he was awake when I arrived."

Matthew shook his head. "Sounds bad. Will you be going back to see him soon?"

"I'll check on him tomorrow. We really need a hospital here," Sam said intently, just as the bell rang in the apothecary.

Sam got up and was at the door when Daniel Koehler appeared.

"I thought I heard your thunderous voice back here?" Daniel grinned at Sam.

"That you did."

"Sound like the same thunder I heard a year or so ago."

"It is. Dan, we need a hospital."

"Is this because of the man you were called to this morning?"

"Him and all the others. Now don't tell me about him and a lot of other strangers filling up the town. Aren't we supposed to serve everyone who needs us!"

"Agreed."

"Dan, look at it this way. If we had a hospital, these outsiders could come here. I could serve the Salem folks better if I were here. And the other sick people in Wachovia, they need a place to come for treatment and rest. They need the best in nursing care until they're well."

"Sam, we've got to consider all of Salem's needs. We're getting ready to build the church. That's a large undertaking."

"I know. I know. And we need it. I believe we need a hospital, too."

"Maybe you need to be on the Ausfer Collegium to see how the money supply is. But that's not what I came about."

All the time the two had been talking so earnestly, Martha had waited for a pause. Now there was a slight one so she quickly interjected, "Why don't you two go into the front room. I'll bring you some tea."

Koehler remarked amiably. "No Martha, but thank you. I must be on my way soon. Sam perhaps we could talk a moment in the apothecary."

Sam led the way into the shop and closed the door. Daniel asked him, "A vacancy has come up on the congregation music committee and we'd like for you to take the opening."

"Why, Dan, I'm honored."

"Will you serve on the committee?"

"Yes."

"We've been promised some new music from Germany soon, a gift from a brother there."

"A man couldn't give a finer gift than to share the melodies he hears in his head and his heart."

The front door opened and Traugott Bagge entered.

Daniel turned and nodded to him. "Good afternoon, Brother Bagge."

"Same to you, bishop."

Again the front door was flung open and a young boy stumbled in. He was breathing hard.

Sam immediately crossed to him. "What is it, Jonathan?"

"Mama. Mama said to come. The baby's sick." He stammered between deep breaths.

The door wasn't closed when two brothers, one married, one single burst in.

The married brother Jacob was coughing. The single brother was scratching vigorously.

Without sounding abrupt, Sam asked what the men needed.

"Doctor, I haven't slept in three nights with this cough. One more night like this would be torture. Can't you give me something?"

Sam listened as the man coughed, then turned to the second man. He rolled up his sleeve, saying, "This rash broke out yesterday. It started red, but there're some blisters now."

Sam wheeled around. "I've got something for both of you." He called at the kitchen door. Martha appeared immediately.

"Get a bottle of the herb mixture for skin eruptions for Brother Earnhardt. Tell him how to make an infusion with it. And Brother Jacob needs some comfrey powder, about one-fourth of an ounce."

Sam went to the kitchen to pick up his bag. Reentering the apothecary, he gave further instructions. "Brother Jacob, stay out of draughts and keep your feet dry. Make a tea with the powder, about a spoonful to a pint of water. Drink a cup at bedtime. During the day, too, if you need it. Brother Earnhardt, wash the red areas with soap. Don't wash the blisters and try not to pop them. Apply the herb solution three or four times a day. And stay away from poison ivy. I'm sorry to leave you, but this young boy has come for me."

Sam pointed to Jonathan who was standing against a wall and looking quite frightened. Gently but firmly, Sam placed his hand on Jonathan's shoulder and guided him outside.

Bishop Koehler left just behind them.

Traugott, usually in the center of activity, had stood by and watched the heavy traffic. He checked his watch as the clock struck five.

Martha filled the prescriptions and took the payments from the men. As they exited, Bagge asked, "Are the girls home from school yet?"

"No, sir. I'll be going for them as soon as I enter these accounts," she answered as she made notations in the ledger. She unlocked a desk drawer and placed the coins in a small box.

"Brother Bagge, won't you stay and have tea with us? Mama and Father are in the kitchen."

"No. Here's the book Sam wanted to read." He placed the book on the table. Martha hurriedly got her cape, telling her parents she'd be back soon.

Bagge and Martha walked down the street together.

"Martha," Bagge said, "I want to send Polly away to school."

Martha was completed overwhelmed at the request. "Why? Where?"

"To Bethlehem. The school there is very good."

"The school here is good, too. She's only seven. She is so young."

"Many girls have gone to boarding school around eight years of age."

"But we'd miss her terribly. The girls would miss her."

"I want to do this for her. She's my only granddaughter. I'll bear all the expenses."

There was something in his tone that Martha could not argue with. He had some rights to Polly that she didn't have, yet she had raised and loved Polly for six years. She had watched over her the same as she had the other girls.

Martha was silent until they reached the corner. "I'll talk to Sam about your offer."

CHAPTER TWENTY-EIGHT

Martha wore a worried look – something quite unusual for her. Sam waited until they were walking along to evening service before he commented on the expression.

"Sam, this afternoon when I walked to get the girls at school, Traugott Bagge was going the same way. It was right after you left. He said he wanted to send Polly to Bethlehem to school."

"What did you say?"

"I told him she was so young and that all of us would miss her."

"Very true. Did he offer any reason for wanting her to go to Bethlehem?"

"Only that he wanted the best education for her. Sam, our girls' school is good."

"Then you think there's another reason?"

"Yes. I have the feeling he sees I'm too busy to give her a lot of attention."

"Martha, you do a good job as a mother. I can tell him that."

"His mind seems made up to me. You know how he is once he gets hold of an idea."

Sam was silent for a few steps. "This is his only grandchild."

"Yes. He reminded me."

"Because of Sister Bagge's condition, he has never been able to have Polly with him except for the briefest of visits. It's not inconsistent with his strong belief in education to want her to go to the best school. He sent his two sons to Pennsylvania."

"Yes, but he didn't send Anna," she replied somewhat defensively.

"No, but wasn't the war going on then?"

"Yes."

"He has made wise decisions in the past. Do you think you can trust him in this?"

What a cruel blow he struck at her, without knowing. She couldn't answer that and betray her own father. How many times will Traugott Bagge and his money be able to buy gifts, education for her and her family? How many more times will he with his financial advantages be able to provide education that her family couldn't afford? Even many of the furnishings in her house were purchased by him for Anna. Bagge, Bagge – was she to be pitted against him always, just as her father had been? If he hadn't come to Wachovia, wouldn't her father have been *merchant*?

Sam squeezed her arm slightly. "Martha. You're about to walk pass the turn."

"Sorry," she murmured as she followed his lead up the slope. She was thankful for the darkness of the night and he could not see her face. She was sure she must be red with embarrassment. Her thoughts had been unkind. At services and at bedtime prayers she would ask forgiveness.

Aloud, she spoke just before reaching the Gemeinhaus. "Dear, we'll do whatever you deem best."

"Then, we'll let Polly take advantage of this opportunity. I'll talk with Traugott after services."

Traugott was willing to make all the arrangements with the school. Martha only asked him to wait to take Polly after her eighth birthday. She believed the separation would be easier then. He agreed to take her up in October when he would be going on a trip for the store. Martha was spared having to spin and sew new clothes and linens. Traugott planned to buy those items in Bethlehem.

Martha did her utmost to make Polly's last few months in Salem happy.

Within the family circle, she strove for a balance between times alone with Polly herself, the four girls together and Polly and Sam some private hours. The latter she accomplished mainly in the late evening by taking the younger girls out in the garden in good weather or by taking them upstairs first for the bedtime routine.

But October 15, the day scheduled for her departure, dawned bright and clear and Polly rode off with her grandfather Bagge in the store wagon. All the Vierlings stood in a group on the walking path and waved until the wagon was out of sight. They turned half-heartily in the other direction. Sam and Martha escorted Henrietta and Carolina to school.

On the way back home they chose the street in front of the Gemeinhaus. Martha preferred not to pass her parents' house, fearing Eleonora might beg to stop, perchance to stay. Martha needed Eleanora's companionship at home today.

As they passed the site of the new church, they slacked their pace to see how the work was progressing. Brother Krause was discussing some detail of the drawing with Brother Marshall.

"Good morning, brothers," Sam greeted them.

They acknowledged his greeting.

"Good to see you out and around Brother Marshall," Sam said approvingly.

"Many thanks to you, doctor," Marshall replied, as he walked over to them "I heard you had accepted the invitation to join the Collegium. Congratulations."

"I pray I can be some service to them."

"I'm sure you will be. Sam, you have a busy schedule now. Just a word of caution. Don't take on too much," Marshall warned him in a kindly, fatherly manner.

Sam smiled broadly. "Brother Marshall from all I hear of your years of devotion, your hours of working for all the people, "he swept his arm in a half circle, "why you set a fine example of how to work hard, enjoy life and live long."

"Thank you again, doctor," Marshall retorted, "but the demands on us are different. I've dealt with the economies. In many times of stress, I could write for opinions from Pennsylvania or to Europe. Your stresses are immediate. Your patients' problems often call for solutions that you must find by yourself, medically that is."

"Ah – but that source up there, guides me as He guides you."

"I trust that will always be so. The strains of decisions, daily, yearly where human life hangs in the balance can take its toll. Martha, take care of him. Help him get his rest and meals, regularly."

Sam laughed. "Now which one of us is the doctor?"

Martha asked, "Brother Marshall, when do you expect the church will be finished?"

"It won't be long. Excuse me, please. I remember something I need to confer with Krause about." He turned and walked slowly down the stake line.

As they continued climbing the hill, Martha said sadly, "I'm sorry Polly won't get to see the church."

Sam rejoined. "Certainly, she will. She'll be back to visit."

At the crown of the hill they stopped again.

Martha took a deep breath. "Autumn smells of apples, doesn't it?"

"Yarrell's apples are about gone." Sam observed as he scanned the orchard. "Martha, can't you vision our house standing on this spot?"

"You still want this property, don't you?"

"True. And I'll have it too."

"Do you think Sister Yarrell will sell?"

"There's an excellent chance. Now that Brother Yarrell is dead, she may not want to look after all this land."

Martha stared down the street. "If we lived here, I could stand on the steps and watch the girls go to school. This would be so handy to the church. And when the leaves are off the trees, I could see father's house. Oh Sam, the more I think about it, the more I like the location."

Eleonora pulled at Martha's apron. "Mama, carry me."

Martha bent down to swoop up her daughter. "I know you're tired, dear. We're going now."

They resumed their walk to First House.

"Sam, I'm glad Polly didn't have to leave until after Eleonora's birthday."

Sam leaned over and took Eleonora. "Let me carry her. Goodness, you're a heavy little girl. Two years old."

Eleonora giggled with the attention.

"Martha, did you realize it's been two years since we had a baby?"

Martha peered at his eyes and saw a twinkle. Her answer to that question was with a very feminine grin and gesture.

All the Vierlings missed Polly in their individual ways and in the family group. One evening Martha sighed upon coming down the steps from putting the girls to bed. She wandered into the apothecary.

"Sam, this break in the family group is hard, isn't it?"

"Um, you have a hard time with the children tonight?" He commented as he thumbed through a book.

"No. Henrietta is taking right over as the oldest girl. She's a natural little mother."

"That should cheer you, my dear." He said. He located what he wanted and read to himself.

Martha ambled back to the kitchen. She decided to set out a sponge for hot cakes for breakfast. She put a dipper into the starter crock, gave a good stir then withdrew it. She watched clean white starter dough slide into the brown pottery bowl. Next, she added equal amount of water and flour.

As she mixed the batter she reminisced of her mama's good gingerbread. "I'll never be the really good cook she is."

One negative thought followed another until she began wondering if she were a good mother. "If I were a good mother, then Brother Bagge wouldn't have sent Polly away. He didn't trust me to raise her. Maybe he thinks I'm not raising the others well either.

I'll have to do better. What does it feel like to leave home? Everybody has done it but me. Mama, father, Sam. Does Sam ever miss his family? It would be so hard to part from mine."

Somehow or other though she felt rejected tonight. She couldn't generate enthusiasm to carry on any creative project; thus she resorted to the ever-present chore of spinning. This she could do and not think, just pedal and pull, stretch and wind.

She continued to feel down for some months. There was one bright spot in late December when Sam received an invitation from some leading doctors throughout the state to convene for discussions of medical matters in January in Raleigh, the capitol of North Carolina.

Martha displayed excitement and pride at Sam's invitation. She was so hopeful that he would accept.

"Sam," she glowed, "it's such an honor."

"I admit I'm pleased that they asked me."

"You will go, won't you?"

"This is a difficult time to be away. There are many illnesses in winter. Who would look after the patients?"

She could not answer that question. There was no other doctor in Wachovia.

"This current illness that is affecting patients' chests, I believe, its going to hit more people before it's over."

"You mean an epidemic?"

"Yes, but please, don't go around saying so. No need to put the idea into people's head."

Martha absorbed the statement as a rebuke. "I won't. I wouldn't spoil anybody's Christmas."

"Martha, I didn't mean to be sharp. Come here." When she did, he put his arms around her. "I'm going to need your help more than ever if this illness does grip the area."

Sam had predicted accurately; the chest illness became epidemic. Patients were seriously ill and required constant care. Martha could not remember a time that the front door had swung open so often with people seeking the doctor day and night.

Martha's parents came down with the sickness. She spent several days running back and forth from the yellow house to First House. Having to take Eleonora along slowed her and she urged the child to hurry. Martha found herself becoming impatient, and on a few occasions, short-tempered.

One day when she returned from one of her nursing visits, the shop was crammed with people wanting teas or medicines to relieve the aches and pains of suffering members of their family. She quickly took off her cape and hung it on a peg. She helped Eleonora get hers off. She dragged a box from under a counter and told the child to sit right there and play.

"All right now everybody. I'll help you in order you came in."

She was filling the last order when Sam returned. He greeted the customer, asking, "Brother, anybody else sick up at your place?"

"No, not yet."

"Good news. I'll be up there later this afternoon."

"We'll be looking for you," the man said and left.

Sam put his bag down behind the counter and saw Eleonora playing with a miniature set of dishes. "Hello there."

"Father!" She jumped up and hugged his legs.

"My it's a pleasure to see someone so well and cheerful."

Martha entered the accounts in the ledger.

"What are you having for lunch?"

Martha answered without looking up from her writing. "Sorry, but it'll have to be cold. When I got back from mama's, the shop was packed. As you see the last person just left."

"May we have some hot tea?"

"If the kettle hasn't boiled dry." She closed the ledger and returned it to the drawer. In the kitchen, she lifted the kettle. "There's hot water."

Systematically, she set out the bread, cheese, cold ham and preserves.

Sam came in bringing Eleonora and put her in the high chair at the table. "Um, look what we've got." He cut her a slice of bread, then walked to the bucket to wash his hands. "In our new house, I'm going to put in a sink for washing up. With a drain. We'll use fresh water for every hand washing."

"Thank you. Then I won't have to empty anymore water."

Martha and Sam sat down to eat. Halfway through the meal, Sam commented, "This is a good dinner, Martha, but in the current cold weather, something hot would be welcomed."

Without thinking, she snapped, "Yes, it would. But I can't be three places. Down nursing Mama and Father, here helping in the shop and in the kitchen."

"Could you have a soup pot simmering, like most women?"

"No. The smell of soup makes me sick."

Sam threw her a sharp look. "You're not getting ill, are you?"

"I don't know what's wrong with me. I'm snapping at you, everything annoys me . . ."

"And soup smells make you sick."

Martha put her elbows on the table and her head between her hands.

Sam calculated a moment. "Martha, could it be another baby is on the way?"

She jerked her head up. Her eyes sought his to determine if he were teasing. No, he wasn't jesting.

She figured, too. "Sam, how could I have been so busy to loose track of days, months?"

Since Martha was usually not short-tempered any time, not even during pregnancy, Sam was not pleased with the sign, but he did not tell her so. "Now that we know, you will cut down the excessive activity." He held her eyes attempting to sound both authoritative and seeking her consent.

"What can I cut out?"

"First, let's start with what you have to do. Take care of Eleonora, prepare meals."

"Answer the bell when you're out," she added.

"We will get someone to help with your parents."

"With both of them sick, the rotating married nurses are hardly enough to tend to all their patients."

"Soon there may not be many of those available. What about a single sister to live with them for a few months, or at least until they're back on their feet, their strength regained?"

This was one time Martha couldn't use the excuse her parents preferred her. Sam needed her more at home. "All right."

"I'll check around while I'm on my rounds." He rose from the table, went to her side and hugged her. "Take care of yourself, my love." She reached a hand to his face. "Thank you for caring and for . . . and for the new life."

Back in the apothecary he pack his bag and left.

Martha washed Eleonora's face and hands then took her upstairs for a nap. Martha laid down for a few minutes rest herself and was soon sound asleep.

Sam did locate a single sister to live with the Mikschs. She was a twenty-year-old sister who had been in service to one of his patients who had died during the epidemic. The sister was grateful to find immediate employment. Martha met her at the yellow house to show her around since both Matthew and Maria were too sick to get out of bed.

Arrangement for the sister's salary was made by Sam. At first, Matthew objected. When Sam explained that he needed Martha at home and that it would be more costly to employ someone for his house and shop, Matthew consented to let him take care of the payments.

Martha snatched any extra opportunity for rest that she found during the day so that she could be up when Sam returned from rounds. She always had food and drink ready for him and clean clothes and fresh water to bathe. After the fourth month of pregnancy, food odors did not make her nauseous so she tried to keep a pot of soup hot. If Sam were making a call to a house that she knew had no one well enough to cook, she sent a crock of soup and some bread.

She told him, "There's so little I can do to help anybody directly. I can't even take a turn at nursing now."

Once, he returned soon after leaving. His steps were heavy on the cellar stairs. By his slow walk, Martha feared he might be ill. He came in the kitchen, set the crock on the wash table. She walked over to clean it. Picking it up, she knew by the weight it was still full. Questioningly, she sought his face.

"There's no one to drink it."

"Oh, no. So many are leaving us."

"There may be more. There's so little I can do. No medicine cures the sickness."

"But Sam, you're making them more comfortable with what you give them. Some of the patients are recovering. Look at Mama and Father. They're getting better."

"Rest, good nursing and not coming down with something else—are helps."

"They need you to tell them what to do and when. Sam, I know that your presence gives them a boost and courage. And you say you need me. Now, I'm saying that you need some rest, too. Can't you stay an hour and lie down?"

"I'm not tired."

The shop bell broke the quietness of the moment. Sam disappeared into the shop only to come back to her quickly. "Martha, it's someone from the store. Brother Bagge is suffering chest pains. I'll go down."

"Wait a second," she reached for the still warm soup crock. "Take this. There's no one down there to help him."

Sam left with the crock under his arm.

Martha went into the apothecary. She checked on her plants. They were dry so she poured water from a pitcher slowly into the clay pots. The plants had been so full when she brought them inside last fall. During the winter she had pinched back so many leaves to make tea for friends that the plants were sharply reduced in size. She decided to put them out early in the spring then give them a rest. They needed a chance to recover, too.

As she went about tidying the shop, she could smell the rosemary on her hands. She delighted in the fragrance and she longed to be out-of-doors again. Soon, she thought, it'll be time to plant.

Father probably will not be able to help me this year. Her mind wandered on to other people who were sick and lastly to Traugott Bagge. She could not recall his having been sick. He always represented the epitome of physical strength to her. She had been jealous of his ability to go on and on when her father could not maintain so vigorous a schedule. Now in his illness, he was very much alone as far as his household was concerned. His wife and Fredrich were dead; Anna was gone. He'd hoped that Carl would follow him in the store. Carl had abilities, but he had not settled down yet.

Traugott had known much personal acclaim locally and throughout the state, but Martha wondered if he were disappointed in his family life. For the first time she experienced a touch of compassion for this giant in her life.

She was relieved when Eleonora awoke from a nap and called for her. Now she could leave melancholy musings and tend to the normal duties of daily life.

Martha could not attend evening services because there was no one available to stay with the children. She always had evening Bible readings and prayers with the children, after which she paused by each girl's bed for a private chat before blowing out the candle.

Downstairs, she would sing a few of her favorite hymns while finishing her chores. Sam was usually out at night. If he wasn't on a case, he was at the service and at a meeting of the Collegium or music committee or at a rehearsal. Martha always waited up for him. When he came in, she served him milk and bread. He would tell her the latest news of the congregation and comment on the sermon.

One evening he came in looking quite disturbed. Before she could ask, he told her. "It's Daniel."

"I'm sorry. A bad case?"

"It's too early to say, but he didn't look good when I left him."

"Did Brother Benzien preach tonight?"

"He did."

"I'm sure he's a good man, but somehow he doesn't give me

the feeling he has the qualities of leadership that Brother Marshall has. The congregation has always placed such faith in everything Brother Marshall has done."

"Marshall is an unusual man. He is gifted with foresight. He insisted the Unity send someone to learn his job and to become thoroughly familiar with Wachovia affairs before he's called home."

"Brother Benzien really hasn't had a chance to lead yet?"

"You know how it is with Marshall. Even after one of his severe attacks, he rallies, gets up and makes another real contribution to the town."

"Like building the church."

"Exactly. Benzien does take some of the administrative load from Marshall."

"I've known Brother Marshall longer than any of the ministers. I shall truly miss him whenever he does depart."

Martha didn't know it then, but it was Sister Marshall who was to be called home first. Martha's eyes were filled with tears when she heard the news. What a true helpmate she had been to her husband and always so gracious to Martha.

Many people were dying. Likewise, many funeral services were conducted in the saal.

Long lines formed and marched down Church Street to God's Acre. She was glad Sam's instrument was the cello and he did not have to play in the funeral processions of his patients.

Martha had a special interest in Bagge and Koehler, and particularly inquired daily as to their conditions. Sam mostly shook his head indicating no change.

In early April, Koehler appeared slightly improved, but Bagge was weaker. While Sam was visiting with Bagge, Martha heard the trombones announce a male death. She clutched her apron: could it be Bagge? She was anxious to know, but she waited at the house. It wasn't long before a customer came into the apothecary. He told her Bagge had just gone home. He himself was on his way to Bethabara to inform the congregation there.

After the brother left, Martha sat quietly a few minutes. No more would Traugott Bagge walk the streets of Salem, no more quarrel with the neighbors about water stand pipes, or interfere with her father's business . . . what little was left of that. He could not send anymore of her family away to school or separate any of them. Even though she knew Bagge had paid for her early schooling, she never attributed her education to him.

Now things were equaled. He would lie beside the other Moravians, no higher or lower; with the same type of simple, white flat headstone to mark his resting-place, that marked all the other graves in God's Acre.

She anticipated more people from outside the community to attend his funeral than came to the services for most of the brethren. They did. The saal could not hold everybody even though extra chairs were brought in and placed beside the benches. According to custom, Martha marched to the graveyard with members of her own choir. The procession was orderly and dignified as always. She offered sympathy to Sam since Bagge had been his father-in-law and had extended help and friendship since his first day in Salem. Afterwards, Martha wrote a long letter to Polly about the service and the number of people who had come.

It was a sad spring for Salem. More than thirty people died. If there was a bright side, it had to be that many patients did recover. Koehler's recovery was noticeably slow. The congregation showed special concern for his welfare, because the Unity had written a request for Daniel and his wife to attend the Synod in the fall in Germany.

Toward the end of spring no new cases were reported. Martha's parents recovered enough to take care of themselves. They preferred doing without the help of the sister so she returned to the choir house. Again, Martha had more time to check on them.

Sam tried everything he knew to help his friend Daniel. In summer just as he seemed fully recovered, Salem experienced an intensely hot spell. A siege of high fevers and dysentery struck the town. Daniel was a victim. His weakened condition caused him to suffer a great deal. Sam bled Daniel, but his condition still did not improve.

Finally, Sam called in a doctor from Salisbury. After examining Daniel and talking with Sam, the consulting doctor suggested that Daniel take a vacation.

"He needs to get away from his responsibilities. He's using a lot of his energies on his official duties. It appears that everybody's problems are on his mind."

"We're all like that. Keeping right on with the job is natural for us. But you may be right. Yes, a vacation might be the needed treatment."

"Do you know of any place?"

"Only the mineral springs. There're several nearby. Often times congregation members go there."

"There's a place down on the Catawba, shady and quiet. I could make arrangements and send a letter by the next post as to when they could accommodate Daniel and his wife."

"Fine."

"By the way, I hear you do a bit surgery. Would you consider operating on slaves?"

"Yes."

"I've been asked to look at some slaves over the years. A few needed surgery in my view. If I run into any cases in the future, I'll ask the owners to contact you. I'm sure the masters would pay the bills. They have quite an investment, you know."

"Also, a compassion to help them in distress."

"Oh, surely, surely. Well, I'll be on my way."

"We will get the Koehlers ready and drive them down as soon as we hear from you."

A letter did arrive by the next post rider. The Koehlers were on their way the following day.

The weather was so hot that even Martha, who was used to the Carolina climate and who generally enjoyed the sunshine, found it difficult to work outside. Her pregnancy, especially the ninth month, added to her discomfort. Almost every afternoon she brewed a pot of peppermint tea and she felt more relaxed after a cup. She picked many mint leaves for the shop due to numerous calls for the herb. There were a lot of requests for rose vinegar also. She placed the petals in crocks and covered them with boiling hot vinegar. She left the solution for several days, but shook the crocks daily. Then she strained the vinegar into small jars.

Maria observed that the oppressive heat was bothering Martha. She warned her to slow down. "This is your first summer baby."

"But Mama, I've carried them in summer before, and we both got along all right."

Maria didn't say anymore, but she thought back to the hot summers and fevers in Bethabara and knew how disastrous the combination could be.

On August 10 Martha went into labor. Sam walked down to the yellow house to ask if Maria could sit with her for a short while. He was on his way to see a patient and promised to return soon. Maria hurriedly put her own house in order and set some cold foods on the table for Matthew's lunch. She had a second thought and went out to the manufactory.

"Matthew, Martha's in labor. I'm going up to stay with her. If you're not too busy, could Eleonora come down here with you?

"Let me get through salting down this bunch of tobacco, then I'll be up to get her."

Maria had to take the slope slowly. She tired easily. It annoyed her to admit even to herself that gout interfered with her work. Her weight was increasing, too, and she didn't like it, but she couldn't stop it. As she advanced toward First House, she questioned how much longer she would be able to keep up her with the saal dienerin duties. No sooner had she formed the mental question than she answered herself: "Why until I absolutely can't walk to services."

Maria didn't stop to knock. She pushed open the door and closed it quietly in case Martha was dozing. She cracked the door to the bedroom and saw Martha sitting rigidly on the side of the bed, her arms stiff at her side, her palms flattened on the mattress. Opening the door fully, she frowned. "Dear, what is it?" After a minute, Martha drooped and gasped. "Oh, Mama, it hurts so badly."

Maria closed the door, set her knitting basket down and went over to the bed. "Can't you lie down? Here, let me help you." Maria put her hands gently on Martha's shoulders and pushed her back against the pillows. "I'll straighten up your bed. It always makes you feel better to have the sheets tucked in tightly."

Maria's experienced hands pulled the bottom sheet taut all around the mattress. She threw the spread, blanket and top sheet over the footboard. After flipping them a few times, she pulled the sheet up over Martha and folded the other covers across the foot of the bed.

By this time Martha was having another contraction. She gnashed her teeth. Pain distorted her face. Maria had witnessed many sisters in labor and she recognized the signs of a difficult labor. She was worried because Martha had had short, uncomplicated labors and deliveries with her first three children.

"Martha, did you have any breakfast?" she asked when Martha relaxed again.

"No. I couldn't stand the smell."

"I expect you need a little something. I'll fix you some mint tea with a spoonful or two of honey."

Maria poured fresh water from the full bucket into the teakettle, poked up the fire and swung the kettle on the crane directly over the embers in the back of the chimney. She heard a slight noise. Her eyes followed the direction of the sound. Maria had to bend down to see under the table. There sat Eleonora.

"What are you doing, child?" Maria asked, pulling a chair back to have a clearer view.

Eleonora had her chubby hands around a crock. Maria reached out to pull the child forward. As her hands touched Eleonora's and the crock, she exclaimed, "My goodness what a sticky mess. Come on out and let me see what you have."

Reluctantly, the little girl crawled out. Maria took the crock. "Honey! Did you think you were a little bee?"

Eleonora was excited at the joke. She clapped her hands and was surprised to feel them stick together. "Look, Grandmama."

Maria inspected the little hands and smiled. She took a soft linen towel, dipped it into the water bucket, then proceeded to wash Eleonora's face and hands, and the outside of the honey crock. She noticed the child's apron was also sticky so she took it off and sent her upstairs for a fresh one.

Maria took this time to douse another clean towel into the water bucket. She wrung it out over the floor as it was not very wet and flung it around and around as she went into the bedroom.

She sat on the soft feather mattress and wiped Martha's face with the cool, damp cloth.

"Mama, that feels so good."

Maria flung the cloth outward then reapplied it to Martha's wrists. Eleonora came bouncing down the steps. "In here," called out Maria.

Eleonora pulled the handle down and opened the door. "Here, Grandmama," she said as she held out the apron.

Maria folded the damp cloth and placed it on Martha's forehead. She turned and took the apron and tied it around Eleonora.

"Why is Mama in bed?"

"Your Mama doesn't feel good today. I'm going to take care of her like she takes care of you. How would you like to go to grandfather's today?"

"Can I? Now?"

"Soon. Stand over by the window and watch for him."

The child did just that, pressing her face to the glass pane.

Maria returned to the kitchen. She put mint into the teapot and poured in boiling water. After a cursory glance she decided to put some potatoes on to boil for lunch. As she finished peeling the potatoes, the bell rang in the apothecary. Drying her hands, she mumbled, "How does Martha ever finish anything."

In the shop she saw a man with four chickens. He had two in each hand, holding them firmly by their feet but they were flapping their wings.

"Is the doctor in?" the stranger inquired.

"No." Maria answered frowning at the fowl in the shop.

"Well, I brought these pullets to the doctor. He fixed up my arm awhile back. Where can I put them?"

Maria could think only of getting them outside. She led the man toward the front door. She stopped, poked her head in the bedroom door, and told Martha she was going outside a minute and instructed Eleonora to continue watching at the window.

The man with his now squawking chickens had been waiting in the hall; he followed her outside and through the gate.

Maria surveyed the yard. "They're not set up to keep livestock. Let's see."

The man suggested that they kill the chickens right then.

"No, no. No use to eat 'em all in one day. We can wring one neck, but in this weather I'd rather keep the others alive a few days. What about that old barrel over there? Drop 'em in there. They'll be all right until the doctor comes."

The man did as he was bid. He obliged by wringing the neck of one and left the limp fowl on a tree stump in the shade.

Maria asked his name so that she could write it down in the ledger. As she puffed back up the side yard, she thanked him for his gift and his help.

Back inside, she put the potatoes in water, thinking all the time she'd make chicken soup today, chicken and dumplings tomorrow and next day fry chicken and wind up the gift offering with a baked chicken. And poultry broth would be strengthening to Martha. She would save the feathers for pillows. She took the tea into Martha, who was sitting up in bed again.

"I'm not comfortable lying down."

"Well, get up and walk around the room once or twice while I fluff your pillows."

Martha wiggled to the edge of the bed, swung her legs over then carefully stood. "Whew, I like this soft bed, except when I'm pregnant."

"He's here. He's here," chirped Eleonora pointing to the window.

"Good," sighed Maria in relief. "Give your Mama a kiss and come along."

Martha leaned forward to exchange kisses with her youngest daughter. "Bye, dear. Be good for Grandfather."

Eleonora bounded out the door in a brightness to match the summer day.

That was about all that was bright that day. No matter what position Martha chose, none were comfortable. As the day wore on, the heat and humidity became oppressive. Martha tossed about and groaned. Maria continued to apply damp cloths to Martha's increasingly warm body.

Sam had returned around noon saying he had intended to be back sooner.

Maria looked directly at him and stated firmly, "We understand. Now that you're here, I believe you'll realize this patient needs some professional help."

"Sister Miksch, I knew this very special patient was in good hands with you." Sam pronounced cheerfully.

Maria smiled with the compliment.

"Martha, how's it going?" Sam asked as he sat beside her.

"It's not easy like before," she replied weakly.

He felt her abdomen. "It'll be awhile yet. I'll wash up and eat. Call if you need me." He leaned toward her and kissed her forehead then left the room.

She nodded then dozed.

The baby was born in mid-afternoon, another girl. This one, unlike the other three, wasn't strong. Sam and Maria exchanged anxious glances when Martha asked to see the baby. Sam suggested she wait until Maria had time to clean her.

"Besides, my dear," he added as brightly as he could manage, "you're half asleep."

Sam moved to a corner of the room where Maria had covered a table top with a soft clean small sheet. Here, Maria was washing the baby, who neither moved nor cried in protest.

Maria whispered low to Sam, "Is she breathing right?"

Sam's face was grave. He did not answer. Although he stayed near the baby all afternoon, there was nothing he could do to prolong his daughter's life. Martha was awake and alert enough to hold the newborn girl; however, Sam sensed Martha knew the fragility of her life. Even so, it was hard for him to tell Martha that their daughter had been called away so quickly. He comforted Martha with tenderness.

While Martha grieved for her departed baby, she also became more thankful for the good health of her other daughters. Martha regained her strength and pleasant disposition rapidly. She knew she needed to be up and around. Others depended on her.

CHAPTER TWENTY-NINE

"Martha," Sam spoke heatedly, "we've got to have a hospital in Salem *now*."

Martha glanced up from her mending. "I wish you could persuade the Collegium or even the Conferenz to build one since the church is finished."

"I've given up trying to convince them."

"Sam, won't it be necessary to have their approval?"

He jumped up from the table where he had been grinding some herbs. He paced the room. "We're too crowded here. I can't turn the patients away."

"I wish I could do something, dear. I feel so helpless."

"No. I don't blame you. You're a big help to me."

"I want to do more. Would you like for us to move upstairs? You could let the patients have our room."

"No." Sam stopped suddenly in front of Martha. "If we can't have a hospital, Martha, how do you feel about having the outsiders stay in our home?"

"Well, they've been staying here all along. If there's no where else to place them, I'm sure we can manage in the future."

"I've been thinking about the house I've always wanted to build up on Church Street."

"Yes."

"Now may be the time to start it. We could go ahead and build it large enough to house our family and the apothecary and include a room for treating patients and for performing operations."

"Oh, that sounds so reasonable. Can we afford it?"

"We'd have to borrow some money from the Collegium."

"Do you think they'll make the loan?"

"I'll certainly ask. First, I'll go to them about purchasing the land."

The next evening at the Collegium meeting, Sam presented his request for purchasing the land for building a residence and apothecary. He did not meet any opposition on this issue. However, when he told the group that he wanted his house to be located on the crown of the hill, there was a definite negative reaction.

"If you place your house there, you will block the lane."

"When I build, there will no need for anyone to go down there anymore."

"Place your house to the side of the lane, in case someone in the future needs to use that route," a brother suggested.

"Why not place your house further south. It would then be in the center of lots seven and eight?" someone asked.

"A building will be needed for the wagon and the horse. I certainly do not want such a building on higher ground than the house," Sam shot back.

"Why not place that building in back, down the hill?"

"Too low. Drainage would be a problem. And it wouldn't be convenient."

"If you build in the middle, why that street will run up that steep bank straight into your front door," surmised another member.

"Excellent! People will be able to see my house without any difficulty."

"No one else has a house in the center of the street."

By this time Sam was thoroughly exasperated with the brethren's reasoning. "I want my house on the high land. A lot of sick outsiders come to me. If any of them have to stay there to get well, I want them in the healthiest spot. If you refuse my petition to build my house where I want it, then I withdraw my offer to buy the land. Now, I'll excuse myself from this meeting in order that you can finish your discussion without me. Good evening."

The following morning when a brother appeared at First House to inform Sam that the Collegium had voted to allow him to place his house on the top of the lot, Sam simply thanked the brother without any sign of emotion.

Sam called to Martha that he was going down to Brother Krause's. Sam told Krause exactly what he wanted in the house and where he wanted it situated. He instructed him to save all the fruit trees he could. Krause promised that he would start on the plans right after Christmas.

Martha had a happy Christmas thinking about her new home. None of the houses she dreamed about were anywhere near as grand as the plans Krause showed to Sam and her one February evening. He had designed a two-story brick structure with chimneys on either end. There were windows on all sides.

Sam was immensely pleased with Krause's plans. "Exactly what I wanted. That will be a structure to last for a very long time."

Martha marveled, "All of brick. How long will it take to fire all those bricks?"

Krause stated, "Well, you won't be in this house in six months."

Sam asked, "When can you start?"

"Whenever you're ready."

"I'll present your plans to the Collegium this week. I'll be back with you when I hear from them."

Again, Sam heard some negative remarks from the group upon presenting his plans. No one was negative about the house plans. Everyone agreed that the designs were impressive and, that such a building would be an asset to the town. The objection, as with the first request, had to do with the location.

"Brothers, think of the resell value. Who would buy it? I don't know anyone else in the congregation who would want or need a house of such a size," said one member.

"It's not on the Main Street. It would be hard to find a buyer," added another brother.

"Brothers, I need a house of this size now. I don't plan to build again," Sam emphasized.

"The amount of the loan is large. We need to consider this further," concluded the Collegium leader.

"Then I'll bid you good evening," said Sam and he left the meeting.

The remaining brethren continued for some time to debate the issuance of a loan for the house.

Finally, the leader made a point. "Dr. Vierling has been after us for as long as I can remember to build a hospital. Perhaps if we permit him to build this large house, he will have room to take care of the strangers who come to him. Then he won't need a separate hospital."

The Collegium realized the wisdom of this argument, consented to make the loan and approved of the building plans.

The new adventure of house planning and house building drew Martha and Sam closer together. In early 1800, Martha knew she had double reasons to anticipate the future with pleasure. She was again pregnant. She carried the baby well and enjoyed a pregnancy relatively free of complaints.

She looked forward each day to escorting the girls to and from school. They would take the Church Street route to see the progress made on the house. It was a long time between the cornerstone laying in the spring of 1800 and the date of their moving in – June 5, 1802.

Nevertheless, the time was marked by several important events to the Vierlings.

On September 3, Martha gave birth to their first son. She and Sam were delighted with the healthy boy. Soon after the delivery they discussed names. She asked him if he wanted to select a name from his family, and he likewise asked her the same question.

"Martha," Sam said emphatically, "I do so want this child and the girls, too, of course, to grow up knowing the love of the Lord. Let's give him a good start with a good name."

"If we both choose a name from our families, could we use August from mine for my grandfather?"

"We couldn't do better. How about Ernst for my father?"

Martha smiled. "I like that. Let's call him Ernst."

In February 1800, the community experienced a real loss at the death of one of their outstanding leaders—Brother Marshall. Because of his administrative role and of his genuine love and concern for the congregation, there was scarcely an inhabitant who had not known a personal tie with him.

The problems of that year were more happy ones than distressing for the Vierlings. There were constant decisions about the building, planning the furnishings, making the curtains and designing the garden. Krause was doing such a splendid job, that neither of them objected to his laying the herringbone pattern (that had become his building signature) in the gable ends.

There was one community problem that distressed Sam. It was not a new problem, but Sam finally reached the point where he decided some kind of official action should be taken.

One day he was disgusted when he sat down to dinner. "Salt meat again!"

"Sam, that's all we have," Martha tried to soothe him.

"Well, it's not good enough. Everybody in town eats too much of this kind of meat. They need fresh meat."

"But, dear, it's spring. People are planting. They don't have time to butcher. Soon it'll be hot weather and your know there's never been much butchering in summer."

"There should be. People can't be in the best of health with all this preserved meat. How are the patients going to get well without the proper diet?"

"What can you do about it, Sam? You've talked to everybody."

"If I put it in writing, maybe they'd pay more attention."

"Even if they agree with you, how would you suggest the town get more fresh meat?"

"Set up a meat house."

"Not another slaughter shop?"

"No. A market place where people could go to buy fresh meat."

"But wouldn't the meat spoil if it were not sold and had to be kept over several days?" the practical Martha inquired.

"The market could be opened only a few days a week. Set a regular time so that the sisters would know when to shop. There must be a number of outsiders who hunt regularly that would be glad to have a market for their game," Sam said, getting enthusiastic about his project.

"Oh. How would the brothers feel about that?"

"It shouldn't hurt their business. After all most of them are craftsmen. They don't have time or the skill to bring in game. This fresh meat would benefit the whole town. By Jove, I believe, I'll write a letter to the Collegium right now."

He wrote the letter, but it was some time before he had an official response.

However, the elders did approach Sam about another problem concerning the health of the community. They called him to a meeting.

"Dr. Vierling, we have news that the new cowpox serum being used to inoculate against smallpox is highly successful."

"Yes, I've heard the reports."

"We understand that some doctors in Raleigh are using the vaccine."

"They are."

"Could you take a trip down there to investigate the results?"

"I don't see how I can go now. My house is nearing completion. There's so much to do to get the new shop and laboratory set up. And who would look after my patients?"

The elders finally decided to send another brother to Raleigh to find out what he could about the vaccination procedures and results and availability of the vaccine.

Sam endorsed the plan. He told the elders he would inoculate the townspeople as soon as the serum was on hand.

The brother returned from Raleigh with a report that the inoculation program appeared to be very successful. Immediately, the elders ordered vaccine for the Wachovia area.

During late spring, Martha and Sam's days were filled not only with regular duties but also with the added chores of moving into their new brick house. Martha was so pleased that she now had both an outside bake house and wash house. She knew this would eliminate a lot of heat and dampness in the family house during the summer. She looked forward to not having wet clothes and linens hanging about the kitchen and other rooms.

She assisted Sam with the apothecary garden. After the ground had been broken and turned, she watched Sam design the garden. She helped him move the plants, a few at the time.

Matthew, who was aging rapidly, also walked up the hill to oversee the house and garden. He would offer advice about the best soil mixture for certain herbs and how deep to set the plants. He told Sam that he could have any plants he wanted from the nursery. Matthew was ready to give up the nursery because the work was too strenuous.

"Father," Martha said, "when you completely stop gardening, you and Mama can share the harvest from our garden."

"Thank you. On my good days, I'll come up and help you with the harvest. I may not be able to stoop and dig much, but I can still tie up sage and separate the seeds," Matthew stated.

"Those are important jobs. The help will be appreciated," she replied sincerely.

"Martha, this is a mighty big house. Do you reckon you all will get lost or lonely?" He looked around, then commented, "You don't have any near neighbors. No one in the back; graveyard to the right; nothing between you and the church, and you can hardly see the Vorsteher's house from here."

The Vierlings moved into their new house on June 5. Sometime during July, Martha and Sam recalled Matthew's question about getting lonely.

Martha had just registered the name of the last patient of the day. He had come for a smallpox inoculation. She reviewed the recent entries and counted some of the names.

"Sam, do you know how many people you've vaccinated for smallpox?"

"Not exactly."

"Almost eighty."

Sam laughed. "Remember when your father asked if we'd be lonely up here?"

"And that's for only one procedure. I won't add the list of all your patients."

About this time, there was a knock at the treatment room door.

"Come in," Sam spoke up.

Brother Benzien entered. "Good evening to you. Your patients have all left, Dr. Vierling?"

"Yes."

"How are the inoculations progressing?"

"I think we've just about finished with every body who needed and wanted one," Sam answered as he put away the syringes.

"Good. I hope there have been no adverse reactions?"

"On the whole, I'd say the project has been successful."

"You never have given us an estimate of your fees for the inoculations."

Sam turned to Benzien. "I've thought about this and prayed about it. There will be no charge for my services."

Surprised, Benzien responded, "But this has taken a great deal of your time."

"The community has been good to me. I'm glad if I can do something for it."

"Why this is very, very generous of you." Benzien shook hands and thanked him for his generosity.

Martha was immensely proud of Sam and his abilities. Now she viewed him with a new admiration at this very unselfish service. Truthfully, Martha was beginning to feel pride in her new stately house. She was aware that congregation members and strangers alike stopped out front to view the impressive structure. Pride was an undesirable trait that she was urging her mind to temper.

There were areas of the new house that reflected more of her taste and personality. She now had her own furniture in the bedroom and her own curtains. Anna's furniture had been moved to a room for patients and the old hand-embroidered curtains had been folded and stored for Polly.

With a room designed for patients, extra people were not always under foot and Martha could attend to her family duties with more ease. Martha found joys multiplied as she had more time to be a helpmate to Sam. She enjoyed grinding the herbs, cleaning the apothecary, keeping records, and attending to patients.

Her children were healthy and happy. They were all in school daily except Sundays. That is all except the baby. Martha did regret that she had so little time for the girls. When they came home from school, there was supper to prepare and afterwards the cleaning up. Next the family would go to evening services together as often as possible. Then it was time for the girls to go to bed. Occasionally Martha felt she was turning over many of her motherly duties to Henrietta who helped so capably with the younger ones.

Sam was constantly concerned with the spiritual welfare of his children. Occasionally on the way home from service he would talk to the girls about the minister's message or the hymns. He told them that joining the Unity had meant a great deal to him and he hoped they too would see the value in belonging to the congregation. Other times he would quote lines or verses from hymns, such as: "Not on my own counsel, but on God, will I build my happiness."

Within the next year Sam was to see one long-held wish materialize. It came about along with several changes.

The Salem leaders decided to erect a new corpse house north of the recently built church. They voted to tear down the current stone corpse house in the square. Now the old corpse house had previously been the storage area for the town's two fire engines. In discussing where to place the engines, someone suggested erecting a small building on the square facing Main Street. Someone else proposed a partitioned building with the second side to be used as a meat house. The brethren agreed this would be a central place, serviceable for both purposes and convenient for the townspeople.

Sam was pleased upon hearing the good news. Martha was impressed that services in Salem were expanding. She was especially interested in the beginnings of a boarding school for girls. She remembered how often outsiders had requested that the school take their daughters. Martha's own daughters attended the congregation's day school for girls.

One evening when the house was quiet, she said, "Sam, I think the Kramschs were a good selection for the new boarding school."

"I'll be glad to see him resettled in Salem."

"They were both so grateful for your help back last summer when they were so sick. While Susanna was here, she talked to me about the girls' school in Europe. Also about her 'outside' pupil who stayed with her in Hope."

"Now that we've built our hospital house, Martha, the town is finally opening up more to strangers."

"But they're just children, dear."

"The committee will have to screen the girls. After all, someday the town girls may go to school with them."

Following a brief silence, Sam added. "But it's a decision I have no quarrel with."

"I'm glad, because if the girls are ever ill, you will be the one to treat them, won't you?"

"Yes."

"Oh Sam," she spoke softly and compassionately, "you are such a help to everybody."

"And you to me, dear Martha," he returned appreciatively and blew out the last candle for the evening.

In May 1804, Martha gave birth to her second son. He was named Friedrich Benjamin. Martha did not have long to lie in bed and be a patient.

In June, Sam had patients whom Martha felt needed attention. Especially interesting to her were two patients: Miss Caldwell and Mr. Mitchell. Both were twenty-four years old and from the same neighboring county.

Miss Caldwell was the daughter of a Presbyterian minister. She had been brought to Dr. Vierling because she had suffered from a weakness of the mind. Sam operated: he trepanned her skull. Sometime after she left Salem, they were pleased to hear that her condition had improved.

Mr. Mitchell had been totally blind for many years. Sam performed a cataract operation on one of his eyes. He told them a spiritual awakening was talking place in his neighborhood. Other patients of Sam brought the same news.

Martha had occasion to feel sad about one person who was called home during that summer. At one of the afternoon services, she heard the memoir of Brother Joseph Dixson read. He had died in Pennsylvania. Martha recalled the wartime and his trip to the army camp, his work with the boys' school and his wish to become a doctor. She remembered his kindness after the lightning incident. She wondered if she had ever conveyed her appreciation for all he did or tried to do? She lowered her head and prayed silently. "Thank you, Joseph Dixson."

In the fall, another case interested Martha. A man that Sam treated over a two-month period had been brought up in a Christian home, had joined a Protestant church, then left the church. The love, care and concern of the brethren who treated, nursed and aided him made such an impression, that the man said upon leaving that he planned to dedicate his future to the Lord.

With the increase in the number of patients and the growing needs of her own family, Martha was appreciative of the cow that had been given to Sam in payment for services. There were days, when she felt she had saved time by not having to run to the dairy. But on other days, owning a cow, with all its food and shelter requirements in addition to seeing that the milking was tended to, was a time consumer in itself.

She laughed as she recalled Sam telling her the first day of their marriage that she was a city girl. What unusual things people found themselves doing as they grew older. Again, she smiled. "Older. Here I am with a baby and talking about growing older."

However, Martha realized that her parents' growing older was not a matter to be taken lightly.

Sam was concerned about the health of both Matthew and Maria, himself. While he was a believer in people working as long as they possibly could because he observed most of them were happier and healthier when they were contributing members of a society; he encouraged the Mikschs to slow down. He used the identical word duo *slow down* that Matthew and Maria had been saying for years.

One day while Sam was on his way home from the Opizs' farm, he stopped to check on his in-laws.

"Good afternoon, Sam," Matthew welcomed him warmly.

"Good afternoon. Brother Opiz sends greetings to you."

"Oh? You've been out there. How is he?"

"Better. Up and around. Ready to go back to work."

"I'm sure he is."

"Yes, he enjoys being useful. But the farm is now too much."

"That's a nice place he has."

"Beautiful. It would be desirable for a hospital. Sometimes I can't find places for my out-of-town patients."

"Would the Collegium let you use it for that purpose?"

"No. But I'll ask. Speaking of slowing down, you should do the same."

"I've been thinking about giving up my tobacco trade."

"I hear Brother Biwighaus is still hoping to find a small business for himself. He may consider taking over the tobacco business."

"He's a reliable brother. He would probably do well with it.

I'll talk to him then we'll see how matters go," Matthew said thoughtfully.

Sam nodded, then spoke, "I noticed a front step was loose when I came in. It ought to be repaired; it could cause an accident."

"I was intending to have it fixed. That and a few other things."

"What other things?"

"Some plastering and roof repair."

"Those repairs shouldn't wait too long," Sam warned. As he walked down the front steps, he was careful of the loose one. Later that day when he and Martha were having tea, he spoke of his visit to her parents.

"Sam, thank you for dropping in on them," Martha said appreciatively.

"Both of them are getting weaker. I believe your father is ready to give up his tobacco manufacturing and the shop."

"What about mama, the gingerbread?"

"They should be able to continue that for a while longer."

"I'm glad. Father can help mama. And there will be customers, so he will have people coming in to talk with."

"The house is in need of repairs."

"I know. I doubt that father can afford to have them done. It's not like him to neglect things."

"Martha, I'll pay for repairs."

"That is so generous."

"It'll be your property someday. We should help take care of it."

Not long after the repairs were completed on the Miksch house, an evaluation of town property was made. Ironically, the Miksch's house had about the least value—$250.00, and the Vierlings, the most—$3000.00.

Matthew did relinquish his sale rights to tobacco and Brother Biwighaus did acquire the rights. Matthew was a trifle surprised that Biwighaus also was designated as a bookbinder. Matthew wished his old friend well in both enterprises.

"Now that Salem has a paper mill, perhaps there will be some books printed to bind," he told the Vierlings one evening when he and Maria were visiting them just before evening services.

"Father," Martha was amused, " do you remember long ago when I talked of making a book?"

"Oh, yes."

"And I never got around to it. Well, I hope there are, somewhere in Salem, people who will get busy writing now."

"You and I didn't see those two adventures through, did we? But there's still no printer in town."

"Maybe someday we'll have a print shop."

Maria chided them. "With all the other accomplishments you two have claim to, I shouldn't think you'd give that a minute's thought. I declare, Martha, I don't see how you keep up everything here."

"Mama, you were always busy. I just try to keep up with all I saw you do – and like you taught me to."

Maria blushed.

CHAPTER THIRTY

Martha continued to stay busy, taking care of the children, the house, the gardens and the patients. Sam was occupied with church duties and his patients at home and in the out-lying communities. Oftentimes, when Sam was out, Martha would find that the patients or members of a patient's family would want to spend some time chatting. She understood that the people were lonely and a little nervous or apprehensive after an operation or during an illness. While Martha did not seek the male outsiders to converse with, she had learned not to turn away from their questions or efforts at talking.

Many of the out-of-town people coming to Sam found the Moravian town structure unusual. They seemed amazed to learn that the church owned all the property and the inhabitants merely owned the improvements on the lots they leased. Strangers were also surprised at the choir system that grouped the townspeople by age, sex and marital status.

Martha did not like the position of having to defend her religion. She preferred not to discuss customs that were distinct to Moravians with strangers. Occasionally though she found herself drawn in some point.

Once Sam operated on a young man who had to remain in Salem and the Vierling's house for several weeks. The boy's father came and stayed, so that he could help take care of his son. The afternoon before the two were to leave Salem, Sam was away and Martha was showing the man how to make a rubbing lotion of rose petals in alcohol.

"You'll find this refreshes the patient. Keep the lotion in a glass or glazed bottle."

"Sister Vierling, I appreciate your showing me this. I want to thank you for being so kind to my son and me the past weeks. You've done everything possible to make us comfortable," the gentleman said.

"It was a pleasure to be of service."

"This is really about the first opportunity I have had to talk with you. The ladies in Salem don't have much to say to outsiders."

Martha didn't reply. She shook the alcohol solution.

"Your people are certainly kind and helpful to those of us in need. Yet somehow I feel there's a difference here."

Martha looked at the man.

"Don't you feel you're living inside a walled city?" he asked.

"We have no wall."

"No wall of stones or bricks, but nevertheless a wall."

"How so?"

"It's not *imagined*. It's been surveyed. On one side of that very tangible line there's a freedom of air. On your side – there's a strong scent of exclusiveness – an *ours* signal. Do you deny that I, also a sworn Christian, cannot live inside your town?"

"No."

"Then you have a wall, only you refer to it as a law, to keep me out. Also, can you leave this town? Can you build off your church's land and still have privileges of the community?"

"In some cases," she responded.

"Come now. Isn't it extremely complicated?"

"Why should we want to move away? There's everything we want right here."

"Everything you want?" He stared at her with an expression of incredulity. "Perhaps some of your neighbors may want other things, and yet those brothers or sisters may still be very tuned in with God."

"Are you proposing that some brethren may be believers of Moravian theology but do not wish to practice Moravian everyday habits?"

"Just so!"

"The two do not seem compatible to me."

"Could you ever see that man's laws may not be God's laws?"

Martha explained, "Our principle laws are based on the lot. The answers are God directed."

He challenged, "But man *submits* the question to the lot?"

"Yes."

"He writes the questions?"

"True."

"So?"

"The elders are very careful to be objective—and always to be fair."

The man continued, respectful but focused on eliciting answers. "Even if man tries to be fair, can't you see that he is still human and *may be* in error? He may at times be subjective."

"Yes, though without intention to be thus. That's one reason there are several elders involved in submitting questions."

"Admittedly, they've all been raised under the same theologies and practices. Certainly they already think alike."

"Not always – raised alike, I mean. I've lived here all life. I grew up knowing men with all types of backgrounds and nationalities before we became a United States. My parents were Germans, as most of our congregation now, but not everybody was from Germany. And besides, all Germans are not alike. Our merchant and assemblyman was a Dane, others were from England. Many were converts from other religious denominations."

"Are you saying," he prodded with interest, "that they thought alike and wanted to band together?"

"I suppose so."

"Take your merchant, he must have dealt daily with people outside your town in business and in the assembly."

"He often did."

"And your doctors, your husband. They render aid beyond the town limits."

"They are pledged to serve those in need."

"Creditable. But when night comes they pack their bag and return to the fold within the walls."

Calmly, she answered. "This is their home."

"Pardon this very personal question. I trust I will not offend. I do not intend to do so. Are you people *afraid* to stay away at night?"

"What do you mean by afraid?"

"Do you fear you'll lose your strength, your touch with God, if you are separated?"

She paused and reflected a moment before answering. "I cannot answer for the Unity in entirety, only for myself. I have never been away from here, not for a night. I have not stayed because I was afraid. I have stayed because I never felt led to do anything other than what I have done any day of my life. But *if* I were directed to leave, I believe I could do so, though admittedly the separation from my family and the congregation I have known all my life would be a wrenching pain to bear."

"I see."

"As for *coming home at night* from the labors of the day, do not all people like to return to some particular home, even though all the world is God's, and we should feel at home anywhere in his world? Isn't it comforting to have a special place to go, where you know you will be welcomed and loved, a place to rest from the major troubles of life?"

"You have spoken of every man's desire." The outsider looked at her with respect and admiration. He folded his arms as he leaned back against a ledge. "Aye, Sister Vierling, your faith is unarguable. You almost *persuade* me there's a bit of perfect heaven here. I wonder though, if I stayed long, would I see brothers take issue with brothers and sisters crossing sisters."

"In unimportant matters. In essential things, there is unity." She considered briefly. "Or a continuance until there is a new accord."

"Beware. It's those little things, if they are repeated day after day, that wear away the finished fabric. If the crossings persist, then will the Unity hold together under the continuous stress?"

"I trust so; however, I will heed your warning. I'll take care not to cross my sisters."

The hard years of wartime had been lifted from the surface of Martha's mind, but its stamp was deeply etched, as were other acts or vivid impressions of childhood. Many could be recalled without difficulty. And a similar pattern resumed during the unusual chain of events in 1805.

The chain really had its beginnings in the late summer and fall of '04. The area enjoyed a record wheat and grain harvest. The cattle were fatted. Milk was produced in abundance. Butter more than met the local needs.

But conditions were in direct contrast in '05. The wheat and grain crops were nil. Prices of both soared. Salem had shipped its grain to other markets. Later, adverse growing conditions continued and there was no pasture for the cattle, no grain for the livestock. Soon the milk supply dwindled and for the first time butter was an almost non-existent luxury.

This sequence of conditions wrecked the economy of many families as well as made obtaining daily bread difficult.

Martha's children had not been through such lean times before. They complained about having to go without milk, butter and cheese. Martha explained to them about the shortages during the Revolutionary War.

One Saturday afternoon, she took all the children down to the yellow house. She entertained hopes that her parents could help the children understand the current situation. As the children burst into the Mikschs' house, one and all shouted, "Grandmama, is the gingerbread ready?"

Maria and Matthew were seated in the front room. Matthew was polishing apples.

"My, my. Looks like we have company here," he commented pleasantly.

"Gingerbread," they all repeated. Martha closed the door. She cautioned the children to mind their manners and not to ask for things. Wait to be offered.

"Children, there's not any gingerbread today," Maria told them. Immediately, they looked dejected. "I couldn't get any flour or butter."

"You mean there's a shortage here, too?" spoke Eleonora in amazement.

"Oh, yes, indeed," Maria emphasized with a definite nod.

"There're probably a few nuts on the tree outside," Matthew said. "If you young ones will come with me, we'll shake 'em off and you can help me crack them."

They jumped up. Running for the back door, they argued as to who would climb the tree to shake it first.

As Matthew slowly raised himself, Martha said, "Thank you, Father."

He patted her shoulders as he passed her. "I'll get my hat. Don't want to be bombarded with nuts."

After he went out, Maria said, "Even if I had the ingredients for the gingerbread, I doubt if anyone would have the money to buy it."

"Mama, are things that bad now?"

Maria shook her head. "I'm getting too old to be keeping up with all this. Martha, your father and I are giving up our saal diener and dienerin responsibilities."

"No?"

"We've already talked to Brother Benzien. They're giving us a love feast next week. I want you all to come."

"We will, Mama. How many years has it been?"

"Thirty years."

"You've given good service. Everybody says so." Martha fought back tears.

"It's been a privilege."

That night at bedtime, Martha told Sam about her parents' situation. "They are both aging so rapidly. Mama doesn't get about at all well. Sam, I wish I could help them. Just checking in everyday isn't enough. They've always done everything they could for me."

"Martha, would you like to bring them here to live with us?"

"They'd like that."

"Would you?"

"Yes. Thank you for all you kindness." She walked over and hugged him. After reflecting a bit, she asked, "Where will we put them?"

"The girls could double up. Martha, the boarding school is going to have lots of room in the new building."

"You are suggesting that the girls become boarding students?"

"They could be. It worked fine for Polly. Martha, they'd still be close by. We'd see them at services."

"It sounds like when I went to live in the sisters choir house." She was silent for awhile. "I'll think about it." She laid her head on Sam's shoulder. It was sometime before she went to sleep. Memories of people going and coming, thoughts of gaining and losing, visions of spring and winter kept surging and ebbing behind her closed eyes.

Matthew and Maria moved in with the Vierlings. Sam set about to sell the Mikschs' house. He was immediately informed by the Collegium that the board had the first option to buy any house once the original lease-holders of the lot were not using it. Sam was not too pleased with the statement; but, as typical of him, he abided by the rules. He ceased his efforts and the Conferenz purchased the house.

Martha had anticipated that her days would be easier when her parents came into her home. She would no longer have to arrange things so that she could check on them. To the contrary, she found she was spending more time talking with them whenever they were in the same room together. Therefore, she was delayed getting around to some of her other jobs.

One morning Martha peeled three quarts of potatoes and put them on to boil. She planned to have potato soup for lunch, potato salad for supper and to have enough potatoes for bread and sugar cake. She felt rather pleased at having routine matters so well under control that particular morning. She sang a favorite hymn as she hung out the wash. She paused to pull a few weeds in the kitchen garden.

She was surprising happy pumping a bucket of water. She went directly to her parents' room and filled their water pitcher.

"Father, it's a beautiful day. Would you like to walk to the boys school to get Ernst at dinner time?"

"That boy is hard to walk with. He wants to run."

"You have to tell him to slow down."

"I have. I have. He doesn't seem to hear me."

"Father, I'm sorry. I'll speak to him. He must learn to mind. I can't imagine his not respecting an older person."

"Don't be too hard on him. He's only a child."

"You wouldn't have let me act disrespectful. Mama, do you need anything?"

"I want to wind this yarn. I'm knitting some socks for the girls. Can you hold the yarn?"

Martha expected the process would be long: nevertheless, she disliked refusing her mother. "Let me check on Sam's patients and fill their water pitchers. I'll be right back."

Maria was slow at the winding. Gout bothered her joints so she had difficulties with her hands. Martha knew she should be moving on to other chores, however she returned to help her mother.

"Martha, if the girls don't have anything else to do right after lunch, I'll show them how to start the socks."

"All right. I'll hunt some needles," Martha consented with the knowledge that if the girls had a knitting lesson she'd have to complete their duties. Suddenly, Martha sniffed. "What do I smell?"

Matthew and Maria inhaled deeply. He said, "Smells like something's burning."

Martha gasped. "The potatoes." She hurriedly put down the yarn and dashed to the kitchen. She pulled the iron pot forward. She pushed the top slightly ajar. Smoke and fumes of burned potatoes escaped. Quickly, she repositioned the lid and removed the heavy pot, carefully taking it to the back yard. Sam came to the back door. "Martha, what's that smell?"

"The burned potatoes. I thought you were down the street seeing a patient."

"I was. I saw several. I'm back for dinner."

"It's not ready." She stood by the pot and stared at it. "Now there'll be no potato bread, nor salad for supper, or sugarcake for breakfast. Not even soup for lunch. I'm sorry, dear. I should have been tending to the cooking. Instead, I was helping mama."

Sam came down the steps and Martha walked over to him. He asked directly, "Don't you need some help?"

"Help?"

"Someone to do some of the chores. You are carrying a heavy work load these days."

"Sam, I've never had any help. I wouldn't know what to tell someone to do."

"I'll ask the pflegerin if there's a sister available – preferably one who's already trained. Would you rather have help to cook or wash or clean?"

"Wash and cook, and to bake."

Sam put his arm around her shoulder and accompanied her up the steps.

After evening service, he walked down to the Sisters House to check on a patient in the sick room. He also talked with the pflegerin about needing a sister to work in his house. She talked with the sisters later but had to report to Sam that no one was interested in or available for that kind of work at the present time.

She was reluctant to make a suggestion to Sam but she did so anyway. "Dr. Vierling, since none of the sisters can serve you now, have you considered hiring a negress?"

"I hadn't thought about it. However, I certainly will consider it. Thank you."

The pflegerin hesitated in suggesting any outsider for a position in town that the sisters could fill. However, she knew that Martha Miksch had always been known to work at a constant, highly productive level and as such it might be hard to find anyone wanting to work with her at her performance standard. In the light of this, the pflegerin was persuaded to offer an alternative. If Dr. Vierling thought his wife needed help, then surely she must.

Dr. Vierling did locate a negress to assist Martha in the house. Martha was glad now for her years of teaching; otherwise, she would have felt totally lost at directing the work of another person.

She found her time was quickly consumed with other responsibilities. The two boys were a lively combination, seemingly more energetic than the girls had been when they were small. She wished that Sam had more time to be with them.

When he was away, she especially enjoyed having her parents in the house to keep her company. When they were feeling well, she could leave the youngest ones in bed and attend services. In the afternoons, she could occasionally attend the married people's choir meeting. Sometimes she accompanied Sam on short trips in the area. And she continued to help him care for the patients in their home hospital.

"Martha, I've just had a letter in the post from a Mr. Williams in the Greenville area of South Carolina. He wants to send his son up here for treatment."

"What's wrong with him?"

"An infection on his leg."

"Do you think you can find someone to lodge him?"

"I'll try. We do have a number of patients around town."

"While you try to think of someone and answer the letter, I'll see to dinner."

Among the extra jobs that Martha had her new helper's assistance with was in preparing a room for the patient from South Carolina.

"After you finish washing that bed, please bring in the whitewash and we'll start on the walls," Martha instructed the negress.

Martha folded the clean sheets and spread that had recently been boiled, dried and ironed.

After the walls were whitewashed and the bed made, Martha

burned a cone of lavender powder to give the room a more pleasant smell.

"Sam," she asked as she entered the apothecary, "what is the young man's name?"

"Thomas."

"And how old is Thomas?"

"Eighteen."

"Well, everything is ready. Is the wagon that's bringing him coming directly to town, or do you have to go meet him?"

"He's coming to town. I gave directions to the house. Martha, I'm sorry I couldn't find a room in town for him to stay in."

"That's all right. People always help out when they can. He's young and it's a long way from home. Maybe it'll be good for him to stay here. She bent over Sam as he worked at the table and kissed him. "You're such a good doctor."

Without looking up, he asked half-jesting, "Is that why I get a kiss?"

"That's why you get a kiss on the cheek."

He raised his head this time and looked at her directly. They exchanged an intimate glance.

Outside a wagon creaked up the hill. A loud voice yelled, "Whoa! Whoa!"

Martha and Sam walked to the front of the room and peered out the window. "That must be the Williams boy."

Both of them went outside.

The wagoneer inquired, "This Dr. Vierling's?"

"Yes. I'm Dr. Vierling."

"This is Thomas Williams from South Carolina."

"I'm expecting you. Good afternoon, Thomas. Have you had a good trip?" Sam asked as he walked around to the side of the wagon.

"It was bouncy, sir."

The wagoneer said, "We knew it wouldn't be too smooth, but his father thought this would be better than a chair or a stage. He could keep his leg out straight in the wagon."

"Can you stand, Thomas?" Sam asked.

"Not very well, sir."

"Can you slide down to the end here? We'll help you." Sam motioned to the wagoneer to come assist him.

When Thomas eased himself to the open end of the wagon, the two men helped him put his legs over the back edge. Thomas placed an arm around the shoulder of each man and put his weight on his good leg. Between them, he hopped up the steps to the house. Sam directed them into the treatment room.

"Now, let's have a look at your leg," he told Thomas "Um. Has it pained you much?" Sam asked while examining the large sore on the boy's leg.

"Yes, sir."

"It's swollen. I'm going to have to lance the infected area. Then I'll put some salve on it."

"Yes, sir."

The wagoneer said he'd wait outside. Martha offered the man a cup of hot coffee and some bread and cheese, which he willingly accepted. He told Martha he was to pick up some supplies to take back to Mr. Williams. "Ordinarily, I'd go to a market closer to home, but Mr. Williams wanted to get his son up here. Everybody says Dr. Vierling is a mighty fine doctor."

"Thank you. I hope you'll find all the supplies you need."

"There's a tavern here, isn't there?"

"Yes. Go back down the hill and turn left. It's on the right side about three blocks down."

Sam came to the kitchen door. "We can get him to bed now."

"Thank you for the coffee and food ma'am." He helped get Thomas to bed then left the home hospital.

Sam returned to tell Martha that Thomas was asleep.

"How does his leg look?"

"It's quite swollen. The infection appears to have been there a long time."

During the weeks and months that followed, Martha prepared many bandages for Sam to use in dressing the infected leg. Matthew was a help in grinding dried herbs for various medicines.

There were days when the swelling subsided and Sam thought the infection might be lessening, only to discover in a day or two that the sore was inflamed again. This was a stubborn case. One evening he was especially perplexed and his feelings were expressed during family prayers. "Oh, Thou who has greater healing powers than I do, please look upon this fine boy. Keep him in Thy tender care during this night. Protect him. Guide me."

The children also prayed for the Lord to look after Thomas. They had come to like him. He was one of the younger patients who stayed at their home. His particular illness didn't prevent their seeing him. The boys could go into his room and talk to him. The girls weren't allowed in, but they did special things for him, such as bringing in an ear of Indian corn at Thanksgiving and a holly sprig in early December. They were even permitted to embroider a handkerchief for him at Christmas. However, they always let their mother present the gifts. Sometimes they waited unseen at the door to hear his reaction.

These adventures gave them interesting things to talk about at school.

Christmas this year was a happy occasion for the Vierlings, especially for Martha. The family enjoyed good health and her parents were with her. She had help to attend to the less pleasant household chores. And Sam was enjoying a unique relationship with Thomas.

Every treatment that Sam used interested Thomas. He would ask Sam why he did this. He wanted to know what reactions to expect. He inquired eagerly about the medicines. The young man's questions stimulated Sam, and he took the time to explain as much as he thought could be understood. Thomas' interest and enthusiasm in medicine grew daily. His admiration for Dr. Vierling kept pace.

Thomas marveled that Dr. Vierling could take care of so many patients at once. He spoke of this several times.

"It appears you need some help, sir, another doctor."

"What we need is a hospital," Sam informed Thomas.

"Are there plans to build one?"

"No. I continue to ask."

"Is there any reason that the town objects?"

"I asked to use the farm below the Wach."

"What did they say?"

"Use the still house."

"Is that a suitable place?"

"I'd take it, if it were. The Collegium really wants to give up the distillery business. It has a deficit."

Thomas was extremely sympathetic. "I trust they'll build a hospital, sir."

"I appreciate your concern."

After Thomas had been with the Vierlings about five months, Sam finally pronounced that Thomas was cured. Thomas asked about the stage and possible connections so that he might return home that way as instructed by his father.

The family discussed the current stage schedule. Sam told them that Salem was trying to get the new post road routed through town. The leaders had sent a message that with the opening of the new boarding school that the road would be a convenience for the families traveling with their daughters and others visiting the girls.

When March 4, the day for Thomas' departure came, the Vierlings were sad to see him leave. When the stage pulled out, the girls commented how nice South Carolina men were.

Martha suddenly became inspired. "Sam, with the new routes and with the congregation stage going to and from Pennsylvania, why can't Polly come for a visit? I'd love to see her."

"Martha, that just might be possible. I'll look into it."

The girls became excited about seeing their half sister again and reminisced about her on the way home.

Sam rushed into the kitchen the first day of May, all excited. He was waving a letter.

"Why, Sam, whatever have you received?" Martha paused from pouring milk into a pitcher.

"A letter from Thomas. You'll never guess what he has written."

"Please, tell me."

"He wants to return to Salem to study medicine with me!"

"How marvelous!" She reflected his excitement. "What are you going to tell him?"

"Martha, he'd make a fine apprentice. He is quick and intelligent. He has a great deal of interest and enthusiasm."

"And he knows about pain. I think he'd be compassionate."

"It would be good to have someone to help."

"Yes, it would. Sam, do you think the Conferenz would permit an outsider to be an apprentice here?"

"I don't know. I wasn't a Moravian when I studied in Berlin. I was a doctor first. I asked to live in a congregation town."

"I do hope they'll say yes."

Sam did go the ministers to discuss Thomas' request. He told them that he could certainly use an apprentice. There were no local boys who had applied to learn medicine.

When he was asked about Thomas' religious intentions, Sam could not answer.

The Conferenz gave serious consideration to the request and consulted the regulations of the synod. They informed Sam that unless a man wanted above everything else to unite with the Brethren that he could not be taken into such an agreement. They could not break with regulations and they feared doing so would set a precedent.

Sam understood and wrote to Thomas that he could not accept him as a student. Somehow, the heart to push for medical improvements on a community basis went out of Sam after this encounter with the Conferenz.

Martha sensed his disappointment and she did her best to cheer him. "Sam, changes take time. Maybe someday they'll come around to seeing the need for the things you've asked for."

"It'll have to be at someone else's request."

"Well, if that proves the case, you have certainly laid the ground work. You have planted the seed."

Two days later Martha was helping the girls finish getting ready for an afternoon service. She was braiding Eleonora's hair and Henrietta was tying Carolina's apron strings. "Henrietta,"

Martha said, "have you heard the teachers mention any special plans for their festal day tomorrow?"

"Mama, haven't you heard?"

"Heard what?"

"There's not going to be any festal observance."

"You must be mistaken, dear. The single sisters always celebrate their choir festal day. Remember last year? They had that lovely celebration in remembrance of opening their house twenty years ago."

All the girls clustered around their mother. "It's true, Mama." "We heard some of the sisters talking." "They are so upset."

Martha looked puzzled. "But I can't imagine why not?"

Henrietta added, "Because the Conferenz won't let them. They say, and I think the lot must have been used, that they weren't showing the true spirit of sisterly love."

At this news, Martha was so astonished that she did not say anything else. Henrietta watched her mother knit her brows as she completed the braiding. "Mama, what are you thinking?"

"I don't know. Rather I was trying to remember something I'd heard. But I can't quite recall what it was." Before she could finish, her attention was drawn to the hall. Ernst was marching by and Benjamin was following. Both were carrying themselves like soldiers on parade. Ernst's voice echoed down the hall. "Halt, soldier."

Martha walked swiftly to the door. "Ernst. What are you doing?"

"Playing soldier, Mama."

"This is not a game that we allow you boys to play."

"But the big boys do. We've seen them in the square."

"If you must copy them, please, follow their best examples of behavior."

"Can we shoot things that make loud noises on the Fourth of July?"

"Certainly not! That's a day to recognize Peace. Shooting is not appropriate."

"You take all the fun out of games. C'm Benjamin."

Benjamin picked up his stick and placed it against his shoulder musket fashion. He started marching and counting one, two, one, two. Martha reached down and retrieved the stick. Benjamin cried in protest and tried to grab it.

"No! There will be no more pretend guns," Martha uttered firmly.

Benjamin continued to cry and struggle to regain his stick. Henrietta came to her mother's aid and distracted her youngest brother. "Let's go down to the kitchen and see what good things the cook is fixing for supper," Henrietta said and carried Benjamin downstairs.

Martha said half to herself, half to Carolina and Eleonora, "War. There always recurs talk of war. Our country is not even at war, yet its presence is felt."

Carolina suggested, "It could be the war in Europe. When we don't get the newsletter from Germany and people can't go back and forth across the ocean freely, everybody always says it's because of the war."

Eleonora added, "A girl at the boarding school told us that her father said the English stop our ships and search them. And now we won't be getting any shipments from England."

Martha was surprised at how much of current world affairs the girls knew. She thought her own horizons had been widening, but the girls were surpassing her in some areas.

Even Salem appeared to be expanding its boundaries. However, its expansion was a protective measure as opposed to one of growth.

Charles Bagge, Anna's brother who had moved about frequently over the past years, had built a new house and opened a store a few miles southeast of town. The Salem congregation decided to claim all lots on either side of the road from the Salem town boundaries out to Charles' store. The congregation made arrangements with the Wachovia administration to exchange this section of land for another strip.

Matthew added his pieces of information about the congregation, too, as he joined the family conversations. "Remember when I raised some questions about the marriage of a couple?"

"About it's not being submitted to the lot, Father?"

"Yes. Well, I heard today that she has left him." Everyone looked surprised. Matthew continued, "She took all the things she had before they were married. And she took a good amount of grain."

"Father, this has certainly been a strange year. I don't understand all that is happening. Am I out of touch with the heart of things?"

"No, I think not. But we might well ask if some in the congregation are losing touch with the heart of life. We have yet to see what the disregard of a few will do to the unity of our people."

CHAPTER THIRTY-ONE

A New Year brought renewed joy to Martha. She found she was again pregnant and the baby was due in June. Polly wrote that she wanted to accept the invitation to come for a visit.

Happily, Henrietta and Carolina busied themselves preparing for Polly's visit.

Henrietta asked Martha, "Mama, can we make new sheets for her bed?"

"Dear, there's such a shortage of linen. With so few people weaving anymore, we have to really be careful about how we use what we have. Put the best pair on her bed though."

In the middle of April when the Salem stage rounded the square, everything and everyone was ready for the visitor. As soon as Henrietta recognized the stage, she asked her teacher if Eleonora could run up to the house and tell her parents that the stage had arrived.

"We're expecting our sister from Pennsylvania," Henrietta explained.

"Of course, she may," answered the teacher.

"Eleonora, go tell Mama and Papa that the stage is here." Henrietta instructed her youngest sister.

"Why should I go? Can't you?" Eleonora protested.

"Because I'll go down to meet her. She might not remember you."

"She will remember me!"

"She may and she may not. Now please, go to the house." Henrietta insisted in her most persuasive voice.

Eleonora went on her errand, but she did not run. After all, for the past few months all she ever heard was "Polly, this" and "Polly, that" from her sisters. They had chatted constantly about their half sister and it seemed to Eleonora as if they had excluded her entirely from their plans and preparation.

When Eleonora told her parents that the stage was in town, they too became excited and dropped what they were doing and rushed down to the square. Everybody was embracing Polly and offering to take things for her.

Finally, Martha noticed Eleonora was lingering in the background. "Eleonora," she beckoned. "Come speak to Polly. Polly, you remember Eleonora, don't you?"

Polly opened her arms to Eleonora. "Of course, I do. You had a birthday just before I left. You were a little girl then."

Throughout Polly's visit, Eleonora continued to feel excluded from the older girls' talk. However she did find something new and pleasurable to fill her time at home. When the baby was born, Eleonora helped her mother take care of the newest family member. She had always seen Henrietta help out with the children. Now in doing this job, she, too, felt older.

Martha knew from her long experience with young girls, that those of Eleonora's age seemed drawn instinctively to babies.

There was one thing Martha wasn't absolutely sure of: Why she and Sam chose the name Traugott Theophilus for their new son? Was it because Polly was visiting and the Bagge connection was so much with them? Or was it because time had reduced her feelings toward the very large figure of Traugott Bagge? No matter what the reason, she decided to call the baby Theophilus.

During the summer, Sam asked Polly if she wanted to return to Pennsylvania, saying, "You're welcomed to stay with us if you want to."

"You're all being so good to me. I like Salem, but I would like to finish school in Bethlehem."

Polly was enthusiastic about life in Bethlehem and she conveyed this spirit of enthusiasm to Henrietta and Carolina.

When Brother Benzien informed Sam that he, his wife and

son were going to Bethlehem in September, Sam made plans for Polly to return with them. It was a tender farewell that the family shared. Martha and Sam did not know when they would all be together again. Polly begged her father to let the girls come someday to visit her in Pennsylvania.

"We'll see," he promised, but reminded her, "we're not a traveling family."

The Vierlings had scarcely settled in a routine again, when Sam became extremely busy. Influenza had struck in the Wachovia area. Before the epidemic was over, most every family had had someone down with the illness. Reports received from other localities made them aware that influenza was widespread throughout the United States.

Martha worried about Sam running day and night treating the sick people. She wondered how he had the strength to continue some days, but he always did. Matthew suggested to Martha that it was because Sam did not always depend on his own strength or medicine to heal people.

Sam did take his physician's role and his commitment to it seriously as was evident in a decision he was called to make.

Martha, bringing in the mail, said with surprise. "Sam, there's a letter here for you from the governor. Whatever do you think this is about?"

"I don't know," he said as he took the letter and slit it open.

Martha saw his face wrinkle in a perplexed manner. "Listen to this," he spoke to her. "The General Assembly of North Carolina has named me as Justice of the Peace. The Governor has enclosed my commission."

"Sam, that's such an honor."

"Martha, I've never sought such a position. I've not even expressed a desire for it."

"That makes it more an honor," she remarked happily.

"Why would the assembly suggest my name?"

"You're well known, dear. Think of all the people you've treated over the years."

"Because I'm a good doctor, doesn't indicate I'd be a good Justice of the Peace."

"We need good men for those duties, too. I remember Dr. Bonn was a Justice of the Peace."

"Martha, that was a long time ago. There weren't so many patients, so many people in Wachovia then."

"It seemed that there were a lot of people here then. Soldiers, strangers. There were many passing through."

"Perhaps he was the man for the job, the Justice of the Peace. Now there are others who could fill the office. Surely someone has more time to do so."

"But, Sam, they've already commissioned you, according to the letter. What can you do?"

"This is a call that is not right for me. My calling is medicine. As I see it, my profession simply doesn't allow me to accept this commission. I shall have to decline."

In some ways Martha was disappointed because she believed he could have served well in the new office; however, she did respect his decision.

For a woman of forty-one years, Martha still had much energy and a zest for life. She never had learned to walk slowly or pursue her work in a leisurely fashion. By staying on top of her tasks, she could go with Sam on short calls around Wachovia provided there were no patients in the house needing close attention.

One December day Sam asked Martha to accompany him to Bethania. She was free to go and accepted with enthusiasm. "Sam, let's take Theophilus. He hasn't been out much lately. He'd enjoy the ride."

"All right. I'll go hitch the horse to the chair," Sam replied.

Martha dressed Theophilus warmly for the winter day. She put on her own long cape, then bid her parents goodbye.

The day was sunny but cold. The trip to Bethania was pleasant and made in a relatively short time. Martha enjoyed refreshments at the home of Sam's patient. Theophilus toddled around the strange house investigating everything in sight.

On the way home, Martha commented on how much she was enjoying the outing. Theophilus was bouncing on the seat so Martha lifted him onto her lap. "The chair bounces enough without your help," she told him kindly. "Look, Theophilus. Do you see that little bird? He has a black cap."

Her attention was fixed on the chickadee on a tree branch near the road. She was pointing toward the bird when suddenly she felt the chair shake and tilt. She slid against the side of the seat. She turned and saw the horse shy to the right. Sam instinctively leaned left, keeping control of the reins. "Steady there!" he said as the horse tried to back up. The chair didn't give. When the horse raised his fore feet, Martha instantly tightened her hold on the child, drew a deep breath and jumped from the slanted chair.

The frightened horse brought his hooves down, then lunged forward. She continued to keep a firm grip on the boy. When they hit the ground, she tucked her head down and both she and Theophilus rolled over several times. As soon as they ceased rolling and lay side by side on the hard, rocky ground, she released her hold on the boy. He began to cry the sounds of a hurt and frightened child. Martha pushed herself into a sitting position, then she leaned over to Theophilus. She asked as she inspected him, "Are you hurt?" She carefully touched his limbs and body and was relieved to feel no bones were broken. She was thankful he was wearing very thick clothes.

Pulling him up to a sitting position, she discovered his face was scratched and bleeding. "Ssh, Theo, ssh. You're all right now."

She tried to soothe him. At the same time that she reached inside her pocket for a handkerchief, she scanned the road for Sam and the chair. She spotted the chair jerking along behind the galloping horse. Sam was leaning toward the upward side of the chair. He was pulling back on the reins and yelling whoa loudly.

The horse turned sharply to the right. The chair upset. Sam was caught underneath. And the horse continued to gallop. Martha screamed as she saw Sam being dragged underneath the chair.

She scrambled up, shouting, "Sam, Sam!" She started to run

down the road. She stopped, grabbed the child, hoisted him to her hip and rushed on. She watched the horse headed toward a big boulder by the roadside. She shrieked. The horse veered, a chair wheel hit the edge of the boulder. The horse broke loose and the chair stopped in the middle of the road.

Martha pulled her long skirt up with one hand. She held Theophilus close to her with the other hand and arm and ran in a broken stride down the road.

When she reached the overturned chair, she sank to her knees and put Theophilus on the ground. "Stay right there!" she spoke authoritatively.

She swiveled toward the chair. It was upside down. Sam was lying in the road with his legs partly beneath the chair.

"Oh, Sam," Martha cried in despair. His face was cut and bleeding. His eyes were open.

"Martha, are you and the baby all right?"

"Yes. Are you?" She glanced at his hands and saw that his leather gloves were scraped but not cut through. His clothing was torn, but she could not tell whether he was cut or otherwise injured.

"My legs. It hurts to move them. Is the chair on them?" He lay quite still.

Martha peered below the chair. "It's not resting on them. Should I try to lift it off?"

"It would be too heavy," he reasoned.

"Sam, can I pull you out? By the shoulders? I'll be careful."

Slowly, Sam raised his arms and bent his elbows. "Oh," he moaned. After a moment he said, "I think there are no breaks." Then he moved his head up and down and side to side very slowly. He lifted his shoulders slightly.

"Take hold of my shoulders and pull. I'll let you know if you should stop."

Theophilus remained seated, though he started crying again.

" Ssh, baby. Mama's helping father." Martha spoke to calm both the baby and herself. She knelt on the ground at Sam's head and slid her hands under his shoulders. Cupping her hands around his upper arms, cautiously she began to pull. His body moved a couple of inches. She scooted backwards and pulled again. Inch by inch, she cleared him from beneath the chair.

Martha shifted around so that she could see Sam's legs better. "How do they feel?"

"There's some pain. I don't think they're broken. Can you check?"

Martha very gently moved her hands over his legs. "I can feel no bones protruding." She paused and gazed down the road. She wrinkled her face, cocked an ear and turned back to Sam. "I believe I hear a wagon."

She rose and stood on tiptoe. "I'm sure I hear something moving." After a few minutes, she spotted a wagon coming from Bethania direction. "It is a wagon, Sam. I think . . . I think, it's the store's wagon."

As soon as she was sure she knew the approaching wagon, she ran down the road toward it. "Brother Kreuser. Brother Kreuser!"

Kreuser, the Salem storekeeper, pulled up the reins and shouted, "Whoa," to his team. "Sister Vierling?"

"Brother Kreuser, am I glad to see you. Our chair turned over. Sam's hurt. Can you help me?"

He jumped down from the driver's seat on the wagon and followed Martha a few paces to where Sam lay.

"Dr. Vierling," said Kreuser as he squatted beside him.

"I think there are no breaks, but my legs are painful."

"This ground is cold, doctor. We ought to get you off here. Can you sit up?"

"Give me a hand. I'll try."

Kreuser held his arms out straight and Sam raised himself to a sitting position. Again he tried to bend his legs. The grimace on his face signaled his pain to the two on-lookers.

Kreuser directed Martha. "We can take him back to Salem in the wagon. I'll move the supplies to one side and spread the tarpaulin on the floor. You and the baby can ride up on the front seat with me."

Swiftly he re-arranged the items in the wagon bed. Then he brought the wagon as close to Sam as possible. "Dr. Vierling, Martha and I are going to move you to the wagon. Now you're bigger than we are, but we can do it. We'll each get on a side. Place your arms around our necks. When we stand up, you pull. Just let your legs drag. That way you won't have any weight on them."

Sam did as he was told. With some effort on the part of all three people, Sam was hoisted onto the back of the wagon.

As Martha was working to drag Sam up far enough into the wagon so that the tailgate would close, she said, "This reminds me of the day you helped take Thomas Williams from the wagon."

Trying desperately not to groan, Sam remarked, "I wish Thomas was going to be there when I get home."

Theophilus was running around the side of the wagon crying and calling, "Mama, Mama."

Sam put out a hand to Martha. He caught one of her hands and held it. "I'll be all right. Better tend to Theo. Your hand is scratched," he commented with surprise.

Quickly, she withdrew her hand. "It's not much."

She slid out of the wagon and Kreuser closed up the back end. Martha reached down and gathered Theophilus in her arms. She took him around to the wagon front and lifted him up to the seat. He cried.

"Now Mama's coming." Martha found a footing on the side of the wagon and hoisted herself up.

Kreuser got up on the other side and clicked to the team. They lurched forward. Martha had never endured a road so bumpy. She thought it was partly because she was so concerned about Sam.

Once when Sam moaned, Martha turned to Kreuser and said, "I'm glad we aren't far from home."

Kreuser asked, "Did you see which way the horse bolted off to?"

"He was headed toward town the last I saw of him."

"Well, I expect you'll find him in your barn when you get home."

"I hope so. Brother, do you think there's a brother at the choir house who can go for the chair?"

"Probably so. Maybe this evening. If not, tomorrow."

"I surely would appreciate your attending to the recovery of it for us."

"I'm glad to do it." Kreuser reached into his coat pocket then handed a piece of molasses taffy to Martha. "The baby might like that to suck on."

Martha asked Theophilus to open his mouth. He did and she put the candy into his mouth. He sucked on the sweet piece, now more contented and laid his head against her arm.

As the horses pulled the wagon up the steep street that led directly to the Vierlings' front door, Martha saw her father on the stoop. Vigorously, she waved her hand to him.

When the wagon halted, Matthew called out. "The horse came home alone. I thought something might have happened."

"The baby and I are all right. Sam's hurt. Tell Mama to turn down the bed. Send Henrietta to take Theophilus."

Matthew hastened into the house and was back in a few minutes. Henrietta followed him. Martha handed Theophilus to her.

"Henrietta, wash his face and hands with some rose vinegar."

She took the toddler and disappeared into the house. Martha hurried to the back of the wagon to help Kreuser get Sam out.

"Doctor," Kreuser said, "this may hurt, I'll have to pull you out, feet first."

Kreuser pulled as easily as possible; even so he could tell Sam was gritting his teeth.

"Wait a minute," Sam said. He put his palms flat on the tarpaulin, raised himself up so that his hips cleared the floor and inched forward. He repeated the movements several times.

"Fine. Now Martha and I can get you," Kreuser grinned approvingly.

Young Ernst came running out the door. "Let me help."

The wagoneer spoke, "Hold the door open."

Ernst dashed back up the steps and pushed the door ajar.

At that instant Brother Fredrich Meinung was passing and saw the predicament. "Here, let me assist you."

Martha gratefully stepped aside. "Thank you. Can you take him on up to the bedroom?"

Martha preceded the men. "Mama, thanks for doing the bed."

The men came in and placed Sam on the bed.

Maria spoke to Martha. "Why don't you let the men finish putting Sam to bed. You come on downstairs and let me have a look at you. His nightshirt is there on the bed, brothers."

Although reluctant to leave her husband, she knew it was best. "Sam, I'll check on Theophilus."

He waved to her.

Maria closed the door behind them. "Martha, your hands are a sight. Come in the treatment room and let's have a look at you."

Slowly, almost awkwardly, Maria moved from the effects of her gout. Martha recited the events of the accident. "It's a good thing you thought so quickly and jumped out," Maria declared.

"I don't even know if I thought what to do," Martha stated.

"Well, I'm glad you're still quick on your feet."

Martha and Theophilus suffered only a few cuts and bruises. However, Sam incurred serious injury to his leg muscles and ligaments. He was confined to bed for several days. Upon first getting up, he discovered his legs were weak and he could not stand for very long at a time.

During these convalescent days, Martha stayed nearby Sam to help him in any way possible. She was glad it was winter and there were few outside chores. She took her sewing to the apothecary so that if he needed anything out of reach she could hand it to him.

One afternoon when they were so working, Brother Benzien came in. After an exchange of greetings, he asked if Sam were seeing patients again.

"Yes, indeed. I can see patients here. I should be out on calls next week. Brother Benzien, this accident has made me more aware than ever that Wachovia needs another doctor."

"I understand. The area has grown. It's good to get more craftsmen in town and fine to see many of our young people remaining here, marrying and starting families. And of course, you have your out-of-town patients."

"Don't forget the boarding school girls. They make quite an increase. By the way, please remind the inspector that the girls should not be allowed to enter school if they have any diseases. The best way to keep the girls healthy is to keep contagious diseases out of the school."

"I'll remind him. If we can locate another doctor, how do you feel about his settling in the Bethania area?"

"That sounds like a good choice. It would cut down on some traveling. What about the apothecary? I'm all set up for it here?"

"I'll speak to the Conferenz and the Collegium. If you want to keep up the apothecary, and this is a more central place for the people to obtain medicines, then any new doctor could be limited to dispensing patented medicines."

After Benzien left, Martha said, "Sam, I hope another doctor will come. You can use some help. I just wish it could he somebody you had trained."

"That would have been convenient. But a new man may bring in other opinions, the latest methods and that could be good for the community. Martha, could you hand me that journal from the table. There's an article I want to read."

She gave the journal to him then put the mending in her basket and left the room.

Wachovia did secure a doctor, Brother Friedrich Schumann, and he and his family moved to Bethania. He immediately became busy serving the people in that area, and Sam concentrated on Salem, the southern and eastern sections of Wachovia.

As Sam resumed a full workload, Martha was forced to spend more time waiting on her parents. Maria suffered a great deal of pain and her joints were so stiff that she could seldom walk about her room. Martha would go to the room in the morning and help her bathe and dress. She would brush Maria's hair, braid it and secure the ends. Whenever Maria was out of bed, she insisted on wearing the traditional cap. After Martha assisted her into a chair beside the window, Maria often would be there until the following mealtime.

One morning Martha walked into the apothecary to ask Sam if there was anything she could do to relieve her mother's pain or ease the stiffened joints.

"We're doing all we can now, dear. Your good nursing is helping her more than you realize. It's your father I'm concerned about."

"Father? But he's up most of the time. He comes to meals," Martha answered strongly.

"Yes. I am glad he can get about and do for himself. Martha, he's showing signs more than ever of weakening."

This was an evaluation Martha couldn't absorb easily: her father was getting weak and old. Surely, if Sam saw reason to comment on it to her, it must be so. Immediately, she sought Matthew. She found him as usual at this time of day, sitting alone in the garden. Martha sat down next to him on the bench.

"Well, Father," she began with a forced note of cheerfulness, "are you deciding where to put a new bed?"

"No, my dear. I'll leave that to you. I'm basking in the sunshine. I thought I'd get out while you were with your mother."

"Would you like for me to walk with you to the square? Some of your friends might be down thereabouts."

"I don't feel like such a long walk today. You may go back in. I'll be fine." Matthew patted her hand and then removed it. He stared straight ahead as if gazing or thinking to himself.

She rose, bent and kissed his head.

The next couple of months, Martha spent whatever time she could with both Maria and Matthew. She witnessed her father's rapid decline. He stopped going outside at all. He stayed in the room with Maria except for meals. Or he would suddenly talk to her about his childhood in Germany. He found pleasure in reliving happy times of the past.

When Matthew could no longer take care of himself and Maria was staying in bed most of the time, Sam told Martha, "We have to get somebody to help nurse your parents."

"But, Sam . . ."

"I will not hear any arguments. It's too much for you to do by yourself."

Martha knew by Sam's sharp expression that there was no need to resist. "Well, let me think if there's anyone that they would like to have around. It's such a confining situation, I hesitate to ask a young sister."

"What about a couple? It's easier for two people to turn someone in bed."

"And they would be company for each other. Sam, didn't you tell me that the Opizes were ready to leave their farm and they wanted to come nearer Salem?"

"I did. Sound thinking, my dear. They would be very good with Maria and Matthew."

"Father always liked Brother Opiz."

"I'll talk to the Opizes and the ministers. You decide on the sleeping arrangements in the house."

When Martha counted the house's occupants and the number of beds, she knew some drastic arrangements would have to be made. Henrietta was already staying at the boarding school. Now it appeared as if she would have to enroll Carolina and Eleonora. Martha reasoned that Henrietta would have only a year longer to stay in the school, then she would be old enough for the Single Sisters House. Therefore, if she allowed the other two girls to enter the school now, Henrietta could make their transition to the school easier. The Opizes could sleep in the girls' room.

Sam approved of Martha's plans. Both of them followed through with all the necessary arrangements.

Martha had held to some hope that her father would get better with someone to take care of him. While Matthew responded with appreciation at Carl's attention, he continued to decline. And one morning he didn't wake up when Martha called him. He had gone home quietly in his sleep.

She called to Sam who came with Carl and removed the body. Martha gently broke the news to her mother. The two shed tears together.

Finally, Maria dried her eyes and said brokenly, "Martha, we must be thankful he was spared pain at the end. He was a good man. He will be missed. He's in a happier place now."

Martha attempted to end her tears, but she couldn't staunch the flow thus left the room. Downstairs, Sam met her and put his arms comfortingly around her. He guided her to their bedroom and closed the door. He let her cry against him 'til the tears ceased of themselves. Drained and drooped, Martha rested against his strong chest within his supportive embrace.

"I'm ashamed to cry like this. I should be joyful he's now in the Lord's presence, but Sam I'm not ready. We've been so close."

"Martha, your father was ready."

"That's true. I must stop thinking about myself."

She let Sam and Sister Maria Schmid prepare the body for the corpse house. She knew the married choir would have brothers take turns to watch over him since she had no family of age to do this.

Because of Sam's profession, Martha was accustomed to death. Somehow, neither the closeness nor the frequency of those deaths helped sufficiently to heal her heart. She found the steps from the church to the graveyard, were steep and hard to take. After the coffin was lowered into the ground, the closing choral, which she had always thought was so lovely and comforting, failed to bolster her and she had hoped it would. On the way home the line "Our steps are safe and sure," echoed in her mind. She began to whisper, "My steps."

"My steps," she thought silently, "are now to comfort Mama."

Martha soon realized the strength of her mother's faith and acceptance of things as they were. It wasn't a spiritual comfort that

Maria needed most now. It was physical attention and the Opizes were taking care of that. Martha's regular duties held no interest for her. She felt strangely out of sorts with the world.

She was nervous and jumpy. One minute she hovered over Theophilus, fearful to let him leave her sight. The next minute, his squeals and childish exuberance exhausted her. Rather than scream at him or the other children, she made excuses for trips to the yard. Once out there, she merely wandered around. For the first time, she neglected the garden. Plants were drying up, turning brown and dying. She couldn't face the endless death.

Sam urged her to go with him to Bethabara one day late in summer. She finally consented. During the trip out, she was tense and talked little. Sam did not push conversation. He knew his wife well. He allowed the horse a slow gait, giving the warm sun, the patchwork of nature's colors, the fragrance of the season's grasses and flowers, time to register and thereby work their own healing messages.

While he examined his patient, someone served a cup of mint tea, a slice of freshly baked bread and blackberry preserves to Martha. The tea was cool and soothing and the food delicious and comforting. Martha was so rarely waited on that she offered to help in the kitchen, but the hostess insisted that she remain seated.

"I know you're always busy doing for everybody else. Now sit still. Let me serve you for a change."

Martha began to relax. The friendliness of the woman, the warmth of the sun streaming through the window panes and the scented tea, combined to dissolve the unhappy coldness that had lain upon her.

Soon after Martha and Sam started on their return trip, their chair passed through a grove of trees. The land was low and damp. A creek ran near the road.

"Whoa!" Sam pulled up on the reins.

Leaping down, he explained to Martha, "There should be some fern down here. I want some for our creek bank."

He walked a few paces to the creek. He stooped beside the

bank and pulled several mature ferns. He returned to the chair, took a cloth from under the seat and carefully covered the roots. He laid the ferns in the shade under the seat. Then he turned again to the creek. He bent over and picked something else. Martha was puzzled by the smile on his face as he neared the chair.

"I thought you might like these." He continued smiling as he held out a bunch of tall wild flowers.

"Why, Sam. They're violet gentians." She took them and deeply breathed their fragrance. "What a surprise and a treat. Thank you so much."

So the restlessness, the tension, the feeling out-of-sorts with the world that had clouded her life recently, vanished. It was as if the holding of the gift of gentians had warmed her hands and her heart.

She slipped her arm around Sam's and gave it a gentle squeeze. He tilted his head toward her. She smiled up at him and he smiled back.

He thought to himself, "If only gentians could do so much for all my patients."

CHAPTER THIRTY-TWO

Just as soon as Martha suspected that she was pregnant, she told Sam.

"What good news," he replied warmly. "How do you feel?"

"Very well. No. More than that. I feel everything is right. I feel like singing."

Sam laughed. He was inwardly pleased that Martha had regained her cheerful attitude. Actually she whipped through her chores so rapidly that he cautioned her on several occasions to slow down.

"Sam, anyone would think I was an old lady the way you stay after me."

"In your condition, one could hardly say that."

Even though Maria was bedridden, she was alert, and she noticed the change in Martha's disposition. In the late fall, one afternoon Martha was holding a cup of tea and helping her mother drink with the aid of a horse weed stem. Maria turned her head slightly to indicate that she had had enough. Martha put the cup down.

"Martha, there's something different about you. You're happier than in a long time."

"Mama, I'm going to have another baby."

"Good, dear. Life must go on." Maria smiled and closed her eyes.

Martha was aware her mother was in much pain, yet she scarcely ever complained. She was grateful for the attention and care that was given to her.

As the old year was closing and Martha prepared to attend the watch night service, she checked in on her mother. "I know they will mention father tonight. I'll tell you tomorrow what they say."

"Thank you, dear. I'll be with him soon. No, don't say anything. I'll be ready."

Maria proved right. On January 16, 1811, Maria's life came to an end. As Martha leaned over to give her mother a farewell kiss, she felt the new life inside her quicken.

She could not grieve at her mother's passing as she did her father's. Her mother had suffered during her last years. And Martha had to feel some comfort in knowing that her pain had finally ceased.

Martha found that her duties in the house were considerably lessened. She spoke about this to Sam. "There's so much less to do, do you think we could do without Carl and Christine?"

"If you consider we can, we should be able to. Do you want to wait until the baby comes?"

"I can manage by myself. Theophilus will be four soon. He can start day school. He can walk with Benjamin and Ernst."

"Right. Speaking of growing up, Ernst will be ten in the fall. Be thinking about his staying in the school."

"You mean sleeping there?"

"Boys that age do, you know."

"It seems we're giving up all our children."

"I don't see it as giving up. They are being educated. They are learning to live with other people. The school masters are devoted to their care."

"And they will be home for meals."

"Yes, you'll get to see them everyday. I think you should plan to keep help for the kitchen."

The first day of April, a farm became available for the Opizes so Sam helped them move. Martha bid them farewell and thanked them for the tenderness they had shown to her parents.

Later that same month, Henrietta ran breathlessly into the house at the vesper mealtime. "Mama. Papa!" she shouted, rushing back to the kitchen.

Martha was pouring water into the teapot. Sam came in from the apothecary. They both showed concern at Henrietta for it was unlike her to run, rush or be overly excited.

"Sit down. I want to tell you the good news," she directed them.

"What is it, dear?" Martha's voice filled with curiosity.

"You both know how much the boarding school has grown. They are having so many requests from girls or rather girls' families all over the state."

Sam said, "We know."

Henrietta continued. "They've had to turn down so many girls. And Papa there are so few girls schools in the south that they don't have any other place to go."

"Henrietta, how is this good news for you?" Her mother wanted to know.

"Because the school has finally decided to open a fourth classroom. And two new teachers will be needed."

"Oh, Henrietta," Martha gasped, "you've been asked to be one of the teachers!"

"Yes, Mama."

"Congratulations," Sam offered.

Martha stood and hugged her daughter. "You'll be a good teacher, dear."

"Henrietta, did you know your mother was a teacher when I first came to Wachovia? She was a whirlwind."

Their daughter gave them a perplexed look as if she didn't comprehend the comparison.

Martha immediately blushed. "I was seventeen, too, when I started. Of course, the school was much smaller then."

The other children came in for the vesper meal and Henrietta shared her news with all of them. Carolina was both excited and saddened to learn that Henrietta would move into the choir house. Eleonora wanted to know if Henrietta would be her teacher.

Henrietta reasoned, "I expect they'll start me in the little girls' classes."

The boys said they were glad their sister wasn't going to teach them, although they agreed good-naturedly that she would be a fine teacher.

Henrietta was placed in the third classroom with a slightly older and experienced teacher, Sister Susanna Peter. Martha went to visit Henrietta in her room the first Sunday she was in the choir house. While there, she overheard some gossip that sounded vaguely familiar.

"Do you think the glove business is really straightened out now?" "It should be. We're only to turn over our gloves to Brother Kreuser." "Is he going to sell them in the community store?" "No. He'll take in the cut leather supplied by Brother Schulz, turn that over to us, then we'll give the finished gloves back to Brother Kreuser. He'll get them to Brother Reuz." "Then Brother Krausch won't be selling them anymore?" "I think not. Anyway, I'm glad this conflict is settled."

Martha remembered when her father had sold gloves in the yellow house to help the sisters. In a way she was sorry Brother Krausch couldn't sell them, too, especially since he had a shop in that same yellow house. However, she had lost tract of many business dealings in the town and deferred making a statement.

Henrietta spoke to Martha. "It's time for services. I don't want to be late. Brother Reichel is preaching his last sermon here. Mama, did you know his son Benjamin is going to stay here as a teacher of the little boys?"

Martha immediately detected a difference in the way her daughter said Benjamin's name, but she declined to comment on it.

She really missed her oldest child's motherly type of help at home. Carolina didn't take over naturally when her services could have been most useful. And Eleonora wasn't consistently helpful. However, both of them could be counted on for assistance when they were directly asked to do a certain task.

On the morning of May 4, Martha gave birth to another daughter. From the moment, the baby was placed in her arms

Martha felt a surge of tenderness that she had not known with her other children. A bond of love flowed between them from that first day and strengthened through the years.

Brother Benzien came to baptize the baby, Elise Wilheimine, in the afternoon. When night descended and the rains poured, there was no church litany. Martha was glad they had chosen the afternoon baptism.

The baby was quickly nicknamed Eliza. Martha found special pleasure in taking care of her. An afternoon in late May, Martha had finished feeding Eliza and she was enjoying a few quiet moments rocking and singing to her. She heard Sam drive up in the carriage and turn into the barn. In a few minutes she heard his footsteps on the outside stairs to the front door. Then she heard a second pair of footsteps. The front door opened and closed.

Martha stopped singing, glanced up and saw Sam followed by Brother Benzien. She welcomed them.

"Good afternoon, Sister Vierling. How's the baby?" Benzien inquired.

"She's such a good baby. Brother, will you stay for a cup of tea? I was waiting for Sam before having a cup myself."

"Thank you, but no. I can't stay long. I came to discuss a request that has been made to Conferenz."

"Well, please, have a seat," Martha suggested. Both men sat down. Martha and Sam waited to hear what the Conferenz needed.

"You know that Carl Bagge has a young son, Carl N."

"Yes. He's about six years old, I believe," commented Martha.

"That's right. Brother Bagge thinks it's time for his son to start school and he wants him to come to Salem."

Sam said, "We've been pleased with the little boys' school. Will young Bagge be staying in the Anstalt?"

"That is where the request comes in. Brother Bagge asks that the boy live with you."

"With us?" Martha spoke, surprised.

"Those are his wishes. We discussed the matter at some length in Conferenz meeting. We agreed that your large family and your own heavy load of patients, doctor, were quite sufficient to keep you both very busy. However, we simply could not think of any other home in town to place the boy," Benzien concluded.

Sam and Martha exchanged questioning glances as if each were saying to the other: What do you think? Do you want to accept another child? Another Bagge?

Finally, Sam told Benzien that they would discuss the request and give him an answer soon.

He thanked them. "I doubt if I need to mention this, but Brother Bagge can well afford any cost of arrangement. I want to tell you that everyone in the community appreciates all that do in its behalf," Benzien said sincerely.

After Sam walked with Benzien to the door, he put his bag in the apothecary, then washed up. Meanwhile he thought over the request. It had been a long time since his home had harbored a Bagge. He thought about Anna in their short time together and about Benjamin working in the First House shop. He remembered young Carl coming to visit both of them, prior to their passing. Could he in some way make it up to the family by taking the young boy? No. He quickly dismissed the question. If he took the boy in, it had to be for the boy's sake only.

Martha, too, was doing some silent soul searching as she got up and took little Eliza to her cradle. This quiet was too good to last. Am I ready to take on the care of someone else's child? I've raised one Bagge child. But it was Sam's child, too. I did enjoy bringing up Polly. She's turned out to be such a fine girl. She's ready to make a good wife. Oh, boys are so much noisier than girls. Carl N. would be Fredrich's age. How would Carl's coming affect Benjamin and Theophilus' relationship? Fredrich Benjamin. Benjamin Samuel Bagge . . . She had not thought of Benjamin Bagge in such a long time. He had died while working with Sam. She often wondered if his death had been the reason that Sam did not actively seek another young apprentice? Again, she wished the Conferenz had allowed young Williams to apprentice to Sam. She sighed accepting that wasn't the problem at hand. Today she had to think whether or not she could bring Carl Bagge into her home in a loving and friendly acceptance. Did he look like Anna? Did he have golden curls? Was there always going to be a Bagge in her life? She remembered once thinking there would be no more Bagges around here. How long ago that seemed at this moment. Why does Carl Bagge want his son to live with us? Is he trying to say he holds no bitterness for the past? Does he want his son with the closest family he had? Surely his reasons are positive ones. How does Sam feel about all this?

Martha called to Sam that the tea was ready. As he joined her, she asked, "Do you want us to take the Bagge boy to live with us?"

"It'll be all right with me, but I will leave this up to you. Most of the responsibility will fall on you. Brother Benzien said the Conferenz had already decided that if Carl came to us, they wanted him to stay, sleep that is, in the Anstalt when he becomes eight years old."

"I don't see how we can turn down the request for help, so tell them we'll be glad to have the boy."

Sam learned that Carl N. Bagge would not be arriving until August. Before that time, Sam had occasion to make other arrangements. On a visit to Sister Reuz he realized part of her health problem was loneliness now that her husband was dead and that she was reluctant to move into the Widows House.

"Sister Reuz, how would you like to take in a school boy?"

"Why, doctor, I would like that. I could stay here and I'd have someone in the house with me at night."

So it was that young Bagge was put in the care of the widow. Martha walked down on the day of his arrival and told both Carl and Widow Reuz that she would be happy to have Carl come up to see his cousins whenever he could. As it turned out, Carl N. proved to be a well-behaved child who was liked by the widow, his schoolmasters and classmates. While Martha was pleased with the knowledge that everything had turned out profitable in this situation, she was spared any foreknowledge of the double tragedy that was again to strike the two families.

For now, Martha's life moved along smoothly: that is as evenly as life can ever be expected to progress with seven children and a doctor's patients coming and going under one roof.

She found a new delight in chatting with Henrietta when she could get away from her lessons and school responsibilities long enough to come for a cup of tea. Martha was interested in hearing about the courses of study offered to the girls, their special festival day programs and their dormitory life.

Henrietta told her mother about the novel customs of some of her students. Martha sensed in the telling that Henrietta had not been swayed by the contact with the outside girls. However, the mother began to wonder about her younger girls for their relationship was on a peer level unlike Henrietta's of teacher to student.

"Mama," Henrietta repeated, interrupting Martha's private thought, "have you heard that the same brother has asked again for the teacher to be his wife?"

"No, I haven't heard. Is she going to accept him this time?"

"She still says no. Mama, I'm so fond of her. She's been so much help to me in teaching, but I don't understand her."

"In what way, dear?"

"In not accepting what the lot approves."

"I'm happy you feel that way and I hope you don't change. Sometimes it's hard to accept the lot." Henrietta wrinkled her brow, puzzled with the comment. "But in all incidents that I know of, it has proved wisest."

Throughout the next two years, Martha heard other reports about marriage proposals to teachers. Some the girls refused; one, the father of the girl refused. While all the marriage refusals did not weaken Henrietta's view of the Unity's procedures, Martha had reason to be concerned about Carolina and Eleonora's opinions. Whenever such events were mentioned in their presence, they shrugged off the importance of the lot.

"Mama, the girls at school say that their religions don't have such laws"; or "They can talk to boys any time they want to – that is if they have been introduced"; or "They don't have to leave town if they marry someone from another religion."

At times Martha wondered about all these new seeds being sown in her daughters' gardens of thought. The best she reasoned that she could do was to double her efforts at teaching the Unity beliefs that she had learned as a child from Maria, Matthew, the ministers and teachers, and beliefs which had proven true and comforting to her through the years. Only Martha found that during the short times the girls were with her that they scarcely listened when she went into one of her guiding principle talks. And, too, there were everyday, practical matters that she had to discuss with the girls in their times at home. She had to work out a private system of reinforcing the values she believed worth keeping. She learned to continue showing her concern for their physical comfort with small, but necessary supplies; their need for individual attention with birthday remembrances and occasional personal notes; and for their spiritual enlightenment, one sentence sermons; and for their moral growth, her motherly advice.

Martha, as well as the remainder of the community, had other concerns both national and local going into the year of 1812. The United States disagreements with England were heading the country toward war. There were some changes in the Wachovia leadership that called for adjustments.

In November 1811, Brother Benzien had died. A few months previous, Brother Herbst had been appointed as pastor to Salem. The town gained a new deacon at Christmas time when Brother Benjamin Reichel was ordained. In January 1812, Brother Herbst died. Again, shifts in responsibilities were made in Salem and Fredrich Meinung once more assisted in Wachovia administrative affairs and Brother Peter acted as pastor and presided at meetings.

The congregations were in the position of having to make many decisions locally. One of these decisions involved the Vierling family in several ways. Sam was made aware of a particular crisis when he was asked to an emergency meeting of the Conferenz.

Brother Peter told Sam, "There is a man from Philadelphia in our tavern. He was taken ill yesterday. Dr. Schumann is attending the man and has reported to us that he has smallpox. Dr. Schumann has advised us to inoculate with smallpox, everyone that has not had the disease. He advises this because there is no cowpox material on hand."

Sam spoke bluntly. "Then we should get some cowpox vaccine at once."

"Then you are not in favor of giving the smallpox?"

"Indeed I am not. Most of our people have been given the protective pox."

"What about the boarding school?" Reichel asked.

"We did not give the cowpox to the children in Wachovia without first consulting the parents, surely it would not be advisable to give inoculations to the boarding school girls without their parents' consent."

"Dr. Vierling, we'll send a messenger immediately to Raleigh for the vaccine. When it arrives, you can inoculate the people in town who need it and Dr. Schumann can take care of the people in his area."

When Sam returned home and told Martha about the meeting, she immediately wanted Theophilus and Eliza inoculated.

"Sam, why did they call in Dr. Schumann?"

"I didn't ask. There could be several reasons. Let's view this as fortunate for us. Since I have to treat the boarding school girls, I would not like to see smallpox start there. Hence, I'm blessed I do not have to be around the tavern patient."

"If such an epidemic spread through the school, the parents might not want their daughters to come back."

"Most of the parents know that we do everything we can to protect the girls. But you are correct, a smallpox epidemic would be bad publicity."

A few days later, a meeting was called of all schoolmasters and housefathers. Sam attended the meeting. When everyone was assembled, Brother Reichel called the group to order.

"Brethren, we have a matter which has arisen we'd like your

opinion on before taking any action. A traveler staying in our tavern is ill. Dr. Schumann was called from Bethania to take a look at the man. He has diagnosed the man's illness as smallpox."

The brothers at once turned to each other and registered surprise, then they mumbled to one another. After giving the men a few minutes to vent their feelings and exchange brief comments, Reichel called them to order again.

"I understand your first concern is for the health and safety of your charges. Let me assure you that no one who has been in contact with the stricken man has in turn been in any contact with your students at the schools; or in your houses to the best of my knowledge."

"Brother Reichel, most of the residents have been inoculated against smallpox by Dr. Vierling. Won't that keep them from getting the disease?" a brother asked.

Reichel replied, "Dr. Vierling, can you answer that question?"

Sam kept his seat. "That's the best preventive we have. However it's not totally effective for everyone."

"What about the youngest children and some of the older newcomers who haven't been inoculated; can they be inoculated now?"

Sam answered. "They can. A messenger was sent to Raleigh for vaccine and he returned with it late this evening. Any of you or your families who haven't had an inoculation can come to the apothecary anytime the next day or two and I'll take care of you."

"Brother Reichel, what do the school masters suggest we do?" A father inquired.

"We talked with the Conferenz and recommend that gatherings of the children cease until we see how this disease goes."

The men nodded in agreement.

Reichel added, "If we have your consent, then we'll dispense with all children's meetings until further notice. With this, goes our recommendation that the boys and girls stay at home and not be allowed to congregate on the streets or go into shops."

The men shook their heads in consent.

A brother who was both a father and a craftsman spoke in a somewhat disturbed voice. "This will be very bad for business. Every time there's an epidemic our trade is at a stand still. And it's low enough now in the winter months."

"Brother, everybody sympathizes with you craftsmen. And one reason we called this meeting was to work out some kind of plan whereby an epidemic can be avoided for the health of the people and the trades."

"Dr. Vierling," a brother asked, "do you have any suggestions to make?"

"I certainly would continue to limit contact with the patient. In fact, the patient should be isolated."

"He can hardly be isolated at the tavern. Whoever waits on him there, has to be around everybody else in the building."

"If you keep a smallpox patient at the tavern, everybody up and down and across the state will know about it in a week."

"Can he be moved?"

Reichel asked generally to the crowd. "Does anyone know of a house or a place?" No comments were made loud enough, or in the form of a proposal.

Sam's big voice topped the low mumbling. "There won't be any volunteers from this group. Everyone here has children in his house. I can suggest a place for consideration. However, this should come from the Conferenz or Collegium: you understand this traveler is not my patient. Most of you know Brother Carl Opiz. He was in my house helping take care of the Mikschs. Well, Brother and Sister Opiz are on one of the town farms just outside of town. If Dr. Schumann gives permission to move the man there, I'm sure the Opizes can be counted on to give him good care and they'll be cautious."

Reichel said, "We appreciate your recommendation. We'll pass it along immediately."

Dr. Schumann agreed to move his patient to the Opizes' farm.

He told Carl and Christina how to care for the patient and that the congregation specifically wanted the man isolated from other people.

Somehow, sometime during the three days that the ill man was at the Opizes, a mulatto who was renting a nearby farm on the Wach came into contact with the patient. On the third day there, the patient died. A rider was quickly charged to inform Dr. Schumann in Bethania.

Another messenger was dispatched to Salem where he contacted Reichel, who in turn alerted Sam.

"What do you propose we do now, Dr. Vierling?"

"Bury the man as soon as you can. Bury him on the farm."

"We should have some type of service."

"That would be appropriate," was Sam's response. "Some of the brothers, perhaps those without children at home, could go down to the farm. Tell Carl to burn all the bed clothing and the patient's clothes. Tell him to clean everything in the house and to whitewash the walls."

Within a few days, Dr. Schumann was called to the farm of the mulatto. The man had become quite ill and smallpox was suspected. The doctor verified that the mulatto had smallpox. Next, he rode into Salem to confer with Br. Peter.

"This new case disturbs me. It may not be the last," Schumann worried.

"It's certainly not a favorable report to hear of any new cases. However, it is the only one so far," Br. Peter spoke reassuringly.

"Don't you think some more drastic protective measures should be taken?"

"Not at the present. We'll appreciate your continuing to care for this patient. We'll send you word if the disease spreads to Salem."

Later the same day Br. Peter talked with Sam. "I told Dr. Schumann that we wouldn't be changing our preventive approaches at this time."

Sam was in accord. "The protective pox and the isolation procedures appear to have worked well. If there were to be any outbreak in Salem, I would have expected it by now. The traveler was in the tavern several days before being moved to the farm, which is probably where the mulatto came in contact with him. Our problem now is to minimize contact with the mulatto."

When a week passed and no other smallpox case was reported and the mulatto showed signs of recovering, the entire area breathed a sigh of relief and offered prayers of thanksgiving. An announcement was placed in several newspapers to inform people, especially parents of boarding students, that the smallpox crises had passed.

The days continued in a more accustomed pattern for several months. It wasn't until mid-June 1812 that the United States declared war against Great Britain. This news brought no pleasure to the people of Wachovia, nor did the subsequent dispatch – a call for seven thousand volunteers in North Carolina.

The Moravian congregations decided to maintain their position of not bearing arms; however, at the first announcement of war and militia call, they refrained from making a rule or issuing statements or seeking outside official judgment concerning the alternative for their brothers who were enlistment age. Sentiments indicated that the congregations would help the brothers with free-will contributions and from diaconie funds.

The older boys and apprentices had been born since the Revolutionary War and therefore had no experience with either the hardships or unpleasantness of war. The war talk that sifted down to them made the events remote but exciting. The ministers were aware of the boys' attitudes. With the Fourth of July memorial celebration coming up, they elected to read at a congregation meeting an open letter, which the Bethlehem Conferenz had composed last year in an attempt to keep worldly practices out of their celebrations.

The reading of the letter did not have the effect the ministers had hoped for; instead, several of the boys paraded around with cockades in their hats.

Upon hearing of this disrespectful act, Sam summoned his sons to his shop as they came in for the vesper meal.

"Boys, I trust that you were not involved in anyway. War is a very serious, very dangerous condition. It is not to be played at. As Moravians, as Christians, as human beings, I want you to have the highest regard for your fellowman and for his right to live unmolested, without persecution. Never let the disregard for another person's life be upon your conscience." He charged them in a firm, calm and caring tone.

Brother Peter decided to speak again to the young brethren. He did this in connection with their preparation to communion. He asked the boys to consider their spirits, and to remember the doctrines of the Christian faith, which were those of the Unity. If after doing this, they found that they did not like the ways of the Unity, then they should withdraw under their own free will.

The boys showed that they seriously considered the words because the Salem Fourth of July celebration was conducted in a peaceful manner.

CHAPTER THIRTY-THREE

The September day was clear, sunny and warm proving that summer weather was still hanging around the rolling hills of Wachovia. The tulip trees had changed their leaves to a bright yellow and a few maples showed streaks of red and yellow, but most of the hardwoods were as green as the Carolina pines.

Martha reached up and pulled a couple of choice apples from a low hanging tree limb. She placed these into a basket that was almost full.

"Mama, hurry, please. I know they'll be ready to go." Carolina pleaded as she came to the back door.

"I'm coming," Martha answered as she stopped to pick another apple.

"Everybody in Bethania probably has apples, Mama."

As Martha walked up to the house, she noted, "It's nice to have a change though. They may not have this variety."

"Apples are apples."

"Oh no. Some are for cooking, some for eating," Martha informed her impatient daughter. "These are especially delicious for eating. If you get hot or thirsty along the way, you'll be glad you have them along."

"Mama, I don't want to walk down to the Sisters House with all these baskets. What will Henrietta and Sally say?" protested Carolina, as she surveyed two other baskets of food.

"The boys will help you. Ernst, Benjamin, Theophilus! Come

along. Carolina is ready. I'll walk down to the Sisters House with you. Let me get my cap." Martha went in by the back door.

"Boys," she said as the trio raced into the kitchen, "take the baskets outside the back door and leave them at the Sisters House entrance on your way to school. Please, don't run. Theophilus won't be able to keep up with you." While she tied her ribbons, she told Sam she'd be back in a few minutes and asked him to listen out for Eliza.

While walking down Church Street, Carolina said with longing, "I wish we could wear the kind of clothes the girls at school wear."

"I've noticed at services that the boarders do have a variety of styles. To me they don't appear any more serviceable than your dress."

"They look prettier. And they should be easier to put on without all the lacing."

"And easier for somebody to sew without all those eyelets."

"Oh, Mama, may I have a different style when I get my next dress?"

"I will start paying more attention to all the dresses, then we'll talk about it."

"Thank you, Mama." Carolina's face changed to a happy expression.

The front door of the Sisters House opened and Henrietta and Sally Fetter stepped out. While they were exchanging greetings, and Martha was telling Henrietta to give the apples and foods to the ministers, the store wagon pulled by two horses and driven by a lone teamster came up beside the square then stopped in front of the Sisters House.

The teamster, a young man with a courteous manner, apologized. "Brother Kreuser regrets he can't drive you sisters to Bethania. He's giving me the day to take you out."

"We appreciate that," replied Martha. "I'm Sister Vierling. These are my daughters, Henrietta and Carolina. This is Sister

Fetter. She's going to help Henrietta lead the singing at the service."

"I'm Willihelm Obert. Called Will." the young single brother said to Martha. He simply nodded to the girls. "There are a few supplies in the back, but I left space for the girls to sit."

Will hopped down and opened the tailgate and assisted the girls up, then he put in the baskets and closed the gate.

"Will you start back as soon as the love feast is over?" Martha asked Will as he took his seat up front again.

"Yes. I'll unload the supplies after I take the sisters to the church. We'll be ready to leave after the service."

"Be careful," Martha called as the team started around the square.

Back home Martha told Sam that she needed the children to help wrap and store some apples for winter, also to help peel and cut some for drying.

"Sam, the boys are a big help when they are home. I'll miss Ernst when he goes to the Anstalt to sleep."

"We'll get the fall garden work finished before he goes."

"What do you think Ernst will do later?"

"What do you mean?"

"For a profession or a trade?"

"I don't know."

"Is it time we thought about it? In a few years he'll be apprentice age. Do you think he'll want to be a doctor?"

"He doesn't apply himself very long to a task, and he doesn't take his studies as seriously as he could."

"I've noticed that he has little interest in the patients. Does he ask questions about the apothecary?"

"Not since he passed that first curious stage when he was a little boy. We'll just have to see how his interests develop the next few years. Right now I have to mix some medicines for several patients."

"I'll take Eliza out to the herb garden and finish picking the mints. Oh, a young brother named Will drove the store's wagon this morning. He was polite and respectful, but I do wish a married brother could always drive the single sisters."

"They do whenever they can. It's hard to spare any brothers for trips in the fall. There were at least three sisters riding out?"

Martha nodded before turning to the bedroom to pick up Eliza who was just awakening from her morning nap. After dressing Eliza, Martha carried her outside and let her toddle around the garden as she worked. The weather was so pleasant and Eliza was entertaining herself so happily that Martha was reluctant to go inside, thus she continued working in the gardens until dinnertime.

About noon Sam strode into the yard to tell her that he was walking down to the Widows House to take some medicines. Martha lead Eliza over to the water bucket which was kept on a tree stump outside the back door and washed the little girl's face and hands and dried them with a towel that hung on a peg beside the back door. She cleaned her own face and hands and together they went inside.

Martha had prepared the family's dinner early in the morning along with the picnic for the girls. She set Eliza in a high chair near the table and gave her a thin slice of cold toast. After placing the meal on the table she sat next to Eliza to feed her. As she offered spoons of applesauce to the eager eater, she realized how much she was enjoying having the kitchen to herself again. Now that her responsibilities were fewer, she had told Sam that she could do without the kitchen help, so Sam released the helper. Martha was appreciative of the fact that she and Sam had not been burdened with financial worries as her parents had been. She was grateful that Sam was generous and had allowed her the extra help that had meant so much to her while her parents lived with them. Her frugal nature and her thrifty upbringing, could not permit her to take advantage of his generosity; thus, whenever she knew she could do without something, she did without it.

Martha's musing was interrupted by the ringing of the apothecary bell. She wiped her hands on a dishtowel and hastened to the front room. Fredrich Meinung stood there with his hand on the bell. His face was flushed, his body tense.

"Where's the doctor?"

Before she could answer the boys bounded noisily up the steps. She peered to see if Sam were with them. He wasn't.

To Fredrich she said, "He walked to the Widows House."

"There's been an accident out on the road."

Martha put her hands to her face. "Not the Bethania Road?"

"No. The Friedland Road. I came by right after it happened."

Fredrich appeared shocked; Martha asked him to sit down to rest a minute and added that she would send Ernst down to get the doctor.

Ernst was off in a run. Martha went to the kitchen and told Benjamin and Theophilus to go ahead and eat and to watch Eliza. She returned to the apothecary.

"Brother Meinung is anybody in the congregation involved?"

"The Bagges from Friedland."

"Carl Bagge?"

"Yes. And his wife."

"Any of the children?"

"One. A little girl." Fredrich put his head in his hands.

Martha glanced out the window and spotted Sam approaching rapidly up the hill. Ernst was running beside his long-legged father. She said to Fredrich, "Here comes Dr. Vierling."

Meinung sprang up and rushed out the door. Martha had never seen him in such an anxious state. From the window she watched him talk excitedly to Sam. Sam pointed to the stable and Ernst and Fredrich headed that way. Sam dashed into the house and shop.

"Martha, I'm taking Fredrich's horse out to the Freidland Road. He and Ernst are following in the wagon." Quickly, he put some things in his bag. At the door, he turned back and kissed her, then left.

The behavior of the two men led Martha to expect the worst.

After a hasty lunch, she cleaned the kitchen and put Eliza down for a nap. She tidied an unused bedroom in case it was needed and checked the clean bandage supply. The boys finished gathering the apples from the ground, drawing water from the well, then returned to school. Martha was pouring water into a kettle on the hearth when she heard the wagon clattering outside. She finished then ran out.

Sam stopped the horses, tied the reins to a post and gently shook Ernst, who roused, then climbed down without glancing backwards.

Sam walked around to Martha. "The little girl, Carolina is dead. Carl and Christina are injured, but they are going to live."

"I have the beds ready," Martha spoke weakly. She reached over and placed a hand on Sam's arm.

"Good. Fredrich and I will carry Carl and Christina there. We'll come back and put the girl in the treatment room"

Everything was blurred for the next few hours to Martha as the patients were transferred to beds and she prepared Christina for examination while Sam checked over Carl. Martha helped Sister Schmid lay out the little girl before she was taken to the corpse house. All the while images of Henrietta and her own Carolina jogging along in a wagon as she had bid them goodbye earlier that day haunted her. These visions became entangled in the ones she had not let disturb her for the past several years: scenes from the accident when the chair overturned with Sam, and she had had to escape with young Theophilus. Horses! They're such unpredictable creatures. Horses and chairs, wagons: they're all so dangerous.

Martha didn't feel relief until she saw Carolina come in around suppertime. Henrietta had gone to the Sisters House. From the happy glow on Carolina's face, Martha knew the day must have been pleasant, but she didn't ask about the trip.

The Bagges were not unconscious. They knew their child was dead. Peter arrived to give them comfort. Sam eased their physical pains with sedatives.

He told Peter that he couldn't tell the extent of the injuries yet and that he wanted Carl and Christina to remain in bed in his house a few days at least. "We can be thankful they are conscious and have control of their limbs."

The Bagges were sore and their heads ached so that keeping them flat in bed was no problem. As their aches and pains subsided and their grief lessened, they began to move about more in bed and soon asked to sit up.

Carl inquired of Sam what the prognosis was. "You should be up and around at the end of the week. In another week or two you'll be doing everything you always did."

"We can't thank you enough for all you have done for us."

"I didn't do much. You and Christina lay here and let your bodies heal naturally."

"Don't sell yourself short. You were the one who decided what should be done and *I* can tell you that I was in a lot of pain and now I know I'm better."

Peter entered the room as the two men were talking. "Brother Bagge, it's good to see you up again. You'll be asking Dr. Vierling when can you go home next."

"That was my next question, brother. There's another question I'll be asking soon. I talked this over with Christina yesterday. Since being here, I know how much I've missed being in Salem. I want to move back," said Carl sincerely.

"Brother Bagge, don't you want to think about this longer, after all you have so many business interests in Friedland," Peter rejoined.

"No. My family wants to return," Bagge said emphatically.

"You know of course, that we already have the community store and we have no plans to open another one."

"I don't intend to open a store."

"And Brother Kreuser is managing the store here very satisfactorily."

Bagge gave an understanding smile. "Yes. I know he is. I won't ask or expect to manage a store for Salem, but I would like to serve the community. I'd like to work in its behalf in any way I could be most useful."

"Brother Bagge, when you return home, if you still want to move to Salem, write to the Conferenz."

"I will."

He did. He informed the Conferenz that some months would be required for him to get his varied business activities in order and for him to complete his term in the state assembly before he could move, if the Conferenz and lot approved. The Conferenz put the matter to the lot during a meeting. The reed drawn held a *no*. Bagge was notified of the drawing. Later, the Conferenz resubmitted the question of Bagge's moving to Salem. This time a *yes* was drawn. It wasn't until a year later that the Bagges were able to move to Salem. And in the years following, Carl Bagge did serve the congregation in several roles.

Ernst's reaction to the accident and his later lack of interest in the apothecary were signals to his parents that he wouldn't follow in his father's profession.

One business that did interest Ernst was the community store. Martha often allowed him to run errands to the store. He would come in and tell her whom he had seen and describe any new articles offered for sale. He kept her informed as to when Kreuser was sending the wagon to Pennsylvania.

"Mama, Brother Kreuser is going north tomorrow and he's taking Brothers Will Obert and Jacob Schulz with him."

"Will Obert? Oh, that's the young man who drove the girls to Bethania," she recalled.

"Yes. I'd like to go on a trip someday. The store workers make more trips than anybody in Salem," Ernst stated.

"They travel when they have to buy more supplies. I suppose Kreuser is taking the two younger men to train them in buying."

"They have to buy American goods now, don't they?"

"Yes. With the war cutting off most foreign trade, American craftsmen should be able to sell their products more readily."

As the war continued into another year, the congregation missed their much looked forward to communications with the Central Unity organization. At times the awareness of war was brought directly into the community, especially when groups of soldiers marched through. Some of the townspeople acting on their own initiative offered food and drink to the soldiers. When the Conferenz heard of the hospitable acts, they approved. They even encouraged people to continue the acts of kindness. It was one way they could show their appreciation that the Moravians had been exempted from militia duty.

One letter did get through to a Salem congregation minister who had relatives in Germany. The letter described the terrible warfare being experienced in Lusatia and Silesia. Martha felt compassion for Sam knowing that he hadn't heard from his family in a long time. When the Conferenz asked in Salem for a donation to send to the battle-weary congregations in Germany, Sam made a generous gift and Martha volunteered to take collections in the married choir. The people contributed as they were able and the collection was sent as soon as a safe passage was possible.

Sam was concerned about a local inhabitant's welfare. On one of his visits, he discovered Sister Louisa Herbst, the elderly widow of the deceased minister, in a weakened condition and her health generally much declined. When he asked her how she managed to get up and cook for herself, she replied that she didn't. She got her food from one of the ministers.

Sam told the ministers that the widow needed better care. He suggested that they obtain the services of a special sister just to look after her. The ministers made an effort to find someone to take care of Sister Herbst, but they had no success.

Martha knew about his concern and one day asked if the Conferenz had done anything to help Widow Herbst.

"Not yet. I can't understand why there isn't someone in this whole community who can care for the woman."

"If you can't locate a sister to stay with her, why don't you place her in a home?"

"I can not think of one family that would take her in. She's so weak. She'll take much care."

"What about us, Sam? We have room. There're only Theophilus and Eliza sleeping here now."

"My dear, it's a big responsibility. Do you feel up to it?"

"Yes, but if I find I need some help, I'll ask you."

"That would be a surprise," he exclaimed.

The widow did move in with the Vierlings and Martha soon adjusted to having an elderly person to care for again.

When the Salem Conferenz learned that Dr. Schumann had been offered a position in Lititz, Pennsylvania, they discussed the advisability of trying to keep him in Wachovia. They were aware that considerable friction had arisen in Bethania and that the town seemed split into two groups: one following Schumann and one another brother. Therefore, Schumann's leaving Bethania was one possible way to restore some degree of harmony to that community. The Salem leaders had to seriously consider whether or not this problem could arise in Salem. They believed they could avert such a crisis. And, too, foremost in their minds was the knowledge that the area needed more than one doctor and there was difficulty securing Moravian doctors for the congregation towns. Therefore, they voted to strengthen their effort to get him to re-locate in Salem.

When the ministers approached Dr. Schumann, he told them he would like very much to move to Salem. He informed them that he had already written to Lititz that he could not possibly leave Bethania before the fall of 1814, and he would not object if they offered the position to someone else. He also told the Salem ministers that he could not move prior to that date. Since Dr. Schumann preferred to come to Salem and because the Conferenz was firm in its appeal, the matter was laid to rest.

Meanwhile, Sam was steadily occupied treating his out-of-town patients, mostly surgery cases, and the people around Salem. He was overworked during the measles epidemic that hit the boarding school. In all, there were one hundred twenty cases of measles. Then in the fall many residents were attacked by influenza.

One evening he came home late and checked on the progress of one of his out-of-town surgery patients. After examining the man, Sam sat in a chair beside the bed.

"Tired, doctor?"

"A bit. Sometimes after I've been on my feet all day, my legs give out, partly from the accident a few years back."

"While I've been lying here, I've been counting the houses in Salem. Not counting the choir houses or the academy, I'd say there are about thirty houses."

"Thirty-six."

"Doctor, you have many people to look after."

"Fortunately, they're not all sick at once."

"But when an epidemic is prevalent, doesn't it seem like it?"

Sam got out of the chair slowly. "See you in the morning. Rest well."

Martha was waiting up for him in the kitchen. When she heard him in the apothecary, she walked in there. "I have some water hot. Would you like a cup of tea?"

"What I'd really like is some sleep, but I'll take some tea with bread and cheese first."

Martha returned to the kitchen and rinsed the cleaned teapot with hot water. She poured that out, added tea leaves and more boiling water then set the pot aside to steep. She sliced some sourdough bread and cheese.

"Sam," she said as he came to the table, "Henrietta came by this afternoon. She wanted to know what I thought about her going to Pennsylvania on a trip with Sister Benzien and her daughter."

"When are they leaving?"

"Next week. She was very excited about the prospect."

"Did she give any particular reason for wanting to go?"

Martha poured tea for both of them. "She said to see Polly and the baby. You know it would be nice if some of our family could visit Polly. None of us have met her husband."

"Henrietta could give us a good account of Pennsylvania and Polly's family."

"Does that mean you give your approval of her trip?"

"Yes."

"The trip should be good for her. She's worked so hard in the school."

"She's a dedicated worker, like her mother; however, I don't see you taking a trip."

"It's different for me. I don't need to get away. I remember young people can get restless." She paused, then said with a twinkle. "I might surprise you one day and want to go to Pennsylvania."

"Oh, that would surprise me. Here you've lived all your life in two blocks of Salem. And you seem content. Are you?"

"I am. That's because all I want is right here: a family to serve and love; friends to share our days with; your patients to nurse and comfort."

"Thank you, my dear. And now there's a tired and sleepy husband ready for bed." Sam stretched his long legs, yawned and stood up. He ambled on to the bedroom while Martha picked up the candle and followed him.

CHAPTER THIRTY-FOUR

Even in the peaceful settlement of Salem, one thing Martha learned that she could count on was change: and with it, personal adjustments. While Henrietta was in Pennsylvania, Martha missed having the late afternoon cup of tea with her and keeping in touch with the boarding school activities. Carolina and Eleonora seldom came home: they ate and slept in the Sisters House and had their laundry taken care of there also. Martha's visiting was limited due to the constant care necessary for Sister Herbst.

Eliza was in the little girls day school now, thus Martha zipped through her household duties during those hours. When possible she timed her outside errands to coincide with school dinner hours in order that she could walk with Eliza. Other times the young boys accompanied her. Ernst, at thirteen, preferred errands on his own. He liked to go the post office or the community store for his mother.

One Spring afternoon after the children had returned to school, Martha picked a bag of coffee beans from the table where Ernst had deposited them from a trip to the store. She was in the process of putting a handful of beans in the grinder, when her mind began to concentrate on Ernst. She left the beans in the grinder and stepped into the apothecary where Sam was studying a new surgical technique in one of his journals.

"Sam, may I talk to you?"

"One minute."

Martha waited patiently until he stopped reading and looked up.

"It's about Ernst. I know we need to make some plans. He's almost fourteen."

"I've talked with him and he still shows more interest in the store than in anything else."

"How would you feel about his working with Brother Kreuser?"

"Brother Kreuser is a fine person and a good merchant. Ernst could learn a great deal from him."

"You won't be disappointed if he doesn't go into medicine?"

"Not if he doesn't want to. I will be disappointed if he doesn't continue some form of study."

"If he works in the store in the daytime, do you think any type of night classes can be arranged?"

"One of the schoolmasters might have some specific knowledge in an area that's not covered in the regular school. I'll inquire. And I'll talk with Brother Kreuser about taking in Ernst soon. Martha, doesn't Kreuser have several brothers helping him now?"

"There's still the Obert young man, but I believe Ernst told me that Jacob Shultz had a farm on the edge of town and that he might be moving out there soon."

The tinkling sound of Sister Herbst's bell ended their conversation.

"Sister Vierling," the elderly woman spoke softly, "I'm sorry to disturb your rest."

"That's all right. I wasn't resting. What may I do for you?"

"Could I please sit over there in the chair by the window? The sunshine looks so warm. My old bones get cold, even in bed sometimes."

"Let me put your shawl around your shoulders. The house does get chilly. I get so warm working that I forget the stoves up here need wood. But you ring your bell whenever you need anything." Martha talked gently with her as she helped her settle in the chair. "I was about to make a pot of coffee. Could I bring you a cup?"

"Yes, thank you. And could I have some sugar?"

"And no cream, is that right?"

Sister Herbst smiled at Martha. Martha smiled back.

Down in the kitchen, Martha ground the coffee beans and placed them in the pot along with some fresh water. She took two mugs off the hutch. She checked the sugar bowl; the contents were low so she decided to refill it. The sugar canister was empty. Martha was chagrined that she had not realized the shortage when Ernst went for the coffee. Because Sister Herbst wanted coffee now, and somebody else was sure to need sugar for supper, Martha decided to make a quick trip to the store.

Sam was busy with a patient. She hurriedly told him she would be out for a few minutes. Usually Martha stayed at the house if Sam had someone in so that she could tend to any household problems. However there were fewer of them to arise unexpectedly now that the children were all in school. Sometimes she stayed so she could assist Sam if he needed her.

Martha walked out without her cape, only a scarf about her shoulders, on the warm, sunny afternoon. She trotted along the dirt street, her basket swinging freely on her arm. When she was a half block from the store, she recognized Eleonora. The girl turned back toward the store but did not see her mother. It appeared to Martha that Eleonora was smiling at someone inside the building.

Martha raised her hand and waved but Eleonora turned and walked away very rapidly toward the Sisters House. Martha never forgot that Sam didn't like for her to run or shout; therefore, she didn't try to stop Eleonora by calling out or rushing after her. Instead, Martha walked into the store and placed her order. While waiting for the sugar cones, she glanced around to see whom Eleonora might have been smiling at. There were no sisters in sight, only a few married brothers shopping and two clerks. Martha was puzzled. Thinking she was mistaken, she decided not to say anything.

Within a few days, Sam talked with Brother Kreuser about Ernst learning the merchant trade. Kreuser expressed his pleasure that Ernst wanted to work in the store and said he could come anytime. Sam discussed the situation with the Collegium and gained consent. The board recommended that Ernst continue for awhile to sleep in the Anstalt.

Next, Sam broached Ernst's continuing his studies at night with the schoolmasters. They agreed to give Ernst whatever time they could.

Ernst was exuberant about his new status. For the first few days, all he could talk about when he rushed home from the store for meals was what he had done that day. He talked at length about how helpful Jacob Schulz was. Ernst took pride in lifting heavy barrels and sacks.

The next trip Martha had to make unexpectedly to the store was also in mid-afternoon, shortly after Ernst began working there. Before entering the building, she paused to look at the new window display of ladies gloves. As she glanced upward, she saw Eleonora and Carolina talking and laughing with Will Obert and Jacob Schulz.

Martha retreated a step in complete surprise. Regaining her composure, she held her head up and proceeded into the store, directly toward the merry foursome. She had no notion of what she would say. She simply knew that the group had to disperse — certainly into two separate sections: one male and one female.

The girls had their backs to the door. It was Will who first spotted Martha coming determinedly towards them. His laughter stopped so abruptly that Jacob turned toward the door. As soon as he recognized Martha, he shook his head sideways and frowned. Both girls turned slightly to see what changed the young men.

Eleonora blushed as she saw her mother. Carolina gasped. The young men cast their eyes downward, embarrassed, and Jacob rearranged some nails in a keg. Will feverishly dusted a barrel top.

At that moment, Ernst tramped up the steps carrying a large sack. He dropped it near the railing at the top of the stairs. Pushing it over out of the walkway and looking up, he saw his mother and he gave her a job-well-done-wasn't-it grin.

"Hello, Mama."

"Hello, Ernst."

The short conversation served to break the girls' temporary inertia and they flustered around Ernst.

"Ernst, we came to see how you like work!" "Ernst, I didn't know you could lift such a heavy sack!"

Ernst looked pleased with the praise, but then he appeared confused. Martha said crisply, "Eleonora. Carolina. Tell your brother goodbye. Then we three will go home."

The girls meekly did as they were told.

Ernst, the businessman, asked his mother as she turned to leave, "Did you need anything, Mama?"

For an instant she reversed her position. "Yes. Some salt. Please, bring it at supper."

As his mother and sisters departed, Ernst thought they acted strangely. He looked to see if Will or Jacob had noticed, but they were working industriously without talking. They continued to do so until quitting time.

Martha took the two steep inclines to her house in a fast clip. The girls remained several steps behind her although they endeavored to keep up with her. She didn't speak a word until they reached home, then she told them to wait in Eliza's bedroom until she called them.

Martha needed a few minutes alone to think and to regain her calmness. She acknowledged to herself that she had acted hastily, but she did not regret having done so. However, she wanted to be careful not to misjudge their actions. Hadn't that happened to her right there in that block of town, twenty some years ago? Well, she concluded, she'd reserve judgment until after the girls had a chance to explain themselves.

Composed again, she searched for Sam. He wasn't in the shop, so she tried the treatment room. He was with a patient; therefore, she went into the kitchen and piddled around. When Sam was free, he found Martha.

"Did you want me?"

"Yes. The girls, Eleonora and Carolina, were talking and laughing with the two store helpers this afternoon. I wanted you to be present when I heard their explanation."

"I am surprised."

"So am I. They're upstairs. I'll call them." Martha left the room and in two minutes she returned with the girls following. She sat down at the table and the girls did likewise, looking innocent and folding their hands in their laps.

Martha spoke first. "Girls, I asked your father to listen to the reasons for your behavior. I considered this was only fair to you. I have told him what I witnessed: your talking and laughing with two single brothers in the store."

The girls eyed one another. Carolina being the elder decided to speak first. "Mama, we told you, we went to see how Ernst was liking the store."

"Ernst was not in the store. He was in the basement."

Eleonora added, "We wanted to check the glove supply to know how many pairs we needed to make this month."

"Eleonora, the gloves were in the window, no where near where you were standing."

Silence.

"We didn't do anything wrong, Mama," Eleonora continued bravely.

"Do our congregation rules permit unnecessary conversation with the brothers?" Martha asked.

"No."

"Then you were breaking a rule and that is wrong," Martha spoke decisively.

Sam regarded the girls keenly. "Carolina, have you been secretly seeing the young men in question?"

"No, Father," she responded quickly.

"Have you, Eleonora?"

"Me, neither!"

"Have either of you girls made any private agreements?"

Carolina immediately said no. Eleonora hesitated.

"Eleonora, why do you hesitate?" Sam was beginning to scowl.

"Father, I haven't seen Jacob secretly, only in the store and at services." She took a deep breath, then continued. "But I do like him very much. I believe he likes me, too. He hasn't made any proposals."

"If he were to ask for you, then you would give your consent?"

"Yes, Father."

"I appreciate your honesty. Carolina, what are your feelings for Brother Obert? Are they of a friendly nature?"

"Oh, yes."

"More than a friendly nature?"

"Like Eleonora, I'd accept a proposal."

Martha showed her bewilderment. "I can't understand how these situations developed without my knowledge." And silently she wondered if they would have gone so far if Henrietta had been around. Surely, she would have been close enough to observe the girls going and coming to the store or lingering after services.

Vaguely, she became aware Sam was speaking to her. "Martha, do not blame yourself. What we must do now is talk with the young men. Girls, you may go back to the choir house. We'll talk again later."

The girls each came forth and hugged and kissed both of their parents, saying, "We're so sorry." "We didn't want to cause a problem."

After the girls left, Martha leaned back. "I understand what they said. They can not really prevent certain emotions from being aroused, but I wish they had not acted upon the emotions. Or spoken deceitful alibis. Oh, Sam what if Will and Jacob do not feel as they girls have been led to believe?"

"If not, then the girls will be unhappy. There's no need to speculate on any of this. I'll go now and ask them both to meet me after services tonight."

Martha trailed behind Sam to the door. She stood on the stoop and watched him go down the hill. "Dear, dear Sam, you can only guess how they'll feel. *I know.*"

That evening Martha asked a married sister to sit with Sister Herbst so that she could attend services. Eliza begged to go but Martha told her she would have to stay home. Martha wasn't sure how long the talks would last and she wanted to be there with the girls.

After the service was over, Martha beckoned the girls with a glance. As the crowd thinned, they made their way to her.

"Your father is speaking with the young brothers. I'd like for you to wait here with me, in case there are any questions to answer."

While the women sat silently in the large church sanctuary, Martha began to hum almost inaudibly, a favorite hymn. Carolina and Eleonora gave no indication what they were thinking: they remained quiet and composed, just occasionally Carolina shuffled her feet and Eleonora twisted her hands.

Inside the conference room, Sam was first confronting Jacob who was doing his own twisting. He kept switching his tricon from hand to hand. "Brother Schulz, what do you have to say about this afternoon's episode?"

"Sir, no harm was meant. Sisters Eleonora and Carolina had come into the store and asked to see Ernst. While they were waiting, Brother Obert and I were talking to them. We knew Ernst would be up soon."

"Are you in the habit of talking with the sisters so freely?"

"No sir."

"Just to Eleonora?"

Jacob blushed. Sam repeated the question.

Jacob looked Sam straight in the eye. "Yes sir. I plan to ask the Conferenz to allow us to be married."

"Without recourse to the lot?"

"Yes sir, if they'll permit it. She is the only sister I have any desire to marry."

And this Sam understood. He said, "When were you planning to make your request?"

"I'd like to make it now, or rather at the next meeting."

"Why so soon? Eleonora is only seventeen."

"I have a farm on the edge of Salem, but outside of the town. I want to move out there in a couple of weeks. Brother Kreuser knows this. I'd like a wife to go with me."

Sam couldn't help but like this sensible young man. He felt that Jacob would take proper care of Eleonora. He extended his hand in friendship. "The ministers are waiting in the next room to speak with you."

As Jacob exited, Will entered. Sam asked him to describe the afternoon episode. His story supported what Sam had already heard.

"Brother Obert, have you any understanding with my daughter, Carolina?"

"No, sir."

"Do you have any plans for your future that include her?"

"My plans are indefinite." Sam made no comment. Will shifted his weight from one foot to another and kept his eyes downcast. "I've been with the store several years, but I do not have a position equal to a master tradesman, and certainly not a professional man."

"Everyone has his own place to serve."

"I'm not certain where my place is."

"Then you are not ready to establish yourself?"

"No sir."

"In view of this, I'm asking you to refrain from speaking to Carolina or making any attempt at seeing her."

John nodded. Sam did likewise in a manner of dismissing him.

Sam picked up his hat and joined the women in the sanctuary. "I've spoken with both of the young men. They are talking with the ministers."

"Should we wait?" Martha asked.

"We'll wait a few minutes." He sat across the aisle from Martha in his usual place.

Shortly, Brother Peter entered. "I apologize for keeping you. Carolina, Eleonora, your parents have already spoken with you about the value of obeying congregation rules."

"Yes sir," the girls said together. "We meant no harm," added Eleonora.

"We hope you decide now of your own will to abide by the

rules and not to seek any further relationships with these brothers."

"We will," they promised quickly but without heart.

"Brother Vierling, I will be speaking with you again in a few days. Good evening, sisters." Peter returned to his study and the Vierlings left the church by the front door.

Sam told Martha to walk ahead to the Sisters House with Eleonora while he walked behind with Carolina.

"Carolina, Will Obert while a brother, does not belong to our congregation. He's here to learn the merchant trade and to work with Brother Kreuser. His position at the present is not a stable one or a permanent one. He says he is not ready to establish himself."

"Father, you are telling me he is not ready to get married?"

"That's what I'm relating. Now that you know this, you understand how unwise it would be for you to make opportunities to see him?"

"But Father," Carolina shook her head in disbelief. "I believe Will likes me. I like him so much."

"When people are considering marriage there are more important things that have to be dealt with first. The brother must be able to support a wife and a family. He must want to settle down."

"Don't you think it's important for a brother to *like* the sister he's going to marry?"

"Liking each other before marriage can be helpful. But do not forget that many brothers and sisters do not even know their mates prior to the lot decisions and the weddings."

"Father, I don't want that! I want to marry somebody I love and like!" Carolina cried.

Sam stopped to face Carolina. "Marriage now with Will Obert is out of the question. You must forget about him."

Carolina hung her head. She and Sam resumed their walking. As they reached Sisters House, Carolina swiftly kissed her mother goodnight and darted up the front steps and into the house. Eleonora bid her parents goodnight and went inside too.

Martha and Sam headed back up the street to their own home.

"Did you have any satisfaction from your talks with the young men?" Martha asked as she held on to Sam's arm.

"They were honest. Jacob is ready to settle down and he wants to marry Eleonora."

"But she's only seventeen?"

"Do you think she's too young?"

"I was thinking about Mama and myself. We were older. But Eleonora has had experience at home with children. Would the lot have to be consulted?"

"If Jacob moves outside of town, I would think not."

"And if Eleonora married him, she wouldn't be a member of the Salem congregation anymore."

"No, but she could still come to services. If we give our consent, there would be no reason for anyone to look upon the marriage in anyway critically. We'll know what the Conferenz thinks in a few days."

"What about Will Obert? Does he want to marry Carolina?"

"He is not ready to take a wife."

"Oh. Is that what you told Carolina?"

"Yes."

"I'm sure she is disappointed."

"The fact really didn't penetrate."

Martha shook her head sadly, as she and Sam walked up the steps to their house.

The next morning after Martha finished the wash, she went up to a bedroom where Eleonora had stored the things she had made before moving into Sisters House. Martha raised the lid from the large wooden chest and peered inside. The chest was almost empty. There were a stack of linen napkins, another of dishtowels and an assortment of handkerchiefs and scarves. Martha realized that Eleonora had two sets of sheets, several pillow slips and hand towels with her. Also she had blankets and a bedspread. But Martha knew the yards of cloth it would take to make curtains, tablecloths, clothing and extra bed covers. She regretted not encouraging the girls to spin more. Weavers were scarce for the needs in town. She chastised herself for not exerting energy and time to see the weaving done.

Closing the lid, Martha decided to check the other girls' trunks. Carolina's was almost as bare as Eleonora's. Henrietta's was the surprise: it was three quarters filled. Martha fingered the soft, sturdy wool blanket on the top and folded the edges back revealing new white sheets and pillow slips, a large cloth estimated by the number of folds, a smaller checked one, and a number of other items underneath. Martha was amazed that Henrietta had found time to finish so many articles.

Martha resolved on the spot that it was time to train Eliza's fingers to the spinning wheel. She located a basket of wool that she had cleaned and carded with the intention that she would spin it on cold nights. Now it was spring. She'd let Eliza start on this, and then she'd show her how to weave it on the small handloom.

Following the weekly Conferenz meeting, Brother Peter visited the Vierlings.

"Jacob Schulz has asked permission to marry Eleonora and he has asked that it not be put to the lot. This can be done because he will be living out of town."

Sam answered. "Martha and I had discussed this possibility and we give our consent to the marriage. Eleonora needs to be asked formally."

"I'll have the pflegerin ask her," Peter said. "We have found it best if couples marry as soon as possible after a decision is made. I'll talk with Brother Schulz and he can proceed with his plans."

The following evening Martha waited impatiently for Eleonora to run home to talk about the proposed marriage. It was after eight thirty. She had heard the town clock strike twice. Surely the service would be over now. And the pflegerin had found time to deliver such an important message.

To keep herself occupied, Martha sat down in a chair next to Maria's old spinning wheel and inspected Eliza's first attempts at making woolen threads. There were the usual lumps and knots but over all, she was pleased. Next, she picked up her own knitting needles and cast on a long row of stitches thinking she could knit a simple afghan for Eleonora.

The front door opened and closed and Martha heard footsteps in the front rooms, then on into the kitchen. Eleonora entered first, her eyes shining. She ran over to Martha, dropped to her knees and hugged her mother tightly. Over Eleonora's white cap, she could see Carolina standing in the doorway, seething.

Martha looked back down to Eleonora who was speaking to her. "Mama, the pflegerin told me that Jacob proposed. And Mama, thank you so much for saying yes. Mama, I know you'll like Jacob. He's . . . he's just so good; a good worker and so kind."

"I'm glad to hear all this. It seems you know a lot about him."

"Ernst has told me about him," Eleonora said blushing. "Ernst likes him and says Jacob has helped show him many ways they do things in the store."

"Since Jacob is leaving, I'm sure Brother Kreuser appreciates Jacob's giving good advice to Ernst. That will make Ernst more of an asset to the store."

Martha again glanced at Carolina. "Dear, have you offered Eleonora your best wishes on this proposal of marriage?"

Carolina walked into the room. "Yes. If Ernst becomes more valuable to the store, then that will hurt some other worker's chances. Some people might feel that a Salem boy would have more opportunity to get ahead than an outsider."

"If you're referring to Will, you should realize that he is much older and more experienced than Ernst. If he's qualified, he will be a store manager years before Ernst will be eligible." At this Carolina's face began to soften. "With Jacob leaving, I would think that Will's prospects to prove himself would double." With this speculation, Carolina absolutely beamed.

Martha asked, "Carolina, there's hot water in the kettle. Why don't you make us a pot of sassafras tea while Eleonora tells me about the plans?"

Carolina removed her cape and placed it on a wall peg. Eleonora did likewise and started talking in the process.

"Mama, Jacob is moving to the farm at the end of this week. And we are going to be married at the early afternoon service on April 25."

"By Brother Peter?"

"No, Brother Reichel. Jacob's been closer to him through the single brothers choir."

Martha leaned forward and stroked her daughter's cheek. "You're very young dear for so much responsibility."

Eleonora smiled and spoke gaily and confidently. "I've learned much about housekeeping at the choir house this year."

"But a farm life will be so different."

"I think my duties will be much the same as every other married woman's. I may have a few more animals to feed and a few more beans to pick, but, Mama, I surely won't have any more fruit to put up than you have around here."

Martha and Eleonora laughed and soon Carolina joined in the merry reminiscence of the family's fun and squabbles at harvest time.

During the next two weeks while preparations were being made for Eleonora's move, Martha noticed that Carolina's attitude fluctuated between hopefulness, anxiety and depression. Whenever Ernst came in with a delivery, she would catch Carolina taking Ernst aside and badgering him with questions that she suspected were about Will. Ernst always reacted with a shrug of his shoulders and a "I don't know expression."

The day before the wedding Jacob walked to the Vierlings house to help Dr. Vierling load Eleonora's trunk, bed, chest and chair onto the wagon. As the two men moved the objects, Jacob observed that the doctor showed a great deal of strength, initially, especially in lifting heavy pieces, but that midway through the moving procedure the doctor showed signs of fatigue.

Jacob slowed his own pace and asked tactfully, "Dr. Vierling, you'll be glad when Dr. Schumann moves here, won't you?"

Sam replied, "It'll be more convenient for the Salem people to have two doctors. But don't forget, that the congregations to the west still have to be cared for."

"I didn't think of it that way. You could end up doing more traveling?"

Sam didn't answer. He wedged two drawers back into the chest on the wagon.

Jacob resumed his conversation. "Is it true that the Collegium has agreed to let Dr. Schumann bring his slaves to Salem?"

"He won't be living inside the town boundaries, that's why he can keep some of them. It seems he needs somebody full time to tend to his wife."

"Then I guess what I heard about the town building him a new house down on the Wach is right."

"Yes. They'll build this summer."

"The town certainly is being generous to him."

Sam surveyed the wagon. "Everything appears secure. I'll check if Martha has anything to add." He walked into the house and Jacob waited. Shortly, Sam returned with Martha, each laden with a basket.

She said as she tucked hers under the front seat, "These are some foods that will keep a few days."

"Thank you, ma'am."

Just then a brother on horseback rode up to the house. He hailed Sam. "Doctor!"

Sam headed toward the rider. After a brief conversation, Sam returned to the wagon. "Jacob, can you manage without me?"

"Yes sir. Brother Kreuser told me Ernst could get off this morning if I needed him."

As Jacob pulled off, Sam spoke to Martha then went inside for his bag. When he had saddled his own horse, he rode off alongside the other man.

The following afternoon Eliza went with Martha and Sam to the service. They remained outside to speak to Eleonora when she arrived. Eleonora and Carolina came within a few minutes. Eliza ran down the walk to greet them.

Martha overheard Eliza suddenly and pointedly ask, "Carolina, why aren't you getting married first? You're the oldest?"

Carolina looked surprised. "It's not fair, is it, Eliza?" A smug smile crept over Carolina's face as she bent toward her youngest sister. "But maybe it won't be long before I'm a bride, too."

Martha beckoned the girls inside. Each found seats in their own choir sections. The afternoon meeting was as usual, short. Carolina scanned the brother's section several times during the service. She was beginning to display a fretful face.

Carolina muttered to herself, "Where can he be? Certainly he'll be here to see his friend married." Jacob and Eleonora were summoned to the front of the church. Carolina's attention was divided between watching her sister's marriage service and glancing around to see if Will had arrived. This was the event she had been anticipating for the past two weeks – because she just *knew* if he could see Jacob and Eleonora married that he would be spurred to ask for her to be his wife. She had known that Will liked her since the day she had gone to Bethania. Eleonora had told her last night that Jacob had invited him to the love feast to follow the service.

This time as Carolina's eyes searched the brothers' row, she spotted Ernst among the older boys. Instantly, Carolina reasoned that if Ernst were out of the store, Will would have to stay to help Brother Kreuser.

The separation of the past two weeks, and the desire to know the effects of today's wedding on Will overcame Carolina's better judgment. As soon as she considered it was polite to leave the love feast, she sneaked out of the church when she was sure no one was looking at her and walked rapidly to the store.

There were only a few customers inside. Brother Kreuser was weighing some nails for one of them. Carolina didn't see Will. She was embarrassed and wasn't sure how to ask about him. She turned to a display near the wall.

Soon Kreuser walked over to her. "Did you run out of something over at the church?"

"No. I . . . I wanted to get a gift for Eleonora. I wanted her to have it to take to the farm with them today."

"Oh."

Carolina quickly picked up a small glass pitcher. "I think she'd like this one."

Carolina knew it would cost most of the money she had earned lately, but at the moment she was more interested in information than money. She swallowed to gain control of her voice. "You don't have any helper today?"

"I'm by myself for an hour or so. Jacob invited all the single brothers to the love feast after the wedding."

"There were many there, but I don't recall seeing his friend Brother Obert," Carolina spoke softly and slowly for this probing was very difficult for her.

"No. Will left early this morning," Kreuser said.

She stared directly at the store manager. "Left?" Her voice was weak.

Kreuser had observed Carolina and Will smiling at one another on several encounters in the store. Secretly, he suspected they had spoken to each other when he was not in the room, but he had never mentioned this to anyone for he had no proof, just suspicions. Now he tried to be kind and gentle to her.

"This morning before the store opened, he said he decided last night to go home to visit his parents."

Carolina put her hands on the counter in an attempt to physically brace herself while she asked, "Will he be back? Ernst, Jacob will want to know."

"One can't be sure with these young brothers, but I doubt he'll return. He took everything with him. I hear he didn't ask them to hold his room at the Brothers House."

Carolina picked up the pitcher that Kreuser had wrapped and placed on the counter. "The gift will be appreciated," he said.

Carolina managed a slight nod and left the store. She could hardly keep the tears back. She couldn't return to the choir house yet, so she took the diagonal path through the square. "Why did he go? Why couldn't he have told me goodbye? What did father and the ministers say to him? Were they too harsh? Did they threaten him? He liked me! I know he did!"

As she approached the gate at the other end of the square, she saw a group of people standing around the church steps. She reached in her pocket for a handkerchief and blotted the tears before they trickled down her face.

She crossed the street and headed toward the church. Eleonora sighted her and started in that direction. Carolina doubled her pace and soon had her arms around Eleonora. Then the tears spilled. Eleonora cried, too. As Eleonora pulled away, she said, "Carolina, I'm not going far. We'll still be able to see each other."

Carolina looked down and remembered the gift. "Here is something for you and Jacob."

Eleonora turned to show Jacob the package. "We'll have a gift to open as soon as we get to the farm."

Jacob said, "Thank you, Carolina. Shall we be on our way, Eleonora?"

Eleonora hugged her parents and brothers and Eliza and told Martha how beautiful the love feast had been. Then she and Jacob walked down the hill towards their farm. Sam asked the younger children if they wanted to walk with him to the blacksmiths. They were delighted to be allowed the remainder of the afternoon off from school, and they started down the hill in front of Sam.

Martha had been holding Carolina close at the waist since she had given the gift to Eleonora. Now she asked, "Come home with me. I think you need some private time."

Carolina nodded. Together they slowly climbed Church Street hill. Martha spoke gently. "You went to the store, didn't you?" Again Carolina tilted her chin up and down. Martha added, "To see Will?"

Carolina choked back a big lump in her throat. "Oh, Mama, he's gone." Again tears rolled down her cheeks.

"Dear, don't let's cry on the street. We won't talk until we're home." Martha reached in her pocket and pulled out a fresh handkerchief, which she gave to her daughter.

Reaching the house, Martha managed a cheerful tone. "If anyone saw tears, they would assume they were for Eleonora, the tears of happiness."

Martha led Carolina to her own bedroom and left her there while she checked on Sister Herbst. Sister Sampson had volunteered to sit with her during the wedding. Martha thanked her, gave her some love feast buns to share with her family, and briefly reported the worship and marriage services.

When Martha returned to the bedroom, Carolina was lying on the bed. She was crying. Martha sat down beside her and stroked her hair. She could see that the pillow was wet.

"Carolina, you thought you loved him, didn't you?"

"I do love him, Mama."

"There will be a good man for you dear someday. You'll make a brother a fine helpmate."

"I don't want to marry anyone else. He will come back."

"You expected he'd come to the service, too. You kept looking for him."

"Oh, Mama, don't hurt me."

"I'm not trying to, dear. I know you're unhappy. I know how you feel. But have faith. The best, and the right, will happen to you."

"You don't know how I feel. You've always had father."

Carolina's words tore a gap from today straight into Martha's past. But Martha's grieving had been done and conquered in private a very long time ago: she could not cut the scar now. She merely stated, "I know."

"I'll never love anybody else."

"You will love. And you will be loved."

The mother posed disturbing questions to herself. Why can't Carolina find solace in the scripture, or why can't the need for service to others be sufficient to pull her out of this over-concern for herself? And faith? Where is the faith to trust that the good things will come to you? Trust and faith. Were they lacking in Carolina's life and in the lives other young people today? If they didn't have these two vital qualities before a crisis, could they hope to gain them at the moment of need?

Suddenly, Martha's more basic thought patterns pierced this current line of inquiry. What's wrong with me? If I doubt now that the Lord is watching after her, where is my faith? If I've failed to give her the guidance to made decisions that bring her peace, then it's my responsibility to help her now.

There is a way to restore peace to her soul. "Be still, Martha. Listen. Have patience. You could be interfering with His Will being done."

Martha stood up and walked to the other side of the room. From her window she could see the yellow greens of April glimmer in the late afternoon sunshine. "It'll be time to tend the gardens in the evenings soon. How good it'll be to get outside."

CHAPTER THIRTY-FIVE

Whatever time Martha had for thinking, she spent planning ways to rekindle Carolina's enthusiasm in the ordinary life of Salem. Carolina wasn't interested in the everyday threads of the community, prompting Martha to embroider the predictable pattern with special events.

When Henrietta returned from Bethlehem, Martha cooked a delicious dinner and invited Carolina, Eleonora and Jacob home to share the meal with the rest of the family. Carolina appeared half-heartedly to hear Henrietta's talk about Polly and her husband and baby. She paid token attention to a description of life in the Sisters Choir House in Bethlehem. After a few days Carolina sank again into a remorseful frame of mind.

Next, Martha asked Carolina to assist her in preparing and serving a vesper meal of cake and lemonade on Eliza's birthday for her schoolmates. Carolina helped make the cake but without enthusiasm.

One afternoon while Carolina was hemming some sheets with Martha, Sam came home bringing letters and journals from the latest post.

Carolina asked hopefully, "Is there anything for me?"

"No. Were you expecting a letter?"

Carolina merely sighed.

"You aren't still thinking Brother Obert is going to write or come back?" Martha commented in an exasperated tone.

"He might."

"Carolina, I do wish you could forget that young man. I do not like to see you waste your days in such thoughts," Sam admonished her.

"I am staying busy," she argued as she held up the sheet she was stitching.

"I've noticed that your mother has put forth a great deal of effort in your behalf lately."

Martha said quickly, "Carolina, I could use your help more often now. Sister Herbst is getting to be too much for me to handle alone. When she's at her weakest and stays in bed, I can scarcely turn her by myself."

Carolina jumped up, "I'm sorry, Mama. I just can't help you any more. It's not my calling to be around sick people. I want to do something on my own. Not be a helper all the time." And Carolina nervously paced the room.

"What do you want to do?" Her father looked intently at her.

"I don't know," Carolina walked back over to the table and took up the sheet that she had been working on. She clipped off the sewing thread and folded the sheet. "I'm through with this. I'm going back to the house. I have some things to do there before supper."

After Carolina left, Sam asked Martha, "Is it true you need help with Sister Herbst?"

"Yes. There's so much to do in the garden during the summer. We have fewer children home or coming in regularly now to help."

"I'll check with the Conferenz for suggestions."

When Sam contacted the group he was informed that he could have the services of a Negro girl for a few days at a time whenever he needed her. He was told that he wouldn't be charged for the girl's services. Sam learned that the Conferenz had been having some dialogue with Doctor Schumann prior to his move to Salem. Dr. Schumann was concerned that he might not be able to make a good living with just a medical practice in Salem and he wanted to explore the possibilities of undertaking a craft. Town leaders were more inclined to assure him a steady patient clientele. They wanted to suggest he take over as the boarding school doctor. Upon hearing the pending proposition, Sam agreed to relinquish this portion of his practice.

While Martha was again adjusting to another worker in her house, she was still attempting to solve Carolina's problem even though she was coming to the realization that Carolina wasn't doing much on her own to forget Will. That problem was in the end going to have to be solved by her daughter herself.

One morning toward the middle of summer, when the girl was in the house to look after Sister Herbst and Martha had finished the baking, on the spur of the moment Martha decided to take a loaf of bread to Eleonora. She had not seen Eleonora for several days. She stooped and picked sprigs from several herbs in the gardens to take along.

Martha had not been fully aware of how closely she had been confined to her house until she experienced a sense of pleasure and freedom on her walk to the farm. As she covered the narrow path to the farmhouse, everything was quiet. No one in sight.

Martha rapped on the closed door and there was no answer. She knocked again, louder. After waiting for a few minutes, Martha pressed down on the latch and the door opened. No one was in the front sitting room.

She called out, "Anyone home?" She listened and she heard groans from a back room. Martha crossed to the door. "Eleonora?"

"Mama," a voice answered weakly.

Pushing the door ajar, she saw Eleonora stretched out on the bed. Her face and hands were very white. There was a strong wretched odor. Martha looked around and saw a pot beside the bed. She immediately walked to the bed, peered at the pot and saw it contained vomit.

She sat on the bed and felt Eleonora's face and hands. "Are you ill?"

"I don't know."

"How long have you been vomiting?"

"Everyday for a week. Just in the mornings."

"Do you ache anywhere?"

"No. It'll pass soon."

"Oh, dear Eleonora. It sounds like you're in a family way."

At this Eleonora rolled over to her side. "I thought it might be summer flu. But I thought it might be the other."

"If you think you're through vomiting for now, I'll empty this pot."

"Please, do."

Martha stayed long enough to brew some peppermint tea and to straighten the house. She also put on a pot of potatoes and beans for their lunch.

Before she left, she told Eleonora to please send Jacob for her if she could be of any help. "I expect you'll be fine after another week or two. Tell Jacob to take good care of you."

"He does, Mama. He's a good husband."

"I'm glad to hear that."

As the year wore on and Carolina's melancholy did not abate, Henrietta suggested to her parents that they let Carolina go to Pennsylvania to visit Polly. Martha latched on to the suggestion hoping a change of scenery would improve her disposition. Sam had no other suggestion to offer so he approved of the trip.

Carolina was surprised at the mention of her taking a trip. She had about given up hope that Will was going to return so she accepted her parents' offer. No definite date was set for her return; however, Carolina decided that with sleeping space so much in demand at the choir house that she would not ask the sisters to hold a bed for her. She had been renting furniture from the diaconie so that her parents could have the use of her old bedroom furniture for their guests and patients.

After Carolina traveled north to be with Polly, Martha had only Eliza of her children at home. Benjamin and Theophilus moved into the Anstalt. Now they were having classes there, sleeping there, going to services with their schoolmasters and she was seeing them only at mealtime. Although she was reluctant to give them up, she felt it might be a wise arrangement, because Sam seemed to have less and less time for them. It wasn't that Sam had any more patients, on the contrary with Dr. Schumann now living near town, he had fewer. But Sam was moving slower, taking longer to drive his rounds and compound his medicines. The apothecary was busier than ever because Dr. Schumann's patients were bringing in prescriptions. Out-of-town surgery requests were still being made, and Sam was trying to handle at least one new case a week.

Martha knew that Sam was interested in and loved the children in spite of his lack of time to show them so. She, being held close to the house by Sister Herbst and Sam's patients, had time to spend with Eliza while she was home from school. Thus their always close relationship grew even more so. They were able to share many of the activities that Martha had shared with her own parents: spinning, dyeing, gardening, preserving, baking and reading.

Working beside Eliza, it was difficult for Martha to realize that she was soon to be a grandmother. "Why I've scarcely stopped having children myself," Martha thought, "and probably still could have some. I feel young. I doubt that I've slowed down a whit." Martha laughed as she thought about how the patients often marveled at how she handled all her duties so efficiently. "If they had been around when all the children were here, they would realize these days are easy."

Of course Martha weighed her ease only relative to her own life and the other wives in Salem. Outsiders judged from a different base. Many of them knew women in other areas who had positions equal to Martha's and those women had household and yard help. When there were two or more patients in the house together, they would exchange views on many issues but they would always include comments on the industry of the Moravian brothers and sisters. One patient questioned once if it could be because of the early training the brethren gave their children. Another said, "Look how many outsiders besiege these people to take their girls into the boarding school. They bring them here a year or two to expose them to the formal studies. Do you suppose they expect them to come away with the discipline that these Moravian young people have?"

Martha was released from one of her major responsibilities with the home going of Sister Herbst. Once again she had more time for choir duties, meetings and her children, especially Eleonora who gave birth to a son.

The next event, which created a change within the family, was another happy one. Brother Benjamin Reichel offered a proposal of marriage to Henrietta. All ministers were still required to submit such questions to the lot. And in this case the reed drawn was yes.

When Brother Peter asked Martha and Sam their opinion of the marriage, before Henrietta was approached, they gave their approval readily.

Enthusiastically Martha said, "Henrietta enjoys the school work so much. Now that Brother Reichel has been appointed to take over as Inspector of the Schools, I feel she will be a very good helpmate." Inwardly, Martha recalled that Henrietta was always interested in young Reichel. Martha believed that Henrietta would say yes to the proposal. Personally, Martha was pleased that her eldest daughter had not been hurried into marriage. She had had time to work, to become self-reliant, and to travel. She handled her students with authority and concern, just as she had her younger sisters and brothers.

Henrietta was surprised at the proposal. She accepted it immediately. The announcement was made at an afternoon service in early May and one week later the young couple was married in the church.

Martha enjoyed her daughters, Eleonora and Henrietta, in different ways now. It was as if their former relationships had expanded. There was more for them to share and to talk about together.

One period that marred the otherwise smoothness of the year was that Sam came down with an attack of fever in late summer. Several people developed the fever with its variety of symptoms and complications. Sam's own case lasted the typical four weeks. Recovery was slow. However, once well, he resumed his normal workload and appeared in generally good health.

Around Christmas time, both Henrietta and Eleonora announced that they were expecting babies in the late spring. Martha was most pleased to learn that both girls were experiencing no difficulties. She made her services available to the girls whenever they needed her and Sam didn't.

Martha wrote the girls' good news to Polly and Carolina. She had a letter from Carolina in February. She opened it expecting a note of congratulations and Pennsylvania gossip. The news was tragic. She rushed into the apothecary.

"Sam, I've just had a letter from Carolina. She writes very, very sad news. It's about Polly. She died in childbirth last month. Oh, Sam."

"Dear Polly," Sam said sadly. "Dear, dear Polly."

"I wish we could have been with her."

"The baby?"

"Dead. I know Carolina will be a comfort to Polly's husband and child."

"She will. It will be good for Carolina to be needed."

"Sam, I'll go tell Henrietta and Eleonora. It won't be an easy task with both of them expecting."

Martha left Sam with his private thoughts. In her mind, past and present superimposed one another. Anna died leaving a little girl and a husband. Polly died leaving a little one and a husband. Somewhere nearby there had been a bit of Miksch, standing, waiting to help in both past and present.

Henrietta and Eleonora were both delivered of healthy baby girls and all the family offered special prayers of thanksgiving.

Sam had two interesting surgical cases in the summer. The first one came in June, a man named Joel Willis, a Quaker from Guilford County. Mr. Willis had a leg injury that wouldn't heal and he was brought to Sam. Mrs. Willis accompanied her husband. The couple stayed in the Vierling's home. Mrs. Willis cared for her husband relieving Martha of that duty. She waited on her husband with love and devotion and he responded affectionately and kindly to her. Martha was considerably impressed. She spoke of this love to Sam and the ministers who visited Mr. Willis.

For Martha, who had not traveled out of Wachovia, and to whom very little of the ways of the outsiders was first hand knowledge, a chance like this to observe a married couple from another community under a trying situation for several weeks, was an educational experience. She was impressed. She felt good inside knowing there are loving people elsewhere.

Everyone who met them during their stay appreciated the devotion of the Willises and their friendliness.

Sam treated the injury with all the measures possible in an attempt to save the leg. When these procedures failed and Sam saw the severest consequences ahead if he didn't operate, he consulted Mr. Willis. Mr. Willis was willing for Sam to do whatever was necessary. Sam removed the leg below the knee and believed the operation was successful. Mr. Willis remained for sometime for observation and convalescence. As he grew stronger and the leg healed and no complication set in, he and Mrs. Willis repeatedly thanked Sam. They made preparations to return to their own home. Martha was sorry to see them leave, having enjoyed their company.

A month had barely passed after the Willis' departure when Sam was summoned to Bethania at the request of Single Sister Elisabeth Ranch. Sam rode out and examined Sister Ranch. He diagnosed her problem as cancer. He told her that the sooner he could operate the better her chances of recovery would be.

She asked, "What do you think the outcome will be?"

"No one knows that but the Lord, Sister Ranch."

"Ah, true."

"But you and I will do the best that we can. When can you come to Salem?"

"Tomorrow?"

"Tomorrow will be fine. We'll fix a room for you at our house. You can rest tomorrow and we'll operate the day after."

Martha prepared a room and a couple drove the sister to town. The morning of the operation, several Bethania single sisters walked to Salem to be there during the expected difficult procedure. They were concerned for their friend.

This display of love and friendship touched Martha. The sisters waited in the choir house saal during the operation. Martha promised to walk down to tell them the outcome as soon as possible.

She knew that Sam bowed his head in prayer before he began surgery and she was certain the sisters in the saal were praying; so she, too, standing by to assist Sam, whispered reverently, "Thy will be done. May we in some way help relieve this sister from her physical suffering."

Sam's extensive medical skills were needed in removing all the cancer. He worked long and carefully and finally he was satisfied that he had done his best. He and Martha stood beside Sister Ranch's bed after the operation and watched the direction her immediate recovery would take. Her color, pulse, breathing were good.

Sister Ranch spoke to them calmly. "Is it over?"

Sam looked relieved, "Yes. You were a good patient. All looks clean now."

"Thank you, doctor."

Martha said, "The sisters are anxious to hear. I'm leaving for a few minutes. Dr. Vierling will be here."

All the way to the Sisters House, Martha's feet want to pick up and run. She had to force herself to walk at a discreet tempo. The day was sunny and she was glad to be outside on a joyful mission. She was so proud of Sam and his ability to heal people. Her own part had been so small, but what a privilege it was just to have a part in his life and service.

When she delivered the good news to the Bethania sisters, they wept with joy. They offered to give whatever nursing assistance was needed. During the two weeks that Sister Ranck stayed with the Vierlings following her operation, the women fulfilled their nursing promise. Martha again experienced that happy feeling of knowing the love that people had and showed for others.

Within a few months Martha was to know a similar period of trial and the next time she was to assume the major nursing role.

Henrietta stood gazing out the window until the customer left the apothecary and was out on the street again. She wheeled around toward her father.

"I need some medicine for Benjamin," she said piqued as she handed him a slip of paper.

"Henrietta, this is written by Dr. Schumann?" Sam read the prescription, puzzled.

"Yes. Haven't you heard of the Conferenz deal with Dr. Schumann?" She sounded irked.

"No, I haven't," Sam responded truthfully.

"Dr. Schumann has offered to take care of all the ministers and their wives."

"That's generous."

"For a fifty dollar retainer."

"Oh."

"But he'll charge for the medicines. Father, I was so angry when the ministers accepted his offer. It's not fair to you."

"Dear, don't be angry. No one promised me certain patients when I started here."

"I know. That's why it's not fair. You've built up your practice with no guarantees, no retainers."

Sam moved over to his supply shelf and drew down a brown glass container. He set a weight on the scales, then measured ingredients into a bottle.

"Father, even though Benjamin is school inspector, he's a minister so he comes under the retainer. I do, too, but I'm not going to him. And I want you to take care of the baby when he comes."

With humor Sam said, "My practice is increasing again."

Henrietta smiled. "Father, you're such a good man."

Sam handed her the small bottle. "Go on back to the kitchen. Your mother will want to see you."

Henrietta headed toward the back of the house. Sam inserted a cork in the container and replaced it on the shelf. He entered the transaction in his ledger marking it as customary for his in-laws, no charge. Proceeding with the actions routinely, he thought about the news that Henrietta had reported.

As he had told her not to be, he wasn't angry, yet something about the transaction cut him deeply. Had the ministers lost confidence in him as a doctor? Where they provoked because he still performed surgery for outsiders? Surely the latter couldn't be the reason, for that would refute everything our brotherhood stands for – service to those in need and call upon us. Why did they accept Schumann's offer? Weren't they satisfied with my services? Except for when I had the fever last summer, I've always been available to them. Do they think I'm too weak to attend to them? There have been days I've felt not up to snuff, but I worked on. No one knew, and now I'm fit as ever. I don't need the money. We'll get along on the surgical fees and those of the other congregation patients, that is if they don't all follow the ministers' lead. There's no need to worry. It's done. It has to be accepted.

After that day, Martha observed that much of the heart went out of Sam. His spirits were low. He showed little enthusiasm for any subjects that she tried to draw him into conversation about. She couldn't charge him with neglecting his patients or the apothecary but everything he did seemed to be from habit and without spirit.

He did show an interest in the birth of two granddaughters: Henrietta's first child and Eleonora's second. He enjoyed his role as grandfather and occasionally stopped by to see the grandchildren while he was out calling on patients. He was almost unhappy when Henrietta announced excitedly in August that she and Benjamin were going to Pennsylvania and were going to take the baby.

"Father, we must take her, otherwise Benjamin's parents may

never see her. Benjamin believes that once his parents get to Germany that they won't be coming back. He may not see them again."

"By all means, you should go. I trust you three plan to return to Salem," Sam said with a touch of his old humor.

"Of course, we do, early in November when the Salem stage returns," she promised.

Martha wrote a long letter to Carolina and encouraged all the other family members to do likewise. She made the rounds of the houses and collected the letters and delivered them to Henrietta to pack with her luggage. When the day for the trip rolled around, she and Sam walked down to the stage at the square to say goodbye.

As the wheels of the stage turned down the road, Martha experienced a heaviness of heart. She wanted so much to talk to Sam about it, as if talking could take away the weight. But Sam seemed remote. She knew full well that he did not want to discuss the past, and her apprehensions now were related to the past: she had watched this stage roll away with Polly and now she was dead. She had seen it disappear down this same road with Carolina, and she had the feeling that Carolina would not be back. The weight was not regarding the Reichels traveling. She knew they would return. But somehow today she sensed a gloom and wanted to talk it away, only there was no one to share a conversation.

CHAPTER THIRTY-SIX

Theophilus signaled his arrival for vesper meal by banging the front door as he entered the house. "Mama," he cried all the way to the kitchen.

Martha, pouring milk, asked, "What is it, Theo?"

All in one breath he blurted, "Look what I brought, hazel nuts." He held up a large makeshift burlap sack.

"Why where ever did you find so many?"

"I didn't. Charles N. and Master Schulz collected them." Theophilus recited all this to his mother as he worked to loosen the knots in the cord tied around the bag.

Martha finished setting out the bread and jams and offered to help him. "Get a basket and we'll put the bag in it before we untie the cord. No need to have to gather the nuts from the floor. Thank you."

"Mama, these will be good in the cakes for harvest Thanksgiving."

"Um. They will. Please, tell Charles N. thank you."

Benjamin came bounding in the back door. Wiping his hands on his trousers after having washed them outside.

"Benjamin, I'll be needing you and Theophilus on Saturday to help with the fruit."

"Can we come in the morning?" Benjamin asked as he spread pear preserves thickly over a slice of bread.

"Isn't Saturday morning your time to clean the Anstalt?"

"They can get along without us, can't they, Theo?" Benjamin's eyes begged his younger brother to agree.

"Um hum. I'd rather pick apples in the morning. Brother Schulz is going to take the class in the wagon to get sand down by the river on Saturday afternoon."

"In whose wagon?"

"Brother Statz's."

"He has a small wagon. There won't be room for all you boys. If you're through, go down to the springhouse and bring up some cream, Benjamin. Theophilus, you bring in some wood and stack it beside the fireplace."

While the boys scampered out, Martha cleared the table. She put the basket of nuts on a corner table. "I wonder where Sam is. He's been gone since lunch. Maybe he stopped at Eleonora's."

Later when he arrived, Martha could tell by the drag of his feet that he was tired. As he closed the back door, she tried to act cheerful. "Did you see Eleonora this afternoon?"

He dropped on a chair near the fireplace. "I stopped by. She sends her love."

"Could I get you some tea?"

"I had some there."

"Is there anything wrong?"

"I suspicion the fever is about to start. You know the people who have the farm below Jacob's?"

"Yes."

"Jacob told me the man is sick. Fever, headache, no energy."

"Did you see him?"

"No. He's not ready to see a doctor. Jacob was trying to get him to see one."

"I hope you told Eleonora to be careful, especially about the babies."

"I did. We've had such healthy years of late. As far as the fever is concerned. Up until last year that is. I was hoping that was the exception. Well, I'll go along to the apothecary until supper. Might as well get some purgatives and prespirants ready."

It was a little over a week before Sam was sure there was fever in the town and on the outskirts, both among his own and Dr.

Schumann's patients. On the tenth day after the sand gathering adventure, Benjamin came home during the afternoon to tell his father that his teacher Brother Schulz was feeling feverish. He asked his father if he could come down to the Anstalt to see Brother Schulz.

"Of course. I'll go right now."

Benjamin walked down Church Street with his father, taking two steps to Sam's one. "Father. He really looks sick. Today in class he dropped like those over-ripe apples on the tree."

"Did he fall to the floor?"

"No. To the bench. He sat there while we wrote."

"I'm glad you came for me."

Benjamin beamed at the praise from his father. They entered the Anstalt together. Sam went to Thomas Schulz's room on the first floor and Benjamin joined his classmates upstairs.

The young schoolmaster was lying on his bed. He raised his head as Sam walked across to him. Even in the dim interior Sam could see that the patient's skin was flushed.

"Benjamin tells me you're not feeling well," Sam said as he pulled a straight chair close to the bedside.

"No, sir. The fever came upon me suddenly this afternoon."

"Any other complaints?"

Thomas switched positions restlessly. "I don't feel good. No matter what position I lie in, it doesn't feel comfortable. I am too weak to stand," he moaned.

Sam gently examined Thomas, then stated, "You have the fall fever, Thomas. You should stay in bed. Can any other masters conduct your classes?"

Thomas nodded his head.

"I'll leave some medicine for your fever with one of the masters. I'll have him bring you your meals."

"I'm not very hungry."

"You need some nourishment and liquids. Try some teas and soups. I'll see you again tomorrow."

The next day when Sam checked on Thomas, he found the

young man's fever slightly elevated. Sam instructed the other school masters to let Thomas sleep as much as possible and to remember to take him his meals and tea. "And keep the boys out of his room," Sam added.

"Yes sir. While you're here, could you take a look at Charles N. Bagge? He feels quite warm to me," said the first master.

Sam followed the teacher up the winding cantilevered steps to the third floor dormitory. The master walked down the central aisle and stopped at the foot of one of the small wooden beds.

"Carl," he called quietly.

The small, fair-haired boy rolled over from his side to his back. "Yes, sir?"

The master came around the side of the bed. "I asked Dr. Vierling to come up to see you."

At this, Sam joined the master at the bedside. Carl N. was wrapped up in a quilt. Sam leaned over and asked, "Are you cold?"

"No. I'm hot."

"Well, let's take the cover off and have a look at you."

The master stepped aside. Sam helped Carl N. disentangle himself from the quilt. When Sam pressed gently on Carl's stomach, the boy yelped with pain. Sam finished the examination and motioned the teacher to the end of the room.

"The fever is starting. Send Benjamin down to the Bagges' house. If there's anyone there, he should go home."

"Yes, sir." With that reply, the master hastened down the wooden steps. In a few minutes he was back.

Sam continued. "If his family can nurse him, it'll be better for him and the other boys. We'll send all his bed things with him, all his clothes. His mother can wash every article before they're brought back. After he leaves, have the bed and floor around it, scrubbed."

"I'll do it myself while the boys are at supper."

"Good. If you have tea prepared now for Brother Schulz, bring a cup up and I'll try to get Carl N. to drink some."

The brother went back downstairs to the first floor kitchen.

Sam pulled up a chair and sat beside the boy. He had his eyes closed, but he was not enjoying a restful sleep. His small hands were clenched over his abdomen. Sam reached over and placed his hand over the curly blond hair. He touched the fair skin that now was flushed. How much like Anna he is, Sam thought. Fair, gentle, sweet.

Once again the master climbed the stairs to the sleeping quarters. Sam helped Carl N. prop up in bed and held the cup to his lips. The boy took several sips.

The wooden steps creaked foretelling the approach of others. The master looked toward the door. First, he saw Carl N.'s father, then Benjamin.

Bagge acknowledged the master with a nod then moved quickly and directly to his son's bed. Carl Bagge carried himself in a confident, self-assured manner, that reminded one of his father, Traugott.

"Dr. Vierling, you sent for me?" Bagge asked with an energetic concern.

"I asked Ben to find out if anyone was at your house. It looks as if Carl N. has the fever. I think you and Christina could give him more care at home."

"Yes. We'll do that." Bagge bent close to his son. "Carl, I've come to take you home."

Carl smiled with effort. "I'm sorry to be a bother, Father."

"No trouble, son." He scooped the boy easily into his arms.

Sam said, "Ben and I will bring his things right behind you."

At suppertime, Sam came in and Martha could tell immediately by the wrinkling of his brow that Sam was worried. She seldom saw that particular countenance.

"An especially bad case, Sam?"

"Carl N."

"Oh no."

"I don't like to see the young ones take the fever."

"Is there anything I can do?"

"He's at home. You might like to send a pot of meat stew down to the school. Thomas will be in bed awhile. Be sure to clean the pot thoroughly when you get it back."

"Speaking of meat, the market hasn't been open lately. I wish it'd get back on a regular schedule. There should be more butchering with the colder weather coming," Martha prognosticated.

Somewhat wearily Sam promised, "I'll appeal to the Collegium. The gunsmiths should encourage the long hunters to bring their game to town."

Before Sam finished his supper, the apothecary bell was rung. He wiped his mouth as he rose. Martha pleaded, "Do finish eating. I can ask whoever it is to wait."

He motioned with his hand for her to keep her seat. "No. I'll go."

After a few minutes Sam stood in the doorway. "I have to ride out to see Peter Sampson on Bethabara Road."

She heard him go out. She heard him open the barn door. Shortly, she heard him close the door and ride away. She wished Ernst weren't staying at the Single Brothers and having to take all his meals there. They saw him so seldom these days. She thought how much help he used to be with the stable chores. Nowadays Sam had to feed and water the animals and groom the horse. The younger boys weren't home long enough to do more than routine quick chores or to run errands. However, Martha reasoned it all balanced: if they were home often, they'd create more work for her.

No matter what Martha said to Sam in reference to his work schedule, he kept on meeting all demands placed on him. She begged him to rest more, something she hadn't done since their marriage. Unconsciously perhaps she was remembering the siege of fever he had last summer. Following that illness, Sam appeared weak to Martha and the children, but he tried to give the impression he was as healthy and strong as ever and appeared determined to prove it by continuing to do as much as before. The family observed that for him to accomplish as much, he had to spend more hours at tasks. Their observations were of his performance of home chores and work in the apothecary. The latter he under took often at night as the fever cases claimed much of his attention during the day.

One evening as he was compounding medicines in the apothecary, Martha walked in.

"Brrr," she said shivering. "Sam, don't you think it's cold in here?" She stepped to the iron stove and touched it cautiously. "The fire must have gone out?"

"What?" Sam wiped his head with his shirtsleeve.

Martha moved to the table where he was working. "Are you all right?"

"Yes. It's hot in here."

"It is not! It's cold. Sam, your face is red. Do you have a fever?" She reached out to touch him.

He pulled his head back and put his own hand to his face. "*I'm all right.* Just tired." He turned the lamp wick down. "Let's go to bed."

Martha led the way to their room with her flickering candle.

During the night, Martha awakened two or three times because Sam was tossing and turning in the bed. Toward morning, he relaxed so Martha did not wake him when she got up. She had breakfast cooked and Eliza ready for school by the time he came into the kitchen.

She looked up at him and answered his questioning glance. "You had such a restless night, I thought you needed the sleep."

Sam sat down at the table. Eliza kissed him goodbye.

Martha said, "Eliza, wait a minute. I'll pour your father's coffee and serve his egg, then I'll stand on the steps and watch you."

As Martha pulled her scarf from the wall peg, Eliza asked, "Mama, why don't you wear a shawl like the other mothers?"

Wrapping the scarf around her thick blonde braids that were crossed high over the top of her head, so they stood up like a crown, Martha replied, "I don't have a shawl."

"You could knit one."

"I don't like shawls." Martha opened the front door and closed it behind them. The air had an early morning frost chill to it. "Shawls make me think of old women."

Eliza hugged her mother. "I don't think you're old, even if the boys do." Eliza bounced down the steps and ran down the hill to school.

The ages and stages of children, Martha mused, how predictable. If only she knew what lay ahead for herself. Re-entering the house, she tried to recapture scenes of her own mother's life and behavior at the age she was now. All she could recollect was the war, its aftermath, the economic struggles and the visits she made from the choir house and her call to come home to help. At this point, Martha ceased the internal inquiry, deciding she didn't feel as old as her mother must have been at the same age, with the realization that her life had not been filled with the hardships Maria had endured.

Martha's thought drifted toward her own children's lives, which had been relatively free of inconveniences, denials or threats. She wondered if in the future, they would appreciate the advantages they enjoyed and the heritage afforded them by the pioneering endeavors of those first eleven settlers in Bethabara. Could they even understand the reasons for the tenacity of those courageous men and the brothers and sisters who soon followed and stayed; or share the vision of those who planned Salem, cut it out of wilderness and persevered to govern every aspect of its existence?

Because Martha was not given to such a deep level of "why and if and could be" probing, especially early in the morning, she shook her head vigorously as she unwound her scarf and entered the kitchen.

Suddenly, Sam jumped from his chair, almost tipping it over and bolted out the back door. Martha wondered what that was all about. She peered out the window and saw him headed toward the necessary. She hung up her scarf and began clearing the table.

When he returned, she was peeling potatoes. He said one word to her – diarrhea.

"Oh. I guess you won't be seeing patients today?"

"Not if this continues."

And the condition did. Sam made several more trips to the necessary. A few people came to the house to ask Sam to come to see some member of their family. Martha relayed the messages to Sam. He sent the people home with instructions, medicine and the word that he would come when he could.

By the end of the week Sam was in bed himself, finally admitting he was "slightly down" with the fever. Martha stayed busy nursing him and laundering his clothes and bed linens. The diarrhea persisted in spite of the maidenhair fern and milk drinks she boiled and other concoctions she administered at Sam's direction.

During the second week of his illness, his fever continued to rise. He became jerky. Martha bathed him with cool water several times a day. At night she gently sponged him with rose alcohol and massaged his muscles. That week and well into the next, his temperature remained high. Often he would blurt out sounds as if he were trying to talk. Usually Martha couldn't make sense of the words. Once or twice she thought she understood him to cry, "Fair, fair and . . ." She wondered if he were meaning "Anna."

Again, in his delirium, he repeated several times, "Master. Master. Master." It sounded like a question. Then Sam added, "Schoolmaster."

"You mean Thomas Schulz?"

Sam nodded.

"He's better. He held his class this morning."

Sam showed relief on his face and dozed awhile. Later, he jerked and pointed to his throat.

Martha put a horse weed stem in a cup of tea and held it close to his lips. Sam sucked the liquid, then dropped his head back to the pillows. "Carl. Carl N.," he said.

Martha couldn't bring herself to tell the complete truth of the little boy's grave condition. "His temperature is down. Christina sent word yesterday. She asked about you."

Sam tried to shake his head, but that small gesture appeared to be too much exertion. He groaned slightly and attempted to pull his knees up to relieve the pain. After he dropped off to sleep, Martha left his bedside to prepare some lunch for herself and Eliza.

The bell rang and she changed her direction toward the apothecary. Brother Peter was in the shop.

"How's Sam today?"

"This is the worst time. If he gets through this week, he should improve next week."

"Please, call on some of the brothers to sit with him if you need help."

"Thank you. I will."

"I have some good news for you. A man on horseback came into town today. He stopped at an inn yesterday for the noon meal. Our stage was there. He saw Henrietta and Benjamin in the dining room. They should be here in a couple of days."

"I'm so glad. Henrietta will be a big help with Eliza," Martha spoke with happiness and relief.

She was always reticent to admit that she needed any physical support, but at this moment in her life she looked forward to the assistance she knew she could and would have.

Henrietta did come through and take care of Eliza and give the boys their meals. Martha could now concentrate on nursing Sam through the last painful days of the fever's course and through the slow recovery period. And life did proceed along the route Martha anticipated, but not for long.

It was Benjamin Reichel who walked up to break the news to Martha that Carl N. Bagge had blessedly passed on. "The child had suffered so much pain, Sister Vierling."

"Yes, Benjamin, I know. So have Carl and Christina. They've lost two dear children. The Bagges have known suffering," Martha spoke with genuine compassion. "Sam has had to see so many of Anna's family buried."

Reichel looked at her momentarily confused.

She clarified her statement. "Anna Bagge was Sam's first wife. She was Carl's sister."

"I'm sorry. I forgot. Shall I tell Sam now?"

"Please, do. He's much improved today. He should be up most of the day. I hope he returns to work very slowly. He was quite sick, you know."

Sam was more upset than Martha had expected he would be about Carl N.'s passing.

"He was so young. This fever is so hard on the little ones. We need to find what causes this disease," he said.

As Benjamin left, his mind was on Sam's comments and he continued to turn them over while he walked to Dr. Schumann's farm. He took the low road out of town. Crossing the Wach bridge, he surveyed the stream. The water level was low; nonetheless, he deemed the flow sufficient to turn the mill water wheel. He considered the recent congregation public auction of the mill. It was getting harder to manage the various enterprises. It was fortunate the mill was purchased, for flour and grains were essential to the people.

Nearing Schumann's farm, Reichel spotted several swampy places. Brush had been piled at random along the river edges creating barricades so that rainwater did not drain off properly. Reichel recalled seeing no standing water like this, in years past, certainly not before Schumann's house was erected on the land.

Reichel threaded his way through a field then along a footpath to the Schumann yard and front door. The doctor answered the knock.

"Good day, Brother Reichel."

"Good morning to you. I came to inquire about the fever. Do you think the epidemic is subsiding?"

"There have been fewer cases reported this week, but I doubt it's over yet. This is one fever that takes patients a long time to recover. I know I'll be busy with all I can handle for the next few weeks, taking care of my own patients and Dr. Vierling's."

"I was just up at his house. He seems on the mend."

"That's good news. I don't expect he'll be seeing patients any time soon. Perhaps he will be back at the apothecary work first."

"Have you run short of medicines?"

"Not yet. But we could."

"Let me know if you have any special needs."

"Well, I do have a need. I want to farm that acreage that joins my land."

"The wooded section?"

"That's right. Of course, the timber would have to be cut and the underbrush cleared."

"You may present your request at the next Conferenz meeting."

"I'll be there, or write a letter."

Reichel inquired about Sister Schumann's health, stated that he would continue to use all health precautions at the boarding schools and finally bid the doctor goodbye.

As Reichel recrossed the farm and gazed once more at the piles of debris and standing pools of water on Schumann's land, he vowed he'd speak to the Conferenz in an effort to have them encourage Schumann to clean up the land he had now, instead of allowing him to try to handle more acreage. The town hadn't experienced a fever problem in years. In fact, the fever recurred at the time this farm was cleared. Reichel wondered if other farmers along the riverbanks were also hindering natural drainage. He thought if the lands were tended properly, perhaps the town could regain good health.

Martha worried about Sam. He was pushing himself too hard on his first few days out of bed; however, he kept reassuring her he knew what he was doing and he was aware of his limits.

There were things he needed to do himself: compound certain prescriptions and answer some mail, he declared.

Likewise Martha knew when arguing with Sam was in vain. She pursued her own routine in silence, although she listened and watched closely in an unobtrusive manner.

A week after Sam had been up and around the house, Martha went into the apothecary to tell him dinner was about ready. Sam stood up from the bench where he had been working. He started to walk, when without warning he realized he couldn't move his legs. He thrust his hands forward and grabbed the side of the table. His face paled.

"Sam," Martha cried, "what's wrong!"

He steadied himself. "My legs. They're weak."

"Sit down," she urged and rushed to his side.

He dropped heavily to the bench. "It's nothing. It'll pass. Just the old chair injury."

She offered to help him to the bed. He waved her on. "Go back to the kitchen. I'll be there in a few minutes. The children are due. Get ready for them."

Martha wanted to stay to aid Sam, but she also wanted to obey his wishes. Obedience won the brief debate and she returned to the kitchen.

Sam did not want to acknowledge the possibility he was having a relapse; nevertheless, he knew the signs and suspected that was the case. And if it were true – well, relapses were usually of short duration. He managed to walk to the kitchen table and drink some tea. He listened with interest as Theophilus talked about his new shoes and how they helped him run fast on the brothers' meadow where the schoolmaster took them sometimes in the afternoon to play ball. "Some days he doesn't feel so good so we don't go out. If he's well on Sunday, he's promised to let us walk out to Eleonora's farm, like we did last Sunday." Sam paid attention to Benjamin's describing his new math studies and Eliza showing with her hands the size of the new sampler she had begun.

After the children returned to school, Sam told Martha there was a prescription he needed to refill after which he would go upstairs and lie down for a rest.

Late in the afternoon, Sam hadn't come down. Martha went to the bedroom to ask what he wanted for supper because she had noticed that he didn't eat any lunch. When she entered the room, Sam was lying quietly on the bed. She tiptoed closer. How very pale his face was. He was fully dressed, but for the first time Martha was shocked into the realization that he was very, very thin.

"Sam," she whispered.

His eyes opened wide. He lifted his head from the pillow.

"It'll soon be suppertime," she said softly.

"I'm getting up," he replied. When he began to raise himself, he discovered he had little strength.

"Why don't you stay in bed? You've been working long hours these past few days."

Again he attempted to rise. Martha extended her arm to help him. He did stand. His legs wobbling, he sat down on the bed.

"May I get your nightshirt, Sam?"

He nodded yes.

After she helped him change clothing, he stretched out and pulled the covers up. She returned to the kitchen where she fussed at herself for forgetting to ask what he wanted to eat. Sam had no appetite that night or the next morning. When he didn't even mention getting out of bed the next day, she realized he was having a relapse. He seemed to weaken by the hour. About suppertime, she was alarmed. Sam was so quiet, so acquiescent. She sent her Benjamin to the inspector's house for Benjamin Reichel. He came in a hurry. Martha explained her concerns, and then Reichel went in to see Sam. When he rejoined Martha, his face was grave.

"He doesn't look good, but relapses are not uncommon. We should know tomorrow. I'll come up early. Do you need someone with you tonight?"

"No. I'm all right."

Martha slept very little that night. Sam lay so still that she sat up in a chair near the bed for fear her tossing would disturb him. When the first morning light woke Martha, she crept to the foot of the bed. He was still asleep. She eased out of the room and added wood to all the fires. She drew water and put some kettles to boil. She tidied herself, prepared breakfast and woke Eliza. She warned her to be quiet so that her father could sleep.

After Eliza left, Martha checked on Sam. "Are you awake?"

"Yes."

"I'll open the curtains." After she hooked the tiebacks on the nails, she turned toward the bed. Sam was whiter than ever. His eyes stared back at her. She dropped her gaze.

"I'll have to stay in bed. I'm too weak to get out."

A fear clutched Martha's heart. It was as if he could see through her bodice and blouse.

"Have no fear, Martha. It has been a joyful life."

She swallowed hard. She projected the brightest face she could summon. "Can I bring you some fresh milk? I stewed some apples. Benjamin Reichel is coming up soon."

"I'll try some."

She brought the milk and food. She propped Sam up on the pillows against the headboard then held the bowl and cup near for him. The efforts to eat and feed himself were exhausting. Martha put the dishes aside and brought warm water, soap and towel and bathed him. She had just finished straightening the bed when Reichel knocked on the door.

Martha left them alone and took the dishes to the kitchen. She was washing up when Reichel entered.

"Sister Vierling, do you think we should call Dr. Schumann?"

Martha watched the drippings from the last washed plate fall into the tub. To Reichel, she murmured, "We owe it to him to call upon all help."

"I'll go for him now."

"Please, take Sam's horse."

Dr. Schumann came and examined Sam. He prescribed medicines and procedures of nursing that Martha was already familiar with.

Henrietta left the baby with one of the married sisters and came to help her mother. At noon, Benjamin was sent to inform Eleonora of their father's relapse. Theophilus appeared frightened at the sight of his father so ill and colorless.

Sam beckoned him to come beside the bed. "Just a weakness in the legs, son, like your schoolmaster. Tell him to take care. Don't run him too hard." Theophilus buried his head in the bedspread and cried. Sam stretched out his large, though now quite thin, hand and rested it on the boy's head.

The next morning, Sam asked what day it was. Martha reminded him it was November 13.

"The most memorable festal day. We should be at service, Martha."

She repeated Sam's sentiments to Reichel later that day when he paid them a brief visit.

He proposed, "I could bring the communion elements here."

"Sam would really appreciate it. He always looked forward to this particular service."

Martha straightaway told Sam the good news. He smiled and appeared happier than she had seen him in weeks. During the short service that the two of them shared only with Brother Reichel, Martha drew closer in spirit to Sam than she had been for some time. They had known the closest touching of the body, the shared delights of raising their children, the strengthening ties that only the death of a child could bring, the rewards of serving their neighbors in illness; but this was a new spiritual bonding – the partaking of communion in which they sensed the nearness and peace of Jesus.

A short time later Sam lost the ability to speak. For the succeeding two days he did not give any indication he was suffering pain. He made no motions for anything to be done for him, although he recognized acts and gestures for his comfort with a kindly expression.

Eleonora brought her little boy and baby girl near the bed and held them up for him to see. Henrietta brought her infant daughter. He smiled fondly at them.

As the news spread throughout the town, that Dr. Vierling's departure was expected, many brothers and sisters came up the hill to be with him and the family. When the end was apparently near, the ministers gave their blessing. Some married brothers and sisters sang hymns around the bed.

While the room was filled with visitors, Martha sought a bit of rest in the kitchen. She sat at the table. On it someone had placed the hazelnuts. She reached out and rubbed them with her fingertips, thinking about Charles N. who had brought them. And Sam liked hazelnut cake. Who would eat the cake now?

Henrietta poured a cup of coffee and toasted a slice of bread for her mother.

Brother Reichel joined them. "Do you know if Brother Vierling has written his memoir or started it?"

Martha stared at him, "Why no. He certainly didn't expect . . . expect this illness to be fatal. It would be unlike him to write about his past or himself. He lived each day – with a care for the future."

"Could you please, write one?" Reichel asked.

"No."

"You know more about him than anyone else."

"No." Martha repeated firmly. She jumped up from her chair and walked over to the window. "The rain has stopped."

Henrietta glanced at her husband and indicated she would speak to her mother. She approached Martha.

"Mama, I know it's hard to think about these things, but even *if* father would rally, someday, the things he's done, the really fine things need to be written down."

"Henrietta, I cannot do this. Your father never spoke much of the past. He said yesterday is over. We plan for tomorrow. He never bragged about his service or his work. Whatever he has done, has been done; the deeds will live on in the hearts and memories of those he helped."

Henrietta tried to reason with her. "Mama, memoirs are our custom. There will have to be one to be read. And Mama, you should start one of your life so that later we will know . . ."

"I will not. Please, don't ever ask me to do that. My only job has been to be a helpmate. I've never done anything on my own. The less said about me the better."

Martha stood erect and walked out of the room.

Henrietta said, "Benjamin, the older children and I will write the memoir for father."

He went over to poke the fire and add a log.

Henrietta asked him, "If father dies, what will become of the house? It's so large."

"I'm sure the Conferenz will wait until the delegates return from the Synod in Europe to make any decisions. However, I expect they'll buy the house for official use."

"So many friends have come to see father," Henrietta commented as she heard voices from another room.

"Your father will be a hard man to replace. He was, is an excellent surgeon and apothecarist. The town will need both."

"Can't the boys, Theo and Ben, be given permission to live at home if Mama stays on awhile?"

"If she requests it."

"I can't see Mama in the Widows House."

"Don't you think she'd go?"

"If she had to, she would. She obeys all the rules. But Mama is an out-of-door person and I don't see the Widows House as the best place for her."

Some visitors wandered back to the kitchen. Reichel greeted them and Henrietta offered refreshments.

Martha returned to sit beside Sam's bed. She placed her hand on his. He couldn't move his hand to clasp hers; however, he acknowledged her presence with his eyes. More brethren filed into the room and Sam seemed to recognize each of them

The people in the room resumed their singing. Martha tried to sing with them but could not. The words hung in her throat. Sam closed his eyes. She sat for a long time... until restlessness stirred her. All her days heretofore had been active because of a positive drive: there were things to do and she did them. Now... what could she do? How could she be a helpmate? All her life had been a preparation for or a fulfilling of this duty. Helpmate. Helpmate.

"Oh God," her soul cried, "how can I help this good man? His whole life has been dedicated to helping others in their illness. Where, or where is there someone now to render aid to his dying body?"

Her soul wept, her body racked. She could no longer bear the lamentations of the household filled with people. She sought the garden, sought solace among the evergreens she knew so well. Frost had weeks ago killed the annuals. Now the perennials were brown and drooping.

"I must come tend the garden soon."

Her long skirt caught on a dead limb projecting in the path. She halted to free the material. Involuntary was her action of carefully lifting the soft cloth so as not to tear the threads. She pulled the limb free from its half-concealed position in the boxwood. For a short distance she carried the limb along the path with her, then dropped it on a small woodpile. When she came to the herb plot, she stopped. Tears formed in her eyes. She could not see, could not tell one herb bed from another. For the second time in her life she sank to her knees and let the tears wash down her face. Both times were for grieving for the lost of Sam from her life. She sat back on her heels, her hands in her lap.

"How can I bear this new burden of separation? It will be harder than the others. I will be alone."

She lowered her chin.

Her tears ran freely.

And then all was quiet.

Her body was limp.

Her eyes drained.

Her fingers reached forward to push herself up.

Dirt and leaves clung to her wet hands.

She brushed them on her skirt.

She pulled her apron up to dry her face.

Something familiar.

What is it?

She took her handkerchief from her apron pocket.

Blew her nose.

Now, what is that fragrance?
Rosemary.
Rosemary?
Rosemary for remembrance.
Rosemary for the Presence.
She raised her head.
She looked toward the sky.
There was still a streak of light.
"Thank you, Lord.
I'm not alone.
I have your promise to be with me always.
And I will be with my children.
I can still be a helpmate.
My roles of teacher and mother, can continue with
My children.
Your children."
She stood up.

Martha Miksch Vierling walked through the garden to the house. Her private grief behind her, she was ready to help the others through the pain that was to come.

ACKNOWLEDGEMENTS

I especially thank the Historical Publications Section with the North Carolina Division of Archives and History for permission to use as reference sources *Records of the Moravians Volumes 2,3,4,5,6, and 7*.

Many of the characters in this historical fiction lived in or were associated with the Wachovia area during the years 1780 through 1817. The intent has been to portray as accurately as possible an outstanding group of people who were among the founders of the United States of America. Records were kept almost daily of activities in Salem, the central town of the Wachovia area in North Carolina. Some characters are entirely fictional.

I appreciate the assistance of the Moravian Church Archives in Winston-Salem, NC, with research of lines from hymns that are included in the text.

And I thank the following:
Snyder Photography, Inc. for cover photograph of single sister at dye pot beside Miksch fence
Sarah Dixon for sketch of Miksch House and Manufactory
Bethania Moravian Church for the opportunity to direct and teach in the weekday school
New Philadelphia Moravian Church for the kindergarten teaching opportunity
Old Salem for its excellent education program
Friends who read and encouraged me to share the manuscript

BVG